Humphrey Hawksley's face and voice are known to millions
through his broadcasts on BBC TV news and radio. Behind
the fluency of his delivery is a formidable intelligence,
backed by a deep knowledge of his subject. From 1986 to
1997 he worked mostly in Asia, covering conflicts from Sri
Lanka to the Pacific and, in 1994, opened the BBC's first
television bureau in China. He is the co-author of *Dragon-
strike: The Millennium War* and author of two acclaimed
thrillers, *Ceremony of Innocence* and *Absolute Measures*.

Also by Humphrey Hawksley

CEREMONY OF INNOCENCE
ABSOLUTE MEASURES

with Simon Holberton
DRAGON STRIKE

DRAGON FIRE

· **HUMPHREY HAWKSLEY**

F/488925

PAN BOOKS

First published 2000 by Macmillan

This edition published 2001 by Pan Books
an imprint of Pan Macmillan Ltd
Pan Macmillan, 20 New Wharf Road, London N1 9RR
Basingstoke and Oxford
Associated companies throughout the world
www.panmacmillan.com

ISBN 0 330 39156 9

Copyright © Humphrey Hawksley 2000

The right of Humphrey Hawksley to be identified as the
author of this work has been asserted by him in accordance
with the Copyright, Designs and Patents Act 1988.

All characters in this publication are fictitious and any resemblance
to real persons, living or dead, is purely coincidental.

All rights reserved. No part of this publication may be
reproduced, stored in or introduced into a retrieval system, or
transmitted, in any form, or by any means (electronic, mechanical,
photocopying, recording or otherwise) without the prior written
permission of the publisher. Any person who does any unauthorized
act in relation to this publication may be liable to criminal
prosecution and civil claims for damages.

3 5 7 9 8 6 4 2

A CIP catalogue record for this book is available from
the British Library.

Typeset by SetSystems Ltd, Saffron Walden, Essex
Printed and bound in Great Britain by
Mackays of Chatham plc, Chatham, Kent

This book is sold subject to the condition that it shall not,
by way of trade or otherwise, be lent, re-sold, hired out,
or otherwise circulated without the publisher's prior consent
in any form of binding or cover other than that in which
it is published and without a similar condition including this
condition being imposed on the subsequent purchaser.

For my father and my mother

ACKNOWLEDGEMENTS

Although *Dragon Fire* is a novel, it draws extensively on factual material and was written after conducting dozens of interviews with experts involved in the scenario described.

I would like to thank those who helped, but cannot be named because they still have jobs in sensitive areas. I can, however, thank (in alphabetical order) Khaled Ahmed, Ravinatha Aryansinha, Mirza Aslam Beg, Andrew Brookes, Rupak Chattopadhyay, Mani Dixit, Roger Dunn, John Elliott, Gavin Greenwood, Bharat Karnad, Tanvir Ahmed Khan, James Lyons Jnr, Raja Menon, Abdul Nayyar, Tseten Norbu, Samdhomg Rimpoche, Kate Saunders, Sreenath Sreenivasan, K. Subrahmanyam, Terry Taylor, Ashley Tellis, Malini Thadani, Karan Thapar and Gregory L. Vistica; BBC colleagues Malcolm Downing, Adrian Van Klaveren, Richard Sambrook, and Fred Scott; Bharat-rakshak, the Tibet Information Network, the International Institute of Strategic Studies in London, the Institute for Defence Studies and Analysis in Delhi, the Institute for Strategic Studies in Pakistan, the Rand Corporation and the Federation of American Scientists; researchers Sitara Achreja, Brigid Bowen, Victoria Connor, Chanel Khan and Chloe Lederman, who worked against deadlines and an ever-changing brief, and Dipanker Banerjee and Ashok Mehta, who made invaluable corrections and suggestions for the text. Sadly missed was Simon Holberton, my co-author from *Dragon Strike*. Any mistakes are, of course, my own, and for those who spot them, remember it is only fiction.

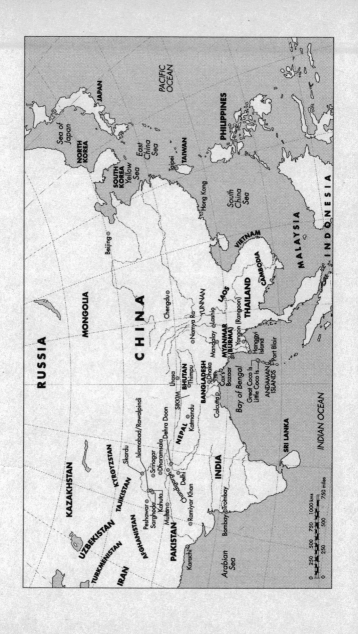

LIST OF CHARACTERS

AUSTRALIA

Keith Backhurst – Defence Minister
Malcolm Smith – Prime Minister

CHINA

Kang Suyin – Ambassador to Moscow
Leung Liyin, General – Defence Minister
Tao Jian – President
Tang Siju – Second Deputy, Chief of the General Staff
Tashi – Chinese agent in India
Teng Guo Feng – Ambassador to Islamabad
Jamie Song – Foreign Minister
Lhundrub Togden – jailed Tibetan Buddhist monk

INDIA

Indrajit Bagchi – Home Minister
Colonel Neelan Chidambaram – commander,
Baghla (Wool) sector
Major Gendun Choedrak – Leader of Special Frontier
Force operation
Amrit Dhal – Group Captain, No. 24 Squadron
'Hunting Hawks'

Hari Dixit – Prime Minister
Captain Tsangpo Jamyang – Second in charge of
SFF operation
Corporal Vasant Kaul – Singh's tank driver
Unni Khrishnan – Chief of Army Staff and Chairman of
the Joint Chiefs of Staff
Mani Naidu – Director of the Intelligence Bureau
General Prabhu Ninan – Western army commander
Lieutenant General Gurjit Singh – Commander, XXI
Armoured Corps
Prabhu Purie – Foreign Minister
Chandra Reddy – Special Secretary, Research and
Analysis Wing
Shanti Tirthankara – anti-nuclear activist

JAPAN

General Shigehiko Ogawa – Director, Defence
Intelligence Headquarters
Shigeto Wada – Prime Minister

NEW ZEALAND

Michael Hall – SBS Royal Marines sniper
Harriet Sheehan – Prime Minister
Benjamin Leigh – Defence Minister

PAKISTAN

Mullah al-Bishri – Islamic leader
General Sadek Hussein – Special Defence Attaché to Beijing

Javed Jabbar – Ambassador to Beijing
Yasin Kalapur – Air Marshal and coup leader
Dr Malik Khalid – missile physicist
General Mohamed Hamid Khan – Chief of Army Staff
and coup leader
Ahmed Magam – deposed Deputy Finance Minister
Captain Mohammed Masood – Khan's
aide-de-camp
Saeed – Stinger marksman

RUSSIA

Nikolai Baltin – Ambassador to Beijing
Vladimir Gorbunov – President

SINGAPORE

John Chiu – Prime Minister

TAIWAN

Lin Chung-ling – President

UNITED KINGDOM

Christopher Baker – Foreign Secretary
Martin Cartwright – BBC Asia Correspondent
Martin Evans – Head of South Asian Department
Eileen Glenny – Press secretary, Prime Minister's office
David Guinness – Defence Secretary

General (Rtd) Sir Peter Hanman – BBC
television commentator
Max Harding – BBC television presenter
Sir Malcolm Parton – Permanent Under-Secretary, Foreign
and Commonwealth Office
Anthony Pincher – Prime Minister
Darren Scott – BBC Asia cameraman
John Stopping – Chairman, Joint Intelligence Committee
Robin Sutcliffe – Head of News Gathering, BBC
Lord Mani Thapar – Indian businessman

UNITED STATES

Milton Ashdown – Ambassador to Moscow
Ennio Barber – Presidential adviser
Tom Bloodworth – National Security Advisor
David Booth – Head of CIA
John Hastings – President
Joan Holden – Secretary of State
Stuart Hollingworth – Commerce Secretary
Alvin Jebb – Defense Secretary
Charles Nugent – White House Chief of Staff
Reece Overhalt – Ambassador to Beijing
Arthur Watkins – Ambassador to Islamabad

PROLOGUE

In a perfect world, communities aspiring to development should not go to war. But time and time again common sense is turned on its head. Even societies whose standards of living are rising rapidly use the excitement of nationalism to balance either the treadmill of economic growth or the weakness of corrupt leadership. Yugoslavia, Iraq and swathes of Africa at once come to mind and danger signals are now flashing in Pakistan, India and China.

In May 1998, both India and Pakistan carried out nuclear tests, elevating hostilities to a new, more menacing level. Asia, still wracked with poverty and conflict, now has three declared nuclear-weapons powers.

India and Pakistan have been in conflict for half a century. Pakistan and China have a long-standing military alliance. India and China have already fought one war and disagree on how to handle restless nationalism in Tibet.

But a far more forceful momentum is also sweeping across those two enormous countries, a sense that as empires come and empires go, at some stage the power of the United States will wane and another great power will rise up to move into the vacuum. This ambition, and an impatience to force events, has made Asia an unpredictable and dangerous place for all of us.

China's naval advances into the Indian Ocean and occupation of islands in the South China Sea are evidence that it is willing to anger its neighbours in order to test its military reach. India's determination to press ahead with its nuclear programme and name China as its main long-term threat suggests a deeper degree of hostility than at first realized.

Both countries have weak conventional military systems and only minimal nuclear forces. But that is no guarantee that either country will not make a military bid for regional leadership in the years to come.

In *Dragon Strike: The Millennium War* (Sidgwick & Jackson 1997), Simon Holberton and I described a scenario in which China takes control of the South China Sea. It attacks its long-standing enemy, Vietnam, occupies the Spratly and Paracel groups of islands, and deploys submarines in the sea lanes to the Indian Ocean. When the United States intervenes by sending a warship into the area, it is sunk by a Chinese submarine with heavy loss of life.

Pacifist Japan reacts by carrying out a nuclear test, uncertain that it can continue to count on American military protection. Much of South East Asia, looking to the long-term future, gives tacit support to China.

American, British, Australian and New Zealand warships fight their way into the South China Sea. As China's fleet faces destruction, American satellite imagery shows nuclear missiles being prepared for launch.

The prospect of a nuclear attack on an American city is enough to force a rethink in Washington about how to deal with China.

Simon Holberton and I described *Dragon Strike* as a future history. *Dragon Fire* is even more so. Developments in Asia are moving so fast that on several occasions my writing was overtaken by events. What was fiction one day became historical fact the next.

The characters of the novel are more the individual countries than the people who run them. Loyalties, betrayals, aspirations and scars of history are played out on a political and military stage through the eyes of India, Pakistan, China and others.

If China and India's security aspirations for Asia converge with each other and with those of the United States and Japan, there is no cause for alarm. That, however, would be an ambitious formula. If either China's or India's intentions are being underestimated and the danger signs are swept under the carpet, the impact on world peace could be the most catastrophic since the end of the Second World War.

Briefing

Tibet

Tibet forms a strategic buffer between India and China, and Beijing is uncompromising about policies there. Chinese troops invaded Tibet in October 1950, a year after the Communist Party victory. In 1959 Tibet's spiritual and political ruler, the Dalai Lama, was forced into exile during an uprising against Chinese occupation. Since then, he has lived in India. The international community recognizes Chinese suzerainty – or control – over Tibet. Although Tibetan nationalism has won great sympathy in the West, the Dalai Lama's campaign of non-violence has failed to deliver back the homeland. Many of the younger generation have become frustrated and have proposed a more confrontational approach against China. Little known to the outside world, the Indian army maintains a unit of Tibetan commandos, specifically trained to operate in Tibet behind Chinese lines. It is known as the Special Frontier Force.

Dehra Dun, Uttar Pradesh, India

The Antonov-32 transport plane was parked at the end of the runway, half hidden from view by a camouflaged screen. The airstrip at Dehra Dun, in the foothills of the Himalayas, was mainly for civilian use and was guarded by only unarmed policemen. Although a cantonment town, steeped in military tradition, Dehra Dun was not like a town in Kashmir or the Punjab, considered to be under any serious threat of attack from terrorism.

Fifteen minutes before take-off, a company of men secured the Dehra Dun airstrip. They tied up the police guards, held them in the civilian waiting area, and made radio contact from the control tower, giving an all-clear for take-off. The Antonov taxied onto the runway, laden with thirty men and equipment, weighing in at 24,000 kilograms. The pilot let the aircraft cover 2,000 feet of runway before lifting off.

It climbed sharply to 25,000 feet and turned. The winter had been mild this year. Much of the snow had melted already on the lower ground, and the night was dark and clear as only the air sweeping through the Himalayas could be. For those in the Antonov, the awesome, inhospitable and magical mountains were home, land they should have fought harder for long ago and land worth dying for. Instead of flying due east, the pilot took the longer route over Nepal, because there was no effective radar or air-defence system to cover it. They would be briefly vulnerable over the Indian state of Sikkim, then move into the airspace of the tiny Himalayan kingdom of Bhutan, where the pilot would take the plane down to the lowest altitude possible among the mountain peaks.

The man leading the operation, Major Gendun Choedrak of the Special Frontier Force (SFF), had been lucky to get his hands on an AN-32. It first went into operation in 1986 and was chosen by the Indian forces over its British, Canadian and Italian rivals. Its capability over the treacherous wastelands of the Siachen Glacier was second to none. The cargo ramp was superb and enabled loads to be dropped by drag parachutes. It handled excellently at high airstrip altitudes, being able to take off from bases as high as 14,500 feet, and it had set new standards on payload-to-height ratio and for sustaining altitude.

The men were equipped with AK-47 assault rifles, MP-5 sub-machine guns and 9mm Uzis, all more suited to close-quarter engagements than the standard commando issue of 7.62mm assault rifles and Sterling Mk 4 sub-machine guns. Thirty paratroopers were on the plane, four of them qualified marksmen, using the 7.62mm SGG-2000 sniper rifle. The commandos had discarded their uniforms for civilian clothes. Most carried cyanide capsules first used by the Tibetan fighters during the uprising. Many had photographs of the Dalai Lama in the top pocket of their shirts. The Indian air-force livery on the plane had been replaced by Chinese military markings. Chinese charts and books had been put in the aircraft to be found among the wreckage in case of a crash.

Seven days earlier, Choedrak had infiltrated two hundred men across the border in units of four and five. They were disguised as herdsmen and lightly armed, although many units carried mortars and anti-tank weapons. Sixty were to go to the Tibetan capital, Lhasa, even travelling with livestock and, when suitable, making themselves known at

Chinese military checkpoints in the hope they would be recognized and let through on the way back. The others were to lay up to help with the escape. They were equipped with tiny, frequency-hopping radios, and Choedrak had heard nothing from them so assumed they were now in position and safe.

Using GPS satellite positions, the Antonov navigator programmed a course through the valleys to avoid detection by Chinese radar. The plan would only work if the weather held and the paratroopers could drop from as little as 1,000 feet. The men expected 10 per cent casualties. The injured would be on their own until the operation was over. The pilot's speed was just over 480 k.p.h. He announced they had reached their cruising altitude, and the men settled down for a two-hour journey.

They were commanded by his immediate deputy, Captain Tsangpo Jamyang. Choedrak himself was not on the plane.

Choedrak would be flying in by helicopter. He was thirty-seven years old and a member of the Khampas, a warrior race from eastern Tibet, which had led the 1959 resistance against Chinese occupation. His father had joined the Special Frontier Force on 14 November 1962, the day it was set up, when India had just been defeated in a border war. The SFF was based in Chakrata, 60 kilometres from the Himalayan city of Dehra Dun and 300 kilometres south-west of the Tibetan border. It started with twelve thousand men who were trained specifically to conduct covert operations behind Chinese lines. It became a tested rapid-deployment force, skilled in rock climbing, sabotage, airborne operations, spy photography, surveillance and guerrilla warfare. Choedrak remembered the SFF fighting in Bangladesh, Kashmir, on the Siachen Glacier and during the Kargil war of 1999. But he had never had the chance to go into action against the Chinese in his own country.

Choedrak sensed that several Tibetans in the Special Frontier Force suspected his operation, but were keeping their mouths shut. Commandeering aircrew and mechanics could only be done under limited secrecy. When he told his Tibetan colonel that he wanted to take 150 men on a training mission to the Siliguri corridor just south of Darjeeling, permission was given without question.

As the Antonov climbed on the first stages of its journey towards Lhasa, Choedrak was more than 1,600 kilometres away in another aircraft, an Mi-26 helicopter with sixty SFF commandos. It was ungainly, noisy and for weeks he had tried to get something more suited to the operation ahead. With eight thirty-five-metre rotor blades, the Mi-26 was the world's most powerful helicopter, but it was purely a logistics aircraft, not designed for fast manoeuvres or offensive action. Its armaments were defensive. The sealed flight deck and passenger compartment directly behind were armoured, and the crew had state-of-the-art night-flying instruments, including an active interference system against heat-seeking missiles.

Thirty minutes earlier, the Mi-26 had landed to refuel at an SFF Wing Headquarters outside the town of Rabangla in the mountain state of Sikkim, just fifty kilometres from the Tibetan border. With auxiliary fuel tanks the Mi-26 had a range of 2,000 kilometres. Choedrak planned to go in with full tanks just in case there was a chance to fulfil the mission and fly back out again.

Getting hold of the Mi-26 had been one of the most complex tasks of the mission. Choedrak had commandeered it from the Indian air force's 126 Helicopter Unit, based in Chandigarh, claiming it was needed for a counter-insurgency training exercise operation (COIN) near Darjeeling. This was the area where India's tense north-eastern states were joined to the rest of the country by a narrow strip of territory only 110 kilometres wide. Nepal lay to the west and Bangladesh to the east. Over the past ten years, insurgencies had spread from the east and the region was wracked with separatist violence. For Choedrak it was a perfect cover.

He identified a Tibetan pilot willing to fly and faked an intricate set of orders, originating at the helicopter base in Chandigarh. The aircraft was flown to the SFF headquarters in Chakrata, 110 kilometres to the east, where it landed under the cover of darkness. Once there, all Indian markings were removed and the helicopter was painted in desert/snow camouflage colours, with streaks of green and small Chinese military markings on the fuselage. From Chakrata it flew at low level, barely 250 feet above the ground across Nepali airspace, into Sikkim 1,200 kilometres away.

The tiny military base had received a message from Chandigarh that the aircraft was on a classified special forces mission and needed refuelling. Faced with a commando unit of blackened faces and Choedrak's forged order papers, the base commander gave the SFF what they wanted.

The weather was clear when the pilot lifted the aircraft off from Rabangla. The stars over the plateau were more brilliant than he had ever seen them before. With its cruising speed of 250 k.p.h., Choedrak expected to be over Lhasa in two hours and probably dead an hour after that. He had not told his family. A letter was to be sent to them from Chakrata. Choedrak turned to the pilot, who gave him the thumbs-up signal, and pointed the helicopter through the mountains to rendezvous with the Antonov and the guerrilla fighters who should be on the outskirts of Lhasa waiting for them.

Drapchi Prison, Lhasa, Tibet

In the past week the beatings had started again, just like when he had first arrived at the prison sixteen years before. They had forgotten about his good behaviour and his proclaimed loyalty to the Communist Party as if they had never happened. Six days earlier, shortly after 0500, they had hauled him out of the cell alone. Outside the temperature hovered just above freezing. They hadn't let him put on his shoes and his skin was torn on cold, hard ground as they dragged him across the yard. They kicked him and hit him behind the knees with a metal rod so that he stumbled. Once in the interrogation room, they said they were going to kill him. Then they tied him up to the wall and gave him electric shocks.

Lhundrub Togden, aged fifty-three, a Buddhist monk from Gangden Monastery in Lhasa, had three years of a nineteen-year sentence to run. After that, he would begin an eight-year sentence for organizing riots – and by then he would be sixty-four, if he survived.

'You are accused of splittist activities,' they said to him. 'You are a subversive organizing the dismemberment of the Motherland.'

Togden remained silent. Whatever he said, the beatings would continue. After he had refused to speak for one whole session, they had pushed him into a close-confinement cell, the opposite to solitary, where there was no light, little air, no sanitation and prisoners were crammed together as tightly as possible in conditions which made sleep impossible.

The next day he was given nothing to eat until the evening when, close to collapse, he was handed a steamed bun and broth, so watery that he was unable to taste any vegetables or meat. He survived using the mantra 'Om Mani Padme Hum', a six-syllable invocation to Avalokiteshvara, the Buddha of Compassion, of whom the Dalai Lama is regarded as an emanation. By reciting it endlessly, he disciplined his mind into a tranquil meditation so that he barely felt the blows or the pain.

Under prison regulations, they could torture, deny sleep and limit meals without referring to higher officials. But Togden understood the system and psychology of Drapchi. They would not move him from the Fifth Division, nor would they seriously injure or kill him, without direct permission from Beijing. He was a special-case prisoner, well known to groups such as Amnesty International, and Hollywood film stars had personally named him a 'hero of peace'.

Togden was made to run with a bag of rocks on his back for hours on end. For years he worked in the greenhouses where temperatures would reach more than fifty degrees Centigrade. At one stage he suffered from fluid retention, becoming grossly bloated, with his cheeks and eyes puffed. He recovered from that, but his dramatic swings in size and weight left him looking gaunt and ghostlike. He spent two years in solitary confinement and a year ago was sent back to the Fifth Division, the section specially created for male political prisoners.

When news leaked out that Togden had finally been moved, Choedrak was approached to rescue him. Togden was the most commanding Tibetan figure who advocated a campaign of violent insurgency against Chinese rule. Once freed, he could change the future of the whole resistance movement.

*

Togden was in state of semi-conscious meditation, forcing away the pain which wracked his body. Shortly after ten in the morning, he heard the first burst of gunfire to the south, coming from the old city, near the Jokhang. This time, however, it was not unarmed defenceless civilians who were fired upon by the Chinese police. Men from the Special Frontier Force, who had walked for days over the rugged and freezing Tibetan plateau to reach the capital, had infiltrated the city like peasant warriors from another age. They came into Lhasa from the north along the Beijing Nub Lan, and only when they were interspersed with the crowds of people in the narrow streets around the Jokhang did the first unit throw back their grubby Tibetan coats to reveal the weaponry of modern commandos. From then on their chances of survival were minimal.

They threw two grenades into the police station at Bharkor, followed by a burst from two AK-47 assault rifles. The men then split up into pairs, heading north; two went past the Snowland Hotel to Beijing Shar Lam, the other two up through the Jokhang, Nangtseshag, past the Lhasa Department Store, and meeting up with the others outside the Jebumgang police station. People were running back and forth in a familiar pattern indicating the start of trouble. Police opened fire above their heads, but their volley was met with a devastating assault from the SFF Tibetans. Five policemen died. Two Tibetans were hit in the exchange, stumbling and falling. Civilians rushed forward to help, but by the time they got there both the commandos had bitten cyanide capsules and were in the throes of death.

Police ran out of the building, firing into the crowd, killing and wounding civilians: the figures are still unclear as to how many. Screams were heard all over Jokhang, bringing people out of their houses, and word spread rapidly that the armed uprising had begun, just like in March 1959. The Khampas were back to liberate their country.

With four- and five-man units, the SFF were able to attack ten different positions throughout Lhasa, spreading confusion and drawing and thinning out the Chinese forces into separate parts of the city.

Three units struck the Armed Police Auxiliary building and the Satellite Earth Station along Ngachen Lam. Two and a half kilometres to the west, the radio and television station on Lingkor Nub Lam was hit with two rocket-propelled grenades, then raked with small-arms fire. They attacked the Tibetan Military Area compound, which housed a battalion of PLA soldiers, firing from the northern bank of the Kyichu River, careful to avoid hitting the women and children's hospital in the north-east corner of the compound.

From a stolen police jeep, they fired into the Armed Police Headquarters along Chingdrol Kyol Lam, drove straight on half a kilometre to the east, pulled up, set up a mortar and fired four rounds into the compound housing the Tibetan civilian administration. This was the first unit to come under attack from the PLA rapid deployment force, which was operational within ninety seconds of the firefight breaking out in the Jokhang.

A Chinese WZ 551 armoured personnel carrier drove straight towards the SFF mortar position. Its 25mm cannon was silent, but the 7.62mm heavy machine gun cut a swathe of destruction through the small guerrilla unit. The last commando fell as the fourth mortar round was let off. Then two Chinese Z-9 helicopters, based on the French-built Eurocopter SA 365 Dauphin, were in the air with searchlights. Crews of other Chinese helicopters, including three Sikorsky S-70 Black Hawks, were being called in, and this was just what Choedrak had planned for.

With its camouflage colours and Chinese markings, Choedrak's lumbering Indian Mi-26 helicopter flew into the Plain of Lhasa north across the tributaries of the Kyichu. It was over the city, on schedule, fifteen minutes after the fighting began. Choedrak could see crowds gathered around the Jokhang, fires burning in the police stations and the muzzle flashes of gunfire. Special Chinese army units were closing in on the narrow streets of the old city, moving cautiously, knowing they were entering a nightmare of close-combat urban warfare. More troops were pouring in along the Ngachen Lam from the PLA's main Tibetan headquarters just to the east of Lhasa.

Seconds later, the helicopter was over Drapchi prison, which seemed quiet, with light morning traffic. Looking north towards the mountains it was as if nothing untoward was happening at all. By now there were other helicopters in the skies, but there was too much confusion for the Mi-26 to be noticed. Choedrak listened for the AN-32.

'Keep flying,' he ordered.

The pilot held a northerly course to Sera monastery in the foothills of the Gyaltsen Mountain, then turned west-south-west down to the Kyichu, making a circle of Lhasa so that he would come back to Drapchi from the east. The SFF infiltration force was in action throughout the southern sector of Lhasa, with up to sixty men engaged in combat. Forty remained in reserve, retaining their disguises, to stagger deployment over the next thirty minutes between the breakout at Drapchi and the escape.

'There he is,' said the pilot. 'Two o'clock and coming down fast.'

'Thank God,' said Choedrak.

Choedrak saw the Antonov's silhouette plunging out of the morning darkness. He recognized the distinctive turbo-prop engine casings above the wings. It came down in a spiral to avoid anti-aircraft fire, and just when it seemed certain the plane would not be able to pull out, the nose levelled and the rear ramp came down. The wings tipped and paratroopers tumbled out, their chutes opening straight away, the men identifying their positions in the prison compound, concentrating hard with only fifteen seconds between the jump and the landfall.

The sudden roar of aircraft and the mushrooming of white chutes were followed by the crackle of small-arms fire as half the paratroopers landed inside the camp, their job to hold down the Chinese troops for the few minutes of the operation and blow the two gates leading to the prison compound.

The two gunners on the Mi-26 shot out each of the watchtowers. Already, men lay dead and wounded on the frozen ground of the military camp. But enough were engaging the Chinese in a fierce firefight to hold the gate leading from the camp to the prison.

Other paratroopers made it into the prison itself. Ten men took cover between the clinic and the wall of the women's prison, setting up a lethal field of fire along the main road running through the compound. Five men set up a position between the fence and the First Division building, laying down covering fire for another four who were working on explosives on the prison gate.

The helicopter came in due south over the Sera Lam road into the city, the pilot skimming the traffic and bringing the aircraft to hover a few feet off the ground opposite the shabby main prison entrance. It led into a military camp. The second gate went into a sort of ante-chamber to the prison, then there was the prison gate itself. Each section was protected by three layers of electrified fencing and the compound was overlooked by six watch-towers, each manned by two guards with searchlights and heavy machine guns. Division Five, where Togden was held, was the furthest point from the prison entrance, sealed off in its own compound with its own gate.

Choedrak was the first out.

A searing explosion ripped away the main gate, hurling debris into the air, and the men from the SFF ran through the flames into the chaos of the military camp. Their firing was controlled and highly skilled, hitting the Chinese, identifying their own and shouting commands in Tibetan, using their own language in their own country for the first time.

The second gate was shattered with plastic explosives, then the gate to the prison compound itself was destroyed and the men ran in, relieving those who had been holding the ground. Each had an intricate knowledge of the prison from the diagrams they had studied, each four-man unit responsible for a specific task. The aim of the operation was to free as many prisoners as quickly as possible onto the streets of Lhasa, destroy the prison and deliver Lhundrub Togden to India or Nepal.

The Antonov was on a course due south, flying at the dangerously low level of 300 feet to avoid Chinese radar and air defences, which would now be on high alert. For the next twenty minutes, the pilot was relying on luck to reach the border with Bhutan, 200 kilometres away, before the Chinese air defences brought him down.

A squadron of six fighters scrambled from the Chinese air-force base just north of Lhasa. They were Shenyang-12 or J-12 fighters, Chinese-built, but based on the Russian-designed SU-27, more than enough to take on the lightly armed Antonov-32 and Mi-26.

Seven more Chinese helicopters were in the sky, but, amazingly, the Mi-26 was still flying undetected. When the alert at Drapchi was sounded the Armed Police Headquarters and Tibet Military Area command headquarters were themselves under attack from SFF units. The message came through not that there was an attack on Drapchi, but that there was a riot. Then the radio operators were killed and their equipment smashed.

As soon as the last paratrooper was out, seconds after the main gate was blown, the pilot took the Mi-26 up again, flying south towards the Kuru Sampa, the main southerly bridge across the Kyichu River. Chinese reinforcements from the east were entering the city, but the area around the bridge was still clear. The pilot brought the helicopter down on the northern banks of the Kyichu, dropped off twenty commandos and delivered another twelve to the southern edge of the bridge at the beginning of the Tibet–Sichuan Highway. Looming above them was the Bhumpa Mountain, where they were to flee once the helicopter was out of action.

1,500 metres to the south-west armoured vehicles came out of the PLA's main depot south of the river, heading towards the bridge. Tibetan fighters saw them, melted into the rocky terrain and watched them pass.

It would only be minutes before the helicopter was identified as an enemy aircraft. The pilot's most dangerous task now was retracing the flight path to Drapchi. He flew low over the Jokhang, now an orange glow of burning buildings and street-fighting. Then it fell quieter below him until suddenly he was above the flames curling up from the prison compound itself.

The first burst of tracer anti-aircraft fire cut a line of speckled yellow and white in front of the cockpit. The gunners returned with a long burst of theirs and the pilot brought the helicopter down into a hover above the prison compound.

SFF units had taken high positions in the prison buildings and watchtowers. The winchman released the ladder from the helicopter, and the pilot identified Choedrak, running through the smoke, with the prisoner, Lhundrub Togden.

The Mi-26 was not designed for such elaborate work and the pilot had difficulty keeping her steady. Togden was on the ladder first, as commandos set up fields of fire in protective layers around him. The Drapchi prisoners formed a human barrier at the gates of the prison, where Chinese troops were now trying to get in. As Togden was on the ladder the first Chinese mortar landed in the prison compound with a ferocity which caused panic among the prisoners. The Chinese later admitted that twenty-nine were killed or wounded with that one mortar shell.

Choedrak was the next up on the ladder. It swayed precariously, but the winchman's hand was there to haul him in, while the pilot took the helicopter up and turned the nose south again. A second mortar landed right inside the prison and exploded beneath them.

Heavy machine-gun fire from the ground cut through the fuselage, killing the starboard gunner. Choedrak took the weapon and kept firing at troops moving in on the prison perimeter. He saw a Tibetan commando raise his weapon above his head in a salute as the helicopter cleared the prison wall. It was the finest salute Choedrak had ever seen: a Tibetan fighting for his country, proud, brave, determined, and holding his post so others could escape. A happy man about to die.

The pilot, too, sensed he had only minutes to live. He kept the helicopter low and fast, skimming the rooftops and twisting to avoid the high buildings. Another round of machine-gun fire hit the tail, striking the rudder control which at once became sluggish. He kept her height at barely 100 feet. He saw the roadblock set up by the SFF units north of the Kuru Sampa, already under attack by two Chinese armoured cars coming down from Samchen Dong Lam. One APC was stopped in a jarring explosion, hit by a rocket-propelled grenade from the Tibetans. The helicopter flew overhead in a deafening roar, following the line of the bridge, an agreed signal to the men on the ground that Togden was on board and they should move on to the next stage.

The SFF explosives unit detonated the charges laid under the bridge. The road collapsed into the river, leaving their own men on the northern banks cut off from escape, but blocking the Chinese pursuit.

'Out now,' the pilot ordered. The aircraft was barely airworthy. He just managed to control its descent again, keeping her steady above the road, recognizing the Tibetans on the ground and holding off Chinese armoured vehicles. 'Everyone,' he repeated, turning in his seat. 'Not a man left on board.'

As the last paratrooper jumped off, he regained enough height to move the wrecked machine towards the PLA barracks. He could have landed her on the road and surrendered. But that would have been the act of a coward. He saw his fellow Tibetans, distant shapes now, taking to the mountains. He got the helicopter to 150 feet, then let it drop, guiding it down until the last few feet to make sure that it shattered in the middle of the highway, spewing out oil and burning fuel, wrecking the thoroughfare with twisted parts and lumps of aircraft metal which would block the PLA attack for the vital minutes that Togden and Choedrak needed to get away.

Briefing

India

British rule in India officially began in 1858, although the East India Company had been extending its grip there since the 1760s. Through trade and conquest, it controlled areas from the southern coastal region to what is now northern Pakistan. By the early twentieth century, there were growing demands for independence, pushed forward by the non-violent campaign of Mahatma Gandhi. The culmination was the partition of India in 1947, with Islamic Pakistan ruled by the Muslim League and secular India governed by the Indian National Congress. The unresolved issue of Kashmir led to the first Indo-Pakistan War, and India's development was plagued by other insurgencies on its borders.

During the Cold War India remained non-aligned, but forged a close relationship with the Soviet Union. Its economic policies were protective and socialist, and the United States viewed it as hostile. In the nineties, the country lost its secular umbrella and elected a government based on Hindu nationalism. It became a nuclear power and proclaimed China its long-term threat. Tibet simmered. The war in Kashmir continued and India remained the world's biggest democracy.

Hari Dixit, the Indian Prime Minister, slapped his hand
on the conference table in his office and angrily pulled out
a chair. 'Why do I have to find out what is happening from
the Chinese?' he snapped at the two men standing in front
of him. 'It's your job to tell me.'

Mani Naidu, the director of the Intelligence Bureau,
which handled internal intelligence, and Chandra Reddy,
Special Secretary of the Research and Analysis Wing,
responsible for external intelligence, were unlucky enough
to be the first members of the National Security Council to
arrive for the meeting.

Twenty minutes earlier, Dixit had been holding meetings
at his official residence at 7 Race Course Road. He was a
tough medical doctor in his early sixties, who through sheer
political brilliance and some brawn had moulded a coalition
to keep his party in power. Three years earlier, he had
suddenly risen to political fame, from the obscurity of being
Chief Minister in Andhra Pradesh. His policies had concentrated on disease prevention, health education, housing,
education and information technology, and had become a
model for Third World development. The press hailed him
as the only genuine leader India had had since Jawaharlal
Nehru, a man who could balance the needs of the poor
with the national aspirations of the world's greatest
democracy.

The unexpected visitor to the Prime Minister's residence
was the Chinese Ambassador, who came in person, unan-

nounced, his lower lip quivering with rage. 'Unless my government has an immediate explanation as to why Indian troops have invaded Chinese sovereign territory,' he spluttered, 'I am instructed to tell you that China will consider itself to be in a state of war with India.'

The British High Commissioner telephoned. The Russian Ambassador sent a hand-delivered note. Dixit blocked calls when he heard that the American Ambassador was also trying to get through. He ordered a meeting of the National Security Council at the Operational Directorate, which was a military crisis centre near the Prime Minister's office in South Block. On the way, Dixit spoke to his Foreign Minister, Prabhu Purie, who told him: 'It appears a renegade unit of the Special Frontier Force was responsible, sir, but the Chinese are refusing to accept this explanation.'

The telephone line from the Prime Minister's white Ambassador car was encrypted and secure. The car had been custom-built in Calcutta by Hindustan Motors with bullet-proof tyres and windows, and an armour-plated chassis. Special Protection Group (SPG) officers changed the number plates at least twice a week.

Two SPG cars pulled out in front. The one closest carried a scanner to detect missile attacks. Two more cars flanked the Ambassador behind and an ambulance followed the convoy. The driver and an SPG commando with a Sten gun were in the front, while the Prime Minister sat alone in the back.

The route varied each time he travelled from his residence to his office. This morning the convoy headed along Akbar Road and on to Vijay Chowk, just below Raisina Hill at the foot of the Central Secretariat complex. The final leg took it up towards the elegant red-stone buildings of South Block, designed by Edwin Lutyens in the final days of the Raj and now the nucleus of government for the world's biggest democracy.

The car turned into gate eleven near Rajaji Marg, and Dixit saw his two most senior intelligence officials drive in just before him. As he stepped out of his car, Dixit could only wonder whether he was to preside over an era of yet more war.

Tibet was the silent, dangerous front which had been swept under the carpet for more than half a century, dormant, but never forgotten. On his way in, Dixit walked past walls covered with photographs of men who had won the highest Indian award for bravery, the Param Vir Chakra.

His private secretary was waiting at the lift and they rode up together to the first floor, turning left towards the room marked OPERATIONAL DIRECTORATE. There had been no time to separate the tables, which had been moved together for a meeting of twenty-five people late the night before. The officials of India's National Security Council pulled up chairs and sat down. Present were the Prime Minister, the Foreign Minister, the Defence Minister, the Home Minister, the National Security Advisor, the heads of the Intelligence Bureau and the Research and Analysis Wing, the deputy chairman of the Planning Commission and the chiefs of the Army, Air and Navy. The Finance Minister, who would have been present, was out of the country.

Briefing

China

Modern China grew out of years of colonization, civil war and internal conflict. Mao Zedong's Communist Party took power in 1949. But it was not until 1979, after Mao's disastrous economic and social policies, that genuine reform began. Western democracies fashionably courted the one-party state with encouragement and investment. The China boom years were temporarily halted by the 1989 Tiananmen Square killings, which underlined China's intention to remain an authoritarian power. The Chinese leadership believed that political reform would lead to uncontrollable violence. The army and police maintained a repressive presence in Tibet. Missile, aircraft and naval development was aimed primarily at deterring Taiwan from declaring independence. China's stated long-term goal was to become the leading regional power in Asia. The return of Hong Kong in 1997 was hailed as a victory over years of humiliation by foreign powers. By the end of the twentieth century, China was jostling with the United States, wooing and threatening South-East Asian neighbours, and warily watching Japan. Then, after India's nuclear tests in 1998, China was forced to begin changing focus.

F/ 488925

Zhongnanhai, Beijing, China

'The Indian Ambassador** is insistent that a renegade military unit is responsible,' said the Chinese Foreign Minister, Jamie Song.

'They were Tibetans, trained by India and using Indian equipment,' said the Chinese President, Tao Jian. 'We must decide on a suitable response.'

'We have declared martial law in Lhasa,' said Tang Siju, the third man present and the Second Deputy Chief of the General Staff. Tang had served as defence attaché in London, Washington and Berlin, although his German tour was cut short when it became clear he was heavily involved in covert intelligence gathering. His brief now was intelligence and strategic gathering, but his grasp of Western military technology, coupled with his hawkish views and uncompromising discipline against internal dissent, gave him power far above his status. As debate within the Chinese leadership swung between authoritarianism and reform, Tang was often tipped as a successor to President Tao. Jamie Song was on the other end of the pendulum's swing.

Three of China's most powerful men walked along the shore of the lake known as the Central Sea in Zhongnanhai, the walled compound in which the Chinese leadership lived and worked. The air was filled with spring blossom swirling like snowflakes, although it had been a cold night and tiny wafer-thin ice clustered in the corners, showing that winter had not quite passed.

Tao nodded, but Song blanched.

'Our policy in Tibet, more than anywhere else, will impact on our global position,' Song argued. 'Since the 1989 Tiananmen incident and the Dragon Strike event, we have skilfully become a role model for the developing world.'

'Tibet is an internal matter,' said Tang bluntly. 'The incursion by India has given us an opportunity to act. We should not lose it.'

Foreign and Commonwealth Office, London

Local time: 0800 Thursday 3 May 2007

'**Do we know** where Togden is?' asked Christopher Baker.

'We don't, Foreign Secretary,' said Sir Malcolm Parton, the Permanent Under-Secretary and the civil servant in charge of the Foreign Office. 'If he's alive, he's probably hiding out with ten or twenty of the guerrillas, trying to make their way to India or Nepal.'

'With the Chinese army in hot pursuit, we assume,' said John Stopping, the Chairman of the Joint Intelligence Committee. 'Even if he turns up in Nepal, his final destination will be India.'

'And if he doesn't make it?' said Baker. 'If the Chinese get him?'

'That would be a more settled outcome,' said Sir Malcolm, exchanging glances with Stopping.

'If he gets to India?' pressed Baker.

'The Indians might give him asylum with the usual conditions that he doesn't engage in political activities,' Sir Malcolm explained. 'They might feel he's too hot to handle and pass him on to a third country. Wherever he is he will become a focal point for violent resistance against Chinese rule in Tibet.'

'And how's China going to react to India's inadvertent incursion?'

'President Tao will milk it for everything he can,' said Stopping. 'But quiet diplomacy through the Security Council should keep it in check.'

The Foreign Secretary stood up, looking at his watch,

indicating that the meeting was over. His mind was far away from China, a country which he didn't like and didn't understand, and which didn't fall in the British or European hemisphere of world affairs. The press were still running with a story about his numerous infidelities, no doubt leaked by his soon-to-be ex-wife. The House of Commons Foreign Affairs select committee was homing in on a bribery scandal in Malaysia, about which he had known nothing. Apparently, the papers on it had been sent to him at the bottom of his red box one weekend six months earlier.

His Under-Secretary had made a valiant attempt to defend him, so, when Sir Malcolm called asking for an urgent early-morning meeting, he reluctantly agreed. The presence of John Stopping, Chairman of the JIC and soon to be appointed Ambassador to Beijing, indicated that something both secret and significant was afoot. The JIC was not directly involved in policy-making, and Sir Malcolm had not made it clear why he had insisted on bringing Stopping along. The most obvious colleague would have been the Director for Asia–Pacific.

But right now he was running late for a breakfast meeting at Downing Street with the Prime Minister and the new German Chancellor. 'Draw up some options, will you, Malcolm,' he said, putting on his jacket. 'Apart from that my instinct is to keep our mouths shut. It seems that Britain's most pressing concern is if Lama Togden turns up alive and says he wants to live in Clapham.'

The White House, Washington, DC

Local time: 0300 Thursday 3 May 2007
GMT: 0800 Thursday 3 May 2007

'I think you need to wake the President on this one.' Reece Overhalt, the American Ambassador, was speaking to the White House Chief of Staff, Charles Nugent, from the secure communications room in the Embassy in Beijing. Nugent was propped up in bed, eyeing his clock and trying to sound polite.

'I don't see it, Reece,' said Nugent. 'You say it's an Indian cock-up. If we woke the President every time a Third World government screwed something up the man would be a walking zombie.'

'China could lose it,' Overhalt insisted, 'become uncontrollable.'

'Well, let them lose it in the morning – Eastern Standard Time.'

Briefing

Dharamsala

In 1959, after the Dalai Lama fled Tibet, the Indian government allocated the town of Dharamsala, nestled in the mountains of northern India, for him to use as his headquarters. The Dalai Lama lived there in a modern compound, while buildings off the steep little streets housed the institutions of the Tibetan government-in-exile. One of those buildings was the Tibetan Parliament.

Chandigarh, India

Local time: 0300 Friday 4 May 2007
GMT: 2130 Thursday 3 May 2007

The call from his controller interrupted his light sleep. Chandigarh was never quiet, with the blaring of a horn or the crunching of gears on the busy road outside his room. It was only a week since he had been rotated, the beginning of his second tour of duty in Chandigarh, the city chosen many years ago from which to launch an attack on Dharamsala. His operational name was Tashi and he was a graduate from the People's Liberation Army Foreign Affairs College in Nanjing. Unlike most educational institutions specializing in international issues, the Foreign Affairs College avoided employing foreign teachers, to try to ensure that its graduates were not recognized when they were sent overseas.

Tashi was a Tibetan, who had spent a year at Johns Hopkins University in the States. He was a member of the Chinese Communist Party and an employee of the Second Department of the General Staff Department, responsible for training agents in intelligence-gathering abroad. Largely unknown, however, was its added role in carrying out covert military operations on foreign soil.

Tashi was a sleeper agent. His controller used just two Hindi words to alert him to the mission. Tashi exercised for fifteen minutes, showered in cold water, which spluttered and dribbled. He lathered his scalp, then stepped out of the shower to shave it in front of the mirror, watching the contours of his skull as clumps of hair fell into the basin.

The orange and maroon saffron robe was folded in his bag, and he shook it out, watching the dust fly out around the room. He wrapped it round him, checking the pockets he had sewn on inside. A driver was waiting when he walked outside his building, and he followed him to a red Maruti jeep. If they talked Tashi had been told to address the driver as Sattar, but they travelled in silence.

At Una, the road forked into little more than two country tracks, and Sattar had to ask the way. Tashi wound down his window to let in the fresh morning air. As they climbed the mountain, the countryside became emblazoned with orange and blue spring flowers, sometimes beautiful, sometimes wrecked by the poverty of the villages. After the first bridge across the Dehra River, when the pine trees began, Tashi slipped the grenades into the pockets of his robe, two on each side.

After Lower Dharamsala, which was still a predominantly Indian town, Sattar took the longer but better route to Upper Dharamsala or MacLeod Ganj, driving round by the Gorkha Army Cantonment at Forsyth Ganj. As they climbed and wound round the mountain the view became more and more spectacular, stretching right down the Kangra Valley on one side and up to the mountains, heavily covered in snow, on the other. The Gorkha battalion was fighting in Kashmir and only a skeleton staff looked after the building. But Tashi wanted to see it for himself, to check how quickly professional troops would arrive after the operation. The sentry boxes were mostly deserted and rusted padlocks hung on many of the gates. The windows of the officers' mess were even boarded up.

Kashmir was sucking in the Indian troops. There were almost three-quarters of a million men there now and still the war went on, funded and fuelled by Pakistan, Afghanistan, Iran and a dozen other Islamic countries wanting to cause trouble. Tashi wondered why India had allowed the Tibetans to open up a second front in China. It just seemed crazy to him. He checked his watch. The journey had taken just over five hours. In half an hour his job would be over. They left the cantonment area and passed the church of St John's in the Wilderness, where Lord Elgin, the Earl of Kincardine, was buried. The road was busy, half-blocked with three-wheelers and monks walking slowly in clusters.

Sattar drew up just before the bus stop. European backpackers, in loose, grubby clothing, some with Tibetan beads hanging off them, unloaded their luggage. The stench of the streets was dreadful, with open drains and rubbish piled up everywhere. No one seemed to be cleaning it up. Filthy water ran through rivulets in the road and gathered in potholes. A sign said *Welcome to the Little Lhasa in India*. If this is what Lhasa would be like under Tibetan rule, thank heavens the Chinese have it, thought Tashi.

It was just after 0915. Question Time in the Parliament-in-exile started at 0930. They called it Question Time to satisfy the Western democracies, but it was nothing more than a recitation about waging war against China. Tashi would wait five minutes and then go in. Sattar manoeuvred through the squalid little town and headed down Nawrojee Road towards Lower Dharamsala.

He stopped just outside the compound which housed the small Parliament building. Tashi got out of the car. The pockets held the weight of the grenades well and he felt for the pistol with his right hand. He pulled the robe around him against the morning mountain wind, waiting while Sattar turned the car, then he walked briskly, his head lowered to avoid eye contact with other monks.

He walked under the arch of the compound, looking right towards the offices of the Tibetan security, which he didn't consider a threat – the .38 would see them off if they suspected him. He kept his pace as he took the two steps leading to the Parliament building, ignoring the office marked Dept of Religious Affairs on the right. Directly in front of him were wooden pigeonholes, each stuffed full of memos and newsletters.

He went to the left, taking his bearings from the faded sepia pictures of Mahatma Gandhi and the Dalai Lama.

His left hand moved to a grenade and his right opened the double doors inwards. A wooden screen blocked his view and he stopped. There were no voices behind him. No one chasing or suspecting him. There was no hurry. Hardly a face turned to look at him. A naked light bulb hung from the ceiling over a centre desk where clerks took notes. The room couldn't have been more than 550 square metres, and there were two rows of seats on each side, each with shared microphones which could deflect the grenade throw. A deputy on the right was speaking, leaning across the microphone, and the room was a mixture of saffron robes, business suits and women in striped Tibetan aprons. The red light of a cheap Panasonic camera showed that it was recording the proceedings.

Tashi moved to the left, so that he had a clear line to the Speaker. He drew the pistol, taking the safety catch off and used his left hand to clear the robe. He fired at the Speaker's head, hitting him twice, and as the first scream of panic reverberated around the chamber he threw a grenade towards the last bench by the window. A second grenade he rolled on the floor straight down to the Speaker's chair and the third he tossed to his right, the pins coming out smoothly just like they had when he practised, and he kept the fourth as he backed out of the door.

The grenade in one hand, the pistol in the other, he ran until he was out of the building, then slowed to a fast walk. Three explosions tore through the small room, and Tashi turned, like an onlooker, watching as the victims stumbled out.

Sattar was waiting, the car door open, engine running, and drove off as soon as his passenger got in. Tashi pulled off the robe and struggled into a shirt and trousers. They edged painfully down through Lower Dharamsala, passing an ambulance and a police car before they got to the bottom. An army helicopter hovered over the Dalai Lama's compound. Sattar kept going. Neither man spoke and eventually they were clear. An hour later, just before Palampur, Sattar pulled up past an Ambassador car parked on the left side of the road. This was where they parted company. Tashi left his weapons and robe with Sattar. The Ambassador driver gave Tashi an envelope with his new identity.

The second driver was called Sadek. Like Sattar, he had been trained for Kashmir and was part of the Lashkar-e-Jhangar, the people who had tried to assassinate the Prime Minister of India.

Zhongnanhai, Beijing, China

Local time: 1430 Friday 4 May 2007
GMT: 0630 Friday 4 May 2007

'It was a complete success,' said Tang Siju, the intelligence and strategic planning specialist for the Chinese military.

'We deny involvement and in private negotiations stress that it was purely defensive,' said President Tao Jian. 'We do not want it to become a wider issue.'

They walked in silence past two Zhongnanhai guards. The President had insisted they meet in the grounds, to ensure that the conversation remained completely secret. No Chinese President had survived in office by trusting confidentiality to the walls of his own offices.

Tao stopped walking and stood on the shore of one of the man-made lakes in Zhongnanhai. He brushed away blossom which had fallen on the shoulders of his overcoat. 'China successfully reasserted its regional strength with Operation Dragon Strike, and before he died I promised Comrade President Wang Feng that our stability and prosperity would be safe in my hands. We have an understanding with Japan, and America now knows its limited role in regional affairs. The governments of South-East Asia look to us for advice.'

'Particularly when it comes to handling the West over accusations about human rights abuses and democratic reform,' agreed Tang.

The Chinese President turned to him and smiled. 'Exactly. The status quo in Taiwan and Hong Kong is acceptable to everyone. Only India is the problem and its emerging ambition to compete with us as a regional power.

The sub-continent is an area of unpredictable madness. It worries me.'

'We may have an opportunity to control India before it gets out of hand,' said Tang.

'He who excels in resolving difficulties does so before they arise,' responded Tao, quoting from Sun Tzu's essays on *The Art of War* written in 500 BC. 'I am interested to hear what my strategic planner has to say about it.'

'I was telephoned this morning by General Hamid Khan, Pakistan's Chief of Army Staff,' said Tang. 'He has offered to open a second front again in Kashmir, should we need it.'

'I would like to think we can handle India without Pakistan's help,' said Tao.

'Pakistan is our oldest military ally,' said Tang. 'It would be a quicker solution.'

Prime Minister's Office, South Block, New Delhi, India

Local time: 1200 Friday 4 May 2007
GMT: 0630 Friday 4 May 2007

'Is the Dalai Lama safe?' snapped Hari Dixit.

The Home Minister, Indrajit Bagchi, answered Dixit's question. 'He was in his complex and was not a target, sir.'

'Casualties?' said Dixit to the table at large

'Twelve dead,' said Bagchi. 'The Speaker of the Parliament was shot with a pistol. The others died of shrapnel wounds. Seventeen wounded. Three are expected to die.'

'Responsibility?'

Bagchi referred to Mani Naidu, the head of the Intelligence Bureau. Naidu glanced down at the e-mail printout in front of him. 'Witnesses say it was a single monk, a very cool operator by the sounds of it, who let off two shots at the Speaker before throwing the grenades. He escaped during the mayhem that followed. We may have picked up one of his team near Palampur after the Bhat Vihan Bridge was blown—'

'Blown?' said Dixit.

'A bridge across the Dehra River on the main route down from Dharamsala was destroyed by terrorism, exactly one hour and forty minutes after the attack on the Tibetan Parliament.'

'And your suspect?'

'He was alone in a Maruti jeep,' said Naidu. 'We found a .38 pistol – we are checking it against the rounds which hit the Speaker – with plastic explosives and a Pakistani-made hand grenade. He is a known member of the Lashkar-e-Jhangvi, the most extreme of the Islamic groups operating in Kashmir and Pakistan.'

'They were responsible for the attempt on your life, Prime Minister,' said Chandra Reddy, head of the Research and Analysis Wing.

'I know who they are,' said the Prime Minister impatiently. 'What I don't know is why Pakistan would want to take the Kashmir war into Tibet.'

Briefing

Kashmir

The disputed territory of Kashmir is a legacy of the violent partition between India and Pakistan. It has never known peace. India and Pakistan fought wars over it in 1947, 1965, 1971 and 1999. Since 1949, UN monitors have been posted along a Line of Control (LoC), which has become the border between Indian and Pakistan in the disputed territory. But Kashmiri fighters have continued to go back and forth across it. In 1989, Pakistan organized a new armed insurgency in Kashmir which is continuing today. After more than fifty years the ghost of Kashmir continues to threaten peace in South Asia.

Srinagar, the Kashmir Valley, India

Local time: 1530 Friday 4 May 2007
GMT: 1000 Friday 4 May 2007

He was fifty years old, too old and out of shape to have
trekked through the mountains for three days and nights,
through the LoC, into the Vale of Kashmir and hiding out,
protected by men young enough to be his sons. He wasn't
a member of any of the groups. He had been for a short
while part of Jamaat-e-Islam, but after Afghanistan he had
lost his fire.

He had fought the Russians for five years and had been
trained with the Stinger hand-held missiles sent in by the
CIA. He was good with the Stinger, understanding how it
homed in on heat emissions from the aircraft – helicopter
or fixed-wing, it didn't matter – and he was better than
most at working a way around the decoy flares which easily
seduced the missile away. The Stingers had given the Afghan
war a new life, then suddenly it was over. The Soviet forces
withdrew and the Stingers were packed up in their boxes.
Saeed Khalid retired to a smallholding just across the border
in Pakistan.

He heard that the Taleban government in Afghanistan
had kept some of the Stingers and that Pakistan's Inter-
Service Intelligence Directorate had others. The CIA didn't
get any back, that was for sure. The politicians said the
Soviets had withdrawn because of Gorbachev and *glasnost*.
But men like Saeed who had lived in the mountains and
seen friends die in the war didn't like that explanation. When
they shot down the helicopters, the Mi-28 Havoc gunships
with their 30mm cannon on the nose and AT-6 spiral missile

pods on their pylons, and the Mi-24s which came in like death on the villages, Saeed knew the Stingers had made the difference. Without airpower, the Russians were nothing. Altogether mujahedin fighters like Saeed brought down 270 Soviet aircraft, a success rate of almost 80 per cent.

He opened the box and saw the launcher, all in pieces. He lifted it out carefully, feeling the same rush of excitement as when he had assembled his first weapon after training all those years ago.

When the phone rang in his house outside Quetta near the border, Saeed had recognized the voice, quiet, persuasive and commanding. He knew he would have no choice but to obey the Chief of Army Staff of Pakistan, General Hamid Khan, his friend and tutor, who had trained him with the weapon which defeated the Soviets in Afghanistan.

'You are the only one I trust and the only one I know who can use them,' said Hamid Khan.

They had strapped the metal cases to the sides of mules and walked them over the hills like they had done twenty-five years before. They travelled by night and hid out during the day and they reached the rendezvous near Srinagar with two hours of darkness left. He was protected by members of the Lashkar-e-Jhangvi, the group he heard had tried to kill the Prime Minister. The rumour was that Hamid Khan had ordered the bomb attack on the car and chosen the place and time.

Saeed had kept track of the groups as they became more and more extreme, the Jamiat-e-Ulema-e-Hind, the Sunni group, Jamiat-e-Ulema-e-Islam, who took on the minority Shias, then the more extreme Sipah-e-Sahaba who wanted to go to war against Iran, and the Harkat-ul-Ansar, the first group into Kashmir, and finally Hamid's very own terrorist group, the Lashkar-e-Jhangvi, the fighters who would win back Kashmir.

The door of the hut opened slightly, just wide enough for two scouts to slip in. They couldn't have been more than eighteen and they didn't carry weapons, because it was safer for them. Their training was in aircraft recognition and they told him exactly which aircraft had just landed in Srinagar and how he should shoot it down. Saeed knew the aircraft well. It was a Russian-made Mi-26, known as the Halo and the world's most powerful helicopter. Saeed listened to the boys talking, about its position on helipad, the flight route they thought it would take out, the mine-field around the perimeter fence and the gap in the Indian defences where they could fire, and run with a chance to save their own lives.

It would be safer than the barren land of Afghanistan, where even in the mountains there was barely a tree to give cover. Even though they had trekked through Kashmir at night, he had seen the deepest green ricefields and a landscape marked by tall poplar trees. They had walked along paths which took them through orchards of apple and plum trees, villages of tall, walled farmhouses made of wood and brick and showing off a wealth he had never seen in Afghanistan.

'We just want to let them know that the Stingers are out of the boxes again,' Hamid Khan had told him. 'Let them know their airspace is no longer safe and that we are in the heart of the valley.'

Indian Army Headquarters, Srinagar, India

Local time: 1600 Friday 4 May 2007
GMT: 1030 Friday 4 May 2007

The Indian Home Minister, Indrajit Bagchi, ushered the three community leaders out of his temporary office in a suite at what used to be the Maharajah's palace, overlooking Dal Lake. It had been a tiring afternoon. From the crisis meeting at South Block he flew by military aircraft to Srinagar. The Prime Minister had wanted Bagchi to go up, rather than the National Security Advisor, to stress a civilian rather than a military future for Kashmir. After twenty years of insurgency, it was time to stop talking about war and start discussing investment.

The meeting with the multi-ethnic Kashmir Chamber of Commerce was to discuss bringing back investment to the Valley. The army had wanted to hold it at the secure civilian complex inside the Badami Bagh Cantonment. But Bagchi was adamant that it should be somewhere with less of a direct link to the war. They compromised on the barracks at the former Maharajah's palace. It had, after all, been the luxury Oberoi Palace Hotel until the insurgency began.

Bagchi preferred to maintain a casual approach, a brightly coloured open-neck shirt, faded denim jeans and soft shoes whenever possible. Bagchi preferred the neutrality of Western dress in a place as culturally and religiously sensitive as Kashmir. Waiting for him in the foyer was General Prabhu Ninan, the Northern army commander, who had been credited making substantive inroads against the insurgency in the past eighteen months. The armoured personnel carrier was parked right up against the palace doors for the five-minute drive to the Badami Bagh helipad, next to the Corps Headquarters. Bodyguards, known as Black Cats because of their black dungaree uniform, fanned out on either side. They were part of the seven-thousand-strong National Security Guard (NSG), created in 1984 after the assassination of Indira Gandhi to meet the emerging threats of terrorism in India. Normally, Bagchi would only have been given local police protection. But with the Dharamsala attack only hours old, the Prime Minister had insisted the more highly trained NSG be used. A high brick wall topped with razor wire protected the palace, which with its panoramic views of the Dal Lake had once been internationally famous as a venue for afternoon tea. At the gates, concrete tank traps had been built to prevent suicide car bombers ramming themselves into the palace grounds.

'The Antonov has engine problems,' said Ninan, ushering the Home Minister towards the door. 'We are taking a helicopter, also with wounded. The weather is becoming problematic. But if we take off in twenty minutes we should be clear of the mountains before it closes in.'

Saeed hid in the thick undergrowth of the Ningali forests 500 metres south-east of the helipad. He recognized the scent of wild briar roses and nearby there was the rush of water from a fast-running stream. The boys from the Lashkar-e-Jhangvi carried the three Stingers and took up positions around him, ensuring he could concentrate on the job. They communicated using sign language and stepped quietly through the undergrowth. The spot, near the stream, had been chosen to cover any noise from the assembly of the weapons.

He unclipped the metal case and bought out the sections: the missile, the disposable launch tube, the detachable grip

stock and the integral Identification Friend or Foe system
which made up the sixteen kilograms of weapon they had
been carrying. Saeed loved the lightweight cool black metal
of the missile which had avenged the misery the Soviets had
brought to Afghanistan. It was designed to be used against
high-speed, low-level, ground-attack aircraft, but that didn't
mean he couldn't go for a lumbering Mi-26.

In the United States Marine Corps the Stinger is a
certified round of ammunition, a use-and-throw-away
weapon, which is what Saeed would do, so that India would
have no doubt about what had shot down its aircraft. He
checked that Hamid Khan had given him the best type of
Stinger they had. It was fitted with a Rosette Scan Pattern
image-scanning technique, which would allow the missile
to distinguish between the target and the Mi-26's counter-
measures, decoys such as flares, chaff or background clutter.
The system also had the Target Adaptive Guidance, which
would steer the missile towards the most vulnerable part of
the aircraft. He would set it for a fire-and-forget heat-
seeking capability. One missile even winging the aircraft
would almost certainly bring it down.

What worried Saeed was his range. He expected the
aircraft to pass overhead, flying south. If it went in any
other direction, moving low and fast, he would have problems with the trajectory. The Stinger's range was just over
four kilometres. He would have to act quickly.

General Ninan saw Bagchi up into the helicopter with his
private secretary, and a crew-member showed them into
the four-seat passenger compartment just aft of the flight
deck. At the back Bagchi could see six stretchers, two with
blankets over the faces of the dead, four with the wounded
and two on drips secured to the bulkhead of the fuselage –

victims of the low-intensity conflict which took place every day in Kashmir. They would be treated at the 92 Base Hospital, often referred to as the Advanced Command Hospital. A doctor looked impatiently at his watch and adjusted the flow to a drip. Ten commandos boarded, followed by Ninan and his ADC, who joined Bagchi in the compartment.

Bagchi put on his headphone and switched on the intercom to listen to the cockpit communication. He watched through the window as another dozen commandos took up new positions around the aircraft. The engine shuddered and the huge eight-bladed rotor began to turn. The helicopter lurched upwards and settled back, and one by one the commandos boarded, the last one jumping up as the aircraft was moving forward, seconds from lifting off.

'The control tower is reporting fighting five hundred metres outside the perimeter fence,' said the pilot through the intercom. 'Should we continue?'

The Mi-26 shook as the pilot held the aircraft back, its wheels settling down again. Ninan looked at Bagchi: 'Did you hear that?'

'Your call,' said Bagchi.

The major in charge of the commando unit made the decision: 'We should go now, sir,' he said. 'Fly north, then double back and we will be clear of the fighting.'

It was a routine Indian patrol. There was no tip-off or betrayal. The Indian soldiers were moving through the plantation towards the stream, pausing to joke with each other, unaware that they were under threat. The fighters of the Lashkar-e-Jhangvi opened fire first. Three Indians were hit before the others could return fire, and the guerrillas went on the offensive to try and flush them out and keep the protection around Saeed. They failed to hit the radio operator in time. He sent out an alert as soon as he heard the first burst of machine-gun fire.

Saeed had his back to the fighting. It was like the war all over again: Soviet troops on the ground. Soon a helicopter gunship was overhead. His experience took over. He had missed the tension, and as he raised the launcher to his shoulder, keeping his eye on the fence, waiting for the helicopter, he felt good, glad that Hamid had called on him to come here.

Still the boys didn't talk. He could sense them running behind him, changing positions, the controlled fire of two of three rounds at a time. He heard a grenade and knew the boys were getting hit, dying as the enemy fire got closer. Then he saw the rotor blades of the Mi-26 rise above the trees, its nose down, the shimmering wave of heat around the engine casing. It turned on itself, but not flying south towards them as it should, picking up speed, keeping low, perhaps two kilometres away already, with a trajectory which made the Stinger like an anti-tank weapon, near-horizontal fire. The missile had an impact force of Mach 2.0, hit-to-kill accuracy.

A boy was right beside him with a second missile, in case the first one missed. He had stayed at his post, not fighting, watching his friends fall, doing what he was told to do. But he pointed up, and a second helicopter was coming towards them, smaller, the Mi-25, with a 30mm cannon in its nose. Saeed knew it. He had shot it down before.

He lined up the launcher's sights towards the airstrip, judging that the Mi-26 was at 500 feet and he fired, turned and took the second Stinger from the boy just as the cannon rounds cut up the ground around them. The boy fell first, then Saeed was hit, the Stinger hurled out of his hand and his torso was torn apart by two cannon shells.

The pilot tried to attain height over the helipad itself, hoping to get to at least 1,000 feet before adopting its flight path. But before that, Bagchi lurched against the bulkhead as the missile smashed into the engine cowling of the helicopter. It exploded instantaneously, tearing off rotor blades and sending the aircraft hurtling back to the ground where it exploded in a ball of fire.

Prime Minister's Office, South Block, New Delhi, India

Local time: 1700 Friday 4 May 2007
GMT: 1130 Friday 4 May 2007

'**Ring them on** the hotline,' said the Indian Prime Minister.

'Ring them and say what?' asked the RAW Special Secretary, Chandra Reddy. 'The weekly conversation was only at noon yesterday.'

'That was yesterday.' Hari Dixit pulled his head out of his hands and re-read the message, which confirmed that his Northern army commander and his Home Minister were both dead, together with twenty-two Black Cat commandos, two nurses, a doctor and four wounded soldiers. A second message sent an hour later said that the launcher for a Stinger missile had been found 500 metres south of the airport, where Indian forces had been engaging Kashmiri insurgents in a firefight.

Two direct lines had been established between India and Pakistan in an attempt to stop skirmishes spilling over into war. The first was set up in the wake of the 1971 war, when the Simla Agreement was signed between the Indian Prime Minister Indira Gandhi and Zulfiqar Ali Bhutto of Pakistan. The line ran between the two offices of the director-generals of military operations. There was at least one weekly scheduled conversation, every Tuesday, and more if cross-border activities intensified. In the late eighties, a second line was created between the two Prime Ministers' offices. Pakistan had feared an Indian invasion from the Operation Brass Tacks military exercises, and there was ongoing nuclear concern by both countries.

Dixit stood up and put his glasses back on. 'We'll go in

gently. Tell them that Ninan and Bagchi have been killed and we want an assurance that they had nothing to do with it.'

Reddy gave the instruction and the two men waited while the call was being put through.

'They're not answering,' said Reddy.

'I don't understand,' said Dixit.

'They're playing games. It's what we did to them during Brass Tacks in 1986. They thought we were going to invade and we didn't pick up the hotline.'

'Meaning . . . ?'

'It's not the Prime Minister,' said Reddy. 'It's Hamid Khan. He's testing our resolve.'

Briefing

Pakistan

Pakistan was created on 14 August 1947 with the partition of India, and the Islamic republic was proclaimed on 23 March 1956. During the Cold War it was regarded as a staunch ally of the West, but since then wove a chaotic tapestry of Islam, Western-style democracy and military dictatorship. Forever feeling threatened by India and ruled by dishonest leaders from within, Pakistan had not yet developed into the Islamic success envisioned by its founders. It was getting poorer and more violent. At the turn of the century, it had recently proclaimed itself a nuclear power and a military government had been installed. Under constant international pressure, Pakistan embarked upon another experiment with democracy, but it failed to pull the country out of its morass. Once again, the army and Islam emerged as attractive alternatives.

General Headquarters, Rawalpindi, Pakistan

Local time: 1645 Friday 4 May 2007
GMT: 1145 Friday 4 May 2007

'**Don't answer it,**' said General Mohammed Hamid Khan.

'It's the Prime Minister's hotline,' said Captain Mohammed Masood, his aide de camp.

'I have instructed the Prime Minister's office to let it ring.'

Khan paced up and down in front of a large map on the wall of the underground bunker which he had made his permanent office in Chaklala, the cantonment area of Rawalpindi. Right now, the whims of a dishonest Prime Minister were the least of his concerns. There were more powerful forces moulding Pakistan's future that Khan planned to bring to bear over the next few days, forces which would end the decades of corruption which had kept his country in the Dark Ages.

'Get me General Tang Siju in Beijing,' Khan ordered, and when the call came through the brief conversation gave him all he wanted.

'Your support is a mark of friendship to the People's Republic of China,' said Tang.

Khan then ordered Masood to drive him through the evening traffic to the run-down tenements of Aabpara District in Rawalpindi. For dangerous journeys Masood often doubled up as Khan's driver. He needed a man whom he could trust completely and who, like him, came from a military family of long standing.

The plain-clothed commandos from the Cherat Special Services Group fanned out on the narrow roads around

Khan's destination. Although their weapons were concealed and they dressed raggedly in an attempt to disguise themselves as the poor, their purposeful movements gave them away immediately as fighting men – but they were identified as mujahedin, whose breeding ground was in Aabpara, not as commandos from the Pakistan army.

Khan stayed in the car while Masood climbed the stairs of the decrepit building. The bodyguards of the Islamic cleric whom the general had come to see challenged Masood and ordered him to hand over his side-arm. Masood responded by drawing the weapon, removing the safety catch and levelling it at the head of one of the bodyguards. He was acting precisely on orders given by Khan.

Khan got out of the car and silently climbed the stairs behind Masood. Then everyone heard the unmistakable clatter of a Huey helicopter gunship overhead.

'Tell Mullah al-Bishri to open the door,' snapped Khan, 'or the armed forces of Pakistan will burn down this street.'

The bodyguard knocked on the door. It opened, and Khan pushed his way through into the room. It had no furniture apart from a low coffee table against the far wall. A red carpet was spread all over, with smaller carpets thrown on top of it and hanging on the wall. The man sitting cross-legged by the coffee table was one of the world's most powerful Islamic leaders. He didn't get up, but waved his hand for Khan to sit down and join him. Masood and the bodyguards stayed outside and the door was closed.

'Yahya was like a son to me,' said the Mullah. 'He was doing you no harm. He was fighting the Jihad and I'm told you gave orders for him to be killed.'

Khan did not answer.

'He was killed in Egypt by a single gunshot wound to the head in the Upper Nile town of Asyut. The gunman came from the Inter-Services Intelligence Agency of Pakistan. I know because we caught him and he said it was you, General, who ordered the death of a freedom fighter.'

Mullah al-Bishri was the leader of the Jamaat-e-Islami, one of the oldest and most deeply entrenched Islamic groups. In a way it was a loose umbrella group for the numerous groups which had based themselves in Pakistan. Jamaat-e-Islami had the biggest network, but others could prove to be equally important in balancing power. The Hizb-ul Mujahadeen was one of the oldest militant groups, made up mostly of Kashmiris. The Sunni Islamic Lashkar-e-Tayyaba represented some of the poorest areas of Pakistan. The Harkat-ul-Mujahedin was an international brigade of fighters, Afghans, Algerians, Egyptians and even guerrillas from Saudi Arabia, people who could pose more of a threat to the stability of the country than the Indian army. And increasingly Khan was seeing the defiant Tehrik-e-Jihad in operation, fighters who came to prominence in 1999 in the battle for Kargil.

He sensed that even Mullah al-Bishri was having trouble maintaining his authority. Al-Bishri had been an ally of Zia-ul-Haq and of Nawaz Sharif, the two Pakistani leaders who held greatest sway over the political arena in the last two decades of the twentieth century. But since then the political landscape had changed dramatically. Over the years, Al-Bishri's own views had hardened, reflecting the country's lurch from a moderate to a fundamentalist Islamic society. He now argued that there were no national frontiers for true believers and that, after the victory in Afghanistan, the next natural battlefield was Kashmir. He predicted that Kashmir would soon be won and had ordered the recruitment and training of young men to fight in the Central Asian republics and even take the Jihad across China's western borders into Xinjiang. One intonation at Friday prayers or one command to his followers throughout Pakistan could bring millions out onto the streets. It was he, more than any other man, who could depose the civilian government, and it was Al-Bishri to whom Khan had to turn for support now.

But the balance of their relationship was delicate. While Khan was a military commander, Al-Bishri would always be an opposition force, a grass-roots activist, a criticizer, but never an achiever. Khan, acutely aware of the cleric's power, also resented it. Al-Bishri's ultimate aim was to form an Islamic combination of Central Asia, Pakistan, Afghanistan and Saudi Arabia to create a formidable global force. Yet Khan knew it would never happen. Saudi Arabia bought its cars and fridges from Japan, Europe and America, and its missiles from China. If Pakistan ever interfered either in China or in any oil-producing country in the Middle East it would be abandoned to the whims of a Hindu India. Khan accepted this. Al-Bishri did not.

When Khan was summoned to his run-down house in Aabpara, the message said he should be there within the hour, showing how out of touch al-Bishri was with the schedules of the outside world. The cleric was an academic, steeped in the Koran and in Islamic writings, far away from the world of satellite telephones, laser-guided missiles and the international banking system used by his fighters. He was their moral compass and their religious legitimacy.

'I am told that the Prime Minister is about to declare himself Amir-ul-Momineen, leader of Muslims,' said Al-Bishri. 'They say that power has gone to his head.'

'I have heard the same,' said Khan.

'But I hear also that you favour cancelling the Shariat law and bringing back a colonial-style judicial system.'

'Yes,' said Khan bluntly. 'The Shariat will not encourage foreign investment in Pakistan.'

'The Shariat is the law for the Islamic people of the world. We do not need their foreign investment.'

'The Shariat is a law ordained in the Koran and Sunnah, the words and deeds of the prophet. Whenever there is no precedent in either of the two sources, then jurists use independent thinking [ijtihad] to deliver their verdict, and this is variable from jurist to jurist. This is not understood or used by the West, and many Muslims consider it unsuitable for trade and business.

'Sometimes, jurists have resorted to using either analogy [quias] or consensus [ijma] to arrive at a decision. Out of the 6,666 Koranic verses, only three hundred have any legal connection, meaning that Shariat jurists have a large scope for interpretation. The international banking system and long-term investors would not operate under such a legal system. Their money will only go where it feels safe, and unless it is protected by the rule of law it will go elsewhere. In order to modernize our country, we may have to compromise on some of its ideals.'

'Saudi Arabia lives under the Shariat and is friendly with the West.'

'Saudi Arabia has oil.'

Al-Bishri sipped his tea and was silent for some time. 'You have studied your subject, General.'

'Yes. I have thought a lot about it.'

'And part of your thinking was the killing of Yahya?'

'China is worried that we are sending mujahedin to cause unrest across its western border. I have to assure them that we are not.'

'What have you told them?'

'We will try to ensure that no mujahedin, whether they come from the Sudan, Saudia Arabia, Bangladesh or Aabpara, will wage war against the People's Republic of China.'

'And in return?'

'They will supply us with enough weapons and political support to defeat India.'

The cleric nodded, then said: 'You are a clever young man, but I fear our people will not understand you. China and investment are not things they know about. The Islamic revolution is a tide, General Khan, which ebbs and flows. It is flowing towards Central Asia and no one can stop it. Not you. Not me. Any man who tries would be a fool. However, perhaps there is a way we can stem the tide at least for our time on this earth, and it is the only way I can guarantee my continued support.'

'What is that?'

'Give us Kashmir, General. If you give us Kashmir, you will be the hero of the Islamic world.'

The President's Office, The White House, Washington, DC

Local time: 0830 Friday 4 May 2007
GMT: 1330 Friday 4 May 2007

'**Is there anything** else?' said the President of the United States. John Hastings stood up, clipping his fountain pen into his jacket pocket. The weekly meeting with the National Security Agency had been routine. His astute National Security Advisor, Tom Bloodworth, had run through the agenda quickly, knowing that the President had elections to think about and a spate of race riots in Washington itself. After the Balkan campaign and with a secured peace on the Korean peninsula, the President had assured the American people that he would keep his eye more on domestic affairs than his predecessor.

'If individual nations are to mature into modern, developed societies, they must learn to take control of their own affairs,' he had said in his inaugural speech. 'Western Europe and America did not reach their present level of wealth and stability without spilling the blood of their own people. Both England and the United States fought horrible civil wars and just because they were many hundreds of years ago does not make the suffering any less for those who took part. We had no NATO or UN to intervene then, and maybe that was the right way to sort out our problems. Since the Western democracies began to see themselves as the policemen of the world, civil war and slaughter has not lessened. The Rwandas, Kosovos and Cambodias continue.

'My words might sound harsh to some. But by trying to help we have, in fact, failed to help. So perhaps if these societies so intent on being enemies with each other know that no one is going to come to their aid, they will think twice about starting a war.'

So far President Hastings had kept his word. In the first two years of his presidency the television networks had become less interested in covering stories of Third World massacres and refugees. It was an electoral gamble, but not a blind one. Hastings ran for the presidency after resigning his post as the chief executive of one of America's biggest news networks. He understood the link between journalists and power, believing that underneath the bravado of many top reporters was the yearning to be a politician.

The first story to test his policy occurred in Liberia, when every man, woman and child in three villages was slaughtered. He refused to answer questions on the massacre, saying he hadn't been properly briefed.

'Why not, sir?' shouted a young women from what had been his own network.

'Just as I haven't been briefed on the 20,614 murders in our own country last year. Nor have I seen the file on the twenty-seven murders which took place in New York last week. That violence is the result of poverty, racism and hatred, no different to the motivation which has created the slaughter in Liberia. The killings there do not threaten American national interests, nor are they a threat to world peace. What do I say to Marilyn Deane, the mother of Brent Deane, aged fifteen, who was gunned down in a Washington DC drugs war last week? What do I say when she asks me to make her neighbourhood more safe? Do I turn round and say: "Don't bother me now, I'm comforting a mother in Liberia"?'

With that retort, condemnation of Hastings's policy petered out and the networks which had been flying crews and satellite dishes into Liberia, anticipating American involvement, pulled out. The massacres continued, but the story ended.

After their assistants left the Oval Office, the President poured his National Security Advisor a coffee and moved from the coffee table on the blue wool carpet in the middle of the room to sit back behind his desk.

Hastings leant back on his chair, his head brushing the yellow curtains hanging from the sash windows, looking out over the front lawn of the White House. Light streaming in silhouetted his figure, which was flanked by the Star Spangled Banner and the Eagle emblem. He lifted a pile of papers out of his in-tray. 'Pull up a chair, Tom,' he said. 'I have to sign papers while we talk.'

'I'm not suggesting we do anything about it,' began Bloodworth. 'But I wanted to mention developments in India to you.'

Hastings sipped his coffee. 'All I remember about India is that it was a very difficult story to ever get anyone interested in. Even when they let off the bomb in 1998. People just didn't really care.'

'Just before this meeting, Kashmiri insurgents shot down an Indian military helicopter with a Stinger surface-to-air missile,' said Bloodworth. 'One that we supplied to the Afghan resistance during the war in the eighties. The Home Minister and the Northern army commander were killed, together with about thirty others.'

Hastings stopped writing: 'Will India retaliate?'

'We're asking her not to, but I fear she will. I've ordered top-level satellite surveillance over both countries. Our ambassadors will appeal for restraint and we will keep a watch.'

'Pakistan?'

'It's on the edge, sir. The Prime Minister has no power. The show is being run by the new Chief of Army Staff,

Hamid Khan. He's a former tank commander. He was on our payroll during the Afghan war to train up the mujahedin against the Soviets. Then he headed up the ISIA, Pakistan's Intelligence Agency's operation, to start the new wave of insurgency in Kashmir. He's certainly no fool and we haven't ruled him out staging a coup in the near future. Khan would have ordered the Stinger operation to bolster his own position.'

'She's not going to do an Iran on us, is she, Tom?'

'Not that bad, sir. But Pakistan is definitely slipping from our grip.'

'Goddamn basket case,' said the President, switching his attention to the documents in front of him, then looking up again. 'And I guess you want a private chat about Tibet as well. I saw it on the news. The Indians have said sorry and that it was a mistake. The Chinese seem to have responded by shooting up the Tibetan Parliament-in-exile.'

Bloodworth nodded. 'Even if it stops there, it means there is a substantive split in the Tibetan resistance movement.'

'I thought the Dalai Lama advocated non-violence,' said Hastings.

'He does. But others are getting impatient. They see the progress made by people like the Kosovo Liberation Army through violence and think they should do the same.'

'And that was a damn shambles.'

The President put down his pen and let Bloodworth talk. 'For months, the Chinese have been asking India to rein in the Tibetans and India has done nothing. Ever since the 1998 nuclear tests, when India named China as her main enemy, relations have been frosty. What I really fear is that the Indians see the Tibetan insurgency as a means of undermining the authority of Beijing. In other words, the Indians are letting the Tibetans do their dirty work for them.'

'And whose side should we be on?' said the President.

'India is the world's biggest democracy and in a constant political mess. China has a seat on the UN Security Council, has helped us with the Balkans, North Korea, Indonesia, you name it. Our trade is huge.'

'So we sit on the fence,' interrupted the President.

'Except I sense our neutrality is about to be severely tested. Our intelligence suggests that Lama Togden, who was lifted from the prison, has not been picked up by the Chinese. We don't know where he is, but he's still free and if he gets out alive he's expected to ask for asylum in the United States.'

Gongkar County, Tibet

The men laid blankets on the cold rocks and lowered the stretcher onto them so that Togden could drink water. Choedrak pulled a bottle out from inside his coat, where he had been keeping it from turning to ice. He tilted it to Togden's lips, chapped and coated with frozen blood, and held his head, while the monk let the water drain into his mouth.

Swiftly deteriorating weather struck Togden down once they climbed into the high mountain passes. For the whole of the second day he had a fever and was semi-conscious. The men carried him and led their ponies rather than ride in order to keep warm. They wrapped protective cloths around their faces to shield them from lashing rain and snow-blindness. Reports kept reaching them of movements of Chinese troops sent in to cut them off, but Choedrak had prepared the route well. Armed units from the Special Frontier Force welcomed them at many villages. They were hiding out along the mountain roads, waiting in ambush for the Chinese.

Once they reached the higher ground, it was easier to hide from helicopters. But the weather was appalling. The pursuit continued, and, before dark, they shot down two helicopters with their heavy machine guns. The Chinese also used new microlights, fitted with GPS and aerial surveillance equipment. They buzzed the Tibetans, flying in driving rain, sending back details of their positions. Then ground-attack aircraft roared in with cannon and bombs.

But the mountains were too dangerous for the pilots to be accurate. They spat fire into the snow and caused avalanches, but never once did they come close to hurting Togden and his party.

Indian Air Force Base, Lohegaon, Maharastra

On the radio command 'Shikar' the aircraft roared along the runway. The early morning sun flashed through the cockpit onto the instrument panels for the two crew and the distinctive tail-fins of the aircraft from No. 24 Squadron 'Hunting Hawks' shook on take-off as one by one the pilots took their aircraft up. Their serial numbers were SB 076, SB 082, SB 083, SB 084, SB 091 and SB 092.

The mission could have been carried out with different aircraft: the MiG-27s from the 'Scorpios' Squadron; the multi-role MiG-29s from the secretive No. 223 Squadron; the French-built Mirage 2000H from No. 1 'Tigers' Squadron; or even the British Jaguars, which had been adapted to carry nuclear weapons. But the six planes lined up at the Indian Air Force base east of Bombay, painted in the national tricolour livery of saffron, white and green, were the cream of the country's air force. Russian-designed but Indian-built, the SU-30MKI was one of the most formidable combat aircraft in the world. Such was Russia's enthusiasm for the SU-30 that many other aircraft projects were starved of cash in order to develop it. As a buyer, India's historic military relationship with the Soviet Union and then with Russia gave it the first option. Once the order was secured, Russia refused supplies to potential enemies, such as China and Pakistan. This was why India had now chosen to make a show of using the sort of airpower that its neighbouring enemies would never now possess.

The SU-30 series was initially designed as a long-range

interceptor, to provide cover for Russia's naval forces and to patrol the enormous and remote border areas. The MKI export version acquired by India had been built with a multi-role added ground-attack capability, and the problems it had encountered in the late nineties had now been solved. The Russian avionics systems had been replaced by French and Israeli cockpit instrumentation suites, with a special feature of four-liquid colour displays for both the pilot in the front and the gunner and weapons-systems operator, on a slightly raised seat behind for better vision. The division of the work-load between the two crew was balanced to ensure maximum range and highest air-superiority endurance. The specialized equipment in the rear cockpit also allowed the aircraft to act as a mini-AWACs and command post. The primary weapon sensor was a Zhuk N001 pulse Doppler multimode radar with a range of 105 kilometres, with which it could track two airborne targets up to 75 kilometres. A secondary weapons sensor was the Infrared Search and Tracking system (IRST), with a 370 kilometre range.

The aircraft had been specially equipped for this mission, and did not carry typical weapons packages. The air-to-air missile systems were limited because India did not expect enemy aircraft to be scrambled and intercepted during the few minutes the strikes would take. A decision had also been taken not to use free-fall bombs, in order to prevent allegations of indiscriminate attack.

The pilots retained their helmet-mounted sights for use with close-combat R-77 missiles in a look-and-shoot capability, together with air-to-surface missile and jamming pods for destroying and disabling air-defence systems. Their main attack weapons were the 30mm cannon, for strafing, air-to-surface missiles, including the Kh-31P anti-radar missiles and laser-guided fire-and-forget missiles, and laser-guided bombs.

When Group Captain Amrit Dhal reached 33,000 feet he sent the single high-frequency radio message 'Checkmate'.

Flying at more than Mach 2, they were less than forty minutes from reaching their target. At high altitude, the SU-30MK had a range of 3,200 kilometres, and 7,250 kilometres with air-to-air refuelling. It would not be used this time; the aircraft were due to return to the big airbase in Ambala, just south of Chandigarh, where they would stay until the potential for conflict had diminished.

After taking off to the east, the warplanes turned north until they reached Srinagar, 1,700 kilometres away. The take-off from Lohegaon was picked up by Pakistani radar operators, but did not prompt any alert. It could have been nothing but a routine operation. At Srinagar, though, the aircraft turned due west and within minutes had burst through Pakistani airspace. The targets were between 3,000 and 4,000 feet above sea level. Five of the aircraft dropped to as low as 2,000 feet above ground as they flew across the Line-of-Control into Pakistani territory.

General Headquarters, Rawalpindi, Pakistan

The photographs of the dead were mostly of young men, but many of the bodies were charred beyond recognition. The villages named on the photograph captions were Kohala, Garhi, Mahandri and Jarad, just inside Pakistani-controlled Kashmir. Houses were in flames. Patches of scorched grass smouldered and lines of refugees were stumbling away along the tracks, which led to safer areas.

The list of the victims was too long for Hamid Khan to do anything but glance down it. He noticed a twelve-year-old girl from Garhi and an eighty-two-year-old man from Jarad. The Indian airstrikes killed 140 Pakistanis, most of them civilians. Pakistan sovereignty had been violated. People were fleeing right along the LoC, an estimated sixty thousand, no longer believing that their army would protect them. The frontier, which had kept the two sides apart for sixty years, was no longer recognized as a valid border.

'What are the Indians saying?' Khan asked Masood, who had brought the photographs into his military bunker office.

'Unni Krishnan,the Chief of Army Staff, said after damage assessment that there may be more strikes. The attack aircraft have returned not to Lohegaon, but to Ambala, which is only a few minutes' flying time from the front. Our radar has detected ten more SU-30MKs also flying up to Ambala, and Mirage 2000 fighters are expected for any future sorties.'

'Artillery exchanges along the LoC?'

'No substantive increase, sir. But continuing.'

Hamid Khan stood up and opened the door to his office to look out on the war room. It was dominated by maps of Kashmir, a scene familiar to Khan throughout his military career. Over the years, the war room had transformed: once little more than a meeting room with dog-eared charts pinned on the wall and the changing order of battle written on a blackboard, now it was alive with colourful computer imagery. One whole wall was taken up with Kashmir itself. Smaller areas were magnified to show details of the shelling on Indian towns like Kargil and Drass; reinforcements in the Pakistan city of Muzafarabad, the capital of the nominally independent Azad Kashmir; and the strategic forward sectors of Tatta Pani, Darra Sher Khan, Bhattal Ghambeer, Khoi Ratta and Pir Badher. A special screen illuminated the tightly guarded sector of Kahuta, the site of Pakistan's uranium-reprocessing plant, a key element of its nuclear weapons programme, which in an air war would be vulnerable to Indian attack. In 1994, both countries had agreed not to target each other's nuclear facilities. But if the conflict worsened, Hamid Khan would have to assume that the agreement was null and void.

Khan knew each of the sectors well. He had fought in them, controlled them, watched men die in them, and he understood enough about the Kashmir terrain to know that the war was unwinnable without a political settlement or the complete defeat of either India or Pakistan. As he stepped out, the colonel in charge of the shift walked straight over. 'The Indian army has ordered the evacuation of two hundred villages along the Punjab border with Pakistan, sir.'

Khan took the sheet of paper the colonel was holding.

'These are from Chinese satellite surveillance,' explained the colonel. 'The town of Khemkaran, population sixteen thousand, thirty kilometres south of the main Lahore–Amritsar road.' The colonel ran his finger down the blurred image of the main street. 'We estimate only five hundred people are left there. The people are moving everything away – household possessions, vehicles, if they have them, even livestock.' He handed Khan another photograph. 'This is what is coming in.'

Khan could see clearly the columns of tanks and artillery shuffling west past the refugees to take up their positions on the Pakistan border.

Briefing

Nuclear tests

In May 1998, India stunned the world when it conducted five underground nuclear tests in the space of forty-eight hours, signalling her emergence as a nuclear power. The exact scope of the programme is still under dispute, but on 11 May, in tests known as *Shakti*, meaning 'power', India claims to have exploded two fission bombs and a thermo-nuclear – or hydrogen – bomb. On 13 May, two more sub-kiloton – or low-yield – weapons were exploded. Pakistan responded. It says it conducted five tests on 28 May and another two on 30 May. Two of the tests are believed to have been low-yield and none thermonuclear. At the time, it was estimated that India had stocks for up to thirty-five warheads and Pakistan had no more than fifteen bombs – although these figures were constantly disputed. By 2005, India possessed 150 warheads, and Pakistan 82. Despite the recent election of a Hindu nationalist government, which had cited nuclear testing in its manifesto, the American intelligence services had failed to detect signs that the tests were about to take place.

National Security Council, Washington, DC

Local time: 2300 Wednesday 2 May 2007
GMT: 0400 Thursday 3 May 2007

'**These have come** in in the past hour, sir.'

Tom Bloodworth, the National Security Advisor, was working alone under a single desk light when his office door was pushed open with a light knock by his second-shift secretary, who was on duty from 1800 until midnight. His office was in a building in the White House grounds, connected by a passageway to the West Wing, where most of the presidential business was conducted.

He opened the folder of photographs which Judy Lewis put on his desk. 'Give me half an hour undisturbed, will you, Judy,' he said, meaning no calls from Asia, which was beginning to buzz at this time. The prints had been processed by the Directorate of the National Photographic Interpretation Center and delivered to his office through a high-capacity fibre-optic cable link. Bloodworth spread out the photographs on his desk just like he had in his early days as one of the twelve hundred specialists at the Office of Imagery Analysis. Now it had become part of the National Imagery and Mapping Agency, jointly run by the Pentagon and the CIA and operated from the Washington Navy Yard.

He had sworn by IMINT (imagery satellite intelligence) for most of his career as an intelligence officer, until May 1998 when India surprised the world by conducting five underground nuclear tests. Four satellites had been deployed full time on India, with cameras powerful enough to read the time on a soldier's wristwatch. Analysts had previously picked out bursts of activity at the Pokharan testing range in 1982, 1995 and 1997, which had led to American questions about the nuclear weapons programme. But they failed to detect India's entry onto the nuclear stage. The CIA was guilty of one of the biggest failures in its history.

Admittedly, the Indians had carried out most of their work at night and under cloud cover when satellite vision was poor. They also knew the time the satellites would be overhead and avoided activity during that time. They used intricate communication codes. Scientists dressed in camouflage uniforms to make them look like soldiers in training. But none of that was an excuse. At the nearby village of Khetolai, a stone and sand Rajasthani settlement with a population of twelve hundred just three miles from Pokharan, even farmers knew. An Indian army major drove there shortly before the tests, warning the villagers that there would be some heightened activity. One villager, who remembered the shuddering of the ground during the 1974 nuclear tests, replied: 'Don't worry. We know you're going to do another test.'

Bloodworth, who then headed the CIA's South Asia desk, called for a list of consumer products used in Khetolai. He found it was among the poorest and most basic communities in India. The villagers used the Parachute brand of coconut oil, made by Marico Industries, and detergents such as Surf, a product of Hindustan Lever; the only luxury of any kind was the Hero bicycle, made in Jalandhar City in Punjab. If these goods were in Khetolai, they would be all over India. Bloodworth set about creating a network of low-level agents, known as HUMINT or human intelligence. Truck drivers and sales representatives would be debriefed on a regular basis to get first-hand intelligence.

Bloodworth used the cover of multinationals such as Motorola, Coca-Cola and Hewlett Packard, together with the more grass-roots retailers such as Hindustan Lever, to ensure that America would know as soon as India conducted unusual military operations anywhere again.

Now, many years later, he was the National Security Advisor, a friend of the President, with an eye automatically glancing towards the sub-continent. The media, and therefore the American public, might ignore it, but Bloodworth knew it was the most explosive place on earth. The photographs in front of him confirmed reports he had been getting from the ground. India was moving a formidable force of armoured vehicles and artillery towards the border with Pakistan. The operation was being run from the Southern Command Headquarters at Pune near Bombay, or Mumbai, as India's financial capital was now called.

The analysts had identified Soviet-made 130mm and 152mm guns mounted on Vijayanta chassis, British-made 140mm guns, together with the British 105mm self-propelled Abbot gun and the Indian Pinaka multi-barrel rocket-launchers. The network of Soviet surface-to-air missile systems was being increased with extra batteries installed in camouflaged positions throughout Jammu and Kashmir, Himachal Pradesh, Haryana and the Punjab – the 2S6 Tungushka air-defence systems working with the Indian Akash missiles. Twenty SA-316B Chetak observation and liaison helicopters had been identified off-base, together with five Mi-25 and six Mi-35 Hind attack helicopters. Two extra mountain infantry battalions had been moved from the Northern Headquarters at Udhampur and were taking up position close to the LoC at Kargil. Columns of regular troops, travelling mostly at night, were pouring into Kashmir. But what worried Bloodworth more than anything was the activity much further south in Rajasthan, with tanks moving out from bases in Jaisalmer and Bikaner, mainly the older Soviet-made T-55s and T-72s. But north of there around the city of Amritsar several of the new T-90s had been spotted, together with the updated version of the indigenous Arjun main battle tank.

Bloodworth's analysts had not found any unusual movements of the nuclear-warhead-carrying Prithvi or Agni missiles, something which would worry him even more. As with all intelligence, the pictures on his desk might only be what the Indians wanted him to see. He assumed that both nuclear and conventional versions of the Prithvi were deployed securely with XI Corps at Jalandhar and further south in the Jaisalmer and Barmer areas. If that was only a quarter of the preparations actually going on, it would mean that India could push across the border from Amritsar at any time and be on the outskirts of Lahore in Pakistan in a matter of hours. She had done it before in 1965, except then neither country was a nuclear power.

Bloodworth pressed his intercom to speak to Judy Lewis. 'Could you get Chandra Reddy in Delhi for me,' he said. 'He's the head of India's Research and Analysis Wing, but tell them the call's both urgent and personal.'

Briefing

Xinjiang

Xinjiang, on China's western border, is the size of Alaska and home to about sixteen million Uighurs, a Turkic Muslim ethnic group distinct from the Han Chinese. Officially it is a semi-autonomous region of China, but Beijing is very much in control and Uighur nationalists want to establish their own independent state called East Turkestan. Since the 1980s there has been an increasing number of bomb attacks and disturbances. Beijing has reacted by flooding the region with soldiers and armed police and encouraging more and more Han Chinese to migrate to the area. Like Tibet, Xinjiang is a problematic area for the Chinese, who are afraid of a creeping Islamization from Central Asia.

Zhongnanhai, Beijing, China

Local time: 1500 Thursday 3 May 2007
GMT: 0700 Thursday 3 May 2007

The car number plates of the Pakistani Ambassador to Beijing, 188 001, were immediately recognized by the guards on the gate of Zhongnanhai, just a few hundred metres west of the monuments of Tiananmen Square. The car's journey past the entrance to the Forbidden City had been tracked by the camera on the corner of the south-west wall of the compound. As it slowed two cameras over the Zhongnanhai gate itself picked it up. Its invitation into the compound was highly unusual. Hardly ever were diplomats allowed into the compound unless accompanying a visiting dignitary.

Despite China's thrust towards modernization, it remained uncompromisingly entrenched in its revolutionary past, reminding its citizens that without the Communist Party they wouldn't enjoy the home ownership, the well-paid jobs, the US dollar bank accounts and the other trappings of wealth. For twenty years since the collapse of European Communism and the Balkan wars, the Communist Party had reaffirmed its view that democracy would only hamper development and heighten the risk of civil war.

Statues of Mao Zedong remained in city squares, and his portrait hung over Tiananmen Gate outside the Forbidden City. There was no debunking of the Monument to the Martyrs of the People, the Great Hall of the People, the museums of Chinese Revolution and History. These were the symbolic institutions which had given China the strength to face down the great twentieth-century powers such as Russia, Europe and the United States.

Javed Jabbar, urbane and cosmopolitan, was Pakistan's Ambassador to Beijing and a graduate of Balliol College, Oxford. His colleague General Sadek Hussein was a veteran of two wars against India, and his government's special military attaché in China. He was a former Chief of Army Staff responsible for building up the close military relationship with China. Jabbar's call directly from Hamid Khan had been unusual, and for a moment he had considered disobeying the instruction. Then Hussein informed him that they had both been invited personally to Zhongnanhai. Jabbar had no choice but to accept.

Jabbar read the Chinese characters painted on the maroon wall as they turned into the gate. *Long live the Great Communist Party*, said one slogan. *Long live the unbeatable thoughts of Chairman Mao*, said the other. Once they were inside, they were joined by two motorcycle escorts, the riders bearing the mark of the personal guard unit of Tang Siju, the powerful Chinese security chief. They were escorted along the broad, uncluttered roads, past the drooping willows and lakes, to a villa at the northern end nestling in its own grounds.

Jabbar was relieved to see the relaxed Chinese Foreign Minister, Jamie Song, on the steps to meet them. By his side was Tang. Jabbar knew the two men did not get along.

Jabbar got out of the car. 'So I finally get an invitation to your inner sanctum,' he said, shaking Song's hand.

'A prime minister or a president would suffice,' said Song. 'Although I gather they spend much of their time hunkered down in Islamabad nowadays, waiting for orders from a general.'

Jabbar cast him a sideways glance, showing an understanding between diplomats, both of them fiercely patriotic and both uneasy about serving autocratic masters.

Song's Harvard education and understanding of the Western media had made him the most famous Chinese politician abroad. At fifty-eight, he was frequently tipped by international analysts as China's next president, but they were predictions which only underscored their ignorance. It had taken Song years to gain the trust of the Chinese Communist Party's inner circle, which was deeply suspicious of his friendship with Western leaders and his flitting back and forth between the government and the private sector. His company Oriental Software had recently been listed in New York and was already a blue chip in Tokyo, Shanghai, Hong Kong and Singapore.

This was Song's second stint as Foreign Minister, a job he had left after his convincing performance during the brief Dragon Strike war. His resignation had been a tactic in order to be asked back and gain political acceptance at the highest level. The Communist Party realized it needed at its centre a man who could count international businessmen and political leaders among his friends. Song was called upon to give advice not only on foreign policy, but also on how to coax in more Western investors. His refrain was that China's economy was on track and its lack of democratic reform was one of the great stabilizing factors in global development. Since the Balkan wars and the collapse of the Russian economy, the Chinese Foreign Minister's views had prevailed.

Song ushered the two Pakistani diplomats into a reception room, dully decorated with calligraphic scrolls hanging from the wall and armchairs positioned next to spittoons, ashtrays and writing tables with pencils and notepaper.

'Let's pull a couple of these round so we can talk properly,' said Song, trying to instil informality into the austere room. He shifted a chair himself while Tang's interpreter ran over to help him.

'Did you guys down the Indian helicopter?' Song went on, dropping the question in casually. The interpreter translated for Tang.

'Out of my theatre,' said Hussein.

'Hamid Khan is both brave and dangerous, if he did,' said Song.

'General Hamid Khan is a very great friend of China,' said Tang, speaking in Chinese with simultaneous translation from the interpreter. He took a seat on the left-hand side of the two main chairs at the end of the room. The others arranged themselves around him while Hussein took out two sheets of paper, one in English and one in Chinese. He gave them to Song and Tang.

'These are the details of the death of a man called Yahya,' explained Jabbar. 'He was a Saudi Arabian, living in Egypt, responsible for some of the worst attacks against Western and Asian tourists there. For the past six months he has been training *fedayeen* – that's Arabic for commandos – to intensify the insurgency in Xinjiang. He was due in Central Asia himself next month. Four days ago, Yahya was killed by a single gunshot wound to the head at the entrance to his apartment block in the city of Asyut on the upper Nile.' Jabbar paused, allowing his Chinese hosts to read the document. 'As you know, the slums of Asyut are a breeding ground for this type of terrorist. Pakistani intelligence agents can infiltrate them.'

Hussein took up the explanation. 'Our Inter-Services Intelligence Directorate has an influence far beyond our borders. Our reputation in some areas is comparable to that of Mossad – even more when it comes to the infiltration of extremist Islamic groups operating from Afghanistan and the Middle East. General Khan asked us to tell you personally and in the greatest confidence how Yahya was killed.'

The double doors at the end of the room opened and a woman appeared with a tray of tea. Hussein stopped talking and the room was silent apart from the rattling of the cups, until Tang barked an order that she should leave.

'Hamid Khan ordered it himself,' said Jabbar as the doors closed. He repeated it in Chinese for Tang and the security chief nodded.

'He is a great friend of China,' Tang repeated.

'You are offering to help us with Xinjiang and Tibet?' said Jamie Song. 'And we'll help you with India.'

Foreign and Commonwealth Office, London

Local time: 0830 Thursday 3 May 2007

'**India has officially** disbanded the Special Frontier Force, whose commandos carried out the operation,' said John Stopping. 'The decision was apparently made before the attack on Dharamsala and Dixit is sticking with it.'

'For which he should be applauded,' said the Foreign Secretary. 'But will it placate the Chinese?'

'Beijing maintains the operation was ordered directly from Delhi. The Indians deny it and we believe them. We have reports of Chinese demonstrations outside Indian missions in Beijing, Hong Kong and Taiwan. We assume the protests have been sanctioned at the highest level of the Chinese government, but they also contain a spontaneous element.'

'I thought that Taiwan and the mainland were enemies,' said Baker.

'Only in rhetoric,' said Stopping. 'It shows us that Tibet – or should I say anti-Tibetan sentiment – is a unifying factor in Chinese nationalism. American and Japanese satellites have identified Chinese troop movements towards the Indian border. Jamie Song, the Chinese Foreign Minister, has apparently told the German Ambassador in Beijing that they are restoring the Sino-Indian border defences to their 1996 levels.'

'What does that mean?' said Baker.

John Stopping deferred to Sir Malcolm Parton, who explained. 'India and China agreed on mutual troop withdrawals from the border area in November 1996,' said Sir

Malcolm. 'Since they fought the war in 1962, they had been near battle-ready. In 1993, they signed a treaty of "peace and tranquility", then in 1996 President Jiang Zemin visited Delhi, and the two governments made a pledge that "neither side should use its military capability against the other". Jiang Zemin spoke of India and China as "major powers in the world" which had "a common responsibility to the whole of human society" to develop themselves as quickly as possible.

'When China withdrew the troops, it freed up about two hundred thousand Indian troops to fight in Kashmir, infuriating the Pakistanis. Their former Chief of Staff, Aslem Beg, even complained to the Chinese army. If the Chinese now reinforce that border – and it's 2,500 miles long – India will have to pull troops back to China from its front with Pakistan.'

'It appears, Foreign Secretary,' said Stopping, 'that China and Pakistan have cut a deal to squeeze India.'

Christopher Baker tapped his pen on the tabloid newspaper lying on his desk, the splashed headline blazing up about his extramarital affair with a Foreign Office interpreter. The Foreign Secretary stood up, taking his jacket off the back of his chair and slipping it on. 'For God's sake keep me informed on this one. I don't want anything buried at the bottom of the boxes. If India has both Tibet and Kashmir to handle I suspect she will become a very dangerous animal indeed.'

Foreign Ministry, Beijing, China

Jamie Song waited until Teng Guo Feng, his Ambassador to Islamabad, was on the secure line, then picked up the receiver. 'Did they receive the imagery?'

'Khan himself was in the war room,' said Teng. 'Parliament is in emergency session, and Khan's been summoned to the PM's office.'

'Good,' said Jamie Song. 'Speak to him now and tell him two things. Firstly, we are having some success in intercepts on the SIGINT from the Indian military command and will let him have them shortly. Secondly, advise him that if our support is to continue, he must follow closely your political advice on how he handles his accession to power. No witch-hunts. No revolution. No personality cults. No personal corruption. If China is to stay with him, he has to win international recognition and respect. Only then will he retain power.'

General Headquarters, Rawalpindi, Pakistan

'The Prime Minister called,' said Captain Masood softly, unwilling to disturb his boss's train of thought.

'Did he now?' said General Hamid Khan. He remembered an afternoon less than a month before when protesters had marched on the Parliament building. The Prime Minister had demanded that Khan give the order to open fire with live ammunition. 'We must teach them a lesson they will not forget,' the Prime Minister had said.

'Let us wait and see what happens, sir,' Khan had patiently replied. The demonstrators delivered their petition and left peacefully.

'What moral excuse would I have for obeying that instruction?' Khan confided in Masood afterwards. 'Pakistani soldiers are not going to protect the ruling classes by killing Pakistani people.'

Now, the Prime Minister seemed intent on interfering in military affairs again by demanding that Pakistan withdraw from the Kashmir conflict. If Khan agreed to that, the streets would run red with the blood of the forces of Islam on the rampage. Kashmir was the outlet for their aggression, yet the Prime Minister could not see it.

Khan picked up another phone and dialled the number himself for the Chief of Naval Staff, who was in Karachi. 'I think the present government—' he began.

The naval commander interrupted: 'You need explain no more.'

He then spoke on the encrypted military line to the

three-star generals in command of IV Corps in Lahore, X Corps in Rawalpindi and II Corps at the central military headquarters near Multan, known as the strike corps. He offered a face-to-face meeting with the Chief of Air Staff in Rawalpindi, but was asked to wait on the line. Then, without introduction, the voice of the air chief said: 'No.' The line went dead.

Khan found the Deputy Chief of Air Staff at the huge Sarghoda airbase in the centre of the country, mixing with the F-16A pilots of No. 9 Squadron. 'The Prime Minister has called an emergency session of Parliament,' said Khan. 'We expect him to order our withdrawal from the Kashmir front.'

'To save his own bloody cronies and US dollar accounts,' replied Air Marshal Yasin Kalapur, a former fighter pilot. 'I bet his bloody wife's nagging him about not being allowed to the London sales any more. Good luck, General.'

Khan got Masood to call up a map of Pakistan on the computer screen in his office. He watched as Masood used green to colour in sections of the armed services upon which he could count. In Pakistan, the army controlled almost all military power. Technically, the Chairman of the Joint Chiefs of Staff was his senior, but that role was adviser to the Prime Minister. Hamid had a line of command. The Chairman did not.

Hamid had spoken to three of the army's nine corps commanders. The air force would hesitate, but the Deputy Chief of Air Staff would bring it into line. The navy, less important in the first hours, was on board. He anticipated confrontation in Rawalpindi because it was the head-quarters of many different sections of the military. He did not rule out exchanges of fire and casualties. But the cantonments around Chaklala were Khan's home turf and within twenty-four hours he expected that the trouble would be over. He shaded in neutral grey the corps commanders he had not contacted at Mangla, Gujranwala and Bahawalpur, and he marked two areas in hostile red, Quetta and Peshawar, both near the Afghan border and both corps commanded by men who supported the civilian administration.

Khan turned to Masood. 'What time will all cabinet members actually be in the Parliament building?' he asked.

'At sixteen hundred, sir.'

Khan closed the country map and brought a city plan up onto the screen. He examined the images from the surveillance cameras around the Prime Minister's Secretariat, the Supreme Court Building and Parliament House, gleaming modern buildings with landscaped lawns, sprinklers and balustrade driveways. Unlike the monuments to modern government in New Delhi, the architectural symbols of Islamabad had not been built by the departing colonial power. They were the creation of corrupt leader after corrupt leader. While citizens scraped for food and soldiers fought in the mountains of Kashmir, the country's leaders lavished money on buildings no Pakistani needed. Khan loathed the ruling oligarchies with their foreign education, property and bank accounts. But he also loathed what seemed to be the only alternative: Islamic revolution and the repressive fanaticism which he had seen in Afghanistan and Iran.

Constitution Avenue, Islamabad, Pakistan

Local time: 1600 Thursday 3 May 2007
GMT: 1100 Thursday 3 May 2007

Hamid Khan arrived for his meeting with the Prime Minister wearing full battle dress and travelling in an armoured personnel carrier. He led a column of ten M113 tracked vehicles down Constitution Avenue to the Parliament building, from X Corps's 11 Brigade, the unit responsible for security in the capital. The column broke into the administrative nucleus of Pakistan, throwing a military cordon of roadblocks around it, sealing off the heart of the capital with a ring of battle-ready armour. Troops took up positions with heavy machine guns. Khan ordered an APC every 200 metres and a main battle tank at the junctions.

The cordon ran right along Ataturk Avenue Ramna 5, north through Ataturk Shalimar 5. Two T-59 tanks blocked the junction with Kyayaban-e-Iqbal, then the cordon of APCs ran around the back of the Prime Minister's official residence, joining the narrow Nurpur Road and Fourth Avenue right down to the start of the diplomatic enclave, where Khan deployed another tank. Infantrymen with bayonets fixed to their G3 rifles were positioned as a human barrier between the armoured vehicles.

He avoided going into the diplomatic enclave itself and ran the cordon west along Isfahani Road, past the Australian, French, Japanese and Egyptian Embassies until it got to Khayaban-e-Suhrawardy. Troops moved into the main government buildings. Parliament House, the Cabinet Offices, the telephone exchange, the state-run television and radio complex and the Ministry of Foreign Affairs all fell within Khan's cordon. The most substantive roadblock was across the highway into Islamabad from Rawalpindi where four T-59 tanks, their 105mm gun barrels horizontal, were parked across the road. An infantry battalion and two Huey Cobra helicopters were positioned behind them, with pilots ready in the cockpit.

Khan turned his 12.7mm machine gun towards the Parliament building. Commandos of the elite Cherat Special Services Group jumped out of the APCs and rushed in to reinforce troops who had just secured the building and its grounds. Not a shot was fired. Not an order was shouted.

The strange quiet which had suddenly enveloped the government buildings was broken by the roar of six F-16 fighters, screaming in at less than 500 feet from their base in Sarghoda. The pilots dipped their wings, circled and flew back again before heading north towards the Muree Hills.

Khan jumped down from his APC. He strode into Parliament House. Commandos, led by Masood, covered him from behind as if breaking cover on the front. He threw open the double doors to the Parliament chamber and walked to the front, his men covering every terrified member with their small-arms, then spreading right round the chamber and taking positions against the walls. Their machine pistols had full magazines, but no bullets in the breech, to prevent any soldier becoming trigger-happy. Khan himself was unarmed.

'Sit down, everybody. Sit down,' shouted Masood in both Urdu and English. 'Don't panic. This is a military takeover. We apologize for any inconvenience caused. You are requested to stay calm, stay down and listen to what we have to tell you.'

Khan mounted the steps to where the Speaker sat and turned to face the Parliament chamber: 'Mr Prime Minister, please lead your cabinet team down to the exit door at the right of the chamber,' he said. 'Parliamentary staff, please assist my men in their job and do not attempt to resist. The remainder of the members must stay in their seats. Mr Prime Minister, will you lead your team. *Now.*'

The Prime Minister had to be yanked out of his seat by his right arm. He was paralysed more by shock than any desire to resist. Other members shuffled in an obedient line towards the exit. Only one, a Deputy Finance Minister, shouted in English: 'This is a disgrace. I warn you, you will never get away with it.' He was wrong. Fifteen minutes later, he was begging for his life.

With the cabinet held at gunpoint in the lobby area outside, Khan turned his attention back to the members. 'I have taken over government, not for power or personal gain, but to save our country from bloodshed,' he said. 'Outside this lavish building, ordinary people are living difficult lives. You, the ruling classes, have let them down. When a citizen comes into contact with the government he faces indifference and extortion. And when they march on Parliament to complain, the Prime Minister commands my troops to shoot them with live ammunition.

'No longer are Pakistani soldiers going to protect the ruling classes by killing Pakistani people. This afternoon, the government of Pakistan was the enemy of the people. As from this moment it will be their friend.

'The educated youth believe that the solution to our problem lies with Islam, not in the ritual sense of beards, bombs and Jihad, but in the faith, discipline and loyalty which the religion brings to people all over the world. Those are the guiding principles of military life. They will now become the guiding principle of our whole country.'

Khan's speech was met with complete silence. No applause. No objection. He stepped down from the platform and spotted Masood hovering in the doorway, his expression indicating that all was not well.

Outside the Parliament building, the members of the cabinet were being loaded into two trucks to be held in custody in a military barracks. The Deputy Finance Minister, Ahmed Magam, was refusing to climb up.

'No! No!' he was shouting. 'I am not getting in and you will not force me.' His voice was raised and as Khan approached he identified uncertainty on a few of the soldiers' faces.

'Get up,' snapped Khan.

'You will hang for this,' spat Magam.

A cabinet colleague put a hand on Magam's elbow. 'Come on, man,' he said. 'Let's do what they say.'

Magam shook off the hand and pushed his way past a soldier, who hesitated enough to let him get through. Khan took a pistol off the nearest soldier, put a round in the breech and held it at Magam's head. 'Get back in line. *Now.*'

Magam took the first half-step of a run. Khan tripped him, pushed him to the ground, face down, and fired a live round in the air inches from the minister's head. Khan stepped back. 'Do you want to die?' roared Khan, emptying the breech, then reloading it again, so that the minister could hear the mechanism move.

'No,' Magam whimpered.

'Do you want to live?'

'Yes.'

'Again. Tell me again.'

'Yes. Yes, please.'

Khan secured the safety catch on the pistol and gave it back to the soldier. The minister, shaking, was helped to his feet by colleagues and climbed into the truck.

Foreign and Commonwealth Office, London

Local time: 1530 Thursday 3 May 2007

'One shot fired, apparently,' said John Stopping. 'To persuade a recalcitrant minister not to stretch his luck. Otherwise a flawlessly exercised takeover.'

Top of the British news agenda of the day were the domestic issues of the single currency and Northern Ireland. The Foreign Office was concentrating on Christopher Baker's upcoming weekend visit to Washington, but the head of Asia–Pacific, who was in fact travelling, asked for a special meeting on the Pakistani coup. John Stopping had been asked to chair the meeting in his place. Stopping was a former Ambassador to Pakistan, and was still chair of the JIC.

The BBC lunchtime radio news had led with the coup in Pakistan, but television gave it thirty seconds voiced over library pictures of the ousted Prime Minister on a previous visit to Britain. Hamid Khan had declared martial law. He banned all reporting and blocked the transmission of all pictures. Few people in Britain knew the Prime Minister, let alone the military strongman who had taken power, and the firing of a single warning shot did not arouse national outrage.

Nevertheless, Pakistan had muscled itself to the top of the Foreign Office agenda, and Stopping turned to Martin Andrews, the young head of the South Asian Department.

'Obviously we're watching things closely,' said Andrews. 'But a military takeover was not unexpected. Pakistan is regarded as a failed state and something had to give. We don't expect it to change Pakistan's foreign policy agenda, although clearly the Foreign Secretary will express concern when he gets to Washington.'

'And who is Hamid Khan?'

'An Armoured Corps officer, Chief of Army Staff and former Deputy Head of the Inter-Services Intelligence Agency, or the ISIA. We're requesting more from Washington. He was one of the key figures involved in the CIA's war in Afghanistan in the eighties. When that finished, he turned his attention to the insurgency in Kashmir and was largely responsible for filtering guerrillas across the LoC onto the Indian side in the early nineties. Three years ago he manoeuvred his way to get the job of Commander X Corps in Rawalpindi in charge of operations in Jammu and Kashmir and the Siachen Glacier. It put him at headquarters and in the most politically and militarily sensitive area, a perfect platform from which to get the top job.'

'Is he a rabid fundamentalist?' asked the head of the Hong Kong/China department.

'No.' Andrews shook his head. 'He appears to be a pragmatist. He is not the hunting, shooting and fishing Sandhurst type. The key elements to bear in mind are that, given India's steady movement away from secularism, it is inevitable there would be a lurch even further towards Islam. After all, Pakistan was created as an Islamic state. I sense that Khan has moved in to prevent the extreme sort of revolution which took place with the Taleban in Afghanistan.'

'The comparison is a bit far-fetched, isn't it?' said the head of the Far East department.

'That's what they said about Iran. We ignored it and we lost a valued ally in the Islamic world.' Andrews paused while the man in charge of the Far East accepted his point. 'In the villages, there is a growing cry for Pakistan to produce its own Ayatollah Khomeini. I think the country has judged democracy as a failure.

'The political class is thoroughly corrupt. Western-educated leaders such as Benazir Bhutto turned out to be disasters. Her successors simply came from different land-owning oligarchies. The ruling elite takes what it can get and puts nothing back. Since Zia ul-Haq came to power in the late seventies there has been a creeping Islamization. Sub-sequent governments have used it to retain legitimacy. The political classes have clung to secularism because that is where their vested interests lie. But the centre of gravity has been shifting for some time. What has become clear is that the political class is incapable of bringing about change.'

'You sound as if you rather admire Khan,' said Stopping.

'I don't know him,' said Andrews. 'But I know where he is coming from. The country is living beyond its means. The religious parties are well organized – particularly in the cities, but they perform badly at the polls because the votes are controlled by the landlords. The army is the only professional institution of any size which works and Khan has stepped in before the conditions created another Iran. Of the two hundred and fifty-odd brigadiers in the Pakistan army, there are thirty known fundamentalists. Of about twenty-five lieutenant generals, there are five fundamental-ists. We should be thankful that Khan is not among them.'

'So does it mean that we should regard Khan as an OK thing for the time being,' said Stopping, 'as long as he keeps his revolver in his holster?'

'On probation, perhaps.'

'I suggest we let things settle over the weekend, then test the waters with the Foreign Secretary on Sunday on the way to Washington.'

Stopping shuffled his papers to get to the next item on the agenda. 'Now. China,' he said, turning to the head of the Far East department. 'I understand we have some intelligence from within Zhongnanhai – from who else, but the Japanese.'

Foreign Ministry Building, Beijing

Local time: 0030 Friday 4 May 2007
GMT: 1630 Thursday 3 May 2007

Jamie Song was driven out of his office compound with the pressing voice of the American Ambassador in his ear on his mobile phone: 'Jamie, let's keep it informal, but we must meet.'

'Reece, it's after midnight.'

'Drop by the residence for a drink. Give me fifteen minutes of your time.'

'Things are tricky at the moment.'

Jamie Song and Reece Overhalt trusted each other completely and that is partly why each had got his job. Overhalt was a key player in defusing the earlier Dragon Strike crisis, when both Washington and Beijing had gone on to nuclear alert. When he left as Chairman of Boeing, it seemed only sensible that he should go to Beijing as Ambassador. In the interim, he helped Song float Oriental Software successfully on the New York Stock Exchange, sealing an already long-standing friendship which stretched back to post-graduate days at Harvard. Both China and the United States were aware of the huge ideological and cultural chasms between them, and if any two men could keep the lid on simmering issues it would be Overhalt and Song.

Song hadn't risen to the top of both global business and the last surviving Communist autocracy without an in-built safety valve that detected disasters. He sensed that while the new deal with Pakistan would largely go unnoticed, the mayhem which was mushrooming over Tibet and the Lama Togden could test the limits of their statesmanship.

'Just what hell is going on in Lhasa?' pressed Overhalt. 'The networks are comparing it to Phnom Penh after Pol Pot took over.'

'You want the truth, Reece?'

'Absolutely.'

'I haven't got a clue. Tibet comes under Tang Siju, a deputy chief of General Staff. You want his mobile number? I'm only the Foreign Minister.'

'Jamie, don't do this, for Christ's sake. Drop by the China World Hotel, if you don't want to be seen at the residence. You've got to fill me in.'

Prime Minister's Residence, Tokyo, Japan

Local time: 0130 Friday 4 May 2007
GMT: 1630 Thursday 3 May 2007

General Shigehiko Ogawa had been in the waiting room of the spartan official residence for more than half an hour, while the Prime Minister's nightcap with a visiting American trade delegation wound up. Ogawa was Japan's long-serving Director, Defence Intelligence Headquarters and since the Dragon Strike war he had been charged with substantively increasing the human intelligence network inside the centre of power in China.

More than any other power in the region, including the United States, Japan had the ability to feed agents into China's institutions. But it had been painstaking work and there was still a long way to go. While Ogawa knew just about every negotiating tactic in advance from the Ministry of Foreign Trade and Economic Co-operation (MOFTEC), he had failed to make any headway in the Second Artillery Regiment, which controlled China's nuclear weapons programme.

He had, however, thanks to a sickness, had some success within Zhongnanhai. While he was unsure of the value of his intelligence, Ogawa, who was just two years from retirement, felt he should let the Prime Minister know what he had found out, even if it meant wasting his evening waiting for an audience. The intelligence had come by way of the interpreter of Tang Siju, the Chinese security chief. Tang's usual interpreter was off with the flu. The replacement was a spy for the Japanese.

The Americans left noisily, passing through the anteroom, eyeing Ogawa as if he was a janitor waiting to clear up. Then Prime Minister Shigeto Wada greeted him formally and offered him tea.

'I have information that China authorized the coup in Pakistan and has formed a new military alliance with the new government there,' began Ogawa.

'But the two governments have always been strategically close,' said Wada.

'The Foreign Minister, Jamie Song, and Tang Siju, of the General Staff Department, have both given their personal backing to General Hamid Khan for specific support during this crisis.'

He handed Wada a transcript of two separate meetings at which Tang had used Ogawa's agent as interpreter. One was of the conversation within Zhongnanhai with the Pakistani Ambassador, Jabbar, and the Defence Attaché, Hussein. The second was in the military General Command Centre in the Western Hills just outside Beijing. Hussein and Jabbar were with Tang, being consulted on moving extra troops towards the Indian border.

'In order to both threaten and humiliate,' said Jabbar, 'I suggest you concentrate your area of attack on the Thag La Ridge, as you did for the 1962 war.'

Prime Minister's Office, South Block, Delhi, India

Local time: 2130 Thursday 3 May 2007
GMT: 1600 Thursday 3 May 2007

'**We are facing** a scenario which only our doomsday soothsayers would have forecast,' said Hari Dixit. 'A military strongman has taken power in Pakistan on an Islamic Kashmir ticket and China is pouring troops towards our border in a way that is reminiscent of our humiliating war in 1962.'

The Indian press had not yet had time to advise on how Hari Dixit should handle Hamid Khan, but they had had a field day with China's attack on the Tibetan government-in-exile and Major Choedrak's mission into Lhasa. The daring and bravery of the men involved was heralded as if it was a new era of Indian nationalism, and it was conveniently forgotten that the commandos and aircrew were, to a man, Tibetan. The capture of Dehra Dun airbase and the theft of the Antonov-32, the faked flight-plan for the Mi-26, the refuelling in Sikkim and the sheer ingenuity of the break-out at Drapchi had fired the public's imagination. As yet, very little was known about what had happened in Lhasa itself. But reports from Dharamsala implied that Togden was still at large somewhere in Tibet, protected by men from the Special Frontier Force.

The Times of India, regarded as the voice of the establishment, suggested that Prime Minister Dixit should distance himself from the whole affair. 'It beggars belief, during a decade when relations with China have been so difficult, that the government maintained a fighting force of ten thousand Tibetans, stationed them close to the Chinese border and gave them an environment in which to carry out the sort of operation we have just seen.'

The reaction of other newspapers was not so restrained. The *Hindu* agreed with Dixit's decision to disband the SFF, but argued that the 'Drapchi incident and the unforgivable violent response in Dharamsala by the Chinese should be used to pull the festering border problem of Tibet to the forefront of Sino-Indian relations. Until this problem is solved, very little can move forward between the two great Asian superpowers . . . and, on the issue of sanctuary, India would be morally obliged to offer Lama Togden a safe home should he survive his present flight from Chinese-controlled territory.'

The *Pioneer* was among the more jingoistic newspapers. It ran pictures of Major Choedrak and his senior officers with potted stories of their lives, together with intricate military details about the two aircraft stolen for the mission. Togden himself received a double-page spread and was hailed as a 'new global voice' for the Tibetan cause. The paper's columnists called on the Indian air force to give air cover for Togden's escape and for those SFF troops still in India to go in and give him safe passage. 'China has stolen territory from India,' raged the editorial. 'It represses the people of Tibet. It is an ally of Pakistan which has caused immeasurable suffering to the Indian people, and, most importantly, China is not a member of the club of democratic governments. In brief, China is the world's "Enemy Number One".'

'Foreign Minister, what are your thoughts?' asked Dixit once he had convened the meeting.

Prabhu Purie took a few seconds to answer. 'My instincts are to follow the moderate line set down in *The Times of India*, although it would not be a popular one in the present climate.'

'True, there is a groundswell for us to play tough. It is a case where the line between mob rule and democracy blurs.'

'We do have a chance now to create a formula agreeable to both sides,' said Purie. 'Something to be implemented when the Dalai Lama dies.'

'The *Hindu* is wrong,' growled Chandra Reddy, 'and now is not the right climate in which to start.'

'What they are saying,' pressed Purie, 'is that if we want a normal relationship with China, which would include secure borders, trade, equal punching weight on the global stage, we have to sort out Tibet. We could begin by guaranteeing cooperation on sealing the border and checking on infiltration, rather like the Irish government agreed with Britain over Northern Ireland.'

'Then every time someone slips through, we are blamed for conspiring,' said the Chief of Army Staff, Unni Khrishnan. 'With all due respect, we would be creating a diplomatic nightmare.'

'And what about Togden?' said Dixit.

'If they haven't caught him by now, I suspect the SFF will get him out,' said Reddy.

'I suggest we hand him over to a third government,' said Purie.

'Isn't that playing it too safe?' said Dixit. He picked up the *Pioneer*, glanced at its populist front page, tossed it back on the table, then paced back and forth at the end of the room. 'The Chinese are going to bleed this for everything they can. If we give an inch now, before they even begin to cut us up, we will be left with nothing. It was a cock-up, not a conspiracy, but you can be sure they will treat it as the latter.

'There is also a wider element, of values, democracy and where India is heading as a society and as a country. Correct me if I am wrong, but Lundrup Togden is an innocent man. He is a monk. A man of God. He should not have been in prison. The Chinese run a repressive regime in Tibet which is condemned by the democratic world. Therefore, should he choose to seek sanctuary in India, we have no choice but to give it to him and damn the consequences.'

'Even without him,' said Reddy quietly, 'I think the consequences have already begun.' He withdrew a number of folders from his briefcase, each marked in black felt pen. 'These are satellite pictures from overnight, some courtesy of the Americans, some courtesy of Indian technology,' he explained. 'They show irregular movements of men and equipment towards our border.'

The members of the National Security Council were on their feet, leaning over the photographs spread out on the table. 'This is in the west. The circled area is a leftover from the 1962 war on the Thag La Ridge where invasion began. The land is claimed by us, but is under Chinese control and is technically a demilitarized zone.' He brought out three more pictures. 'This is a closer image of the town of Qizl Jilga, and this, gentlemen, is a fleet of helicopters flying in at around 0300 hours this morning.'

Reddy pointed to another. 'The town of Zanda is only two hundred kilometres from Dehra Dun. This is unmistakably a column of armour. These look like 155mm artillery guns, but I am getting confirmation. This photograph is of an army barracks just outside the town of Garyarsa from where a mountain road leads directly to Namgia just across the border.'

He turned to another envelope. 'This file is even more interesting. The formations you see here are infantry. The image next to them is of a troop transport plane. The town is Mazar, in Chinese territory, but worryingly close to Pakistani-controlled Kashmir and only four hundred kilometres from Srinagar. This is not the terrain for tanks, but here and here you will see armoured build-ups, north of the Sikkim border, along the Indus Valley at Demchok and at Chusul in Ladakh.'

'One would have thought they were preparing for this,' said Dixit.

'So far,' said Reddy, 'it seems they are using their reserve supply of border forces. We have no evidence that any reinforcements are being brought in from outside the area.' He opened the last file on the table. 'Now we move more than six hundred and fifty kilometres to our eastern flank. These are similar sort of activities, here around the town of Lhunze and here near Nyingchi.'

Reddy unfolded a larger map of the area, showing the locations of the two Chinese towns. 'They are here and here. This is the border with Arunachal Pradesh and it's only about two hundred and forty kilometres across until you get to Burma, a staunch ally of China's and no friend of ours. China claims Arunachal Pradesh as its own sovereign territory. Only six months ago the New China News Agency said it had a "sacred mission" to reclaim it, as it has with Taiwan. We only officially created the state in 1986 and during 1986 and 1987, after a stand-off with the Chinese we moved our forces closer to the border.'

'If I might add,' said Purie, so softly that he was barely audible, 'we have an enormously strong advantage over Pakistan. With China, I am not so sure.'

'Go on,' said the Prime Minister.

'If we make it clear immediately that we have every intention of going to war with Pakistan if necessary, we will have complete international backing. True, we are a democracy, and they are now a military dictatorship. But the reality is more than that. In diplomatic circles it is known as the Tiananmen effect, drawn from the Chinese killings of democracy protesters in China in 1989. No major power will risk its overall relationship with India because of Kashmir. We are simply too big. That is not, however, the case with Pakistan, particularly since Khan himself has indicated the pariah characteristics of his own government. If it comes to the brink, Pakistan will be left to swing in the wind.'

'But China?' said Dixit.

'While we threaten to demolish Pakistan, Prime Minister, you get on a plane to make a visit of peace to China.'

The White House, Washington, DC

Local time: 1400 Thursday 3 May 2007
GMT: 1900 Thursday 3 May 2007

Tom Bloodworth rang to ask for a meeting with the President and was let straight in to the private office.

'Could you spend five minutes reading this transcript, sir. It explains why Hamid Khan took power with such confidence. It was sent to me personally from General Shigehiko Ogawa, head of Japanese intelligence.'

John Hastings looked up impatiently, irritated that crises in far-off lands were drawing him away from domestic agenda. 'Not if it's to do with the coup in Pakistan, Tom,' he replied.

'It's more than that, sir.'

Bloodworth handed the President a copy of the transcript and kept one himself. 'Jabbar is Pakistan's Ambassador to Beijing,' explained Bloodworth. 'Hussein is the Diplomatic Attaché. Dr Malik Khalid is an eccentric and brilliant missile physicist from Quaid Azam University in Islamabad, and now the predominant figure involved in the missile programme against India. He flew to Beijing on instructions from Hamid Khan thirty-six hours ago – before the coup. Tang Siju is one of the most powerful hawkish generals in charge of strategic planning. Tao Jian is marked in the transcript just as President and General Leung Liyin is the Defence Minister. You'll see there were others present, but we don't have an identification on them.

'The meeting took place in an office off the war room in the General Staff Headquarters, an underground bunker in the Western Hills just outside of Beijing. The verbatim transcription is from the interpreter's own notes. The non sequiturs and gaps are where the interpreter couldn't remember the true record of conversation.'

They began reading through in silence and Hastings had to admit to himself that it was a remarkable piece of intelligence gathering.

Jabbar: You ask why? India must understand once and for all that the threats to our existence must stop.
President: And you want us to give you practical help. Perhaps, Ambassador, for the benefit of those who were not with us earlier in Zhongnanhai, you could explain the thinking behind your policy.
Jabbar: We are aware that Tibet could within days, even hours, become a flashpoint. Diplomatically it is your weakest area of policy. You also have the other vulnerability in the far-western Muslim region of Xinjiang, which has suffered a spate of bombings and riots. Islamic unrest on your western borders and a terrorist campaign in Tibet is your nightmare scenario. It would suck your resources away from development and the economy, wreck your nurtured friendships with the Western democracies and throw China itself into a separatist war.

I have told President Tao that Pakistan will use every means at our disposal to stop foreign insurgents operating in Xinjiang. By that I mean we will intercept them in their countries of origin, be it Afghanistan, Iran, Algeria or wherever. We will intercept them on their way to Xinjiang and, if you wish, we will offer our unique expertise to work with the Chinese security forces on the counter-terrorist operation in Xinjiang itself.
Leung: You're saying you will encourage the holy war in

Kashmir, but fight against it in Xinjiang. It seems an ideological contradiction . . .

Jabbar: You disagree with the policy, General?

Leung: Not at all, Ambassador. I think it is an admirable example of pragmatism.

Jabbar: My colleagues General Hussein and Dr Malik Khalid will explain in detail how we think you can help Pakistan.

Hussein: Until recently China used commercial SPOT and LANDSAT imagery surveillance, which was basic and unsatisfactory. Now, thanks to help from the French and the Russians, your new space surveillance system has just become operational. It's outdated by Western standards, because you have yet to get real-time satellite reconnaissance. But with the launch of the new military photo-reconnaissance satellite two months ago, you are now receiving good intelligence around the Asia–Pacific region. We need constant guaranteed round-the-clock access to it.

You have been helpful in the past day in providing material about Indian troop movements along the Kashmir, Punjab and Rajasthan border. We need that to continue, together with imagery of Indian nuclear installations, air-bases for nuclear-capable aircraft, mainly the SU-30MK, and anything which could threaten the security of Pakistan.

Tang: The Indians get everything they want from the Israelis, who get it from the Americans. I see no problem with this.

President: Agreed.

Khalid: [Inaudible because of soft voice] . . . all know the areas I will be talking about well enough.

In any nuclear exchange, the Indians have two weapons of choice. The Agni is the intermediate-range missile. Agni, gentleman, means 'fire'. The missile project began in 1979 at the Indian Defence Research and Development Laboratory in Hyderabad. The first successful launch was in 1989. The second test in 1992 failed, but tests in 1994 and 1999 were successes. Since then, three more tests have been carried out and we believe this is now a highly sophisticated weapons system. The first stage missile [sic] is solid fuel. The second is liquid. It can carry multiple re-entry nuclear warheads and its range is two thousand five hundred kilometres, meaning it can hit anywhere in Pakistan and a significant area of China.

In a limited exchange with Pakistan, they would choose the Prithvi, their short-range missile. The name means 'earth'. Design started in 1983. The first test was in 1988 and it has three versions with ranges of a hundred and fifty, two hundred and fifty and three hundred and fifty kilometres respectively. All three are now operational, launched vertically from an eight-wheel mobile truck. One Prithvi fired from Indian territory could destroy Rawalpindi within eight minutes of launch with a single 500 kilogram warhead.

Sarghoda, here, [Interpreter's note: Khalid was using a map projected onto a screen] is our main airbase, command and control centre and assembly centre for our 500 kilogram uranium warheads. It is also just two hundred kilometres from the Indian border and vulnerable to attacks from both the Agni and the Prithvi. We have the Hatf series, capable of ranges of eighty, three hundred and six hundred kilometres. Hatf means 'deadly'. We claim the design to be indigenous, but the technology as you may well know is Chinese and originally Russian. The Hatf 2 is a version of the M11 and the Hatf 3 is from the M9, which we also call the 'Shaheen'.

Our counterpart for the Agni is the Ghauri, which we bought off the shelf from North Korea as the Nodong 11. Its range is one thousand five hundred kilometres against the Agni's two thousand five hundred kilometres. But since we brought in the Ghauri, the Indians have modified the Agni to create a completely solid-fuel rocket. The first version of the Agni operated with the liquid-fuel engine design from the Prithvi. The test in 1999 was with a new second-stage solid-fuel booster. The third stage is the war-head re-entry vehicle capable of carrying a payload of a thousand kilograms.

Jabbar: Perhaps Dr Khalid could explain to us laymen the difference between a solid-fuel and liquid-fuel missile?

Khalid: Liquid fuel has the advantage of greater accuracy, The fuel tap, as it were, can be turned on and off to vary the firing distance. It has the disadvantage of mobility. We need at least fifteen vehicles to accompany a liquid-fuel rocket for maintenance and control and we need time to fuel the engines at the launch pad – several hours of preparation have to be allowed.

Hussein: Not much of a deterrent.

Khalid: The solid-fuel Agni can be launched within fifteen minutes of an unexpected alert. Several missiles are kept permanently inside specially modified goods trains. From the outside they look like regular trains. The missile itself is twenty metres long and for the launch it would slide out of the back of one rail car, then be raised by a hydraulic piston. The first-stage rocket motor burns out in less than a minute at an altitude of around twenty-five kilometres. The second stage motor goes a minute later at just over a hundred kilometres. The missile keeps going up to around four hundred kilometres before re-entering the atmosphere. It is built to withstand heat of up to three thousand degrees Celsius. The total flying time to its target two thousand five hundred kilometres away is thirteen minutes.

Hussein: We would have less than thirteen minutes to react, but it would take us twenty times that long to prepare the Ghauri.

Khalid: We had been relying on the North Koreans, who were developing a solid-fuel rocket known as the Taepo Dong. But since rapprochement has come to the Korean peninsula, the missile project has stopped.

Jabbar: In other words we have been left high and dry.

President: Your aim is to neutralize the Indian threat against Pakistan totally. Am I right in thinking this? No half measures.

Jabbar: I think we all agree that if our borders are secure and power is balanced, Asia will be a more peaceful place.

Tang: What is it you need?

Hussein: The East Wind DF-21 missile and launchers and the KS-1 theatre-defence missile.

Tang: The technology?

Hussein: The products themselves. We don't have time to make them.

Khalid: The DF-21 is a two-stage solid-fuel missile which we need to match India's Agni-11 missile. The KS-1 is a short-range ground-based theatre-defence missile, which can engage air-launched tactical weapons – in other words a strike by Indian aircraft carrying nuclear bombs. We would want to import complete batteries of twenty-four missiles, the phased-array radar-guidance station, four missile launchers on trucks and associated vehicles.

Song: It would surely violate the Missile Technology Control Regime – the MTCR. We have agreed not to sell missiles or technology that can carry a payload of more than five hundred kilograms a distance of more than three hundred kilometres. What are the specifications of the missiles we are talking about?

Khalid: The KS-1 has a range of forty-five kilometres and the warhead could be well under five hundred kilograms. The payload of the DF-21 is five hundred kilograms and the range is eighteen hundred kilometres.

Song: Impossible, then.

Tang: No. Not impossible. We have not signed a treaty, but merely agreed to adhere to the provisions of the MTCR. We will be breaking no international law and any sanctions put upon us will hurt the governments imposing them as much as they do us. A year after we adhered to the MTCR in 1987 we sold six DF-3s to Saudi Arabia. Range two thousand seven hundred kilometres.

Hussein: Price three billion dollars.

Leung: I am not completely happy. The idea that India and Pakistan can replicate the nuclear safeguards set up between the Soviet Union and the United States during the Cold War is unworkable. The cost to America of maintaining a nuclear arsenal to match the Soviet Unions was five and a half trillion dollars. The cost to the Soviet Union was the disintegration of its economy. It seems that no one in India or Pakistan has thought through the sophistication needed to manage the policy of Mutually Assured Destruction, where both parties come out of it intact.

Jabbar: No, General Leung. We know that if it comes to all-out war – either conventional or nuclear – Pakistan will lose. We are not seeking a Cold War scenario. And we would, naturally, pass on to you all our intelligence on India's own nuclear weapons programme. It is far easier for a Pakistani to infiltrate than for a Chinese.

Hussein: We also want to put a tactical air-burst bomb onto our Hatf short-range missiles and possibly on the DF-21, if you give it to us. Or an enhanced-radiation warhead.

Tang: Neutron bomb.

Hussein: Correct. You tested the neutron bomb in November 1988 and we understand it became fully developed in the late 1990s – thanks to stolen American technology. If you remember, gentlemen, the most dangerous time that Pakistani and Indian tank forces faced each other was during India's Operation Brass Tacks in 1987. India fielded a quarter of a million troops and thirteen hundred tanks and we genuinely thought they were going to invade. It was the first time that it seriously dawned on us that we needed the bomb.

Khalid: The deterrent effect of a neutron bomb against tank and infantry formations on the battlefield is very high. It is a small thermonuclear weapon, or hydrogen bomb, which produces minimal blast and heat, affecting an area of less than three hundred metres in radius. Everything within that area will be incinerated. But a massive wave of neutron and gamma radiation is thrown out over a larger area. Tank crews would be disabled immediately – although some might take days or weeks to die. But buildings would survive, as could civilians living only a few kilometres away.

Jabbar: If we have a tactical nuclear weapon or neutron bomb, we are convinced that any war between us can be confined to the battlefield. If we do not, we would be forced to escalate straight from artillery exchange to nuclear exchange with no in-between.

President: You will give unconditional assistance against Islamic fundamentalism and all intelligence on India's military activity against Tibet and its nuclear weapons development?

Jabbar: That is correct, sir.

[Interpreter's note: Long silence. Deferring to the President.]

President: Then we have an understanding.

Bloodworth waited for John Hastings to finish before he handed him a folder of satellite photographs. 'These were sent to me personally from Chandra Reddy, head of India's external intelligence. They were taken by India's IRS-ID satellites, which are pretty close to world-class. It means they don't have to beg from the Israelis or us any more, like Tang said.'

'You mean he got it wrong?'

'Totally. The Indian satellites can photograph an object as small as five hundred and eighty centimetres and their panoramic coverage stretches for eight hundred and ten kilometres. They can also operate in three separate bands of light, enabling them to record objects in near darkness.'

The President listened, spread the prints out on his desk and let Bloodworth carry on.

'You can easily make out the shape of a ship in dock there. She is the MV *Baldwin*, Liberian-registered at the Chinese southern naval headquarters in Zhanjiang.' Bloodworth stood up, leaning over the desk to point out the significant features. 'You can see the head of a missile on the railway siding, here. And in this one four hours later, the *Baldwin* heading out to sea, we assume for Karachi in southern Pakistan. Loading began three hours after President Tao gave his assent.'

'When will these be operational?'

'More than a month, sir. But, if I may –' Bloodworth sifted to one caught underneath – 'this is an Antonov 124, the biggest military transport plane in the world. This picture was taken at an airport near Xining in Western China, near the headquarters of the Second Artillery Regiment. If you look in the far right corner and you'll see the fuselage and wing tip of another An-124. This truck here, we think, is carrying the KS-1 theatre-defence missile – possibly also some form of nuclear warhead.'

'What you're telling me is that these aircraft have already delivered their cargoes to Pakistan.'

Prime Minister's Residence, Race Course Road, New Delhi, India

Local time: 0200 Friday 4 May 2007
GMT: 2030 Thursday 3 May 2007

'**Cancel the visit** to Beijing,' said Hari Dixit.

'If you call it off now, the relationship will take years to repair,' said Prabhu Purie, the Foreign Minister.

Hari Dixit screwed one of the satellite photographs into a ball and hurled it into the corner of the room. 'They are blatantly breaking international law.'

'But they regard the SFF attack on Lhasa—'

'That was not authorized by my government. The force which carried it out has been disbanded. If we end up going to war over that, then we would have ended up going to war anyway, over something else.' Dixit turned to the Chief of Army Staff. 'Mr Krishnan, what is your view?'

'At some stage, possibly months ahead, it will become public knowledge that you visited China, well aware that it was secretly shipping nuclear weapons to Pakistan. Unless those weapons are withdrawn – and I doubt they will be – India will have emerged as the weaker of the two new Asian powers. It is similar to the missile crisis when the Soviet Union tried to ship nuclear weapons to Cuba. I agree with Prabhu's sentiments. He is correct about China's reaction. But we have to face them down.'

'Chandraji?'

'I think China's chosen this moment for a shakedown of the Asian powers. I don't know why, sir. But I agree with the Chief of Army Staff.'

'Prabhu, call our ambassador in Beijing and cancel my visit. Give him the reasons. We'll convene a full meeting of the National Security Council and decide how much to release into the public domain.'

Zhongnanhai, Beijing, China

Local time: 0700 Friday 4 May 2007
GMT: 2300 Thursday 3 May 2007

'Prime Minister Dixit has called off his visit,' said Jamie Song. Tang was already with President Tao when Song was shown into his office. No one else was present, an indication of Song's membership of Zhongnanhai's innermost circle.

'Why?' said Tao.

'No reason given. There was no indication that they knew about our shipments to Pakistan.'

'But the weather has been clear,' said Tang. 'Their satellites would pick it up.'

'I don't think that matters,' said Tao. 'If we wish to arm an ally against an aggressive enemy, then we shall do so. Tibet, though, is more sensitive because of the Americans. What did you tell Reece Overhalt?'

'That I was Foreign Minister and Tibet was an integral part of China.'

'Comrade Song,' said Tao, insistent on retaining some old-style Communist Party formalities, 'Comrade Tang and I were discussing the international repercussions of martial law; whether we should declare it in Tibet. I don't believe it is necessary, but we would welcome your view.'

Song chose his words carefully. 'I would certainly advise against using the term "martial law". We will shortly – and by that I mean within the next twenty-four hours – have to make a statement about what is going on there. The cordon Comrade Tang has thrown around the city appears to be holding and no news is getting out. Yet the Western democracies are demanding access.'

'When the West stamps its feet, China closes its doors,' said Tao. 'We have been through this before and survived, and a declaration of martial law would give an umbrella of legitimacy to our operation to crush dissent there.'

'Nothing we do in Tibet has legitimacy in the eyes of the Western democracies. They tolerate it only through gritted teeth.'

Tao interrupted: 'Comrade Tang, how long will the present operation last?'

'We need to retain the seal around Lhasa for at least another two weeks to ensure that the splittist elements are neutralized.'

'And if you loosen it? If, say, a European Union diplomat is taken to Lhasa for a day?' asked the President.

Tang was silent for a moment, then began by addressing Song: 'If Comrade Song can give me two weeks, I can ensure that the Tibetan problem is solved once and for all.'

'How will you do that?' said Song softly.

'I don't ask you the details of your foreign diplomacy,' said Tang bluntly. 'The incursion by India has given us an opportunity to act. We should not lose it.'

'I am concerned about how our policy in Tibet will impact on our global position,' retorted Song. 'Since the 1989 Tiananmen incident and the Dragon Strike war, we have skilfully become a role model for the developing world. The myth that Western-style democracy is a panacea to end global poverty and civil war has been exploded by our achievements. Our human rights policy, once reviled by Western democracies, is now regarded as a necessity to keep economic development on course. Our citizens are proud to be Chinese and proud to be ruled by the Communist Party, and I would not like to see this ruined because of a sudden iron-fist campaign in Tibet.'

'What would you prefer, then, Foreign Secretary?' said

Tang. 'UN/NATO forces running Lhasa?' The security chief cleared his throat and spat into the spittoon by the side of his chair.

'That is precisely what I am trying to avoid,' snapped Song.

President Tao held up his hand. 'Comrades, we are losing our focus. Chinese sovereign territory has been violated from the Indian side. There has been an armed incursion deep inside our country. It is only right that we defend ourselves, and the international community will have to accept that. The problem lies in their interpretation of what we are doing in Tibet. The Indian incursion was the catalyst for a much larger terrorist uprising, which we have to put down. Yet we have seen in places like Serbia that Western democracies only permit an iron fist if it is clenched by one of their own. President Milosevic acted out of principle and paid the price. We will not make a similar mistake. We have been forthright in putting down the rebellion, and we have reinforced our border with India in order to prevent a similar incursion happening in the future. Comrade Song, you are quite right in suggesting we make a statement within the next twenty-four hours and that is why I have arranged for the Defence Minister to brief us.' President Tao stood up. 'A train is waiting to take us to the Western Hills.'

The three men travelled in silence, mainly because of the noise: Muxidi, Gongzhufen, Yuquan Lu, then just as the metro line should have come to an end at Pingguoyan, the train only slowed, went through the station and picked up again. The sides of the tunnel were more roughly hewn and illuminated only by the light of the train. Further along, a few kilometres before the Summer Palace, the tunnel

Lhodrag, Tibet, China

Local time: 0500 Friday 4 May 2007
GMT: 2100 Thursday 3 May 2007

They had been walking now for three days, but Major Choedrak knew the worst was still to come.

He had planned two routes out. The longer was to the south-west to Gangtok in Sikkim, 400 kilometres from Lhasa. In the old days, a single runner could do the journey in six days. With Togden, it could take them up to a month. This was the way Choedrak had wanted to go, because once in India he believed Togden would be safe. His second choice was to go due south to the tiny Kingdom of Bhutan, a journey they could do in five days, if they pushed it hard, which was what the men had been trained to do.

After escaping into the mountains south of Lhasa, Choedrak led the party south-west down the Yarlung Tsangpo Brahmaputra river valley to Chushul, a strategic town at the intersection of the four main highways linking central, western and southern Tibet. It also had a key bridge with a strong Chinese military presence around it. They crossed the bridge with false papers in the early morning of 4 May. Two hours later, SFF units in Chusul attacked Chinese military positions and blew up the bridge, cutting off the main route of pursuit. More units pinned down Chinese trying to cross the river by boat, holding them back until all the Tibetans were dead. As word of the battle in Chusul spread through the community, spontaneous uprisings broke out in all towns in southern Tibet. Hundreds were killed, but thousands of Chinese troops were tied up in crushing rebellions, giving Choedrak the precious space he needed for the escape.

Choedrak kept twenty men with him, putting ten ahead and ten behind at all times. The next centre after Chusul was Gongkar on the banks of Yarlung Tsangpo Brahmaputra, where the Chinese air force kept a squadron of SU-27 ground-attack aircraft. As they hurried south, Choedrak's men fought skirmishes with approaching Chinese troops. Sometimes whole villages would turn out as human barricades across the road to stop armoured vehicles. Once, as they reached the pass in sight of the Yamdrok Tso lake, they heard small arms fire of close combat behind them. Chinese mortar shells killed two Tibetans in the party and wounded another, who took cyanide rather than be captured or delay the party more. It was then that Choedrak decided to strike out due south to seek sanctuary in Bhutan, which was less than 100 kilometres away. The mountain passes were higher, the weather fouler and the refuge less certain.

The Yamdrok Tso was considered by Tibetans to be sacred, a beautiful expanse of blue, grey and white water covering more than 750 square kilometres. They found communities so remote that they were able to rest for a few hours in warmth and recover their strength. When the villagers guessed who Togden was, they vowed that not one Chinese soldier would pass through while any man in the village was still alive. The party headed along a vast high-altitude depression towards the town of Nagartse, which was on the Lhasa–Gyantse highway. This had become the headquarters for the search operation to find Togden. They had another 1,800 metres to climb in freezing temperatures and nine passes to go through before reaching Bhutan.

Choedrak gave a wide birth to Nagartse and for a whole day it seemed the Chinese had lost them. But that morning the microlights had come, then the fighter planes, not hitting them, but slowing them down, making them hide out, unable to move around. After the first air attack Choedrak gave orders for them to shoot down the microlights, breaking their cover, but hitting two – and hopefully deterring more from coming. They had to reach Lhodrag, and then strike out south-west to Langdo, but if the weather closed in, it could be days away, or death on the mountain. The final few kilometres of the route which Choedrak had chosen were along the Monla Karchung glacier pass. It was one of the most awesome journeys a man could make.

Parliament Building, Islamabad, Pakistan

Local time: 0800 Friday 4 May 2007
GMT: 0300 Friday 4 May 2007

Hamid Khan's newly appointed ministers, a mixture of technocrats, Islamists and military officers, took the seats of the former Pakistani cabinet in the Parliament chamber. The elected members were allowed to keep their seats, although many who supported the old regime boycotted the special session. It was highly unusual for an emergency session of Parliament to be called on a Friday morning, and be addressed by a general in full military uniform. But Khan wanted to emphasize the character of his government and make his statement before the imams spoke during prayers in the mosques.

'Pakistan was created under the concept of Hezira,' he began. 'It is the concept that Muslims must not live under tyranny or oppression from other people's faith. Since the partition in 1947, the threat against Pakistan has increased many-fold. India has transformed itself from being a secular state under the Congress Party to becoming a Hindu and nuclear-armed state under Hindu nationalism.'

Khan had planned to mention Pakistan's founders, men like Chaudhury Rahmat Ali and Mohammed Ali Jinnah, but he had accepted China's advice to stick only to policy and avoid the use of personalities and heroes.

'Under Hezira, Muslims remake their lives elsewhere and move from Dar-ul-Harb to Dar-ul-Islam. It is a concept which dates back to AD 622, when the Prophet travelled from Mecca to Medina to escape persecution. With partition, we had hoped that there would be peace between the two countries. But that has not happened. The reasons are plentiful. Human weakness and rampant moral and economic corruption in both countries have kept Pakistani and Indian societies poor and close to war.

'India with its much-heralded democracy has failed to provide any better life for its people than Pakistan with its rotten ruling elite, whether military or civilian. The people of Pakistan, the Cold War ally of the United States, are as pathetically poor as the people of India who proudly chose to be non-aligned. I have heard numerous wretched excuses for the state we are in. We have blamed the British for allowing partition; the Americans for betraying our alliance; the Indians for threatening our existence; the multinationals for exploiting our workforce. The new government of Pakistan has heard all the excuses, but it will no longer use them or listen to them. The hard truth is that Pakistan has been incapable of governing itself.

'Why have Taiwan and South Korea managed their relationships with the superpowers and created decent places for their people to live in? How come Slovenia and Hungary have steered their way out of Communism and into the global village to stability and success? How can other Islamic countries like Malaysia and Jordan balance obligations towards their cultures and religions against the forces of Western influence? The answer is because the governments there think, plan and implement. From today, this is what Pakistan will do as well.'

Khan paused and noticed seats in the chamber filling up. The door at the back constantly swung open and closed as those members who were keeping an ear on the speakers in the lobby decided to come in and see for themselves.

'I will now briefly outline the policies of the new government and then turn to the latest conflict with India.' He rearranged his papers, allowing time for people to sit down.

'Pakistan is now a military dictatorship and it will remain so until our economy is close to First World standards. We will follow the models of Taiwan and South Korea, whose dictatorships were far more ruthless than ours will be. We will not be euphemistic about what we are. Democracy has failed Pakistan. Our foreign policy has not protected us. Our economic policies have not made the people rich. I suggest, therefore, that you give the new government a chance.

'We will introduce strict laws against corruption, based on the Independent Commission against Corruption set up in Hong Kong in the 1970s. Efforts will be made to pay our civil servants enough money so they don't have to take bribes. We will encourage foreign investment, trade and research to create our own manufacturing base. We will work towards opening our border with India to trade, resuming direct shipping routes, increasing air routes and introducing an exchangeable currency. Technocrats, not politicians, will work out the details.

'Those with vested interests will oppose, some violently, and they will be handled forcefully and without hesitation. And to those of you in this chamber who are already plotting to overthrow me, I ask you to consider one thing, and one thing only: count not your personal loss from the new system, count only the country's gain. Think of your children and your grandchildren and the day that they will be able to hold their heads high as citizens of Pakistan without making excuses for the poverty and suffering of our people.'

Khan had been mostly reading from notes, his manner not theatrical, but humble, his voice soft, diffident and at odds with the forthright speech he was making. But now he looked up, moving his eyes around the chamber, accomplishing the personal contact needed to bring the assembly onto his side.

'There is, though, one terrible obstacle to this plan, and that is India, whose policy is to threaten our very existence. India is the only threat we face, and the only real issue of contention is Kashmir. Underlying Kashmir, however, is the unwritten perception that India does not accept Pakistan's right to exist. We live with the flawed inheritance of partition.

'Yesterday, Indian aircraft crossed into Pakistani airspace and attacked our territory. It is not the first time. Perhaps it is not the last. Civilians died and our sovereignty was violated. It is an apt time, therefore, to end the issue of Kashmir once and for all. We will let this one airstrike go unpunished. In return, I am going to take an initiative which may well cost me my life, but could settle once and for all the cancer which the Kashmir dispute has inflicted upon our development.

'I believe that Kashmiris on both sides of the LoC would prefer independence to rule either by Pakistan or by India. In the past, we have claimed the whole region and would perhaps let the southern Jammu area and eastern Ladakh, which has a Buddhist majority, stay with India. But that would mean further partition, and I am not convinced that partition has worked either for either of our countries. Therefore, I am proposing a referendum to be held among all Kashmiris, under the auspices of the United Nations and checked by international monitors. If the vote is for independence, it will be a blow to the psyches of both India and Pakistan. There will be grumbling within the armed forces about wasted lives. But Kashmir will remain a predominantly Islamic society. The war will be won by waging peace. Kashmir will look to us for support in creating the world's newest state, and we will give it unequivocally in our quest for peace. India will play its role. It will also realize that severing Kashmir from both our sovereignties will not lead to the break-up of India. It will mark the beginning of peace, prosperity and development.'

Khan paused, allowing the significance of what he had said to sink in.

'This offer from Pakistan is not negotiable,' he continued quietly. 'If India attacks us again or rejects the referendum, we will punish her so severely that she will end up as a rump of her former self. My government's policy is unequivocal. We will make safe our territory and modernize. Nothing, absolutely nothing, will stand in our way to provide the life that our people deserve.'

Hamid Khan collated his papers, which he had ignored for the last five minutes of his speech. He walked slowly down the aisle of the chamber, as if inspecting a guard of honour on a parade ground, his hands clasped behind his back, the papers rolled awkwardly, holding them more like a swagger stick than the notes from a politician's speech. Just before he reached the door, the first cheer broke out, timid at first and far away. But within seconds it spread with clapping, then the shuffle of feet as member after member in the chamber rose to give the military ruler a standing ovation. Khan stopped, looking around, clearly surprised at the reaction. He turned to Masood more for refuge than anything else. Masood had the door open. The bodyguards stepped back to let the general through.

Khan turned back towards the chamber and held up his hand to speak again. The applause quietened. 'Threats of sanctions from the West have only just begun. For a while, Pakistan will be branded as a pariah state. The members of my government will be demonized as monsters. Pakistani money now in Western banks may be frozen. We will be denied visas. Those of you who manage to travel abroad will be followed and spied upon. Every tool of the Western powers will be used to intimidate us. But ride through it, ignore the arrogance of the developed world, and we will find that the sanctions will fade away.

'No society has developed from poverty to wealth as a democracy. The repression of Victorian Britain was an appalling spectrum of suffering and human rights abuses. The apartheid and racism of twentieth-century America is a blight upon that country's history. Democracy has pulled Africa and South Asia into debt, humiliation and beggary. Autocracy in East Asia has created wealth and self-confidence. We may have democracy, but not in our lifetime, although today the unashamed dictatorship of Pakistan has laid the first seeds towards creating a fairer, juster and freer society than this country has ever had before.'

The members were still standing, but they had fallen quiet. Khan left the chamber in silence.

Back in the Prime Minister's office, Hamid Khan picked up the green hotline telephone on his desk. 'This is Hamid Khan in Islamabad,' he said softly. 'I would like to speak to the Indian Prime Minister, please.'

Prime Minister's Office, South Block, New Delhi

Local time: 1000 Friday 4 May 2007
GMT: 0430 Friday 4 May 2007

'**We haven't spoken** directly before,' said Khan to Hari Dixit.

Chandra Reddy happened to be with Dixit when the hotline call came through, and as the Prime Minister spoke he slipped transcriptions of Khan's speech onto the desk, highlighting the final section about the airstrikes and referendum. The tape recorders were on.

'Only a solution to Kashmir can lead to permanent peace in South Asia, and this is the way to do it,' Khan said. 'I can only remind you that the original idea for a referendum came not from us but from India in 1947.'

'The UN resolution of 13 August 1948 specified that Pakistan withdraw from Jammu and Kashmir, which you haven't,' replied Dixit. 'The second resolution of 5 January 1949 stated that people should be consulted about their future only after the withdrawal and after normalcy had returned. That hasn't yet happened.'

'The resolutions were overtaken by the Simla Agreement of 1972,' Khan said. 'But in any case, all this is long ago. Let's press ahead without dragging up history.'

Dixit interrupted. 'The resolutions still stand.'

'We must focus on the future and not the past.'

'You have been organizing an insurgency in Kashmir for the past twenty years,' Dixit continued, calling in every political and diplomatic instinct to prevent himself from slamming down the phone. 'Two days ago the Northern Army Commander and the Home Minister were murdered

by the shooting down of their helicopter with a Stinger missile.'

Khan paused, then said: 'I have only just taken power. Some things have gone further than I would have allowed.'

'Did you order the Stinger attack?'

'My information is that it was carried out by extremists, attached to the Lashkar-e-Jhangvi guerrillas.'

'Where did they get the missiles from?'

'The Taleban. We have told the Afghan government that we will not tolerate another such incident. All Stingers in the hands of the Pakistan government are accounted for.'

Reddy, hovering behind, wrote TIBET in prominent capital letters and put it on top of the papers in front of Dixit. 'And the attack on Dharamsala,' said the Prime Minister. 'We have a Pakistani suspect, caught with weapons.'

'I know. But I can't add anything. Let us start from yesterday. My intention, Hari, is to end conflict, not begin another one.'

'Well, General,' said Dixit, refusing to be drawn into a first-name relationship, 'I will consult and get back to you within the day. But as you know, the Indian people would be reluctant to permit the incorporation of Jammu and Kashmir into Pakistan simply because the majority of the people there are Muslims. The impact on the Muslims in India would be dangerous and it would threaten the secular basis of our society.'

'Don't talk about history again, Hari,' said Khan. 'India is no longer secular. It is a Hindu state and Pakistan is a Muslim state. Once you accept that, Kashmir will solve itself.'

When Dixit ended the call, Reddy said: 'We can't accept, sir. It would be political suicide.'

'I know,' said the Prime Minister. 'Let's get out a statement saying that.'

New China News Agency, Lhasa, Tibet, China

Local time: 1300 Friday 4 May 2007
GMT: 0500 Friday 4 May 2007

Dateline: Lhasa
Recent disturbances in Lhasa and other areas of Tibet created by a handful of splittists have ended.

Foreign and Commonwealth Office, London

Local time: 0800 Friday 4 May 2007

It was highly unusual for a senior civil servant, particularly one so closely involved in intelligence work, to call in a television presenter for a classified briefing. But John Stopping, Chairman of the Joint Intelligence Committee, had been instructed to do so by the Foreign Secretary and was relieved, in part, to have known the presenter, Max Harding, from a posting in Moscow nearly twenty years earlier. Stopping chose to meet in his office, not for a restaurant breakfast meeting as the Foreign Secretary had tried to suggest. He was suspicious of the press and would never have agreed to be seen socializing with a journalist.

'I understand you have the Chinese Foreign Minister, Jamie Song, as a guest on your phone-in show this morning,' said Stopping, when Harding had sat down. 'I wondered if you might like some information with which to tease him?'

'Like what?' said Harding, who was equally concerned about being fed a line from the British government. Harding was the presenter of *Globe Talk*, a live interview and phone-in show on BBC World Service Television. When his producer rang up the Chinese Embassy in Portland Place to ask if the Ambassador would come on the show, they called back half an hour later offering Jamie Song in a satellite link from Hong Kong.

'It will be a BBC exclusive,' said the Chinese Press Attaché. 'We have not approached CNN because we feel that China's position will be better understood in Europe

than in the United States. You do not need to submit written questions and he will talk about anything you wish.'

Stopping spread a pile of satellite pictures on his desk. 'These are surveillance photographs of Chinese military activities over the past few days, and, during a break in cloud cover, pictures of what look like widespread disturbances in Tibet. You can't use them on the programme and, frankly, without expert knowledge they won't mean much to you.'

Harding stood up and picked up two photographs. 'Go on,' he said.

'We believe that the Chinese are using the raid on Drapchi prison in Lhasa to make an unnecessary show of force against India. We accept India's explanation that a unit of the Special Frontier Force ran amok. We hope that a line will be drawn under the incident and relations normalized. These pictures, however, show substantive troop reinforcements moving in right along the border with India. They have become particularly active in the mountain areas towards Sikkim, where India and China have fought several skirmishes, and the route along which we expect Major Choedrak and Lhundrup Togden are trying to make their escape.'

'Is he still alive?' interrupted Harding.

'We assume so. If he had reached India or Bhutan or if the Chinese had caught him I am sure we would know. If your viewers can bear the geography lesson, mingle their thoughts on Tibet with those of Kashmir, where Pakistan and India have been hammering it out for sixty years.'

'The killing of the Western army commander and the Home Minister and the Indian airstrikes across the LoC?'

'Yes. We think of Kashmir and Tibet as being on separate flanks of India. But if you look at the map they are frighteningly close to each other. Take in that and then

look at the other flashpoints along this border.' Stopping moved to the coffee table and laid a detailed map of the region over it. 'Starting in the west, this tiny pocket of land just north of the LoC – fifteen thousand square miles known as Shaksgam Valley – was voluntarily given by Pakistan to China in 1965. The problem is that the territory was not Pakistan's to give. The whole of Kashmir is claimed by India and there are UN resolutions regarding it. Move a fraction east, and there's this blob of wasteland in northern Ladakh called Aksai Chin, which China took in 1959 when it was building a strategic highway between Xinjiang and Tibet. It's about twenty-five thousand square miles, still under Chinese control, but claimed by India. These areas are among the most difficult places in the world to fight a war. No possibility of moving troops through into Ladakh. No land communication whatsoever. It would be easier on the moon, I would think. But if you look here on the map north of Chushul, east of Pangong Tso Lake, these shapes here are a column of tanks being moved closer to the border to threaten Indian positions.'

Harding was taking notes. 'Give me the origins of the China–India border dispute in a nutshell.'

'At the time, two bald men fighting over a comb. Or two young cockerels flexing their muscles. Look at it how you want,' said Stopping. 'In 1914, when China was in anarchy, Britain signed a border agreement with the Tibetans. It's known as the McMahon Line and stretches 1,360 kilometres along the eastern section of the border running from Bhutan to Burma. It was also initialled by the Chinese representative at the negotiations, but never accepted by Beijing. The area directly south of the McMahon Line to what was the border of British India remains disputed and makes up much of the new Indian state of Arunachal Pradesh which India announced in 1986.

'After the Communists came to power, China and India signed a friendship treaty, the Panchisila Treaty or the Five Principles of Peaceful Coexistence. It was 1954, and Mao was too busy consolidating his power to raise the border issue, although he steadfastly refused to recognize the McMahon Line. Then Chinese troops poured into Tibet, and by 1958, the friendship treaty was out the window and the relationship had deteriorated into open animosity.

'Then came the 1959 Tibetan uprising and the escape of the Dalai Lama to India, which overshadowed everything else. Mao was outraged. The next year, Chou En-lai, Mao's trusted moderate lieutenant, went to Delhi to thrash out a compromise. They were talking about territory where no sane human being would want to live. No oil. No minerals. Just national pride. The negotiations stalled, and in September 1962 there were the first skirmishes. On 20 October China crossed the McMahon Line on the eastern sector of the border and went into Ladakh to the west in a massive incursion; two days later the Indian army defences collapsed. Fighting continued for a month, then China withdrew back across the line. The Indian parliament passed a resolution saying that India "would recover every inch of its sacred soil lost to China". That vow hangs in the mess room of the Northern Command headquarters at Udhampur.'

'This is a lot more than I can say on television,' said Harding, looking up from his notes.

'The Foreign Secretary didn't instruct me to write your script,' retorted Stopping. 'Only to explain to you the backdrop of the conflict. And the nub is this. China was not concerned about the geographical boundaries. As I said, the territory itself is worthless and inhospitable. It wanted India to abandon its recognition of the McMahon Line, which implicitly meant it accepted the sovereign authority

of Tibet. There's been a lull since the '62 war, but the issues are still there.' He ran his hand along the border. 'Along this stretch, China claims this disputed area in Kashmir, and ten thousand square miles from the Karakorum pass. It also claims Arunachal Pradesh and does not recognize Sikkim as part of India.'

'One hell of a lot of areas of dispute between two nuclear powers,' remarked Harding.

'That is exactly the point the Foreign Secretary wanted you to understand.'

Foreign Ministry Building, Hong Kong, China

Local time: 1800 Friday 4 May 2007
GMT: 1000 Friday 4 May 2007

Jamie Song chose to be interviewed in Hong Kong because it represented the modern liberal face of China. Like Tibet, Hong Kong was an autonomous region and an example to the world. If you don't fight the motherland, she will give you all you want.

The spotlight was harsh in Jamie Song's eyes. He asked them to change its angle so that he could look straight at the camera without squinting. He had already changed from a swivel office chair to a straight back, so he would not move inadvertently while in shot. He made sure the sound technician clipped the microphone on the outside of his tie, instead of concealing it underneath, to lower the risk of rustling and interference. He held notes in case the cameramen were asked to do cut-aways to his hand. With nothing to hold, he could appear tense and nervous. With ten seconds to air-time he brushed the lapels of his suit, specially chosen because it was hand-made in Hong Kong. He listened to the opening music and then to Harding's introduction.

Harding: In this BBC *Globe Talk* exclusive, we have the Chinese Foreign Minister, Jamie Song, live from Hong Kong, and with me in the studio is General Sir Peter Hanman, a military consultant with the Institute of Strategic Studies in London. We will be discussing the tension between India and China.

After the dramatic prison break-out in the Tibetan capital Lhasa, by the little-known Indian regiment, the Special Frontier Force, India has said sorry. China hasn't accepted the apology and, as you'll see on the map on your screens now, thousands of Chinese troops are pouring into these sensitive border areas with China. Europe and America have appealed for calm. China and India – and this is one thing they seem to agree on – say it's nobody else's business but their own.

The other complications in this alarming turn of events is that the revered Buddhist monk Lhundrup Togden who was freed from prison in the raid is still at large and believed to be heading for India. Fighting has also flared up again between India and Pakistan in Kashmir. Both are nuclear powers and Pakistan has just been shaken by a military takeover. Jamie Song in Hong Kong, before we start taking calls from our viewers, can you set our minds at rest that China is not trying to stir things up in Asia?

Song: Not at all, Max. Your excellent précis of events sums up the situation. Perhaps, though, I can make a comparison closer to home for Europeans. Suppose renegade troops in the Republic of Ireland burst across the border into British territory in the North and released convicted terrorists from the Maze prison.

Harding: I think you're stretching the imagination . . .

Song: Am I? Many people in Northern Ireland, Ireland and the rest of the world believe Ulster should be part of Ireland – as many believe Tibet should have its independence from China. But the hard facts are that Tibet is part of China and Northern Ireland is a part of the United Kingdom. I dare say there are those within the Irish armed forces who sympathize with the Republican cause, and in my scenario they act on their sympathies, just as India claims commandos in the Special Frontier Force have done. What

would the UK then do? Would it simply accept an apology from the Irish government and continue with business as usual? Or would it put the apology on hold, try to find out exactly what happened and in the interim reinforce the border to ensure that nothing like it could possibly happen again?

Harding: General Hanman. Let me bring you in here. You served many years in Northern Ireland.

Hanman: I can't speak for the government, of course. But in the Foreign Minister's scenario, we in the armed forces would certainly urge the government to do what Jamie Song suggests – reinforce the border.

Harding: All right, we have our first caller, who happens to be in Hong Kong. Go ahead.

Hong Kong: Yes. I want to ask Jamie Song. I have two questions. Firstly, did you know that India kept a commando force of Tibetan nationalists specially trained to fight against Chinese troops in Tibet? And number two. Isn't it time China took the opportunity from this incident to reclaim back the land across the border which is now occupied by India?

Harding: Foreign Minister?

Song: I personally was not aware of the Special Frontier Force, but I am a businessman and diplomat. Of course, I am fully briefed now. China had repeatedly asked India to disband the unit and had pointed out the dangers. India refused until—

Harding: Excuse me for interrupting, Foreign Minister, but can you confirm that, Sir Peter? India ignored Chinese appeals?

Hanman: That is my understanding. But Prime Minister Dixit acted with exceptional swiftness once he discovered what had happened. I don't think China could have asked for more.

Harding: Jamie Song. Your second question. Should China now reclaim land you say is occupied by India?

Song: We are very pragmatic about this. The territory under dispute is not prime real estate in Manhattan or Mayfair. Nor is it valuable like the oil fields of the Middle East. It is a pretty grim and inhospitable part of the world. The main issue here is Tibet. If India opened negotiations for a new border agreement and made an unequivocal statement that it would not support Tibetan independence, we would have absolutely nothing to quarrel about.

Harding: By that you mean India would have to expel the Dalai Lama?

Song: Yes. The Dalai Lama can live out his days in Europe or America. But not on our borders.

Harding: We have a caller from Delhi. A former admiral, I believe. Go ahead, New Delhi.

Delhi: Yes. I am Admiral Ravi Jacob retired. I understand China is moving naval vessels into the Indian Ocean. Could the Foreign Minister confirm this?

Harding: This is in reference to intelligence reports that two *Kilo*-class submarines have passed through the Straits of Malacca into the Indian Ocean. The closest Indian territory is the Andaman and Nicobar Islands and New Delhi plans to protest to the United Nations.

Song: Admiral Jacob, I honestly don't know about that. I could tell you to ask Admiral Li, the head of our navy, but I know he won't tell you, just as I'm sure the British Foreign Secretary Chris Baker has no idea where all the British submarines are at the moment. But I will say this. The Chinese navy has a right and a national obligation to send its warships and submarines into any international waters it wishes. It is a ridiculous notion to suggest that while American and European battle groups can sail the seas at will, those of China are confined to specific areas.

Harding: Sir Peter Hanman, can you enlighten us any more on this?

Hanman: There is nothing new about Chinese naval passage through the Andaman Sea. The Burmese have given Chinese full naval facilities at Hanggyi Island and they have a surveillance station on the Cocos Islands from which they track Indian missile tests. India doesn't like it, but can do nothing about it. The United States didn't like Castro in Cuba and Cuba didn't like the American base of Guantanamo on its territory left over from a previous treaty. I'm sorry to jump around the world so much, but I think it's important to bring in these comparisons. Nobody is special here. Things happen in geopolitical change which governments don't like. But that doesn't mean you go to war over it.

Harding: A call from Seattle. The caller doesn't want to give his name, but has already identified himself to us as a supporter of the Tibetan independence movement. Go ahead, Seattle.

Seattle: What will China do if Lama Togden gets to safety in India?

Song: We will ask India to return him in order for him to serve the rest of his sentence.

Seattle: And if India doesn't?

Song: I think we shouldn't speculate.

Harding: Perhaps, Foreign Minister, this a good opening for you to give us a run-down on what exactly is happening in Tibet. You have sealed it off, banned all foreign visitors, yet Western satellite pictures show widespread civil disturbance in many towns.

Song: Yes, Max, you are right. If I could return to my analogy with Northern Ireland, a small number of Tibetan nationalists have used the Drapchi incident to try to ferment civil unrest. They are being armed and helped by

units from the SFF which appear to have been infiltrated into many areas. And I might emphasize that these soldiers are doing exactly what they were trained to do when the SFF was created in 1962. The Chinese army is trying to stop the rebellion, but in many places our troops are fighting pitched battles with the insurgents. If a similar incident happened in Northern Ireland, I am sure Britain would not allow an Irish delegation into the Falls Road at the height of the disturbances.

Harding: I think they might—

Song: Please. Let me finish, because young Chinese men and young Tibetans are killing each other as we speak in this conflict. We did not start it. India ignited something it cannot control. We have, in any case, just announced that the disturbances are over. I have today issued an invitation for diplomats accredited to Beijing to visit Lhasa as soon as it is safe for them to do so.

Harding: The Tibetan government-in-exile accuses your troops of massacring civilians in their hundreds.

Song: Well, we wouldn't expect them to say we were serving them tea and cutting firewood for them.

Harding: We have a call from Islamabad. Go ahead.

Islamabad: India is also reinforcing its border with Pakistan. Its warplanes have bombed villages, killing civilians in Kashmir. Many of us in Pakistan fear we are going to be swallowed up by India. China is an old ally. I'm pleading with you to do something to help.

Song: Kashmir is a very difficult problem and I don't think there is anything China should do to inflame the situation any more. You are right, though. We do have very genuine and strong links with Pakistan, and China would certainly not like to see her treated unjustly by the international community.

Harding: Sir Peter Hanman, is the Chinese alliance with

Pakistan significant? Is it something we should take into account as tensions over Kashmir and Tibet mount?

Hanman: It exists, for sure. Pakistan's military is largely supplied by China, including its intermediate- and short-range missiles. China helped Pakistan with its nuclear-arms programme.

Song: I refute that unequivocally. The allegation—

Harding: OK, Foreign Minister, we've taken your viewpoint on board.

Hanman: Up until the 1965 war with India, Pakistan was pretty much a Cold War ally of the United States. India was non-aligned, but regarded as in the Soviet camp—

Harding: Sorry to interrupt, Sir Peter, but it appears we have a former Pakistani Chief of Army Staff on the line from Rawalpindi, General Awan. Why don't we get it from the horse's mouth.

Rawalpindi: Yes. Thank you. During the fifties, Pakistan opted for an alliance with the United States. The question of looking to China began actually during the 1962 Sino-Indian War, when America sided with India, and China offered friendship to Pakistan. In the 1965 war with India, when we were still technically a Western ally, Pakistan was completely abandoned by the United States. We were left without spares. No new equipment was available. We pleaded with the Americans to fulfil their agreements with us and they refused. It was like a stab in the back, and we turned to China. For fifteen years, between 1965 and 1980, there was very little military contact with Washington. China provided everything we needed. She gave us four billion dollars' worth of weapons and didn't charge a penny for it. And I would like to take the opportunity to thank Foreign Minister Song for the complete friendship China has shown us over the so many years.

Harding: Then came the Soviet invasion of Afghanistan.

Rawalpindi: Quite right, Mr Harding. The United States needed its Cold-War ally back and we let them take us. American relations with China were improving at the time, and Beijing, which had no love for the Soviets either, told us it didn't mind. In 1990, the Cold War ended and the Soviets were out of Afghanistan. But the nuclear-proliferation issue raised its ugly head and the United States stabbed us in the back again. We were making legitimate efforts to create a nuclear deterrent against India, yet the Pressler Amendment made all US aid conditional on our not possessing a nuclear device.

Harding: So you went to China?

Rawalpindi: Washington cut more than half a billion dollars of the money it had promised us. Yes, we went to China, and I for one regret we ever again danced to Washington's tune. America corrupted our ruling classes and its support for the mujahedin guerrillas in Afghanistan, created a monster of violent religious fundamentalism which we are now having to contend with. That is why the people of Pakistan and the armed forces support the middle way being forged by General Hamid Khan and his government.

Harding: Gentlemen, I've just been told that the Reuters news agency is sending over dramatic and horrific pictures of the situation inside Tibet. They have been smuggled out of Lhasa to Beijing. We don't know how and we are now going over live to that Reuters feed and I'm told what we are seeing now is a protest outside the official buildings of the government of Lhasa.

The camera was on a position above the crowd and held completely steady, letting the action take place within the frame. Hundreds of demonstrators were at a junction of

two major roads. A traffic light in the left-hand top corner of the screen was smashed. On the roof of a drab government building the cameraman picked up a machine-gun position. The lens zoomed in shakily. Three men manned it, and a fourth, wearing white gloves, had his pistol drawn. He was shouting, but the camera did not pick up any of his sound.

The roar of the protesters came through clearly, though. They were unarmed and included many women and children, most waving banners and carrying pictures of Togden and the Dalai Lama. As they reached an open area outside the compound, an armoured personnel carrier drove out of a nearby gate towards them. The crowd held its ground, mothers bringing their children closer to them. On the roof of the building, the soldier with the pistol was on the radio, gesticulating and pointing. The three men were ordered away from the machine gun. Those among the demonstrators who saw it cheered and held their banners higher, but at that moment the commander of the armoured personnel carrier opened fire straight into the crowd. Amazingly, the Tibetans did not disperse. They stayed where they were, collapsing on top of each other, until the firing stopped.

The screen went to black and returned with the Reuters' satellite feed logo. In the studio Max Harding remained silent for a number of seconds before speaking. 'Foreign Minister Song,' he began, 'perhaps you could tell us what exactly was going on there.'

The director switched the camera to the feed from Hong Kong, but Jamie Song's position was empty. The tiny black microphone which had been clipped to his tie dangled on the arm of the chair and then the link was cut.

Oval Office, White House, Washington, DC

Local time: 0800 Friday 4 May 2007
GMT: 1300 Friday 4 May 2007

'I know it runs against every grain of your new foreign policy, Mr President, but if you do not react to this massacre, we should hand back the campaign money for the next election and retire.' Ennio Barber, aged thirty-five, was one of John Hastings's closest personal advisers.

What Tom Bloodworth gave him in diplomatic and military pragmatism, Barber gave him in domestic and electoral advice.

Within hours of the Tibetan massacre being shown worldwide, political opponents had already been on television calling for sanctions against China. Each had a different comparison, yet each amounted to the same.

It was compared to the Tiananmen Square killings on 4 June 1989, to the slaughter on 20 March 1959 outside the Chinese Transport Centre in Lhasa, and to the 1956 tragedy in Magyarovar, Hungary when eighty-four unarmed demonstrators were shot down by Communist machine guns. There was an emphasis on the word *Communist*, to show that while the United States had defeated the Soviet Union in the Cold War, it had yet to contend with China.

'The relationship with China will sort itself out, Mr President,' said Ennio Barber. 'The question facing us now is what message should you, the President, send to the American people about the atrocities in Tibet.'

With John Hastings and Barber were the National Security Advisor, Tom Bloodworth, and the Secretary of State, Joan Holden.

'I think we have to be careful not to get ourselves into a media-driven policy,' said Hastings. 'I don't care if we keep our mouths shut for another twenty-four or forty-eight hours on this. Tom, could you give us a run-down of what we know happened and what is happening now.'

'The demonstrators were on the corners of Lingyu Shar and Chingdrol Shar Lam,' said Bloodworth. 'It's an area in the south-east corner of Lhasa. Most of them had walked about three hundred yards from Jokhang where more disturbances were taking place. They were unarmed and, it appears, none of the Tibetan Special Frontier Force, which has so effectively infiltrated Lhasa, was with them.'

Bloodworth turned on a television set, ran the video disc for a few seconds and paused on the picture of the machine-gun post on the roof. 'This is a PLA post, put up after the Drapchi raid, to protect the government offices.' He paused on the armoured car coming out of the compound to the north. 'This is the headquarters of the Public Security Bureau, who are a permanent street security presence in Tibet. In other words the PSB regard the streets of Lhasa as their patch, while the more disciplined PLA are under stricter orders of engagement. The massacre, Mr President, was carried out by the PSB, against the specific instructions of the PLA.'

'Which has overall command?'

'In a situation where the PLA is deployed, it should technically be the army,' said Bloodworth.

'So the Chinese might admit to a renegade unit being responsible and we would all be off the hook.'

'I doubt it,' said Joan Holden. 'The Chinese security chief, General Tang Siju, came from the Public Security Bureau. He is one of President Tao's closest confidants and he is very unlikely to let his old friends be criticized for killing rebellious Tibetans. China will speak with one voice on this one.'

'We have satellite surveillance to back up our HUMINT reports stumbling out of Lhasa,' said Bloodworth. 'Protests have been going on just about every day since the Drapchi break-out. Some only a few hundred. The biggest are between three and five thousand people. Many of them are spontaneous, usually sparked off by the police arresting someone. Although supported by normal Tibetans, most of the demonstrators are monks and nuns. Sera, Drepung, Ganden and Nechung monasteries have been closed. We have unconfirmed reports that twenty monks were gunned down in a courtyard at Sera while praying. The Shungseb nunnery has been shut down and the military presence in the Jokhang is so intense that it is as good as closed. We believe the protesters who were shot by the PSB had gone to the government offices after failing to get into the Jokhang.

'The Chinese have put police or army units in all the major Tibetan parts of the city. The ones we know about are in the Barkor area just south of the Jokhang. There's a 7.25mm sand-bagged machine-gun position on the side-street off the south-west corner of the Barkor Square. Two armoured personnel carriers are permanently parked outside the Snowlands Hotel just north-west of the Jokhang, to ensure that no tourists get out, or see out. The same is at the Holiday Inn, the best hotel in Lhasa, although that is not in such a sensitive area. All communications are down. There is no television and the Chinese are jamming the BBC and Voice of America as best they can.

'There's another machine-gun post along Beijing Lu. The restaurants and cafés along there like Tahi One, the Kirey and Banak Shol hotels are crawling with police. Basically the whole Tibetan area which runs around the Lingkor circumambulatory path, around Chakpori Hill and the Potala, is affected by riots and repression.'

'What about tourists?' asked Hastings.

'The Chinese were going to fly them out at night. But things never got quiet enough for them to do it, without them becoming witnesses to the crack-down. They've been confined to their hotels and the windows have been shuttered up.'

'Are there American citizens?' asked Barber

'Almost certainly,' said Bloodworth, glancing over to Holden. 'Joan, do you want to take this?'

'Jamie Song personally assured Reece Overhalt in Beijing that no American had been harmed. Song's view was that it was far better to have a dozen Americans cooped up in a hotel room for a week than have one arrested on spying charges because he's been caught with a video camera. As even the PLA found out, the PSB are a law unto themselves, so Overhalt gave Song the benefit of the doubt and recommended to us that we go along with it.'

'OK, Tom, go on,' said Hastings.

'We estimate that more than ten thousand people have been arrested. Our satellites have picked up the sudden overcrowding of prisons. We've photographed Gutsa in the east of the city, which is a PSB detention centre; Sangyip in the north-east; Utritru – the Chinese call it Wuzhidui – which is usually for common criminals, but is used as an overspill in times of riots; Sitru, Sizhidui in Chinese, which is for prisoners considered to be a threat to state security; and there's a new prison less than a mile south of Sitru. This is where the ringleaders would be taken and where the serious people would be executed and tortured. No one seems to have been taken to Drapchi, not surprisingly – yet this is where 45 per cent of political prisoners are usually kept.

'The number of dead is more difficult to ascertain. But given the killing we know about on video, and given that there might have been others, such as the shooting at Sera Monastery, our analysts put the number of dead so far at around three thousand.'

'Tell it like that,' whispered Barber enthusiastically after a few seconds' silence, and turning to Hastings. 'Just stroll into the White House press room and blind them with detail. Not scheduled. Do it as a "drop-by", when the question is asked.'

'But we're getting asked it all the time,' said Holden.

'Then I'll do it as a drop-by at State,' Hastings suggested. 'Joan can walk in with me.'

'But what's the policy?' pressed Barber. 'We can't tell them what's happening, without telling them what we're going to do about it.'

'Why not?' said Hastings. 'There is no American national interest in Tibet. We have no factories there. We do not sell American products there. It does not border any area which is of vital strategic interest to us. If we don't intervene in Africa any more, why should we in Tibet?'

'Because Tibet's special,' insisted Barber. 'Tibet and the Dalai Lama have a special place in the hearts of the American people. If we abandon Tibet after scenes like this, America will abandon us.'

The red bulb on top of a direct-line telephone on the President's desk flashed, indicating that a call was coming in to his private office from the National Security Agency. Hastings took it, but within seconds put the call on hold. 'Pakistan has launched a major attack on Indian Kashmir,' he said.

Kargil, Ladakh, India

Local time: 2130 Friday 4 May 2007
GMT: 1600 Friday 4 May 2007

Kargil had a symbolic place in the hearts of many Indians as the military sector which repulsed the Pakistani attack in 1999. There was actually very little fighting around the town of Kargil, where the population was ethnically Kashmiri and mostly Muslim. It was the second biggest town in Ladakh, built next to the turbulent Suru River, but had little more than one long main road with smaller lanes running off it. In the past few years, residents had access to all-day electricity after a huge hydro-electric power station was opened nearby. In the spring and summer, the hotels were bustling with tourists. Kargil had two attractions: the awesome mountains and the Indian army which gave visitors a taste of being in a war zone. Hamid Khan chose it as the first community in Kashmir to be liberated from Indian rule.

The roar of shelling began at 2130, battery upon battery of the thirty-year-old American-made M198 155mm howitzers. The guns had a range of twenty kilometres with normal shells and thirty-two with rocket-assisted ammunition. General Hamid Khan did not want to carry out a symbolic shelling. India had rejected the offer of a referendum. In response, he was going to take Kargil and raise the Pakistani flag.

The first rounds fell on the bus station, exploding fuel tanks and sending flames leaping into the cold night air. One of the main bridges was hit, withstanding only minutes of sustained bombardment before it broke, collapsing into the river and cutting off Kargil's main route to the north-east. The telephone exchange just south of the Baki Bazaar road functioned for ten minutes, then went down with a direct hit through the roof. The post office, between the bus stand and the Main Bazaar Road, was pulverized by three hits, together with the State Bank of India next door.

The bombardment lasted through the night, after which Kargil was a scene of burning debris, with barely a building in the centre left unmarked. Just before dawn the shelling suddenly stopped. There was a lull of a few seconds, then the quiet was shattered by the roar of twenty French-built Mirage ground-attack aircraft crossing the LoC. They flew dangerously low, only a few hundred feet above the mountain peaks. Using cannon and laser-guided missiles, two aircraft continued the attack on Kargil, ensuring this time that all roads in and out of the town were impassable. Other aircraft headed along the LoC from the Indian side, hitting anti-aircraft positions and Indian bunkers. West of Kargil, they attacked Dras, the key town west of Kargil on the Srinagar to Leh road, the key Indian resupply and artillery positions at Baltal, Matayan, the strategic command and control post on Tiger Hill and the Toleling feature north of the Mushkoh River. More aircraft concentrated on areas just east of Kargil, where India deployed the bigger artillery units of 105mm guns, the massive 155mm Bofors FH-77B howitzers with a range of more than twenty kilometres and the even longer-range 212mm Pinaka multi-rocket launchers. (These had proved disastrously unreliable in 1999, but were back in action again after being withdrawn and remodelled.) The Pakistani aircraft laid down a lethal line of fire with a cocktail of weapons around Goma, Batalik, Lamayuru and Chorbatla, then climbed and turned back to home territory.

No sooner had they finished than heavier, more cumbersome and ageing American-built F-16 multi-role combat aircraft came overhead. They were equipped with conventional single-warhead bombs with radar airburst fuses to increase the damage on structures and buildings. Cluster bombs sowed a lethal path of destruction, their tiny bomblets throwing out delayed action mines and fragmentation devices to kill people and slice through light structures such as aircraft and vehicles.

The first Indian aircraft were scrambled out of Ambala, Srinagar, Awantipur and Leh as soon as Indian radar picked up the air attack, but they were too late to engage the Pakistanis in dogfights, and the pilots did not have permission to cross onto the Pakistani side of the LoC. That had to come from the Prime Minister and he had only just been woken up.

Hamid Khan's final assault was the riskiest of the operation and began at the height of the bombing raids. A fleet of thirty helicopters, mainly the SA 330 Puma and the Mi-8 HIP C, some with twenty men, others with just four, swept into Indian-controlled Kashmir, meeting little resistance from ground fire. They were protected by a squadron of the Pakistan and Chinese built Super 7 aircraft as they flew low for the sixteen kilometres from the frontier to Kargil. Each helicopter pilot had a designated landing area, depending on the debris caused by the shelling and air attacks. Each unit had area to secure. The pilots dropped the men, from a hover, not letting the skids touch the ground, and headed straight back to the LoC.

It was in that narrow window of opportunity that the Indian fighter pilots found and attacked in a withering onslaught, while coming under fire themselves from the Pakistani Super 7s. Of the thirty helicopters which crossed into Indian territory, only twelve made it back. Three Indian aircraft were lost.

The men on the ground were not mujahedin fighters, but Pakistani soldiers, most of whom expected to be dead within the next few hours. Hand-to-hand fighting with Indian troops began as soon as they landed. But they secured enough of an area just north of the junction of Hospital Road and the Main Bazaar Road to raise the green flag of Pakistan with its white crescent and single star above the town's mosque.

Prime Minister's Office, South Block, Delhi

Local time: 0100 Saturday 5 May 2007
GMT: 1930 Friday 4 May 2007

'I offer my resignation, Prime Minister,' said Mani Naidu, the head of the Intelligence Bureau.

'Refused,' replied Hari Dixit as he took his chair at the head of the table and opened a book in front of him.

'I would like you to accept my resignation as well,' said Chandra Reddy, of RAW, who should have known in advance of Pakistan's attack on Kargil.

'Refused,' said Dixit, running his finger down a page in the book. He looked up at Naidu. 'If we had a Home Minister, he could go, but we don't because he has been murdered. The situation is so grave and the actions of Hamid Khan so unpredictable that to reshuffle my intelligence agencies at this time would be immature to say the least. Within the past thirty minutes, the whole of the Dras-Kargil sector has fallen, and we need to look ahead. Foreign Minister, before we begin on the details could you sum up where we stand diplomatically with China, Pakistan and the United States?'

'Pakistan denies involvement,' said Prabhu Purie, 'although we have the wreckage of their helicopters all over Kargil. We have heard nothing from Hamid Khan directly, but I expect them to call for a UN Security Council meeting in the next few hours. Equally disturbingly, China is racking up pressure both bilaterally and through international institutions. I'm told its troop levels on the border are almost high enough to launch an invasion. Reddy could give more details on that. Beijing has launched official complaints against us to the Human Rights Commission in Geneva.'

'What on earth for?' said Dixit.

'Prison conditions,' replied Purie. 'We treat our prisoners inhumanely.'

'They must be out of their minds.'

Zhongnanhai, Beijing, China

Local time: 0800 Saturday 5 May 2007
GMT: 0000 Saturday 5 May 2007

President Tao Jian had risen to become the leader of the world's largest one-party state on a reputation for incorruptibility and hawkish nationalism. Having gained the support of the economists and diplomats within the Party, he finally won over the military in March 1996 when the United States sent an aircraft carrier into the Straits of Taiwan during China's missile tests. It was Tao, then a vice-minister, who suggested that the then President Jiang Zemin and Foreign Minister, Qian Qichen, be summoned for a dressing down. From the viewpoint of the Chinese military, if the Americans had the nerve to threaten China with an aircraft carrier, China had clearly shown herself to be too forgiving of Taiwan's democracy and too soft in response to international pressure.

On the rare occasions when he had to meet an American official, Tao made it unequivocally clear, albeit as part of a joke, that if the United States attempted such a show of force again China would attack. His favourite parting remark, which he had mastered in English, was: 'We may not be able to hit the Pentagon, but we can vaporize Hollywood.' He became a key liaison figure in pushing through the new policy to down-size the army, modernize it and invest in missiles and a blue-water navy.

Like most Chinese leaders, Tao was a pupil of the works of Sun Tzu's *Art of War*. But he had also been influenced by the Prussian officer Carl Philipp Gottlieb von Clausewitz, whose work *Vom Kriege* or *On War* advocated that war should be seen as an extension of political policy and not as an end in itself. Years ago, when Tao first read Clausewitz, he discussed it with translators and military experts to ensure that he understood the meaning. He then blended Clausewitz with Sun Tzu's teaching that the supreme art of war was to subdue the enemy without fighting. 'War is a matter of vital importance for the state,' wrote Sun Tzu in 500 BC, arguing that the military was the instrument which delivered the *coup de grâce* to an enemy previously made vulnerable. While Sun Tzu argued that 'there has never been a protracted war from which a country has benefited', Clausewitz insisted that 'To introduce into the philosophy of war a principle of moderation would be an act of absurdity. War is an act of violence pushed to its utmost bounds.'

As Tao Jian contemplated his political objective with India, he thought about Hari Dixit. Dixit had offered to come to Beijing and had then cancelled without explanation. He had struck Pakistani positions across the LoC and emerged diplomatically unscathed.

The man might be a follower of neither Clausewitz nor Sun Tzu, but clearly he was a national leader of high brinkmanship and courage. The war about to be waged was not about Pakistan, but about India and China. Ultimately, it was the first skirmish in a fight for global leadership.

Prime Minister's Office, South Block, New Delhi

'How are we fixed militarily?' asked Hari Dixit. The National Security Council had not left the room since convening overnight. Each time decisions were made, messages interrupted the meeting with new developments.

'The Rajasthan and Punjab borders are in battle-ready positions, Prime Minister,' said Chief of Army Staff, Unni Khrishnan. 'We could move on Lahore any time you want. Fighting is still going on along the LoC. A counter-attack has begun to retake Kargil.'

'Casualties?'

'Not clear yet on their side. But we have more than fifty confirmed dead and about two hundred wounded so far. We have drawn up plans to create a buffer zone on the Pakistan side of the LoC, rather like the Israelis did in southern Lebanon. We've named it Operation *Qabza-e-Zamin*, or in English, *Secure Ground*.'

'How would that go down at the UN and elsewhere?' said Dixit.

'Given what happened last night, if we went in now, we could get away with it,' said Purie.

'Can it be done?' Dixit asked Khrishnan.

Khrishnan hesitated: 'At a pinch, yes. It is high altitude and carries risk.'

'What risk?'

'The environment is the most hostile imaginable. Movement through the mountains is painfully slow. It takes an average of ten minutes to cover a hundred yards, five times longer than on the plains. It's even slower with rations, ammunition, weapons, warm-weather protection and communications equipment.'

'But it is the same for the enemy, is it not?' said Dixit.

'They are dug in, sir. I am not saying we cannot do it, because this is what the mountain troops are trained to do. What I am flagging up is the chances of failure and the reasons. The pathways, running along the mountain ledges, are narrow. The men have to walk in single file. If they slip and fall, it is certain death. If the enemy pins them down with machine-gun fire, there is nowhere to flee to. Once out there, each unit is often cut off without a radio link. The high-frequency VHF radios operate on line of sight, so we have to set up relay stations, visible to each other to make sure commanders can pass instructions through to the forward units. And finally there's fatigue. The thin air saps the energy of the men.'

'I assume each battle-front carries its own unique set of risks,' said the Prime Minister, 'and that Kashmir is worse than most. If we go in now we can argue our case on the international stage. Can you do it?'

'If you accept the level of risk, sir, we can give it our best efforts.'

'And the China border?'

'We shouldn't fight there, Prime Minister,' replied Khrishnan, glancing towards Purie.

'The Chinese have diplomatically shot themselves in the foot by breaking the Missile Technology Control Regime and nuclear proliferation agreements,' said Purie. 'They also have a record of backing losers. Cambodia, North Korea and Burma are not shining examples of success. We should persuade Beijing that Pakistan is only going one way and that is towards collapse.'

'And let international sanctions do the rest of our

fighting for us,' said Dixit. 'Is that what you're saying? Khrishnanji, what do you think?'

'I am not as convinced as the Foreign Minister, Prime Minister,' said Unni Khrishnan. 'If China launches a cross-border attack, we will have to respond. Already they have reinforced the border along the Thag La Ridge just west of Bhutan, which is where they made their first advances in the 1962 war. We now know they have sent *Kilo*-class diesel-electric submarines to the Andaman Sea. Two surfaced as they went through the shallow waters of the Malacca Straits and made themselves known to the satellite cameras.'

Dixit put his head in his hands. 'What in Heaven's name are they trying to achieve?' he said.

'They think they can threaten us and win, sir,' said Khrishnan.

Mumbai/Bombay, Maharastra, southern India

Within an hour of the Kargil/Dras sector falling, explosions tore through cities all over India. The first was in Mumbai, the capital of Maharastra, where the state government was fervently Hindu nationalist. A massive car bomb went off on Madame Cama Road, outside the state government offices, near Horniman Circle on the edge of the main modern downtown business district. A security guard on duty was killed.

A second car bomb exploded in Delhi's Connaught Place and over the next two hours there were bomb attacks in thirteen Indian states. The only significant city to escape was Calcutta, the capital of West Bengal, for reasons which only became apparent much later.

The most concentrated violence was in the north-east. Two car bombs exploded in the capital of Arunachal Pradesh, Itanagar; one outside the town hall and the other close to the police station. Bomdi La, the southern town in the Kameng Division near Bhutan, was attacked by three timer bombs and grenades were thrown in the western town of Tawang, the closest major centre to the Bhutanese border.

In neighbouring Assam, guerrillas claiming to be from the once-defunct United Liberation Front of Assam fought running gun battles with police and troops in Dispur, the state capital, and in the second city, Narogong. When the fighting was finished, twenty-nine Indian security personnel were dead, together with more than fifty guerrillas.

Strategically, the most important target was the main trunk road heading north towards Sikkim from West Bengal, cutting across the smallest corridor of Indian territory. It was less than thirty kilometres across at its narrowest. Wedged between Nepal to the west and Bangladesh to the east, this was where the geographical cohesion of India was at its most vulnerable. It was known as the Siliguri corridor or Chicken's Neck. The road, which linked Siliguri and Guwahati, was blown in three places and blocked with booby-trapped empty fuel trucks. Two hundred mujahedin fighters held the position, while Indian infantry and fighter planes tried to dislodge them. It was later discovered that the guerrillas had come over the border from Bangladesh, where they had been trained for the operation by Pakistani and Chinese specialists. Every man would die, but for a short time, Pakistan's dream and India's nightmare had come true. The seven states of the north-east were cut off from the rest of India.

Prime Minister's Office, South Block, New Delhi, India

Local time: 0730 Saturday 5 May 2007
GMT: 0200 Saturday 5 May 2007

'**Let me get** this clear, Prime Minister,' said Unni Khrishnan, the Chief of Army Staff. 'You believe that China and Pakistan have an agreement to sever the north-east militarily, and at the same time move in on Kashmir. But I am convinced China does not want war.'

'No, perhaps it doesn't. But it will go as far as it can by pushing it to the edge.' Dixit put on his spectacles and looked down. 'I think the answer might lie in this memo I have in front of me. It was written to Pakistani Field Marshal Ayub Khan in 1966 by Zulfi Bhutto, who was then Foreign Minister. We should note the circumstances. Pakistan had just been defeated by us in the 1965 war. Bhutto considered the terms of the truce unacceptable and was quoted as saying that Pakistan needed complete victory over India. The only alternative would be Pakistan's destruction as a self-respecting nation. He described the Tashkent Agreement which ended the hostilities as a national humiliation and diplomatic betrayal. Then he outlined his plan, and I am convinced that Hamid Khan has borrowed Bhutto's strategy to use for his own foreign policy. Remember, of course, that Bangladesh was still East Pakistan.

' "The defence of East Pakistan would need to be closely coordinated with Chinese actions both in the north-east of India and also possibly in the regions of Sikkim and Nepal. It would be necessary to provide the Chinese with a link-up with our forces in that sector. I envisage a lightning thrust across the narrow Indian territory that separates Pakistan" – or Bangladesh as it is now – "from Nepal."'

Dixit looked up. 'Bhutto was referring to the Chicken's Neck, exactly the same area which the terrorists held this morning. "From our point of view, this would be highly desirable," he wrote. "It would be to the advantage of Nepal to secure its freedom from isolation by India. It would solve the problem of Sikkim and Tibet."'

'It would also deal with China's claim to Arunachal Pradesh,' said Prabhu Purie, 'and bring Bhutan and Nepal into the Chinese sphere of influence.'

'In short, gentlemen,' Dixit went on, 'that is the price the Chinese dictatorship is asking us to pay for peace. We give Kashmir to Pakistan. Expel the Dalai Lama and much of the Tibetan community from India. Abandon our security obligations to Bhutan and Nepal and renegotiate our borders with a view to handing over Arunachal Pradesh and giving independence back to Sikkim. And it will go like that, chiselling away at us to make us the weaker power in Asia.' He paused, lost in his own thoughts for a moment, then summed up: 'It is not the road democratic India would seek to go down.'

Line of Control, Kashmir

Local time: 0830 Saturday 5 May 2007
GMT: 0300 Saturday 5 May 2007

Unni Khrishnan, Chief of Army Staff, and Ranjit Mansingh, Chief of Air Staff, monitored the operation from the underground command and control centre at the Ambala airbase just south of Chandigarh. Four hundred aircraft were used, including the ageing fighter and ground-attack MiG-21, the MiG-27 tactical strike fighter, the Mirage 2000–5 air-defence and multi-role fighter and the formidable SU-30. They flew from Ambala, from Srinagar in Kashmir itself, Jodhpur in Rajasthan, Hindon near Delhi and Agra, more famous for the Taj Mahal than for waging war.

The first strikes hit Pakistan's Divisional Headquarters in Skardu, taking out air defences, radar and aircraft. The next waves concentrated on the artillery positions sixteen kilometres beyond the LoC, destroying the big guns which had laid siege to towns like Kargil and Dras over the years. Then the Indians laid down a withering array of firepower on Pakistani army bunkers, transport and fuel depots. When the airstrikes ended, India's Bofors 155mm guns opened up to continue the pounding.

As the weather cleared at mid-morning under a bright blue Himalayan sky, the helicopters took off, in one of the most impressive sights of modern military warfare: the sky filled with rotary aircraft, in places blackening the sky like flocks of migrating birds. The plan for such an assault had been drawn up and reworked dozens of times since the first war with Pakistan in 1947. But never before had it been taken off the shelves, dusted down and implemented. At the centre of Operation *Secure Ground* were the Himalayan Eagles, the expert mountain squadron which had pioneered techniques in fixed- and rotary-wing high-altitude mountain flying. The squadron's emblem depicted the snow-capped Himalayas over which its pilots flew every day of the year.

The terrain in Ladakh and Jammu and Kashmir was among the most hostile in the world. The main airbase at Leh was at 3,200 metres. Others in the area were equally treacherous. Chushul was at 4,400 metres and Thoise at 3,000. Arrangements had been made to fly in the AN-32 and IL-76 transport aircraft as the only means of keeping these remote bases resupplied, even at night.

Ladakh itself was snowbound for up to nine months of the year and the AN-32 made routine drops to the men defending the Siachen glacier. Helicopters were the only way to get soldiers in and out.

India planned to take control of sections of the L-shaped piece of territory, 700 kilometres long, which stretched west and south from the Karakoram and Ladakh ranges close to the border with China. Dras and Kargil would be reclaimed, and the Indian flag, troops, supply bases and landing strips would be set up at points all the way to the Pakistani town of Muzafarabad, then further south, passing within eighty kilometres of Islamabad to where the LoC began fifty-five kilometres west of Jammu.

It was one of the most audacious airborne campaigns in military history. The attacking forces divided the LoC into five sectors, each identified by a colour. Red sector covered the area from the Chinese border near Gapsham in Indian territory taking in a triangle stretching up to Skardu and down to the Marol inside Pakistani territory, the next town north of Kargil along the Suru River. Yellow sector covered a much smaller, but more heavily fortified area, taking in Kargil and Dras and aiming to capture territory around the villages of Kakshar, Matiyal, Gultari and Karbos. Blue sector ran along a 160-kilometre stretch from Dras to Tithwal close to Muzafarabad. Orange sector covered the more politically sensitive area from Tithwal to Hajira directly east of Islamabad. White sector took in the final southerly stretch to the beginning of the LoC near Jammu.

To secure ground beyond the whole of the LoC would be too bold. The initial plan was to cordon off the area behind Kargil and Dras between Minimarg and Suru/Indus. A safe corridor was to be created in the Neelam Valley and the Haji Pir pass. Once that had been done, the third objective was territory west of Poonch up to Muzafarabad. Once heliborne troops had taken areas, they would be reinforced with a parachute drop from fixed-wing aircraft.

The first assaults were limited to the Yellow and Blue sectors, where most of the fighting had taken place in the battles over Kashmir and where Indians felt most vulnerable. An assault on the Red sector around the Siachen Glacier region of Ladakh would be pointless until the summer, and by then the dispute should be over. The southerly assault on the Orange and White sectors would be limited to artillery barrages. Unni Khrishnan was deterred from striking any harder there for fear that Pakistan would resort to threatening a nuclear strike. He hoped that there would be a ceasefire within forty-eight hours and that a deal could be reached on India's terms.

The helicopters flew in formations of fifty, keeping to 135 k.p.h., contour flying along the valleys. With each formation was an Mi-26 workhorse, some carrying seventy combat-equipped troops, others up to twenty tonnes of ammunition, weapons, supplies and vehicles. Flanked out from the Mi-26s were the smaller Mi-17 medium transport helicopters. For this first sortie they were mainly carrying troops, with twenty-four in each aircraft. The more versatile assault and anti-armour Mi-25 kept to the outside of the formation, each with an eight-man Special Forces squad, which was to identify and neutralize those Pakistani positions which had survived the airstrikes and shelling.

Flying at 1,000 feet above the formations were four-man Alouette Cheetahs, two in each sector, used for command and control. They also carried high-ranking officers who would command the sectors once they were secured. Others flew with medical crew to evacuate the critically wounded.

Three formations flew low and slow towards Yellow sector, with 1,022 men deployed in the first wave. On dropping them the helicopters returned to bring in another thousand within the hour. The larger helicopters carried platoons of Indian Muslim soldiers, so that there would be one with each landing.

Pakistani resistance was scattered, as if after the overnight battering every man had been left to his own initiative to take out an aircraft. High above, the Indian fighter planes were engaging the few Pakistani pilots who had managed to scramble their warplanes into the air. The Yellow sector helicopter pilots began calling in hits within seconds of crossing the LoC. They were mainly from small-arms and machine-gun fire, but it became clear that this would not be a casualty-free operation.

'Fuel line severed,' the pilot of a Mi-25 managed to report before power was lost. He skilfully brought it down in one piece, but straight into the fire of a Pakistani bunker. While the pilot was wrestling with the controls on the way down, the crew fired a Scorpion anti-tank missile blindly, and raked the area with a four-barrel 12.7mm rotary gun, causing mayhem on the ground. The commandos were out of the helicopter when it was still six feet off the ground, storming the bunker. The corporal in charge just managed to raise the Indian flag before they were pinned down and killed against overwhelming odds.

'Pilot killed,' said another report from a Mi-17.

'Secure Ground Yellow, you are off course,' said the second in command to the leader of a formation, which was trying to get attention with a frantic hand signal that the aircraft's radio had been knocked out. The Alouette, carrying the sector battalion colonel, took over as command aircraft.

As they got closer to the designated landing zones, the formation bunched up. From the ground, it might have looked like precision flying, but in the air it was like a sudden traffic jam, with everyone bobbing around at different altitudes and pilots pulling back and going forward to avoid collisions. The pilots had to have nerves of ice to get through the landing. One wrong position, one touch of the rotor blades and a dozen aircraft could go down. Yet fear of making a mistake affected judgement, with less experienced pilots overcorrecting until their helicopter got out of control. The orders of the first wave were to avoid population centres, set up secure positions and call in airstrikes and artillery to clear the ground for the next wave. The first landings were to go no further than Kaksar and the Shingo River.

But on the ground, resistance was building, and it would be impossible to reach some of the landing zones (LZ) without inflicting an enormous number of civilian casualties. The orders, though, were clear. If civilians stayed around, they should be treated as sympathizers and participants in the conflict.

For many of the pilots, their assailants from the ground were invisible. Ten aircraft came in at only twenty knots under concentrated fire on the northern side of the Shingo and Dras rivers where the Pakistanis had an artillery command and control centre. All that the Indian troops could see were villagers looking up, shielding their eyes from the sun, with the enemy among them firing up with heavy-calibre machine guns. The crews called in hits every other second. The ships were too high for the soldiers to jump and if they did they would be cut down in a withering field of fire. Then a gunner from a Mi-25 opened up on the villagers with the 12.7mm. Other soldiers from the same craft fired into the crowd and lobbed down grenades, killing women, children, animals and the enemy – any living thing which moved against them. Ten aircraft landed. Ten took off again. The men on the ground secured one of the most strategic areas in Yellow Sector.

Further along, directly north of Dras, the pilots had to deal with LZs of up to 4,500 metres. Buildings seemed to grip hold of mountainsides of icy wastelands. It was one of the cruellest places to fight a war, but also one of the most strategic. In the second formation of fifty aircraft, fifteen were damaged and ten were shot down while they foundered around the mountains, dropping off troops. Most of the pilots had to carry out pinnacle landings, which they described as like approaching a raft at sea in a storm. Some of the hilltops soared straight up 300 metres above the valleys and the pilots had to keep the landing spot below the horizon. If they climbed above, they were too low and became buffeted by winds.

The pilot of a Mi-26, loaded with five tonnes of equipment and twenty men, made that mistake. His aircraft became impossible to control and it smashed into the mountain, mushing up like a squashed paper cup. It rolled down the slope, spewing out men and equipment all the way down until it exploded into a ball of fire. Some of the areas were so unstable that the skids would slip on the ice and get caught somewhere, so the pilots couldn't take off. They had to get lift by bringing the nose up first, making sure both skids were free. If one got stuck the aircraft would flip over and crash.

On Pakistan territory across the LoC from the town of Minimarg, eight helicopters came into land amid extraordinary scenes of welcome, as if they were a liberating force. Four Mi-25s landed first and the assault squads set up positions around the rest of the LZ, with the villagers backing away from them, but staying. Then the Mi-26 came down and, as soon as the wheels touched the ground, the men on board four Mi-17s jumped out from a hover, secured the area and began unloading equipment. That was when the Pakistanis opened up. A handheld anti-tank missile exploded against the cockpit of the Mi-26. Machine-gun fire, criss-crossing the LZ, cut down a swathe of men, scrambling to get weapons to defend themselves. Rocket-propelled grenades destroyed two helicopters before the assault units were able to lay down fire.

The battle around Minimarg lasted for hours with the bodies of children lying wounded and dying in between the two sides. Every helicopter was wrecked and it wasn't until the third wave of the Yellow sector assault arrived that India could lay claim to the area.

Prime Minister's Office, South Block, New Delhi

Local time: 0930 Saturday 5 May 2007
GMT: 0400 Saturday 5 May 2007

'**Tell General Hamid** Khan and President Tao that I want to speak to them personally and set a time. Chandraji, see the Americans informally and tell them what's going on. We will handle this bilaterally and regionally. We will not internationalize it. If they want to send special envoys, we will accept them with courtesy, but not as negotiators. If the democratic world wants its values to survive in Asia, they will have to help us anyway.'

'**Prime Minister Dixit** is on the hotline, sir,' said Masood as Hamid Khan, alone in his office, was reading the latest military reports from Kashmir.

'Have all our aircraft left Kashmir?' asked Khan, reaching for the telephone.

'Yes, sir.'

'How many have we lost?'

'Eighteen on the ground. Ten F-16s and eight F-7s, all from the attack on Skardu. We lost two F-16s in dogfights. The enemy lost one aircraft, a Mirage 2000.'

'Cold comfort, Captain. It is my fault for not anticipating their swift response.'

Khan picked up the phone. 'Prime Minister, General Hamid Khan here.'

'General, I will not speak unclearly, nor will I be diplomatic,' said Hari Dixit as soon as Khan came on the line. 'India holds you responsible for aiding and abetting the Chinese attack on Dharamsala, for murdering the former Indian Chief of Army Staff and the Home Minister, and for planning a terrorist campaign throughout India in which many lives were lost.'

'Prime Minister, you are talking rubbish,' interrupted Khan.

'Shut up, General,' snapped Dixit. 'India will continue to form a fifteen-kilometre buffer zone across the LoC. We will attack any military installation, anywhere in Pakistan in order to achieve our objectives. Your attempts to draw

Europe, the United States and China into this dispute will fail. You are an unelected military leader with a history of aiding insurgencies. You are not a man of the modern world.'

'You have twenty-four hours to withdraw your forces from Pakistani territory, Prime Minister,' said Khan. 'And twelve to stop all hostilities.'

'We will stop only when we have achieved the security of our borders.'

'While you are violating ours. Hari, listen to me. For the sake of God, listen. If you were a military man you would understand what is happening. Pakistan cannot respond to Indian airstrikes by sending up its air force. We have four hundred combat aircraft. You have twelve hundred. We would end up being slaughtered. Pakistan has two deterrents against Indian aggression. Insurgency – or terrorism, as you call it – and the nuclear option. The former has kept us enemies for more than half a century. The latter would destroy us both in half a day. We're unlucky in that we don't rule a country like Switzerland, whose citizens are more happy with peace than with war. Our people are warriors. It needs extra-special skills for us to guide it through, Hari. Real imagination.'

'General, that is a very nice speech. But if you are genuine, why are you picking a fight?'

'I am lancing a boil, Prime Minister, like NATO lanced a boil in the Balkans by bombing Serbia. They caused many more casualties than if it had been left to fester. But the problem was exposed so that it could be solved.'

'All right, General. You have one shot. Give me your solution.'

'You set up your buffer between Tithwal and Marol along the northern sector of the LoC and I will not fight back. You will have secured the most militarized sector. I can't let you do it along the western flank because it brings you too close to Islamabad. All hostilities cease. Prisoners are sent back. The dead returned. We then make a joint announcement on a referendum for Kashmir – a referendum which *will* take place. Once details are drawn up, I will do everything in my power to bring back the mujahedin. We have control, as you know, but it's not total.'

'The UN resolution stipulates that Pakistani forces must be withdrawn from the disputed territory before any referendum takes place,' said Dixit, jotting down the points Khan had made.

'If you don't want me to internationalize this issue, let's forget about a defunct UN resolution passed by the very same men who allowed this bloody partition to take place.'

'I'll get back to you.'

'And the invasion continues?'

'Yes.'

Prime Minister's Office, South Block, New Delhi

Local time: 1000 Saturday 5 May 2007
GMT: 0430 Saturday 5 May 2007

'**Thank you for** making the time, President Tao,' said Dixit. 'I am sure you agree that if we talk personally we might be able to see a way through the fog.' Interpreters were on the line. Tao insisted that his Foreign Minister, Jamie Song, join in the conversation, so Prabhu Purie was called in as well.

'I don't see any fog,' said Tao abruptly. 'Your government has maintained a force of anti-Chinese Tibetan guerrillas who have now invaded Chinese territory. You give sanctuary to the Dalai Lama and the Tibetan government-in-exile, which is fomenting disturbances leading to deaths and injuries among Chinese citizens. The Dalai Lama has stayed outside China since the failed rebellion of March 1959 by a small number of splittists of the Tibetan upper class. Since then he has gone further and further down the road of dividing the Motherland. He preaches about his aim of turning the Tibetan Plateau into a holy land filled with peace and non-violence, where people can live in harmony and nature – yet he sends terrorists to Tibet to blow up buildings and kill innocent people.'

Tao was speaking simultaneously with his interpreter who was so efficient in the translation that she must have been working from a prepared text. On a signal from Purie, Dixit let the Chinese President continue.

'The facts of the Tibetan issue are as follows. Tibet under the rule of the Dalai Lama was still in the feudal age with its aristocracy holding absolute power. The democratic reforms in Tibet in 1959 put an end once and for all to the barbarous and backward serfdom. Life expectancy for Tibetans has increased substantially from thirty-six, before 1959, to sixty-eight today. In India, your official statistics show that life expectancy is only sixty-three years. Ninety per cent of the population was illiterate or semi-literate. Now 73.5 per cent of Tibetan children of school age have access to an education. In your country only 52 per cent of the young people can read and write. In old Tibet, there were only two small government-run clinics in Lhasa. The region now has more than a thousand medical institutions, with 2.3 hospital beds and 2.1 doctors for every thousand people.'

'I think I get your point, President Tao.'

'The Dalai Lama did not construct one single road. We have built a road network of more than twenty thousand kilometres.'

'I accept many of those things.'

'It would be better if you waited for the President to finish,' said Jamie Song, intervening in English.

'In the past there were nearly a thousand families of beggars and poor people in areas around Lhasa,' Tao was saying, 'and it was also common to see prisoners in handcuffs, shackles and on wooden trolleys begging along the streets. These scenes have been eradicated by the democratic reforms. The overwhelming majority of farmers and herders now have enough food and clothing. Why, then, is India championing the cause of the splittist Tibetan aristocracy by providing them with men and weapons? What has India's hero the Dalai Lama done for Tibet in all these years? How has he improved the people's living standard? India should know that Tibet is an integral part of China and the splittist Dalai Lama has given no thought to the fundamental interests of the country. He has only tried to spread lies and stir up riots.'

After the interpreter finished the last sentence, no one spoke for a few seconds, until Dixit said: 'We very much appreciate your view of the situation.'

It was Jamie Song who replied, in Chinese, with a different interpreter coming in: 'President Tao has unfortunately had to go to an urgent meeting. He asked me to convey his deep regret that you had to inexplicably cancel your visit to Beijing and would be very happy to receive you in the near future should you be able to find time to come.'

'Thank you, Foreign Minister,' said Dixit. 'I will ask Mr Purie to be in touch with you about that. Meanwhile, as you know our bilateral dispute with Pakistan over Kashmir has escalated this week. We would like your assurances that China will not side with Pakistan to escalate the crisis even more.'

'Human rights are a global issue, Prime Minister. Some of the reports of civilian massacres are difficult to ignore.'

'As are the pictures of your troops opening fire in Tibet, Jamie,' added Purie.

'For China, the Kashmir issue is a dispute between India and Pakistan,' responded Song, 'You must remember though that Pakistan is a very old friend of China. My government is more concerned about the Tibetan issue. I am sure—'

'Excuse me, Foreign Minister,' said Dixit, impatiently, as Chandra Reddy burst into the room, slipping an urgent note onto his desk. Dixit quickly read it: 'I'm sorry, Foreign Minister, I have been told that Chinese aircraft and ground troops have invaded the Kingdom of Bhutan. The King of Bhutan has called on India for help.'

Briefing

Bhutan

The tiny Buddhist Himalayan Kingdom of Bhutan has deliberately made itself one of the world's most isolated countries. A hereditary monarchy was established in 1907 and, with a population of only six hundred thousand, the first king signed a treaty with Britain to safeguard the kingdom against attacks from China. In 1949, after its independence, India drew up a similar replacement treaty. But it was not until 1963, in the aftermath of the Sino-Indian war, that the Indian Military Training Team (IMTRAT) was established in Bhutan, with India supplying military hardware, advisers and trainers for the Royal Bhutan Army. India regards Bhutan as a strategic buffer state. Any attack on it would have to be repelled to preserve the delicate balance of power in South Asia.

China–Bhutan border

Local time: 1023 Saturday 5 May 2007
GMT: 0423 Saturday 5 May 2007

Choedrak and his fighters sat against the mud-brick wall, silently savouring the moment of success. This was one of the greatest moments of the Tibetan struggle. This was why so many of his men from the SFF had died. Togden was recovering with a mug of yak tea and the guards were cranking up the radio to try to get a helicopter in from the capital, Thimpu. Around the hut there was the hum of conversation and the smell of a wood fire. For the final few kilometres, there had been firing behind them, single shots as the Chinese tried to start an avalanche in the Monla Karchung pass. Two SFF men, rotting with frostbite, had volunteered to stay behind to stop them.

Choedrak only had five men left. It took four to carry Togden's stretcher, and they stumbled along the valley of the Bumtang River until they spotted a spiral of smoke. When he explained who they were and who they had with them, the Bhutanese guards embraced them with admiration and brought them into their hut. Word spread around the communities and villagers crammed in to look at the man who was being hailed as one of the great Buddhist leaders of Tibet.

Choedrak dozed and lost track of time and when he heard the steady thud of rotor blades he thought it was the Bhutanese helicopter come to pick them up. He pushed himself up, getting his balance against the wall, and gave an order to prepare the stretcher. Then a machine gun opened up. The bullets ripped through the hut as if it were paper.

Camp David, Maryland, USA

Local time: 2330 Friday 5 May 2007
GMT: 0430 Saturday 5 May 2007

'**You've got to** pick up the phone and talk to the Prime Minister, John,' said Joan Holden, the Secretary of State. 'Conflict between India and China is a whole different ball game than between India and Pakistan.'

'If I talk to Dixit, I have to talk to Tao.'

'Then talk to them both. China has violated the sovereignty of Bhutan just in order to capture a Buddhist monk. It's a ludicrous way of conducting foreign policy. Indian and Chinese warplanes are having dogfights over Bhutan this morning. Nepal has already asked for international intervention. A Chinese squadron has crossed the border into Arunachal Pradesh and they've buzzed the border guards in Sikkim. One Indian pilot chased a Chinese plane almost to Lhasa. The only government with any authority to intervene is the United States of America.'

'On the side of India, or as a neutral party?'

'Neutral,' said Holden.

'One minute,' said Ennio Barber, a map of the Indian subcontinent spread out on his lap. On the coffee table by his side were the latest opinion-poll ratings on the Chinese crackdown in Tibet. 'The American people are already outraged after the massacre in Lhasa. The anti-China lobby in Congress is calling for sanctions, carrier groups and withdrawal of the Ambassador. The works. I can't see the President getting on the phone to Tao and Dixit saying, "America is friends of both countries."'

'But it's true,' said Holden.

'Maybe. But he cannot call for India to stop its military action against China. Firstly, India is a democracy. Secondly, if Chinese aircraft attacked Bhutan, India has a treaty obligation to protect.'

'What exactly is that obligation?' said the President.

The Defense Secretary, Alvin Jebb, spoke for the first time in the late evening emergency meeting. 'China claims suzerainty over Bhutan, which basically means it claims to have control over it, which the international community does not recognize. To give you a parallel, we recognize Chinese suzerainty over Tibet, but not over Bhutan. Because they're terrified of China, the Bhutanese signed two agreements with the British, when they ran India – the Treaty of Sinchula in 1865 and the Treaty of Punakha in 1910. After Indian independence, the provisions of the two treaties were formally incorporated in a new agreement with India, known as the Treaty of Darjeeling, signed in 1949. The upshot is that Bhutan runs its internal affairs, while India is responsible for defence and foreign policy. India has a similar arrangement with Nepal, but Nepal is less afraid of China and more protective of its own sovereignty.'

'Alvin, you're right,' said Joan Holden. 'But your emphasis is wrong. India is not obliged to go to war on behalf of Bhutan. It's got the option.'

'What's happened to Lundrup Togden?' said Hastings.

'We presume he's dead, together with a man called Major Choedrak who devised the whole operation,' said Jebb. 'After the helicopter attacked with a machine gun, the pilot gave the coordinates for an airstrike. Some people managed to escape and headed to the town of Lhedam about fifteen miles south of the border. A Bhutanese helicopter came in from a place called Jakar Dzong, which is the local administrative capital, and picked some of them up.'

'Is Togden alive?' said Hastings.

'We don't know. But the Chinese MiGs came back. They blasted the Bhutanese helicopter out of the sky. Everyone on board was killed.'

'After all that, and they get killed as they cross the finishing line.' Hastings was clearly upset.

'The Chinese went on to bomb the bridge across the river which heads out of the town,' continued Jebb. 'They strafed the roads, killing a number of people, who are mostly Bhutanese nationals of Tibetan origin. It was between these sorties that Bhutan asked for India's help. Indian planes got to Jakar just as the Chinese were heading back and that's when the dogfights started.'

'And they're still going on?'

'Seems so, Mr President.'

'All right. Let's put that on hold for a moment. What's happening in Kashmir?'

'The Indian assault is ongoing,' said Jebb. 'They've set up a buffer zone along the most sensitive part of the LoC. Casualties on both sides are heavy. I understand that General Khan has spoken to Hari Dixit on the Prime Ministers' hotline, but we don't know how it went or whether there'll be a ceasefire.'

'We can't be seen to be sympathizing with China in any way, Mr President,' pressed Barber. 'This is democratic values against dictatorship.'

'We're not sympathizing with anybody, Ennio,' Hastings replied impatiently. 'Frankly, I don't think we should say a damn thing. We've got two border skirmishes in faraway places. Most people know Tibet through the movies and Nepal because of Mount Everest. By the time I get round to explaining what Bhutan is, the whole thing might be fixed.'

The President's Private Secretary rang through on the

intercom. 'The National Security Advisor asks if he could have a quick word. He knows you're in a meeting and wants to join it.'

Bloodworth came in a sports shirt and shorts and looked as if he had been trying to get an early night. He pulled out a batch of photographs. 'These are our own images and show the build-up of Indian armour and artillery along the border with Pakistan. I've just spoken to Chandra Reddy, their Foreign Intelligence chief. He warns us to back off any condemnation of India's military actions. He is convinced that China has flown into Pakistan either a proven tactical nuclear warhead or their version of the neutron bomb, and possibly the DF-21 missile. If that's true, Pakistan now has a credible strategy to deter an Indian armoured advance into its territory.'

'How quickly could he use them?' said Hastings.

'If China has handed them over ready-to-use, as it were, they would be ready now. These pictures are about twenty-four hours old.'

'I don't buy it,' said Holden. 'Why would they break every rule in the book? Peddling nuclear technology. How far does the DF-21 go?'

'Twelve hundred miles,' said Bloodworth.

'Then they're breaking the Missile Technology Control Regime as well. I can't see why they would do it.'

'Why do you say that, Joan?' said Hastings.

'China craves stability. She has enormous internal problems of modernization and unemployment. She needs our technology and trade to develop. Why should she risk all that to support a basket-case like Pakistan?'

'Alvin. What's your view?' said Hastings.

'The Chinese leadership enjoys believing that it could soon be a world power and it expects to play a leading role in Asia much sooner than that. For us in the West, there is nothing so destabilizing as the arrival of a new economic and military power on the international scene. China is in a state of transition, switching suddenly between confidence and insecurity. It is an adolescent, and adolescents are dangerous. It is suspicious of India and distrusts Russia and Japan.'

'What does it think of us?' said Barber, his eyes down studying the map.

'Like many of our friends, allies and enemies in Asia, it sees America as a power in decline, drifting towards an obsession with domestic issues, no longer interested in being the world's policeman. Your policies since coming to office, Mr President, have underlined that view. Your predecessors were thought to be overly strong on human rights and democracy, but short on vision and realpolitik. At least with you, they think they know where they stand.'

'But I'm with Joan,' said Hastings. 'Why now? Why take the risk?'

'Unelected national leaders rarely act rationally,' said Bloodworth. 'Tao sees a window. As Alvin said, he could be taking advantage of our more inward-looking policies. You might not be here three years from now, and a new President could be much tougher and more involved with the China issue. Nor is Hari Dixit a warrior Prime Minister. Hamid Khan is, despite his vision for development. He needs China to balance the power of the Islamic fundamentalists. The United States has proved to be an unreliable ally, so he is willing to ditch us completely and use China to win Kashmir and prove his Islamic and national credentials.'

'In order to control the fundamentalists?'

'Correct.'

'And China?' said Hastings.

'China realizes that India's democratic status is beginning to attract American interest as a counterbalance to its own relationship with us,' said Jebb. 'It is also worried that in the long term India's economic reforms promise a much more successful economy because they are based on an established and impartial judicial and financial system.'

'So India's threat to China is not so much military as economic and diplomatic?'

'Correct,' said Jebb. 'It is very difficult to see India and China confront each other seriously through conventional means. India is, and will remain for some time, the much weaker power. But it could become the moral political beacon for Asia, in a similar role to that played by Japan – a functioning democracy and the rule of law underwritten by the United States and the European Union.'

'For the US, though, China has the far larger interest?' said Holden.

'That's right, at the moment. But China believes that the world needs it as a global player. It studies incremental shifts in the balance of power and is gradually becoming more assertive.'

'What we should bear in mind is that Tao is doing nothing new in sending Pakistan a weapons package,' said Bloodworth. 'China is the main supplier to the military. It designed Pakistan's nuclear-weapons programme. It broke the MTCR in 1988 with a three-billion-dollar sale to Saudi Arabia. It has gunned its citizens down in Beijing's main city square, continued to ban political dissent and carries out ethnic repression in Tibet, Xinjiang and numerous other places. And Joan tells us our largest interest is with China and not India.'

'Let me get this right,' said Barber, folding up his map. 'It seems that for years India has been kept preoccupied with Pakistan. If India was rid of this problem and sorted out its economy it would move from having a local-power role to a much bigger regional role and China doesn't want this. So China fuels the Pakistan conflict and keeps India weak.'

'That's about it,' said Jebb.

'I still don't buy it,' said Holden.

'All right. Let's move on,' said Hastings, 'because I assume Tom wouldn't be in this room with twenty-four-hour-old imagery unless he thought there was a problem.'

'If India invades Pakistan, I don't believe Pakistan's first use of tactical nuclear weapons can be confined to the battlefield,' said Bloodworth. 'There are no safeguards to stop it escalating into a full-scale nuclear exchange.'

'Then it's up to China to stop them, isn't it?' said Hastings.

China World Hotel, Beijing, China

Local time: 1400 Saturday 5 May 2007
GMT: 0600 Saturday 5 May 2007

Reece Overhalt, the American Ambassador to Beijing and multibillionaire businessman, flicked through the television channels in the suite he had personally booked and paid for in the China World Hotel. Jamie Song had called him two hours earlier, suggesting a quick and private drink. But he couldn't come to the Embassy. Nor could the Ambassador be seen at the Foreign Ministry. Since then Overhalt had talked to Hastings and was told to do everything within his power to bring China into line. He had also spent a difficult thirty minutes with the Pakistani Ambassador, Javed Jabbar.

'I honestly don't know what you are talking about,' Jabbar had said urbanely as Overhalt accused Pakistan of getting missiles and neutron bombs from China.

'Would you necessarily know?' pressed Overhalt. 'There is a military government in charge now.'

'Pakistan's institutions are intact, Ambassador Overhalt. Personally, I'm surprised your government isn't giving more support to General Khan. Is it that you find it easier to deal with those singing to the tune of the Taleban or the Iranian mullahs, or are you more at home with buying your foreign leaders so that they are more answerable to America's beck and call?'

'Let's not go down an anti-America road, Javed,' replied Overhalt. 'The MV *Baldwin*—'

'The *Baldwin* is bringing artillery shells from Korea to us. They have supplied us with these shells for years. Journalists who go up to the front have reported it. The fighting in Kashmir ebbs and flows and right now there is an upsurge.'

'Our information is that you are being given the DF-21 intermediate-range missile, which would break international regulations.'

'Your regulations. Not ours,' said Jabbar sharply. 'If what you say is correct, it would be diplomatic madness for both us and China. We have just had a military takeover. There is an Indian offensive going on in Kashmir. We are being accused of terrorism in India. At this very time, to import the weapons you suggest would brand us as a pariah state.'

'Precisely,' said Overhalt.

'Then think again, Ambassador. For God's sake think again. If you don't it will be the end of a modern Pakistan.'

Doubt flitted back and forth as Overhalt ran through his conversation with Jabbar. Doubt about whether Tom Bloodworth had called it right. Doubt about whether Jabbar had been sending Overhalt a message of admission by listing the steps Pakistan had taken towards isolating itself from the international community.

In the middle of his analysis, and more than two hours late, Jamie Song arrived, looking unusually confused and harassed. Overhalt took him out onto the balcony, just in case one of the many Chinese intelligence agencies had bugged the room.

'Sorry, I got delayed. Just as we were about to summon the Indian Ambassador for a third time, a bloody air war broke out over Bhutan.'

'Togden's dead, I gather,' said Overhalt gently.

Song shrugged and leant on the balcony rails looking over the lights of Beijing. 'Reece, I don't know. And, frankly, I would like to say I don't care. But I'm a wiser man than that. Let me give you good advice. Your President's instinct on this is right. Let us sort Tibet and Bhutan with the Indians and it will settle down. If you guys get involved, Europe will get involved, and your politicians will be like lapdogs reacting to the democratic mob.'

'That's how things work nowadays, Jamie. Humanitarian foreign policy.'

'Bullshit, Reece, and you know it. Let me tell you this. You succeeded in Kosovo, Timor and Iraq because these were dying regimes of a bygone age. Milosevic was no new Hitler. Saddam Hussein was no new Ayatollah Khomeini. But India and China are new powers, Reece. In a hundred, a thousand years, when the American empire has collapsed, we will be ruling the world. Let us fight our wars. Let the tectonic plates of history shift naturally.'

'I'm more concerned about the next hundred days,' said Overhalt.

'Then accept what I am saying. If you had ever attended a meeting inside Zhongnanhai, you would understand that the longer we can keep things balanced, the better it is for everyone. It could see us both to retirement. Tibet is one issue about which you don't mess with us. Even a cosmopolitan man-of-the-world like me becomes a crazy nationalist when it comes to Tibet.'

'Those pictures were not very pleasant, Jamie.'

Song glanced sideways towards his friend: 'Nor was My Lai or Kent State, Reece. Nor are the pictures of prison chain gangs in Alabama. One image does not represent a whole nation.'

'Point taken. But I'm not sure how the President would have to react if more of this got out.'

'You lost the Vietnam War because the American public did not like the images of violence coming out of it. That was your choice. But the American people will not decide whether or not we win our war in Tibet. If it helps the President, I'll go on CNN and say precisely this. Lhasa was suffering riots. Just like America suffers riots. We have put them down and arrested the ringleaders. Just like America does. It all started because Indian troops—'

'Renegades, Jamie.'

'You're too big a man to quibble, Reece. Let me finish. We pursued some of those troops into Bhutan, just as you pursued the Vietnamese into Cambodia and Laos; just as you pursue drug traffickers into Latin America. We have achieved our objectives and have now withdrawn.'

'What about Pakistan, then?'

'What about Pakistan?'

'We have information that you're shipping them missiles and nuclear technology.'

Jamie Song was silent for a moment: 'You have this on authority?'

Overhalt nodded.

'They've asked. They've been asking for years. If it's happening, Reece, I don't know. And that's the truth.'

India–Pakistan border, Rajasthan, India

Local time: 1200 Saturday 5 May 2007
GMT: 0630 Saturday 5 May 2007

All stations: Order of March: Charlie Combat Commands, Artillery Group, 4 Brigade. 7 Brigade is to take 2 Field Regiment, 9 Artillery, under command. Helicopter reconnaissance is a priority call. 7 Brigade is to advance to Objectives Cotton and Silk and cut enemy routes north to south. Secure 5 kilometres beyond railway line west. 5 kilometres south of Mirbar Mathello and 5 kilometres north of Rahimaya Khan. None to move before orders.

Lieutenant General Gurjit Singh, commander of the Indian XXI Strike Armoured Corps, closed his eyes to acclimatize quickly to the bright desert sunlight, opened the tank turret and lifted himself out of the cramped and dingy interior. If they were sent in, he anticipated at least seventy-two hours of continual combat before the Pakistani surrender. His ears were already ringing with the constant radio traffic through his headphones. He took them off and jumped down onto the crusty surface of the Thar Desert to allow himself five minutes of clear thinking.

His armoured deployment was as good as he could make it. But even for the new and most tested tanks the Rajasthan sector was one of the most difficult for armoured warfare. The desert was not like in North Africa, where the sand was relatively hard. The surface of the Thar desert was loose and shifting. No wheeled vehicle could handle it, and even tracked vehicles could suddenly get bogged down. There were very few paved roads, and once across the border all Pakistani territory was assumed mined.

Under his command were a thousand main battlefield tanks, an assortment of tracked armoured vehicles and a hundred thousand men. The advance armour would be led by the three-man T-72M1 Ajay main battlefield tank (MBT), whose resistance to nuclear, biological and chemical attack had been proven in exercises. Its sensors could detect chemicals, viruses, bacteria and gamma rays released into the air by an explosion. The filters ensured that contaminated air didn't enter the crew chamber and there would be enough oxygen to continue advancing in hostile conditions for several hours.

Singh's own tank was a T-90, the next model on from the T-72. The electronics were not as stable as the T-72, which was why Singh had deployed them in front. But the T-90 was one of the best-protected battle tanks in the world. It was fitted with an infrared jamming system to disrupt any guided rocket attack. The missile had a range of four kilometres and took less than twelve seconds to reach that distance. The anti-tank missiles were intended to engage tanks fitted with Explosive Reactive Armour (ERA) as well as low-flying air targets such as helicopters, at a range of up to more than five kilometres. The missile was fitted with a semi-automatic laser beam riding guidance system and a hollow-charge warhead with an 80 per cent chance of penetrating a target with 700mm armour. In most situations the T-90 could attack a tank or a helicopter while it was safely out of range itself.

The back-up for the T-90s and T-72s was the Indian-built Arjun, a tank which had failed many of its user trials and was not liked by the army. It had too many technical defects to be trusted to operate alone and the first orders for the Arjun totalled less than 125. The second series was meant to have improved features, but they only led to further defects.

The first advance would bypass small pockets of the enemy resistance. The second wave of T-90s and Arjun tanks would mop up.

Unlike the enemy, Singh knew the positions of every sand dune, bunker and Pakistani tank formation across the desert. He had ordered pictures from IRS-1C satellite when it was at pan 91–53B, taken from a height of 960 kilometres. Some were confined to the smallest tactical area and if needed he could have brought in images right down to the markings on individual tanks.

India and Pakistan had agreed that no military exercises should take place within a hundred kilometres each side of the border. But as soon as darkness had fallen, Singh received the order from Southern Command Headquarters in Poona to advance to within a kilometre of the border. He had now been waiting there for half a day.

Prime Minister's Office, South Block, New Delhi

Local time: 1330 Saturday 5 May 2007
GMT: 0800 Saturday 5 May 2007

'**We're losing on** the higher ground east of Kargil,' said the Indian Chief of Army Staff, Unni Khrishnan.

'I thought we weren't even trying to go in there,' said Dixit impatiently.

'No, but we were reinforcing and the troops helicoptered in had not been acclimatized to high altitude. Usually, they walk up there, taking a couple of weeks to get used to it.'

'How on earth did that happen?'

Khrishnan shrugged. 'It was a mix-up of men. The wrong battalion got on the wrong aircraft.'

'In a military campaign these things happen,' said Chandra Reddy, supportingly.

'The affected area is around Batalik,' explained Khrishnan, 'between the Red and Yellow sectors designated in Operation Safe Ground. The altitude at our higher posts is above five and a half thousand metres. After two hours up there the men went down with acute mountain sickness. The brain swells trying to draw in enough oxygen and you end up dizzy or going mad.'

'I thought all the troops in this operation were mountain-trained,' snapped Dixit.

'They are, Prime Minister. But if they spend three weeks at normal altitudes they have to start acclimatization all over again. The Pakistanis must have known this and threw all their remaining forces against us there, around Jubar, on Muntho Dhalo. The Shangruti post is now in Pak hands and the boys in Kukarthang are hanging on. We don't know for how long.'

'Casualties?'

'In the hundreds, sir,' said the Chief of Army Staff.

'Do the press know about this?'

'They are bound to find out. Although it seems they are concentrating on our successes.'

Dixit stabbed his finger onto his notepad. 'If Pakistan has raised its flag on our territory, then we don't have any successes. What about airstrikes?'

'We can't. They have Indian prisoners in their bunkers, sir.'

'And the good news?'

'We have the beginnings of a buffer zone.' Khrishnan turned to Chandra Reddy for support. 'But this is the most hostile terrain in which to fight and resupply.'

'Can we hold it?'

Khrishnan shook his head. 'No sir, not indefinitely.'

'You said you could do it,' interrupted the Prime Minister.

Reddy came to Khrishnan's aid. 'The mujahedin are throwing themselves at us in human waves, Prime Minister. This is unlike any other conflict we have fought with Pakistan. In war you can never be sure what is going to happen until it begins.'

'Will we have to retreat?'

'We can hold on for a while. But it depends how many casualties we can accept.'

'Foreign Minister, any bright ideas?' said Dixit, looking towards Purie. 'Short of bombing Islamabad.'

'Let's hope that will not be necessary.' Purie fiddled with his papers and took a sip from the glass of water in front of him, showing that he wanted to lance the anger in the room. 'China is the key, Prime Minister. Without China,

Pakistan is nothing. It is a Sudan or an Afghanistan. An Islamic basket-case. Indians understand the conflict with Pakistan and will accept casualties over the short term. They feel nothing about China. They can't hate a place and people they don't know. I urge you. Make peace with China. Move troops from the Chinese border to the Pakistan front and win the war.'

'Make peace with China?' Dixit repeated.

'Yes. Call off the air patrols over Bhutan. Ring Tao and tell him you are on your way to Beijing. We can draw up negotiating panels on border disputes, nuclear disarmament, Tibet and trade, anything as long as we're talking. I would also recommend that you offer to sign over the sovereignty of the Shaksgam Valley to China as a gesture of goodwill.'

'The area that Pakistan gave to China in 1965?'

'Yes. The Chinese have moved troops and artillery in there, but it's a wasteland. Give it to them and, in return, ask that they phase out their military links with Pakistan and join the world of mature nations.'

'Would they?'

'We would make a start.'

'What about Tibet?' said Khrishnan.

'Arrest a couple of Tibetans. Give Tao face within his own Communist Party and you'll have him like an obedient puppy at your heels. As soon as Khan knows you're having meetings with Tao, he's going to think twice about how far he pushes this.'

India–Pakistan border, Rajasthan, India

Local time: 1430 Saturday 5 May 2007
GMT: 0900 Saturday 5 May 2007

First came the relentless explosions of the artillery barrage laid down from the batteries of guns behind him. He had asked for more of the 155mm Bofors FH-77B, which had a range of thirty-two kilometres and were capable of firing ten rounds a minute. But the bribery scandal which had erupted years earlier, when the guns were being purchased from Sweden, left the army with a shortage. Only 410 guns were delivered out of the initial order of 1,500. Of those 120 had to be cannibalized to keep the others operational. Most were deployed on the Kashmir front. General Gurjit Singh had argued for more, but was given only twenty guns for this battle.

The mainstay of the artillery barrage was carried out by the reliable 105mm Indian field guns, with sixty batteries of eight guns each. And the most devastating attacks for the Pakistanis came from the 300mm Smerch and the 212mm Pinaka multi-rocket launchers, mounted on specially tracked vehicles better suited to the desert conditions. These weapons, which went off like machine guns, sent a blistering cordon of anti-tank bomblets and anti-tank mines against the 10th and 14th Pakistani Armoured Brigades of XXXI Corps. They had come down towards the border from their headquarters at Bahawalpur 160 kilometres north-east of Rahimyar Khan and from the south from Sukkur. The Smerch was so powerful that a salvo of rockets could be fired in less than forty seconds with accuracy better than 25 per cent and an ability to cover an area of 672,000 square metres.

Singh received regular updates of the damage being inflicted, knowing that the Pakistanis had no such remote-sensing capabilities. They would probably be getting some intelligence from the Chinese. But, almost certainly, nothing would be forthcoming from the Americans. In the two areas where cloud cover had prevented defined images – around Madagargh and Sandh, about ten kilometres inside Pakistan – Singh had deployed lower-flying aerial drones.

When the artillery barrage lulled, he watched the first vapour trails of the deep-penetrating Jaguars and the agile MiG-27s heading in to bomb airfields, armour concentrations, depots, bridges, roads and enemy command head-quarters. And that was when Pakistani F-16s scrambled from Sukkur, Bahawulpur, Multan and Sargodha.

Singh had deployed the SA-8b Ghecko single-stage solid-fuel short-range anti-aircraft defence system together with the Tunguska-M1 low-level integrated air-defence system with two twin-barrel 30mm anti-aircraft guns and an SA-19 Grisom surface-to-air missile. The missiles were arranged in two banks of four and had a semi-active laser guided capability, infrared and command radar. They had a range of more than ten kilometres and a 65 per cent probability of passing within five metres of the target, when they would be activated by a proximity fuse. The Indian crew fired off two at a time, increasing their chances of a hit and causing crippling damage to the Pakistani sorties. Within the first hour of the airstrike, the main enemy airbases were out of action and Pakistani pilots stuck to defending their own airspace against Indian attacks.

Singh's plan was to neutralize his area of attack, knock out every visible enemy position, and lay down a field of rocket and air attacks to kill any infantry and armoured division which tried to enter the area and then advance. The onslaught must have been horrendous for those on the receiving end. Unit after unit abandoned their secure radio links and Singh listened to networks swamped with calls for ambulances and commanders repeatedly asking for permission to move their positions.

Illuminator shells went off far away so pilots could see their targets more closely. High-explosive shells burst with flashes and plumes of bright yellow and orange fire spiralling up from the desert. All tanks were to avoid population centres, and infantry battalions were to dig in around the villages, laying them to siege. Warfare psychologists would then move in to convince the remaining enemy troops to surrender.

Singh's orders were to secure just one small town, Walhar, which straddled the railway line twenty-five kilometres south-west of Rahimyar Khan. This is where he expected his highest casualties and heavy close-combat fighting.

Earlier, at the headquarters briefing, he had been told to cut the line between Pakistani Punjab and the barren province of Sindh in the south, where fresh weapon supplies were being shipped in through Karachi.

'We have information that a new air-defence system is being delivered from China and will be transported by rail to Rawalpindi, Lahore and Sargodha,' Lieutenant General Jyoti Bose had told the assembled corps commanders. 'If we bomb the line from the air, they will fix it. So this is not a symbolic seizure of land. General Singh has to take control of this arterial rail route, hold it, and prevent weapons supplies delivered by sea in Karachi from reaching the north.

'The main thrust of the Indian advance will be in the north. We will attempt to secure the Shakargah bulge, or "chicken's neck", where we failed in 1971. One Corps will move against Sialkot from Jammu from the north-east and up from Gurdaspur through Narowal from the south-east. We are avoiding the more direct route through Shakargah because of the Ravi and Degh water crossings which lie in the way. A separate attack will be made through the Wagah crossing towards Lahore. Our advances will stop before Lahore and there will be no attempt on Gujranwala or Wazirabad, regardless of the extent of the Pakistani collapse. Sialkot will be taken if possible.

'So, to sum up, gentlemen, Indian forces will go into Pakistan in the south and secure the small railway town of Walhar. Our major assault will be in the north, threatening Lahore and taking control of the Shakargah bulge, which will then come under permanent Indian control. The consolidation to create a buffer on the western side of the LoC in the north will continue.'

Camp David, Maryland, USA

Local time: 1730 Saturday 5 May 2007
GMT: 2230 Saturday 5 May 2007

'**I think we** can get away with it,' said Ennio Barber, spreadsheets and polling graphs laid out on the table in front of him. He was in the room alone with John Hastings, knowing he had less than ten minutes to get his argument over.

'Go on,' said the President.

'Operation Brass Tacks, 1986/7, hardly got a mention on the networks. Yet Pakistan and India were within a hair's breadth of going to war. 1990, India was within one button-push of ordering an airstrike on Pakistan's nuclear facilities. Not one word in the press until it was well over. Kashmir, 1999, is an interesting one. A genuine fighting war between two nuclear powers, hand-to-hand combat, artillery and airstrikes, armour moved to other parts of the border. It was utterly eclipsed by the non-global-threatening conflict in Kosovo. Behind the scenes, President Clinton brokered a peace, yet the general public knew very little about it. October 1999, a military coup in Pakistan. The State Department didn't even elevate it enough to set up a task force in the crisis management centre. George W. Bush, then campaigning for the Republican nomination, made a press-conference gaffe that the coup leader had been elected, and nobody gave a damn.'

'But this time they're shelling across the border right down to Rajasthan.'

'I don't think it matters, John,' said Barber, reverting to the familiar first-name terms the President preferred for private meetings. 'Pakistan crossed the LoC in 1999 and the American people didn't give a damn.'

There was a knock on the door and Tom Bloodworth walked in: 'Sorry to disturb you, Mr President, but India has just declared war on Pakistan.'

India–Pakistan Border, Rajasthan

Local time: 0400 Sunday 6 May 2007
GMT: 2230 Saturday 5 May 2007

'**Ready to move,** General?' The voice of Corporal Vasant Kaul in Gurjit Singh's headphones told him the corps was ready to advance.

Instead of replying directly, Gurjit Singh tapped Kaul's shoulder with his boot, gave the thumbs-up sign, and the tank lurched forward. It was a breathtaking sight, line after line of armour turning the sand of the Thar Desert into a huge dustcloud covering 100 kilometres from end to end. Thirty minutes earlier, ground-attack aircraft had blasted a path through the minefields, so that each of Gurjit Singh's five sector commanders would have a clear path through.

Silk sector took the road through Madargh towards Mirbur Marthelo. Cotton was next through Sandhi towards Ubauro. Gurjit Singh himself was Leather sector, with the road to Sadiqabad. But he would turn south well before that to take Walhar. Wool and Calfskin sectors broke through the border together and separated where the road split just before Islamgarth, bypassing the town. Wool headed towards ruins of Baghla south of Rahimyar Khan. Calfskin advanced more directly north towards Khanpur. As each armoured column finished crossing the border, infantrymen stuck a signboard in the sand saying, 'Welcome to Indian-administered Pakistan.'

But the euphoria was short-lived. The tank commanders were faced with a depressing tableau of the destruction caused by the artillery and air bombardments. For the first thirty kilometres (about the range of the barrage) they met no resistance at all. The desert around them was a smouldering graveyard of charred bodies, destroyed vehicles and arid ground. After the banter of pre-battle nerves, the advance into Pakistan was a disheartening anti-climax. They drove along a moonscape of craters gouged out of the earth by artillery shells, their radios mostly quiet, except for a steady bleep, every fifteen seconds, to tell them that the lines were still secure.

Thirty-five kilometres in, Leather sector sighted the first enemy position. 'Contact dug-in infantry,' said a tank commander. 'Contact. My tanks have engaged.'

The other sectors continued the advance.

'No return fire,' said the commander. 'White flags. Platoon-size position.'

Ten minutes later Silk sector reported coming under attack: 'One tank hit. Hand-held anti-tank weapon ... bunker destroyed.'

'Casualties?' asked Gurjit Singh.

'Two dead. The tank commander seriously injured.'

'Damn!' he snarled, knowing that men would be killed, but angered by the first news of casualties.

Similar skirmishes broke out throughout the afternoon. Prisoners were taken. Bunkers were destroyed. The attacks appeared to be random, as if the whole of the Pakistani command and control system had broken down and individual soldiers had been left to fight wherever they saw fit. Indian aircraft flew overhead with control of the skies. Helicopter crews had the most dangerous assignments, flying into far forward positions to test the enemy fire and reporting back.

'Continue to avoid civilian population centres,' ordered Gurjit Singh. 'But armour remains a threat and must be engaged when seen.'

In the first six hours of the assault, the Pakistani vanguard troops shot down three helicopters and damaged five others with machine-gun fire. They mainly operated in the fast-moving, Chinese-made armoured personnel carriers, which were far more mobile than the Indian armoured formations. They destroyed ten tanks and immobilized another eight others.

Then, in the early afternoon, Cotton sector came under a short but damaging artillery attack. Two damaged T-90s blocked the cleared minefield path and stopped the advance in its tracks. The tank commanders behind had no choice but to sit it out for thirty-five minutes while enemy spotters in hidden bunkers directed fire onto their positions. They heard radio reports of tank crews calling in hits or getting blown to pieces around them. Finally, Indian aircraft silenced the guns, then blew a new path through the minefield on either side of the Madargh road.

The worst confrontation took place with Wool sector around the ruined ancient settlement of Bhagla, where satellite pictures had shown only a token Pakistani presence. Thirty minutes before approaching the area, helicopters buzzed it and failed to draw enemy fire. The crew reported signs of fresh wheeltracks, sandbag positions having been removed, and some civilian movement inside the old settlement walls.

'Bhagla unlikely to present a challenge,' reported the helicopter pilot.

The Wool commander, Colonel Neelan Chidambaram, gave the order to bypass Bhagla and leave behind a token occupying presence until the second wave arrived. But as they came within 275 metres of the main settlement, a fusillade of enemy fire with anti-tank weapons, recoilless rifles and heavy machine guns opened up on them.

'Sustained and heavy anti-tank fire,' reported the commander. 'Request permission to take Bhagla before proceeding.'

General Headquarters, Rawalpindi, Pakistan

Local time: 1400 Sunday 6 May 2007
GMT: 0900 Sunday 6 May 2007

In the underground war room, Hamid Khan leant over the button of the intercom on his desk. 'Hold Baghla at all costs,' he said.

He had decided to make a stand at Bhagla, sensing that General Gurjit Singh would go for Walhar to sever the rail link. It was twenty-five kilometres from the main depot at Rahimyar Khan. Even if India got as far as Baghla, it could reinforce the road and bring in its heavy towed artillery and shell the city.

'Then we need air support, General,' came the voice through the intercom.

'Baghla must not fall,' Khan repeated.

Baghla, Thar Desert, Pakistan

Local time: 1400 Sunday 6 May 2007
GMT: 0900 Sunday 6 May 2007

'**Can you not** bypass Baghla?' said Gurjit Singh, questioning Colonel Chidambaram's decision.

'Negative, sir. The level of fire indicates a substantial enemy force. Our final position is only ten kilometres north of here. Baghla must pose no threat to our position.'

'How long to secure it?'

'Three hours.'

'You have two.'

Chidambaram ordered his vehicles to move towards the southerly and easterly sides of the settlement, giving each line of tanks a clear firing line. Twenty tanks fired simultaneously on Baghla from the south in a massively destructive volley. Thirty seconds later twenty tanks from the east fired a similar volley. Straight after that, enemy positions were strafed with cannon fire. Then Chidambaram ordered his men to hold their fire.

But in the sudden quiet which came after the firing, twenty Pakistani warplanes screamed in at low level, unleashing cannon and missile fire on the tank positions, turning and tearing back again before the Indian air force could make a response. The impact of the attack was devastating. Before Chidambaram could get back on the radio to check on the casualties, the anti-tank guns opened up again from inside Baghla.

'Call in your hits,' ordered Chidambaram.

Some reports came in of damage. Other call signs were silent because the tank was destroyed and the crew dead.

'Request air support on Baghla,' said Chidambaram on the main link to Singh.

'What the hell is going on there, Wool sector?'

'Enemy position with air cover.'

'Fifteen T-90 and Arjun tanks destroyed. Casualties not known. Substantive minefield and anti-tank opposition.'

The Indian air assault on Baghla was later described as the decisive attack which changed the objectives of the war. It was relentless, unforgiving, allowing no room for let-up or surrender. For thirty minutes Indian warplanes pummelled what was no more than a desert ruin. The enemy who had remained to hold Baghla were buried in scorching rubble. No one escaped and Chidambaram witnessed it, wondering with horror what he would find when his units could finally move in.

General Headquarters, Rawalpindi, Pakistan

Local time: 1445 Sunday 6 May 2007
GMT: 0945 Sunday 6 May 2007

'**Baghla has fallen,** sir,' said Masood, relaying the message from the Military Operations Directorate. 'Indian forces are advancing towards Rahimyar Khan. Flanking forces also advancing north.'

'And the situation in the northern sector?'

'We are holding the LoC well. In Siachen we have advanced. But Lahore is threatened. Indian forces are within ten kilometres of the city and are shelling the cantonment area. We have lost General Iqbal Faisal, I'm afraid, sir. The town of Wagah is completely under Indian control. Sialkot is expected to fall within the next forty-eight hours and India will then have control of the Shakargah bulge. We are managing lightning airstrikes, such as the one we carried out around Baghla, but it is difficult to hide the aircraft. Our forward bases at Sukkur, Bahawalpur, Nawabshah, Mirpur Khas—'

Hamid Khan stood up and held up his hand for Masood to stop. 'All right, Captain. Are Dr Malik Khalid and Air Marshal Kalapur outside?'

Without answering, Masood opened the office door and waved in the missile scientist and the new head of the Pakistani air force from the war room outside. Dr Khalid entered with a bundle of diagrams and maps and sat down opposite Khan's desk. Yasin Kalapur carried nothing and stood by the map near the door.

'Is Sargodha still secure?' Khan asked Kalapur.

'The runway and airbase buildings are damaged. But the underground facilities are intact.'

Khalid leant forward in his chair. There was only one reason for him to be summoned. He was not a military man and was unable to discipline his curiosity. 'Are you thinking of the northern or southern sector, General?'

'The southern,' replied Khan. 'We strike once and once only.'

'Then I suggest a mix of the Mirages and the Shaheen, fired from Sargodha. The target range will be between 450 and 500 kilometres. Each missile will carry a 500 kilogram warhead yielding a 20 kiloton explosion.'

Khan shook his head. 'The missiles will be kept in reserve. Both the Shaheen and the Ghauri must be primed and ready for the second strike. But wait until darkness so that, God willing, they will escape satellite detection.' He turned to Kalapur: 'Yasin, are the Mirage 111s and the FC-1s still intact in Samungli and Pasni?'

'Yes, sir. The Indians have confined their strikes to the border areas so far.'

'Good. The F-16s?'

'We have six at Samungli and four at Pasni.'

'The Mirage 111s and F-16s will carry out the toss-bombing attack using the 500 kilogram warheads . . .'

Khalid nodded enthusiastically. 'That will yield a 20 kiloton explosion per weapon.'

'The FC-1 will give air support, particularly if the enemy deploy the SU-30.'

Kalapur nodded with approval. The FC-1 (Super 7) was Pakistan's latest multi-role fighter. Its development had been delayed to equip it with weaponry and avionics which could take on the threat from India's SU-30. The technology was derived from the American F-16 and the Russian MiG-29, particularly the Klomov RD-33 turbofan design. The aircraft was jointly made by the Pakistan Aeronautical Complex (PAC) and China's Chengdhu Aircraft Industrial Corporation, with much of the engine input coming from Russia's Mikoyan OKB Design Bureau. Kalapur had flown one himself and declared it among the finest aircraft he had ever piloted. China would be keen to see the fighter tested in a real combat situation.

'At night?'

'Yes. Once the missiles have been prepared.'

'Captain Masood, have we had confirmation from Beijing that we have complete access to their satellite imagery for the next twenty-four hours?'

'The Ambassador has confirmed it, sir.'

'What sort of strike would you want?' asked Khalid.

'Their doctrine is to destroy Pakistan if we strike first with nuclear weapons. But I don't think Dixit would have the nerve to do that in response to a battlefield strike. Their first targets would be our nuclear facilities. We can assume that Sargodha and Multan would be destroyed and we must ensure that all personnel are in secure bunkers. We will have no more than eleven minutes to respond, probably less by the time we detect the launch.'

Khan stood up and moved towards the map where Kalapur was standing. 'For defence purposes we should strike Chandipur here at 21° 28' N, 87° 00' E, at Hyderabad, 17° 14' N, 78° 21' E and Jullundur, 31° 19' N, 75° 34' E. These are all missile bases. We know that the Agni is in Hyderabad. If you think we have enough warheads, Dr Khalid, I would like to take out the nuclear research facility at Trombay at 19° 02' N, 72° 56' E. But that is more symbolic than strategic.'

'We shall see,' said Khalid pensively. 'And a third strike?'

'It won't come to that,' said Khan. 'But we will have to

retain a credible deterrent for at least one large population centre.'

'Hamid,' said the Air Marshal, 'during the Baghla operation, we would need to carry out air attacks on nuclear-capable Indian airbases. It would mean simultaneous sorties against the Jaguar and SU-30 squadrons at Ambala, the Jaguars at Gorakpur, the Mirages at Gwalior and the remaining SU-30s at Lohegoan. Those are the bases from which we would expect an airborne nuclear strike to take place. If we keep those occupied it lessens the risk of a false response.'

'You're saying, then, that we only react after the detection of a missile launch?'

'Exactly. Indian aircraft will be in action anyway. We want to eliminate the confusion between conventional and nuclear.'

'When would you be ready?'

'Any time.'

'Dr Khalid?'

'If we want to prepare under cover of darkness.'

'Captain Masood, ensure that I have Hari Dixit on the hotline the second the first toss-bomb strike takes place.'

Baghla, Thar Desert, Pakistan

Local time: 0500 Monday 7 May 2007
GMT: 0000 Monday 7 May 2007

Colonel Chidambaram raised himself through the turret of his T-90 and inhaled the night desert air deeply. The empty sky threw out enough light for him to see the ruins of Baghla. He looked more closely through the infrared night-vision binoculars and saw no movement, no sign of human or animal life.

'Ninety minutes from now, at first light, we move into Baghla. Then we will proceed towards Rahimyar Khan,' he told Gurjit Singh on the radio.

'How long will you take to secure Baghla?' he asked.

'It will be done immediately. There is nothing left. What news from the other brigades?'

'They are moving into Walhar at first light and expect one hell of a fight. Silk sector have reached the Uanur River and will hold there. There was only token resistance at Madaghar. Cotton had to take Sandhi after armoured resistance. That is now secure and Cotton is ten kilometres from the rail track. Calfskin took Bahuwalatoba with light resistance, but six hundred prisoners. They are outside Bagh-o-Bahar. You drew rotten luck, Colonel.'

'Thank you, sir. And in the north?'

'I understand we are doing well and that Sialkot will fall within the day. Our luck hasn't been so good in the Batalik sector of the LoC. But a comprehensive ceasefire should solve that.'

Colonel Chidambaram felt better for the briefing, knowing that he wasn't alone in the Thar Desert and that other officers had had problems as well. Many of the tank crews were outside their vehicles, washing, shaving, praying, preparing for the battle to come. Chidambaram was about to jump down and walk around, talking to them, when he heard Singh back on the radio again, an edge in his voice: 'Toss-bomb attack. Toss-bomb attack. All men inside vehicles. NBC suits where available.'

The Pakistani Mirage 111s and F-16s streaked towards the Indian armoured positions, flying at 3,000 feet. Each pilot was trained for nuclear weapons delivery and the toss-bomb loop which would ensure his safety from the explosion. Each had a target specified from the Chinese satellite imagery. Two thousand feet higher the FC-1s were patrolling to head off any attack by Indian fighters.

But not all the aircraft carried a nuclear bomb. Two were nuclear-armed, one Mirage 111 – which Indian intelligence was not certain had been made nuclear-capable – and one F-16. Each aircraft carried one one-kiloton neutron bomb, an explosive device no bigger than a grapefruit. Each bomb had a destructive range of 700 metres, throwing out an 8,000-rad dose of radiation, more than ten times the 600-rad dose needed to kill in a normal environment, but enough to force the high-energy neutrons through the armour protection of the Indian tanks. A few of the tanks might have had depleted uranium shields built into the armour, which could offset the radiation. But that was untested and too expensive to be used throughout the Indian army.

The whole Pakistani squadron of sixteen aircraft came in at high altitude. As they dived they came under withering Indian anti-aircraft fire, which was attacked by the defending FC-1s. An F-16 was hit on its descent and exploded in the air. A Mirage 111 went too low and crashed into the ground. The other fourteen aircraft released bombs as they dived, and continued heading down: because of the airspeed the bombs shot upwards against the force of gravity. Once clear, the pilots pulled the nose up and went into a steep climb, avoiding the impact of any immediate nuclear explosion.

The aircraft were at the height of their climb when the bombs went off. Six were conventional; six were 500 kilogram fuel-air explosive warheads; two were tactical nuclear weapons. They exploded within fifteen seconds of each other, sending out devastating bursts of radiation. Contrary to the common perception of the neutron bomb, the attack did not just kill soldiers and leave buildings and vehicles intact. Anything within the 700-metre range was damaged beyond repair. Those vehicles outside the range were left intact, as were several of the tank crews who had managed to get inside NBC suits and seal up their vehicles.

But after that, many died, from dehydration and heat, abandoned by both sides as contaminated and beyond saving. The alloy steel used in the armour became radioactive itself. When rescue teams finally went in, both General Gurjit Singh and Colonel Chidambaram were found dead in their vehicles.

The area of the southern-Indian armoured advance was declared unsafe for at least forty-eight hours – and by then the world was on a nuclear precipice.

Briefing

Nuclear weapons

At the turn of the millennium, five countries were acknowledged nuclear weapons states. Two had demonstrated a nuclear-weapon capability and it is thought that only one, Israel, with a capacity for about 200 warheads, remained undeclared. North Korea may have produced a small number of nuclear weapons. At the peak of production in the eighties, there were about 70,000 nuclear weapons in the world – with an explosive power equivalent to 500,000 bombs of the size dropped on Hiroshima and Nagasaki. India was thought to hold more than eighty nuclear weapons to Pakistan's twenty-five. China had 400; Russia 21,000; the United States 11,500; France 450; and the United Kingdom 260. Just one 15-kiloton fission bomb explosion over an urban area with a population density of about 25,000 per square kilometre would kill about 200,000 people.

Zhongnanhai, Beijing, China

Local time: 0815 Monday 7 May 2007
GMT: 0015 Monday 7 May 2007

General Leung Liyin rang Tao Jian from the military headquarters under the Western Hills on a direct line straight through to the President's office in Zhongnanhai. 'Pakistan has halted the Indian advance in the south with a tactical nuclear burst,' said Leung. He paused. Tao was silent. Then Leung continued: 'We are ready on the western front.'

'What about the Indian northern positions?'

'Fighting is continuing.'

'All right, General,' said Tao. 'Begin Operation *Dragon Fire*.'

Briefing

Japan

The historical use – or misuse – of Japanese militarism has long been a soul-searching issue for the Japanese. In 1894, Japan defeated China in a brief war and took Taiwan. Korea was annexed in 1910 and Manchuria invaded in 1931. Japanese forces swept through China in 1936 and finally attacked US forces at Pearl Harbor in 1941 – ending in the nuclear-bomb attacks on Hiroshima and Nagasaki in 1945. Japan then drew up a pacifist constitution which 'for ever renounces war as a sovereign right'. During the Cold War, Japan flourished, living under a US security umbrella which protected it against threats from the Soviet Union. In the late nineties, however, the United States urged it to take a greater role in regional defence. Japan quietly redrew its military profile, believing that ultimately its biggest challenge would come from China, whose aim was to overtake Japan as the pre-eminent power in the region.

The Prime Minister's Residence, Tokyo

In normal circumstances, Prime Minister Shigeto Wada would have left it up to his Foreign Minister to summon the Indian Ambassador. But these were not normal times. The nuclear balance of Asia was untested and dangerous. And Wada had to make swift and difficult decisions which would strike right at the soul of modern Japan.

Mandip Singh arrived, looking like a man who had not slept for two days, and when Wada offered him tea he waved his hand and asked for black coffee.

'Will you retaliate?' asked Wada.

'We will,' said Mandip Singh. 'But the question is, will it be nuclear – and I won't know that until you do, Prime Minister.'

'Don't do it,' said Wada with uncharacteristic bluntness. 'For many years we have suggested that we strengthen ties, but your governments haven't listened. Now that this has happened, we have no choice but to insist you do not retaliate. If you do, we will withdraw all aid, Japanese investment will naturally follow and your economy will collapse within months.'

'Unfortunately, millions of Indians don't see it like that. Territory and honour are more important than life and a full rice bowl. Besides, it is out of my control.' The Ambassador was exhausted and didn't mind showing it. 'But I will say one thing. China has decided to use this conflict to become the undisputed regional power. If it succeeds, India's influence will have to diminish, and that

will not be in Japan's strategic interest. We believe it is an apt time to examine the strategic ramifications.'

Wada nodded: 'We don't have the academic luxury of diplomatic evaluations. So I will tell you this in confidence, Ambassador, and use it how you wish. Our intelligence tells us that China is determined to win. They have just activated a military plan called Operation *Dragon Fire*.'

Briefing

Russia

Russia retains an impressive order of battle on paper, but its military power is far less than that once wielded by the Soviet Union. Cohesion, morale and operational effectiveness are all reduced. Throughout the Cold War the Soviet Union retained a strong relationship with India. In the 1990s Russia also began what was called a Strategic Relationship for the Twenty-first Century with China. Russia now supplies substantial amounts of weaponry to both countries. It continues to struggle with its own political and economic reforms. If events go badly in Russia, autocracy could be strengthened, reviving a new era of tension and confrontation with the West and other powers. In the first months of the twenty-first century, Russia made a series of announcements centred on increased military spending and modernizing its nuclear arsenal.

The Kremlin, Moscow, Russia

Local time: 0330 Monday 7 May 2007
GMT: 0030 Monday 7 May 2007

Russian President Vladimir Gorbunov did not need to be woken up. He was an insomniac who often made crucial decisions for his country in the early hours of the morning. In the past few months he had been working on strengthening the alliance between Russia, China and India. His aim was to create a military and political force which would curb the power of the United States and NATO.

A former commander of the Pacific Fleet, Gorbunov was acutely attuned to the undercurrents of the Asia–Pacific. Far more than his counterparts from Moscow and St Petersburg, Gorbunov looked east for his models of development. He admired China, in particular, for the determined way it was pulling itself into the modern age, viewing it more as a role model than a threat.

India was a long-standing ally, as at ease with its democratic institutions as China was with its authoritarianism. Only two months earlier, Gorbunov had been in Delhi to extend the military technology pact with India, which was giving it the weaponry needed to counter the superior forces of China. In 1999, India and Russia signed a Military Technology Co-operation Treaty lasting until 2010.

Gorbunov believed if power between India and China could be balanced, he could lead a population bloc of 2.5 billion people, with a formidable array of nuclear and conventional weapons to limit the United States' influence in international affairs. Many thought of this strategic triangle as a seductive aspiration, but too far-fetched. Gorbunov believed that a military alliance between China, India and Russia was far less ambitious than the chaotic union pushed through within Europe. If he did not try, the second-power countries of the world would forever remain weak against the Western democracies.

It was Gorbunov's initiative, long before he was President, to give away the 30,000 tonne aircraft carrier *Gorshkov* to India in exchange for the purchase of the equipment and aircraft for it, including the SU-27M. Gorbunov had personally authorized the transfer of technology for India's Rajendra phased-array radar system and Akash long-range surface-to-air missile system, making up a limited integrated theatre-defence system against the threat of Pakistani M-11 ballistic missiles.

Although the Rajendra was mostly Indian-built, the Akash was made up of the formidable Russian mobile S-300V Anti-Tactical Ballistic Missile system, code-named the SA12 Giant by NATO and considered superior to the American Patriot system. It was effective against planes, including those equipped with Stealth technology, and various types of missiles, including tactical and cruise.

Each system could protect an area of more than 320 square kilometres, including major cities, from missile attacks.

Before becoming President, Gorbunov had hosted Indian delegations at the Kapustin Yar test grounds, 1,300 kilometres south-east of Moscow. He persuaded them to abandon their national pride and take technology for the Rajendra as well. It could detect ballistic missiles more than 1,200 kilometres away, track sixty-four missiles and aircraft simultaneously and give warnings of at least five minutes to activate the anti-ballistic missile defences. The Rajendra was just what India was looking for.

Gorbunov also strengthened the role of the Indo-Russian Joint Working Group (JWG), which was looking at rearming India's aircraft carriers, upgrading both the T-72 and advanced missile-firing T-90 tanks, providing India with Msta-B guns and KA-30 attack helicopters and purchasing the new MiG-AT advanced jet-trainer aircraft.

But the Russian President's main achievement had begun more than ten years earlier when he was co-chair of the JWG and later a deputy Defence Minister.

'No navy can be considered a force to reckon with unless it has nuclear submarines to control oceans,' he repeatedly told the Indians, while at the same time pushing for Russia to release more technology for India's beleaguered attempts to build a nuclear-powered and nuclear-armed submarine.

He arranged for the Russian submarine-design bureau, Rubin, to cooperate with Indian scientists on the hull and the reactor. The result was a 6,000 tonne displacement hull of titanium steel to give extra diving depth.

Gorbunov's final initiative was the technology for the submarine-launched Sagarika cruise missile, capable of carrying a nuclear warhead and derived from the Prithvi, with a range of 320 kilometres. The Sagarika had put India's navy in a different league. The nuclear-powered submarine had unlimited endurance and mobility. There was no place for a surface ship to hide from torpedoes, and the Sagarika could be fired from outside territorial waters with the capacity to destroy a city.

The obvious targets from the South China Sea would be the Chinese cities of Guangzhou, the southern commercial capital, the southern naval headquarters at Zhanjiang and the coastal bases at Shantou, Xiamen or Fuzhou.

As far as Gorbunov knew, the submarine was still called simply the Advanced Technology Vessel (ATV) and it had not yet gone out for public trials for fear that other navies would pick up and copy its signature for future recognition.

Gorbunov was still authorizing limited help to the Surya intercontinental ballistic missile programme, aimed at creating a vehicle with a range of 12,800 kilometres, capable of reaching the United States. The programme was veiled in secrecy. Not even Gorbunov knew how far advanced it was. But if it ever worked, a missile launched from Delhi would be able to target an area bounded by Raleigh in North Carolina, Omaha in Nebraska and Eugene in Oregon. If it was launched 500 kilometres north of New Delhi, the range could go much further south.

If India declared the Surya, it would then equalize China's DF-32 solid-fuel 12,800 kilometre range missile, whose technical guidance system had been supplied by Russia.

India and China would have only a handful of missiles compared to Russia, which would remain the undisputed leader of the bloc. When all three powers lined up against the United States, Washington would think again about humiliating the developing world and committing another Balkan-style campaign.

But now, suddenly, unity within Gorbunov's tripartite bloc was threatened. Pakistan, China's ally, had carried out the first nuclear attack since Hiroshima. India would respond within a matter of hours. If China became involved, it could take generations for the strategic alliance to recover.

The Russian President postponed meetings with his Defence and Foreign Policy teams, then personally telephoned the Chinese Ambassador, Kang Suyin, who was at the residence but awake. Gorbunov asked her to come straight round. They met alone in Gorbunov's sprawling office, just off the cabinet room. Kang was a graduate from Moscow University and they spoke in Russian.

'I urge you not to get involved,' began Gorbunov. 'If you do, there will only be one winner, the United States.'

Kang nodded cautiously: 'Possibly you are right. But it is more complex.'

'We don't have time for complications,' urged Gorbunov. 'You shared with us the outrage of the Kosovo operation in 1999. You watched as American missiles reduced your Embassy in Belgrade to rubble. We watched as NATO seized territory from one of our closest strategic allies in Europe. All of us, including India, were appalled and have tailored our defence needs to meet future threats from the United States. Against such a global policy, it is not worth defending Pakistan.'

'It isn't Pakistan,' said the Ambassador. 'It is mostly Tibet, and partly Central Asia.'

'Tibet is a wart. She is too small to cause any real damage. We are all concerned about Central Asia . . .'

'Can you persuade India to stop interfering?'

'I don't have time. We need decisions within the hour. But what I can promise you is another six *Typhoon*-class nuclear-powered submarines, ready armed with nuclear missiles, if you stand back.'

'And if we don't?'

'I will have no option but to consider ending military cooperation.'

'That is a small carrot and a big threat.'

'Suyin,' said Gorbunov, 'I have known you for many, many years as we have witnessed the emergence of our two countries. I have envied China in its economic determination. You covet our military arsenal. As I have encouraged Russians to take a lead from you in economic policy, please impress upon your President to take a lead from us on military policy. We have the experience of the Cold War and we know the bitter taste of defeat. If you take the carrot, China will be a formidable naval power in the region. If you fight India over Tibet right now, you will be hauled back fifty years.'

'You're wrong, Vlad,' said Kang, leaning forward in her chair. 'At the end of the Cold War, you stood isolated. The industrialized democracies were against you, as was China. We have gone about our development with greater patience. We experimented with Dragon Strike and found that the United States did not have sufficient backbone for an all-out war. There is a view in Beijing, which I agree with, that this might now be the time to test the challenges on our western borders.'

'You'll play into the American's hands and get the Russian people worried as well.'

Kang laughed: 'You have nothing to worry about!'

'All right,' said Gorbunov. 'But you'll reinforce the view that China, like we were, is ideologically bent on regional, if not world, domination. Once that is believed, co-existence with the United States will be impossible. The pressures to contain the last major one-party state will be immense until you transform yourself into a democratic society. No American president can be seen to be weak with you.'

'But they have been and always will be,' said Kang. 'Your Marxist ideology was very different to ours. You avowed its determination to maintain Communist parties in power, by force if necessary. You intervened in Hungary and Czecho-slovakia, threatened to do so in Poland and even in China. We have no such ambitions, no international network of Communist parties to undermine Western positions. They may think we run a repressive one-party state, but we threaten no Western democracy and we are hauling tens of millions of people out of poverty.'

'So you're going to . . .' Gorbunov paused.

'It's called Operation *Dragon Fire*. Yes, Vlad, we're going to do it. What will you do?'

'Confine it to Tibet and the border, and it will be business as usual.'

As soon as he had walked Kang to the steps of the building and shown her into her car, Gorbunov telephoned the American Ambassador, Milton Ashdown. Ashdown arrived at the President's private office within fifteen minutes.

'Please tell President Hastings that Russia would like India and Pakistan to solve this problem without outside interference.'

Ashdown had made significant contributions to Hastings's election campaign and the two men were personal friends. But he was primarily a businessman who was finding the intricacies of diplomacy difficult. Ashdown also had little time for academic theorists who argued for any alternative system of government which opposed democracy and the free market.

'I will pass on your message. No doubt the President will want to speak with you directly. But, with all respect, if the free world is threatened by nuclear war, the United States will do everything within its power to stop it – not minding whose sovereign territory we violate.'

'That's what I feared,' said Gorbunov.

Newsroom, BBC Television Centre, London

The midnight radio bulletin had just finished. On the second floor, BBC News 24 interrupted its sports news to flash the Pakistani nuclear attack. In another part of the BBC's giant newsroom, World Service Television News had broken into its programming fifteen seconds earlier. Only a handful of staff was on duty in the main news-gathering area, a horseshoe of desks, computers and banks of television screens. The World Duty Editor had made one telephone call to the home of the World Assignments Editor, who was on stand-by.

He then called the Asia hub bureau in Singapore, from where correspondents, producers, camera crew and technicians were despatched to the BBC bureaux in Islamabad and Delhi. They left from Hong Kong, Singapore and Beijing. Reinforcements joined them from Jerusalem, Cairo and London.

Satellite transmission dishes, satellite telephones, portable edit packs, flak jackets and nuclear, biological and chemical (NBC) warfare protection suits were loaded on commercial flights with the reporting teams. Within a few hours, the BBC would have the most formidable news reporting system in place to cover what could become the world's first nuclear war.

Briefing

Burma/Myanmar

Burma, or Myanmar, is a cultural and geographical buffer between East and South Asia. From 1885 until the 1930s, Burma was governed as part of British India. It was occupied by Japan from 1942 to 1945, and won independence in 1948. After just fourteen years of democracy, the army seized power and Burma went into a state of self-imposed isolation. Troops brutally repressed democracy demonstrations in 1988. The regime ignored a landslide election victory for the opposition party in 1990 and jailed its leader, Aung San Suu Kyi. Increasingly shunned by the international community, Burma was courted by China. Chinese engineers built roads and military bases. The army was equipped with Chinese weapons. By the turn of the century, the Hanggyi Island naval base and the Cocos Islands were being built to take Chinese naval ships, threatening India's predominance in the Indian Ocean region.

India–Burma border, Tirap Frontier District, India

Local time: 0600 Monday 7 May 2007
GMT: 0030 Monday 7 May 2007

The attack from the south came as a complete surprise, not least because the enemy troops broke into Indian territory, not from China, but from Burma.

Air support came from Dongkar and Orang in Tibet and Sinkaling, Myityina and Putao in Burma, laying down a devastating gauntlet of fire on the unprotected Indian positions. The main infantry advance came up from Namya Ra, twenty-five kilometres south of the border.

For almost twenty years, since minor skirmishes in 1987, Chinese and Indian troops had successfully and peacefully protected their borders. At the most tense times, almost half a million troops had faced each other. India deployed eleven divisions and the Chinese PLA deployed fifteen. The mountainous terrain, high-altitude climate and logistical supply difficulties deterred either side from starting a protracted conflict there. India had reluctantly allowed China to continue its occupation of the Aksai Chin area, occupied since 1959, and nestling on the border with Kashmir. China claimed, but had left alone, Arunachal Pradesh, to the east of Bhutan which borders Tibet.

In 1996, both governments agreed to reduce the size of their armies on the border, allowing India to deploy more men against Pakistan in Kashmir. But as tensions ebbed and flowed, troop levels climbed back up again. In the past week, Indian satellites had picked up images of thousands of Chinese troops pouring in, threatening the northern border positions. India reinforced its own positions with the Kameng, Subansiri, Siang and Lohit frontier positions.

Neither side seemed to want conflict. This front was cold, inhospitable and bereft of glory. Even though it was May, conditions in the mountains were appalling and no modern army would want to fight there.

The Chinese build-up, carried out in broad daylight, was a massive decoy to the operation planned to the south. The deployment in Burma had been carried out at night to avoid satellite surveillance. India's concentration was primarily on Kashmir. An eye was being kept on the China front. The Burmese border was virtually being ignored.

Troops from the Indian 2nd Mountain Division were unprepared. They tactically withdrew and consolidated enough to stop the Chinese advance five kilometres from Ledo. Once there, both sides secured their positions, but the Chinese army was dug in on Indian territory.

Presidential helicopter Marine One, USA

Local time: 1935 Sunday 6 May 2007
GMT: 0035 Monday 7 May 2007

Tom Bloodworth was interrupted in the middle of a conversation, notifying his office that he was en route from Camp David to Washington. He immediately passed the news on to John Hastings through the intercom on the Sikorsky VH-3D. 'Pakistan has carried out a tactical nuclear strike.'

'Battlefield or urban?' asked Hastings.

'Battlefield. It appears very precise and calculated.'

'India?'

'No word yet. We're trying to get through to Dixit. But Chinese troops have also invaded India through Burma . . .'

Conversation on board was difficult at the best of times. Hastings remained quiet for five minutes, juggling his policy of domestic focus to the nuclear war which had just broken out in Asia. Then he said: 'Get me the details of our task forces in the Indian Ocean and South China Sea. We'll have a full crisis meeting of the Principals' Committee on landing at the White House.'

Prime Minister's Office, Downing Street, London

Local time: 0115 Monday 7 May 2007

The British Prime Minister, Anthony Pincher, was woken by his Private Secretary, slipped on a tracksuit and gym shoes and came down from his flat above 11 Downing Street. The Foreign Secretary, Christopher Baker, had just arrived. John Stopping and Sir Malcolm Parton had been in Downing Street for fifteen minutes. The emergency alert had come through from the Permanent Operations Headquarters in Northwood, north London, which acted as a nerve centre for Britain's military activities around the world.

Next door to the Prime Minister's office the powerful Press Secretary, Eileen Glenny, was at her computer, writing options for a statement to go out on the rolling news channels as soon as decisions had been made. She was determined to make sure her Prime Minister's voice was heard before that of the American President, the Leader of the Opposition or any other European leader.

Across the road, in the basement of the Foreign and Commonwealth Office, officials from the relevant departments were setting up a twenty-four-hour operational working area, known as the Emergency Room. The lead department was Asia–Pacific, with Martin Andrews as head of the South Asian Department taking immediate control. He drafted in experts on nuclear proliferation, counter terrorism, consular affairs, for British nationals at risk, and liaison colleagues from the Secret Service (MI5) and the Secret Intelligence Service (MI6) and other involved regional departments, plus a representative from News Department.

The BBC, CNN and three Web sites were displayed on screens around the room and officials were already contacting embassies, collating the scant information and trying to ensure that the European Community would speak with one voice. But already the French were being obstructive: they had sold Mirage aircraft to both India and Pakistan. Germany, which had been involved in India's nuclear-powered submarine technology, was noncommittal. The smaller countries such as Denmark and the Netherlands were worried that Britain would charge in with its militaristic hat, without consultation, in the wake of whatever the Americans decided to do.

Pincher opened up the Downing Street cabinet room and sat down. The Defence Secretary, David Guinness, was the last to arrive, having come straight from a briefing at the Ministry of Defence on the other side of Whitehall.

'We have not yet detected any response by India,' said Guinness.

'Has anyone talked to Dixit?' said Pincher.

'He's not answering his phone,' said the Foreign Secretary.

'The Indian offensive is continuing across the LoC in Kashmir,' said Guinness. 'Since Pakistan went nuclear, India has also pushed ahead into Sialkot, near Jammu in the north. It might have even fallen, and Indian armour has continued to shell the cantonment area of Lahore. Supply lines are being set up between the frontline and the Wagah border crossing.'

'Meaning?' said the Prime Minister.

'Dixit must be gambling that Hamid Khan won't carry out a second strike. He's sacrificed his southern advance to make Pakistan a pariah state.'

Eileen Glenny came into the room without knocking, took a seat next to the Prime Minister, looked at her watch and glanced at the four television screens banked into a bookcase in the wall with BBC News 24, BBC World, Sky News and CNN showing simultaneously.

'I have three statements, Prime Minister,' she said. 'One, we condemn Pakistan's first use, et cetera. Two, we condemn violence on both sides, abhor Pakistan's first use and call on restraint from India. Three, we point up that India is a democracy and Pakistan is a military dictatorship.'

Pincher tapped the bottom of his pen on the table and turned to the Defence Secretary: 'I read somewhere that we had been in Bangladesh helping with relief efforts. What have we got there?'

'A small task force, Prime Minister,' said Guinness. 'The *Ocean* is still off Cox's Bazaar, after being diverted from exercises under the Five Power Defence Agreement with Singapore, Malaysia, Australia and New Zealand.'

'Remind me about the Five Power Defence Agreement. Is it significant for this scenario?'

'It was drawn up in the 1960s when we were in conflict with Indonesia. We have treaty obligations to Singapore and Malaysia, should they ask for our support. If either government feels threatened, they can call us in.'

'Are the Australian and New Zealand navies with the *Ocean*?'

'After the cyclone, the exercises switched to become a real-life military humanitarian operation. HMS *Ocean* is the command vessel. She has five hundred marines, most of whom are now ashore in the cyclone area, six Sea King helicopters and six Sea Harrier ground-attack aircraft. The Special Boat Squadron is also on board with one of its new VSVs.'

'What do they do?' said Pincher.

'VSV means Very Slender Vessel. They go at sixty knots in all weather and have a range of seven hundred miles, although I'm not sure that it would be relevant to this meeting.'

'It may be,' said Pincher. 'Go on.'

'Prime Minister,' interrupted Eileen Glenny, pointing up to the clock, 'we have ten minutes max before the top of the hour and we need it to be you, not anyone else.'

Pincher nodded, but looked back over to the Defence Secretary: 'If Drake had time to finish his game of bowls in Plymouth, I certainly have the time to know what we have in the Bay of Bengal.'

'The frigate *Grafton* and destroyer *Liverpool* are there with support ships,' said David Guinness, 'together with two nuclear-powered attack submarines, the *Triumph* and the *Talent*. The Australians have their diesel-powered *Collins*-class submarine, the *Sheean*. Singapore has a submarine in the exercise – I don't have the name. After the trouble at the end of Prime Minister Mahatir's rule, the one Malaysian submarine doesn't work. They have sent up a frigate, the *Jebat*. Singapore did have a corvette, the *Vigilance*, which didn't go on to Chittagong. New Zealand has the frigate *Te Kaha* and a support ship.'

'Foreign Secretary,' said Pincher, 'have you been in touch with our European allies?'

'The French and Germans are noncommittal. Neither has made a statement yet,' said Baker.

'The Americans?'

'President Hastings is on his way back to Washington from Camp David. I understand he has called a meeting of the Principals' Committee.'

Pincher turned to his Private Secretary. 'Get Hastings on the phone.'

'President Gorbunov is just coming through from Moscow, sir,' said the private secretary. 'He says it's urgent and is prepared to speak in English.'

'Prime Minister, we must put out this statement,' pressed Eileen Glenny.

'Is there anything about China in there?'

'The border skirmish with India. No. I think it's too tangential.'

'Like hell it is!' said Pincher. He drummed his fingers on the table, thinking. 'All right. Say this. The Defence Cabinet Committee is monitoring developments. A British task force now helping cyclone victims in the Bay of Bengal was immediately put on full alert. We are liaising with our European allies. The Prime Minister is speaking personally to the Presidents of the United States and Russia.' Pincher paused.

Glenny prompted: 'Whose side are we on?'

'At the moment we're neutral, Eileen. Tell them that, but also remind them that India is a democracy and both China and Pakistan are not. Our support has a natural channel through which to run.'

'Is it wise to bring China in at this stage?' said Baker hesitantly. 'We don't want to upset them unnecessarily.'

'If you think Hamid Khan would have ordered a nuclear strike without first consulting China, Christopher, you should spend less time in your mistress's bed and more time reading your brief. Yes, we bring in China right now, and that is what I will be telling Hastings and Gorbunov.'

Eileen Glenny left the room, writing on her clipboard as she went. Pincher picked up the telephone call from Gorbunov.

'President Gorbunov, thank you so much for calling. If any power centre is the key to defusing this crisis, it surely is the Kremlin.'

'Thank you, Anthony,' said Gorbunov in English so

fluent that it was difficult to tell him from a Bostonian. 'I am calling because I am worried about the Americans. I have just spoken to the Ambassador here, Milton Ashdown, who was boasting about the Americans being the only power with responsibility to intervene. It could be disastrous. This is not the nineties. I feel strongly that India and Pakistan, even China if it comes to that, must be allowed to sort out their own grievances.'

'Not if nuclear fallout is concerned.'

'Of course. But we can stop that. China holds the military tap to Pakistan. We hold it to both India and China. I can turn it on and off at will. But if the United States blunders in, Russians will regard you in the West as the common enemy.'

'I am talking to John Hastings in the next few minutes,' said Pincher.

'Tell him that I will guarantee best efforts to stop an Indian nuclear retaliation, if he can guarantee keeping America out of this dispute.'

'The conventional war will continue.'

'And may the best man win.'

State Department, Washington, DC

Local time: 2045 Sunday 6 May 2007
GMT: 0145 Monday 7 May 2007

The land line was open to the Embassy in Delhi. A satellite link had been set up with Pakistan and the secure encrypted connection was being used with Beijing. The State Department's Management Crisis Center was manned round the clock by three staff, specializing in foreign policy, security and the military. They liaised constantly with counterparts in the White House situation room and in the Pentagon.

Ten minutes earlier, the Crisis Center had been elevated to Task Force level. Across the corridor, two rooms were being opened up. One was for consular staff to field calls about Americans living in Pakistan and China. It was linked by a sparsely furnished reception room with a few chairs and a photocopier to the small Task Force room with an oval desk in the middle and ten work stations, four on each side and one at each end. The single television on one wall was on split screens, taking in the rolling global channels together with Indian and Pakistani television.

Just down the corridor outside the Crisis Center area, Joan Holden put down the telephone from Jamie Song in Beijing. The conversation was cordial, wary and noncommittal on both sides. She had also spoken to Christopher Baker in London, and the foreign ministers of Germany, France and Russia. Records of her conversations were being printed out, together with the latest reports from the embassies.

With her informal manner, she had insisted the State Department meeting took place in the Crisis Center, so officers could keep an eye on their work. So far staff from the South Asia and East Asia Pacific Affairs Bureaux had arrived together with officers from the Department of Defense, Consular Affairs, USAID, the PolMil (political/military) Division, and Medical and someone from Public Affairs to handle the press. Experts on nuclear, biological and chemical warfare were expected within minutes.

After the Pakistan coup, the attack on Dharamsala and the SFF operation in Lhasa, the Crisis Center did not stand up as a task force, because no American lives were at risk. Pakistan's nuclear strike and China's incursion into India did not involve the American military and, at this stage, the State Department remained the lead Federal agency to handle the crisis.

A message from the International Atomic Energy Agency (IAEA) in Geneva, which monitors all nuclear risk, came through reporting on the prevailing wind, the blast-danger area and the concentration of population. Joan Holden saw that thinly populated civilian areas were affected, and the blast and wind direction was such that the threat would have diminished by the time the dust cloud reached any significant town. Consular officials reported that no American citizens were known to be in the area.

Holden's executive secretary had already mobilized two thirty-seat aircraft to fly to Islamabad and Delhi in what was known as a non-combative environment operation. Each was medically equipped to evacuate seriously ill or injured American citizens, be they Embassy staff or civilians. There was strict procedure, known as the 'no double standard rule', which meant that all Americans would be treated equally.

Plans were put in place for an 'authorized departure' from both embassies which would allow dependants and non-essential staff to leave. If the crisis escalated, an 'ordered departure' would take place and finally a special aircraft would be on stand-by to evacuate a core of staff who had to stay behind until the last minutes before closing the Embassy.

Given that neither India nor Pakistan were considered hostile governments, Holden hoped she could keep events on track so that didn't happen.

She picked up the phone and talked directly to Tom Bloodworth at the National Security Council in the White House. 'The IAEA say the fallout of the strike can be confined,' she said, hoping he would take her lead to play it softly. Bloodworth's job was to devise a plan according to presidential policy. Bloodworth could hand out hard truths. Holden had to be more measured.

She walked into the Crisis Management Center. 'I've got five minutes for a brief from each of you, then I'm off to the White House,' she said.

Pentagon City, Virginia, USA

Local time: 2045 Sunday 6 May 2007
GMT: 0145 Monday 7 May 2007

A stream of military personnel moved back and forth along the Eisenhower Corridor on the third floor of the Pentagon building, where the Defense Secretary, Alvin Jebb, was preparing for the White House meeting. His personal staff handled the mass of queries coming into his office in room 3E880. Jebb had alerted the Military Command Center in the Pentagon that he would be going there straight after seeing the President. He asked that the Joint Chiefs of Staff meet him in a secure room known as the Tank, so called because going into it was compared to climbing into a tank.

Jebb had just finished a conversation with the Commander-in-Chief, Pacific (CINCPAC) in Hawaii, who controlled American forces in the Asia–Pacific, stretching from the American west coast to the Mediterranean. He had found the nub of what he needed to know. The brand new *Nimitz*-class aircraft carrier, USS *Ronald Reagan*, with forty-three fixed-wing aircraft on board, had just entered the Indian Ocean where it was heading for a port visit to Trincomalee in Sri Lanka. It was travelling with an *Arleigh Burke*-class guided-missile destroyer, USS *Higgins*, an *Oliver Hazard Perry*-class guided-missile frigate, USS *Rodney M. Davis*, and an *Aegis*-cruiser, USS *Vela Gulf*, which was carrying a sea-based theatre missile-defence system, together with support ships and the SSN attack submarines USS *Greeneville* and USS *Toledo*.

The carrier group could either continue its journey into

the Indian Ocean or double back to the Arabian Sea. Its aircraft gave it a power-projection radius of more than 1,100 kilometres. Its cruise missiles could hit either India or Pakistan from where it was now. It was this carrier group which would provide the core of any American military intervention.

Jebb had already spoken to David Guinness, his counterpart in London, who had informed him about the British-led naval force in the Bay of Bengal. The last thing Jebb wanted was for his forces to get sucked into a nuclear war between two developing nations. He agreed with John Hastings that the United States had become overstretched as the world's policeman and if two governments wanted to fight, they should be allowed to.

The plan he was drawing up now was for a short, sharp hit at the nuclear facilities of both countries, like taking air-pistols away from kids in the school playground.

The Situation Room, The White House, Washington, DC

Local time: 2115 Sunday 7 May 2007
GMT: 0215 Monday 8 May 2007

'**I'm sorry, Mr President,**' said Tom Bloodworth, 'we have no idea how the Indians will respond. Prime Minister Dixit is not taking calls, nor is any member of his cabinet. I have even failed to get through to Chandra Reddy, whom I consider to be a personal friend. They seemed to have shut down the Operational Directorate in South Block. We have picked up a new burst of highly encrypted SIGINT from near the village of Karwana about a hundred miles north of Delhi.'

'Meaning what?' said John Hastings.

'If it means anything it is that the Indians have a war bunker out there, probably dug underneath a farmhouse or something. The signals have never been used before, so we would have no way of knowing before now. There is heavy cloud cover over much of India so it is impossible to check on any preparations for a nuclear or conventional response. As yet, we have not deciphered the code being used from Karwana, but we expect to have something within a few hours.'

'By which time Pakistan could be one big nuclear wasteland.'

The Situation Room where the Principals' Committee had gathered was in the basement of the West Wing of the White House, a small wood-panelled room able to accommodate only about two dozen people. The key conference area was protected by bullet-proof glass. The Committee, led by the President of the United States, met in times of crisis and usually comprised the secretaries of Defense, Commerce, State and Treasury, together with the heads of the CIA, FBI and any other Federal agency involved. For this session, the FBI and the Treasury had not been brought in. But Ennio Barber, the President's personal adviser, was there.

'Joan, tell us about American citizens,' said Hastings.

'None killed or injured that we know of,' said Holden. 'A task force has been set up and we're getting a lot of calls. We are advising all American citizens to leave both India and Pakistan.'

'Isn't that a bit panicky?' said Barber.

'The launch to impact time between Delhi and Islamabad is eleven minutes. It would be irresponsible not to get them out. In fact, we're asking the airlines to lay on airlifts from major cities so that any American citizen who wants to leave, can. The Ambassadors in Islamabad and Delhi have made personal appeals to both Hamid Khan and Hari Dixit to have a nuclear ceasefire until this has happened. Dixit, as we know, has gone to ground. The message has been passed through the Indian Ambassador to the United Nations and here in Washington. Khan has responded. He has pledged not to strike again. But he's asked us to get India to pull back and stop threatening the existence of Pakistan.'

'He thinks he can nuclear strike his way to an international negotiating table,' said Hastings. 'Alvin, I don't want you involved in this, but tell me what you've got.'

'A carrier group is off the southern coast of Sri Lanka,' said Jebb. 'I suggest we send it right up into the Indian Ocean. We have a smaller group from the Fifth Fleet led by the USS *John C. Stennis* in the Gulf of Oman which we can get into the Arabian Sea and up towards the Pakistani coast. Power projection from both groups is well over seven hundred miles, so there would be little risk of radiation if there is a full nuclear exchange.'

'How would that leave our forces in the Gulf?' said Hastings.

'We would move in a group behind the *John C. Stennis* from the Third Fleet in the Mediterranean. We have a cruiser, the USS *Lake Erie*, in the Persian Gulf, with the USS *Bataan*, which is an amphibious assault ship, a couple of destroyers and attack submarines. If Iraq or Iran doesn't choose to exploit the crisis, and if the regime in Saudi Arabia is toppled in an Islamic coup, we should be all right.'

Hastings turned to David Booth, the head of the CIA. 'Check that none of that is about to happen,' he said. 'The *Ronald Reagan* should go into the Indian Ocean anyway and we'll make that the focus of our military announcement. I've just spoken to the British Prime Minister. He is making HMS *Ocean* and her support vessels available, and they have the advantage of being much closer to the action, helping with the Bangladesh cyclone.'

'Working under whose command?' said Jebb.

'Britain's for the moment. Should the crisis escalate, Pincher is happy to put his ships under our command, as I'm sure Australia and New Zealand will. The Malaysians, who also have a ship there, will probably back-pedal off.'

'China,' said Bloodworth. 'We must examine Chinese involvement.'

'I think the nuclear issue is more important than a border skirmish,' said Holden.

'The nuclear weapons were given to Pakistan by China,' said Bloodworth. 'I have just been telephoned by General Shigehiko Ogawa, head of Japanese intelligence. Some of you might know that they have an agent within Zhongnanhai. An interpreter. Ogawa told me that China has begun a long-term military and political plan of which its alliance with Pakistan and hostilities with India is all a part. They've called it Operation *Dragon Fire*.'

'You believe him?' said Holden.

'Yes, Joan, I do. I sense that this will not end by us slapping down India and Pakistan. The stakes are much bigger, our involvement far more precarious. I think China is willing to sacrifice Pakistan in order to win regional power over India. It gave it nuclear strike power, precisely because it believed Hamid Khan would use it.'

'Apart from China, who has leverage with Pakistan?'

'Saudi Arabia,' said Joan Holden.

'Talk to them, Joan. Deploy our carrier groups as discussed. Get me Reece Overhalt on the phone in Beijing and keep trying for Hari Dixit.'

'Mr President,' said Jebb, 'without boring you with new technologies, there is a simple interim measure we could take if there is a hint of escalation.'

The President's Personal Secretary working next to the Oval Office rang through on the open intercom, interrupting the conversation. 'Sir, the Joint Chiefs are reporting Indian missile launches against Pakistan.'

Local time: 0720 Monday 7 May 2007
GMT: 0220 Monday 7 May 2007

Wreckage of buildings and planes was still smouldering from the air attacks on the huge airbase. It was as if the facility was already destroyed and deserved nothing like the blistering salvo it was seconds away from receiving. Hours earlier the Prithvi missiles had been primed for launch by engineers from India's 333rd Artillery Group located with XI Corps at Jullunder. Islamabad, Rawalpindi, Faisalabad, Lahore, Sargodha and Multan were all within missile range. Although the Prithvi was capable of carrying either nuclear or conventional warheads, India chose to limit its retaliation to a conventional strike.

The surviving Pakistani radar, already crippled by Indian strikes, did pick up the Prithvi missiles as they re-entered the atmosphere. The command and control system operated from the bunker deep underneath the airbase activated what little was left of the air-defence system. The most effective should have been the KS-1 short-range ground-based theatre-defence missile, recently flown in from China. But the Chinese technicians had fled the day before, and the equipment was too new for the Pakistanis to operate it efficiently. The KS-1 was hidden in nearby wooded land. But by the time the trucks and launchers were made ready, the missiles had struck. As soon as one of the phased-array radar-guidance stations was switched on, Indian pilots took it out with air-to-surface missiles and laser-guided bombs.

More than a hundred assembled M-11 missiles with a range of 320 kilometres were in storage around Sargodha, shipped in years earlier from China. Indian intelligence believed they were in the Central Ammunition Depot in a hillside set away from the base. To make an impact on the bunkers four Prithvi strikes used 1,000 kilogram fuel-air explosive warheads, which created enough over-pressure to do significant damage. Seconds after the missiles struck, wave after wave of aircraft flew in using both laser-guided and free-fall bombs: No. 23 squadron with MiG-21s and No. 5 Squadron with Jaguars out of Ambala, No. 21 Squadron with MiG-21s out of Chandigarh, No. 221 squadron with MiG-23s out of Halwara and No. 3 Squadron out of Pathankot. Two aircraft failed to return. It's thought they were shot down by hand-held Stinger missiles. The onslaught of missiles and aircraft was designed to seal off the bunker exits with so much rubble that the missiles would never get out. On the way back the Indian pilots blasted targets on the Kirana Hills near Lahore where the missiles were also being stored.

A. Q. Khan Laboratory, Kahuta, Pakistan: 33° 54' N, 74° 06' E

Local time: 0725 Monday 7 May 2007
GMT: 0225 Monday 7 May 2007

The town of Kahuta, thirty kilometres south-east of Islamabad, was a closed, military area. Anyone who travelled there without a permit was arrested on suspicion of espionage. It was the site of a uranium mine, which also contained Pakistan's main nuclear weapons laboratory, named after A. Q. Khan, the physicist who pioneered the country's nuclear programme. In the early eighties, Chinese technicians were involved in working on Highly Enriched Uranium (HEU) and production began in 1986. It's thought Pakistan began to build weapons shortly after that. The HEU hexafluoride was made into uranium metal which was then machined into weapon pits. Kahuta was able to produce enough weapons-grade uranium for three to six weapons a year. China's involvement came to light again in 1996 when it sold five thousand ring magnets, enabling Pakistan to double its capacity to enrich uranium.

India suspected that Pakistan had alternative reprocessing laboratories and at least one more within the vicinity of Islamabad. In the late nineties, a heavy-water reactor went critical at Khushab, 160 kilometres south-west of Islamabad, giving Pakistan the ability to make plutonium. This was the nuclear material of choice for missile warheads, because they could be lighter and therefore give the missile more stability. About half the amount of plutonium was needed, making it possible to create a nuclear weapon the size of a grapefruit. Although the success Pakistan had had in creating plutonium was not yet clear, Khushab (32°

16' N, 72° 18' E) was part of the same airstrike operation as Kahuta.

Kahuta was the pride of Pakistan's nuclear programme. It was also within a few minutes' flying time from India, and barely had the aircraft crossed into Pakistani airspace than the laboratory was in flames. The weapons used for this operation had been carefully chosen so as to minimize the risk of nuclear leakage. No deep penetrations or free-fall bombs were used. Laser-guided bombs were the main weapons, targeted on the entrances and exits of the laboratory, with the view of sealing it rather than destroying it. Cluster bombs were dropped around the perimeter of the complex, sowing a path of smaller anti-personnel bomblets and tiny delayed-action mines, with the purpose of maiming staff working there and deterring others from going in. Fragmentation explosives damaged vehicles and light structures. By the end of the raid, the Kahuta laboratory might still have been in action. But its capacity to transfer enriched uranium to any warhead and missile had been crippled.

Samungli Airbase, near Quetta, Pakistan: 30° 14' N, 66° 55' E

Local time: 0725 Monday 7 May 2007
GMT: 0225 Monday 7 May 2007

Until now, PAF Samungli, base for the Pakistani Mirage fighters, had escaped attack. Now, however, it was a prime target because of its involvement in the Ghauri surface-to-surface missile project. In 1998, Pakistan carried out Ghauri's first test flight. It was launched from Malute near the city of Jhelum (32° 58' N, 73° 45' E) in north-east Pakistan and landed within the grounds of the Samungli airbase, west of Quetta. Indian aircraft destroyed both the airbase and the Malute launch site.

Multan, Pakistan: 71° 30' N, 30° 15' E

Local time: 0725 Monday 7 May 2007
GMT: 0225 Monday 7 May 2007

Military sites around Multan were hit by both Prithvi missiles and aircraft. For civilians, Multan was a crossroads in central Pakistan of bazaars, mosques and beautifully designed tombs and shrines, crushingly arid in the summer heat. But the hills around the city were also suspected to be the site of one of Pakistan's main command and control bunkers, built in the nineties and designed along the lines of the Chinese underground war headquarters in the Western Hills outside Beijing. The Pakistani M-11 missiles were stored at the air-force base in Multan, after being deployed ready for use from Sargodha. Indian aircraft began a steady bombing campaign around Multan, flying sortie after sortie, at first destroying the airbase, then keeping up the pressure on the suspected sites of the bunkers.

Other sites which were also attacked in the same air operation were at Gujranwala, Okhara, Jhang and Dera Nawab Shah, each suspected of housing missiles, communication terminals and launchers sent in from China.

Indian military HQ, Karwana, Haryana, India

Local time: 0830 Monday 7 May 2007
GMT: 0300 Monday 7 May 2007

The Karwana underground complex had been built in the late nineties after the Pokhran nuclear tests and the escalation of the conflict in Kashmir. The only noticeable landmark was a sprawling run-down farmhouse with outbuildings, three kilometres outside the village on a 120 hectare estate which had been taken over by the government. A high wall had been put up around one hectare of the property, within which the bunker had been built. It was neither spacious nor cavernous, unlike the one in China. The Prime Minister had his own quarters, but other members of the National Security Council shared rooms and the military personnel involved slept in dormitories. There was one canteen, common shower rooms and the operations room was just under 100 square metres. This was not designed for a prolonged war but precisely for the crisis which was occurring now. Either it would be over within forty-eight hours, or they would all be dead.

Signals were sent and received through antennas concealed in the roofs of the farmhouse building. Air-conditioning units were installed inside the outer buildings. A sewage system ran into an underground river. The bunker operated from a generator fitted into the complex. If that broke down, there were two emergency generators in the farmhouse.

Military staff, dressed up as farmers, had continued working the property throughout construction and the interim period during which it wasn't used. Any satellite pictures or human agents passing the place would have seen a rich landowner's property and nothing suspicious. No transmission, not even a test, had been sent from the site. The encrypted code had never been used before. Once signals began, the Karwana nuclear bunker would have up to two days before being located and an indefinite time before the code was cracked.

Most of the National Security Council flew out to Karwana by helicopter as soon as Pakistan carried out its tactical nuclear attack. The Prime Minister carried with him the nuclear codes and would have ordered a retaliatory strike if any missile launch had been detected from Pakistan while he was in the air. It had not. The Indian air force and 333rd Artillery Group had already drawn up plans for a wave of strikes intended to cripple the military government of Pakistan.

India had almost a thousand combat aircraft. But while the SU30 was a state-of-the-art weapon which could take on anything used against it and the Light Combat Aircraft could hold its own, many other aircraft such as the old MiG-21s were close to obsolete and failed to perform well. For the first wave of attacks against Pakistan, the older aircraft were used, except for the offensive against Kahuta, which needed high-precision bombing.

Reports back from the pilots suggested that Pakistan's air power had either collapsed or that aircraft had been flown to Afghanistan and Iran in order to stop them being destroyed. Dozens of Pakistani aircraft had been used in attacks against Indian airbases in the minutes before the tactical nuclear strike. They had limited success and early estimates were that Pakistan lost more than forty aircraft in that wave of sorties.

It was impossible to know the success of the Indian strikes on the Pakistani missile bunkers. Unni Khrishnan,

India's Chief of Army Staff, wanted to maintain strikes against them, but shift the emphasis to destroying the Pakistani airbases known to have nuclear-capable aircraft. At the same time, he was keeping back far more aircraft than he would prefer, in order to counter the threat from the east by China.

Meanwhile fighting in Kashmir, outside Lahore and around Sialkot had virtually stopped, indicating that Pakistan's central command and control system was close to being paralysed. As soon as Khrishnan heard that the first wave of strikes were finished, he ordered the second attacks to begin.

One of Pakistan's newest and most threatening nuclear-capable aircraft was the Fantan A-5M, recognized by the bubble canopy on its fuselage and pointed nose. It was a single-seater, twin-engine supersonic fighter developed by the Nanchang Aircraft Company of China. Its particular skill was at low-level flying and was designed as a support aircraft for ground troops and ships moving forward in an attack. The cannon on each wing were mounted close to the fuselage, leaving room for racks of spare fuel tanks, missiles or bombs – including a laser-guided nuclear bomb of up to 20 kilotons.

Very few of the American-made F-16 Fighting Falcons remained in service. This was the aircraft used in the tactical strike and three had been lost then to pursuing Indian aircraft. Pakistan had hoped to build up a substantive force of F-16s, but its difficult relationship with the United States had left them without a full supply of spares and unpredictable maintenance schedules. Of the forty originally acquired by Pakistan, only twenty-five remained, in three squadrons. In 1990, the air force had ordered another 71 F-16s, but they were never delivered because of Pakistan's attempts to develop nuclear weapons. When it became clear that Paki-

stan was not going to stop its programme, Washington
ended its military supply relationship. The money so far
paid for the F-16s was returned. The aircraft was not the
weapon of choice for delivering a nuclear bomb, but, by
improvising the electrical system, it could be used for a
nuclear strike on visually acquired targets.

The third nuclear-capable aircraft was the French-made
Mirage, a single-seater, ground-attack and fighter reconnaissance aircraft, which could carry two 20-kiloton nuclear
bombs. Although Khrishnan had details on the whereabouts
of the Fantans and F-16s, a squadron of Mirages had
vanished in the overnight cloud cover and so far remained
undetected. India's counterforce attack planning was complicated by the thirty different airbases in Pakistan which
were able to host the nuclear-capable aircraft. The ten
Major Operational Bases (MOB) were the peacetime bases
for the aircraft. Of those, only Sargodha and Samungli had
been neutralized in the strikes on the missile bunkers.
Chaklala, which would be the main airbase of Rawalpindi, would
be dealt with in a separate operation.

The other seven MOBs, Faisal and Masroor near Karachi, Mianwali north of Sargodha, Minhas/Kamra north of
Islamabad, Peshawar in the north-west, Rafiqui/Shorkot
north-east of Multan and Risalpur in the far north, would
be targeted in the second major operation to start as soon
as the missile-bunker sorties had ended.

Thirty minutes later, Khrishnan would launch a second
wave of attacks against the Forward Operational Bases
(FOBs), which only became fully operational during wartime. Lahore had been taken care of by Indian artillery on
the outskirts of the city. Multan had been attacked as a
missile base. The new targets were to be the southern bases
of Mirpur Khas and Nawabshah, west of Karachi, Murid,
south-west of Islamabad, Pasni on the southern coast,

Risalewala and Vihari, south-west of Lahore, Shahbaz in the centre of the country and Sukkur to the south of Shahbaz.

The other nuclear-capable airfields were known as satellite bases for emergency landing and recovery during both peacetime and wartime. Khrishnan hoped that once Pakistan realized the wrath it had unleashed, bombing these would be unnecessary.

Connaught Place, Delhi, India

Journalists disputed the exact time the riots broke out. Many claimed to witness the first killing, depending where they were in Delhi, or in India at the time. The sturdy communities of Old Delhi, living cheek by jowl in the hot narrow slumlike streets, were old hands at bloodshed, and there it took the same course as it had for generations. The Hindus claimed they were attacked by Muslims. The Muslims insisted they were the innocent party. Nevertheless, after the first flash of violence, slaughter began on both sides.

It may well have been the Hindus who struck first, aggrieved that an Islamic nation had unleashed the bomb on their armed forces. But the issues soon gave way to grievances and blind revenge for a cruelty which had occurred just minutes before. In the mixed slums of other main cities, Calcutta, Bhopal, Patna, Hyderabad and many more, hostilities broke out in the hours after the nuclear strike. Bombay, ruled by a grass-roots Hindu movement, saw some of the worst atrocities against Muslims, allegedly encouraged by the state government itself.

But if the real political issues of communalism and nuclear power were played out anywhere it was in Delhi's Connaught Place. Before the rioting started, a small group of about three hundred people gathered there with anti-nuclear placards. They spaced themselves in groups of about ten right around the outer pavements and stood silently, as if waiting to be engulfed by a mushroom cloud.

'The nuclear bomb is the most anti-democratic, anti-national, anti-human, outright evil thing that man has ever made,' read one leaflet they were handing out, words taken from the author Arundhati Roy, whose writings had made her a figurehead of the anti-nuclear campaign. 'If only nuclear war was just another kind of war.'

It was a strange morning in Delhi. In the first instance, roads out of the capital became clogged with refugees, most on foot or with animals, so that within a few hours Delhi was, in effect, cordoned off with no land route in or out. Government announcements appealed for people to stay at home or go to work as usual. They had some effect, and factories reported that about 50 per cent of staff had turned up. The security forces were exemplary, with hardly a man going sick or choosing his family over his duty.

News of the Pakistani attack had been widely broadcast, but very few understood the meaning of 'tactical battlefield strike' or that they were in no immediate danger. The population acted as if it was living out its final hours, so great was the ignorance about nuclear warfare. Hospitals were overwhelmed with people complaining of radiation sickness. Violence broke out when doctors tried to send people home. Many shops opened as usual, and hawkers around Connaught Place imaginatively created potions and masks which would ward off a nuclear death. Thousands flocked to the temples and shrines looking for solace. Others, looking for someone to blame, killed and rioted.

Soon, however, when the searing of the sun and the cloudless May sky carried through the morning unchanged, impatience and irritation set in, as if India had been cheated of her final Armageddon. Then there were announcements of India's retaliatory strikes, creating a lull in the tension and new excitement. India was neither destroyed nor victorious. Nor had the war ended. When the holocaust failed to appear, the acute personal emotion of waiting for death diminished and tedium set in. The fatalistic citizens of the Indian capital resorted to getting on with the routine of their lives. Those frustrated with pent-up fear and aggression took to the streets again.

The anti-nuclear protesters stayed their ground throughout, understanding more than most the issues involved. But they appeared too knowledgeable for the situation. There was an air of the 'I told you so' about them, as they pushed leaflets into hands of the public and tied their placards to lamp-posts. Nor did they suggest any solution which Indians could have accepted. Should it declare away its nuclear weapons as a result of the Pakistani attack, then India might as well ground its air force and surrender.

The movement had never been a powerful one and the activists protesting that morning were from the educated and liberal middle class. They were brave to be out. Their arguments against nuclear weapons were well thought out and made sense against the backwardness of India. But nations stumble forward more in folly than in wisdom, and the eloquent voice of writers like Arundhati Roy cut little ice against the raw pride of an impoverished nation.

Her name was Shanti Tirthankara, aged twenty-three, a graduate in civil engineering, with a special interest in rural irrigation. She was attractive, bubbly and outspoken, with long, dark hair, which blew back and forth across her face as she read from an article by Ms Roy. Coincidentally, her father, a wealthy businessman from the Jain community, had an office and large rambling apartment in the old buildings of Connaught Place.

Shanti Tirthankara died on the streets where she had grown up. Quite a crowd had grown up around her. 'The air will become fire,' she read in Hindi. 'The wind will spread the flames. When everything there is to burn has burned and the fires die, smoke will rise and shut out the sun. The earth will be enveloped in darkness. There will be no day. Only interminable night. Temperatures will drop to far below freezing and nuclear winter will set in. Water will turn into toxic ice. Radioactive fallout will seep through the earth and contaminate groundwater. Most living things, animal and vegetable, fish and fowl, will die.'

A single rifle shot hit her in the heart, fired by a policeman, and no one found out why because he was beaten to death minutes later. A mob surged, spontaneously, disorganized, horribly cruel, tearing down the anti-nuclear placards, beating the activists and fighting the police at the same time. Petrol bombs were thrown into shops and black smoke curled up on the clear, hot morning, the latest evidence of India's precarious existence.

Connaught Place was burning just as it had done in the great watersheds of history before and Indians died as police bullets tried to bring their great civilization into line. But as the rioters were cleared from Connaught Place, the debris and the bodies left behind, they found another common target for their anger. Communities throughout India were not suffering from nuclear radiation, but from the aggression of misplaced blame. Eight hundred metres to the south-west down Parliament Street lay Parliament House and the offices of government.

Three policemen died as the mob broke through the cordon. Rioters died in the hail of fire which followed. But by now, the mob was thousands strong, many running with burning rags and petrol bombs to attack the seat of power.

General Headquarters, Rawalpindi, Pakistan

'**Sargodha and Multan** are out of action, sir,' said Masood. 'We have lost communications. Kahuta is paralysed. We have lost twenty-three of our thirty nuclear-capable airfields. The pilots have taken the aircraft wherever they can to avoid them being destroyed. Most are in Kabul and Kandahar in Afghanistan, Saravan, Zahedan and Khash in Iran and Kashgar in China. Sialkot is vulnerable and we are facing defeat there. Lahore remains under artillery bombardment.'

'The good news?' said Hamid Khan.

'We are winning decisively in the Kashmir Valley. The Indians have lost thousands of men and dozens of helicopters. They were ill-prepared.'

'What of Rawalpindi?'

'The Chaklala airbase is badly damaged and unusable at present. Apart from that, we do not appear to have been a target.'

'Good,' said Khan. 'So far it is as I had planned.'

'I'm sorry, sir?' said Masood, looking confused.

'We have lost nothing which we need if Pakistan is going to be a modernized state with no external enemies. Airfields can be rebuilt. But we are winning Kashmir and now we must talk to the world.'

'Do you want President Tao in Beijing?'

'No. We will have no communication with China. The signals will be picked up. Get me John Hastings in Washington.'

The Oval Office, The White House, Washington, DC

Local time: 2235 Sunday 6 May 2007
GMT: 0335 Monday 7 May 2007

'**Hamid Khan is** on the line and wants to speak directly to you.'

John Hastings sipped from his cup of Chinese herbal tea, which he hoped would keep him alert, yet calm, throughout the night. In any other circumstances he would have refused the call. Ennio Barber would have warned against the President of the United States speaking directly to a military dictator who had just started a nuclear war. But as Hastings was learning fast, a nuclear war was like no other. The rules had not yet been written.

'Unless you bring your powers to bear, Mr President, Pakistan may soon cease to exist as a nation,' said Hamid Khan.

'You forfeited that right by your actions last night.'

'You are correct. I have forfeited my right to rule Pakistan and I will never again be accepted by the Western democratic nations. But you cannot condemn the people of Pakistan for my actions. They are being blasted by the full might of the Indian air force. They are threatened with a far more powerful nuclear strike. Muslims are being slaughtered in India and riots have begun here in Pakistan. Only the United States has the influence to call an immediate halt to the Indian offensive. Once there is a ceasefire, you have my guarantee that I will step down from office.'

'And who will take over?'

'An interim leader who has full international support.'

Hastings put Hamid Khan on hold and called Tom Bloodworth along to the office.

'So far all the strikes are conventional,' said Bloodworth. 'Specifically against legitimate military targets. Far more than ours were in Serbia. If anything, India's response has been remarkably measured.'

'Will Dixit go nuclear?'

'I sense not. Not if Pakistan doesn't strike again.'

'General Khan, are you still there?' said Hastings.

'Yes, Mr President.'

'I want a statement from you right now on Pakistan radio and television that you will not use another nuclear weapon in this conflict. It must be short, unequivocal and in both English and the languages of Pakistan. When we hear that and have it translated, I will call on India for a complete ceasefire.'

'But people are being killed—'

'Then get a move on and make the statement.'

Foreign and Commonwealth Office, London

Local time: 0345 Monday 7 May 2007

John Stopping, Chairman of the Joint Intelligence Committee, was woken by the telephone ringing on his secure line. Only a handful of people in London knew the number, together with a small circle of colleagues in the international circles in which he mixed. Stopping's career in the diplomatic and intelligence services had forged trust and friendships lasting many years. Often he suddenly found them adversaries amid unpredictable events of foreign policy.

Stopping automatically checked his watch and saw he had been dozing on the office couch for less than twenty minutes. He was surprised but delighted to hear the voice of Chandra Reddy on the other end.

'John, I think we need to look ahead and perhaps we could do each other a favour.'

'Only the greatest optimist would try to look beyond nuclear conflict,' said Stopping. 'Why is Hari Dixit not taking any calls?'

'He is trying to stop a nuclear war, John. He can't do that if he's yacking on the bloody telephone to every head of government who wants to get involved. Don't tell me that Margaret Thatcher chatted to Indira Gandhi during the Falklands conflict.'

'Given that you've just been nuked, Reddy, you sound in remarkably good form.'

'I need Britain's help. No one else can do it.'

'Go on.'

'Can we agree that Pakistan would never have done this without China's backing?'

'Let's say we do.'

'And that China's incursion into India was timed to coincide with the flare-up in Kashmir?'

'Agreed.'

'Then, until a shot is fired across China's bows, the war in Asia cannot be stopped.'

'This is a diplomatic, not a military issue.'

'No, John. It is one for men like us.'

Stopping kept quiet, allowing Reddy to continue. 'The Chinese have been building up the port facilities at the Burmese naval base in Hanggyi. In the past two months they have sent two warships there, the *Kaifang*, a 3,600 tonne destroyer, and the *Anqing*, a 2,500 tonne frigate. Both ships are expendable. They know we could blow both of them out of the water. They also have three or four *Kilo*-class diesel-electric submarines in the Andaman Sea. We spotted them going through the Malacca Straits, but now have no idea where they are. In a conflict like this, the presence of those ships is a clear incursion into our theatre of influence.'

'But not illegal,' said Stopping.

'Kosovo changed the frontiers of international legality.'

'I still don't see how we can help.'

'You have HMS *Ocean* coming down from Chittagong towards Hanggyi Island right now. On board is a unit from the Special Boat Squadron together with a VSV; length 53 feet, three crew plus room for eleven commandos, capable of 60 knots with two 750 b.h.p. diesel engines and stealth technology which enables it to avoid radar and infrared heat sensors and a range of 700 nautical miles. If they went in to destroy the Chinese ships and whatever else they find in Hanggyi, China would think twice about continuing to stir things up on the subcontinent.'

'You're out of your mind,' said Stopping.

'You know I'm not. I estimate that by late afternoon, our time, the *Ocean* will be within VSV range of Hanggyi. Send them in at nightfall. The war could be over by midnight.'

Prime Minister's Office,
Downing Street, London

Local time: 0345 Monday 7 May 2007

'I am not speaking to you as a member of the House of Lords, but as a businessman, a private citizen and an Indian.'

Like John Hastings, Anthony Pincher was drawing himself a completely new set of guidelines. Right now, in the middle of the night, with conventional diplomacy failing, Pincher accepted that he needed to explore unorthodox methods to reach a peace. Military action of any kind against India or Pakistan could create a fearsome backlash which might easily prompt more use of nuclear weapons. That was why when Lord Thapar called from his mansion in Hampstead to announce he was on his way to Downing Street in his Rolls Royce, Pincher instructed that he be let straight in.

Lord Thapar had been ennobled by Pincher as a recognition of the contribution of the Indian community. Both in Britain and the United States they had overtaken any other immigrant group in economic performance and had become a serious lobbying machine, fielding candidates for parliament, making inroads into the City and, most dramatically, contributing enormous expertise and ideas to the information technology revolution. Lord Thapar himself was a second-generation Indian in his mid-sixties, whose wealthy parents had found themselves a victim of the partition, lost everything and decided to emigrate to Britain. While they struggled, impoverished, against the pressures of racism, they ensured that Mani Thapar was given the best the English state education system could offer, such that he won a place at Cambridge, went on to study in France and the United States, then built up a multi-million-pound empire. Only after his wealth was secure did he begin serious investment in India itself, winning business and political friends, and persuading the inward-looking governments to ease up on their investment laws. Hari Dixit was the Health Minister in Andhra Pradesh when Mani Thapar pioneered the building of a pharmaceutical factory there. The two men became close friends, with Dixit using Thapar as his conduit to the West, which he then regarded as arrogant, colonial and interfering. Dixit understood as little about the workings of international business as Thapar did about the aspirations of the rural Indian. They both learnt keenly from each other.

Anthony Pincher was acutely aware of this relationship when Thapar called. He had just finished speaking to an exasperated John Hastings in Washington, who was still unable to get hold of Hari Dixit. With the rolling news media it was becoming a humiliating political issue. Reports coming from France and Germany indicated that Europe might find it difficult to approach the crisis with a united front. Already, there were enough divisive issues over trade, currency and customs control. A nuclear exchange, albeit in Asia, could be the one which finally caused a split.

'Thank you for seeing me at such an inhospitable hour, Prime Minister,' said Thapar while taking a seat. 'I felt I had to get my oar in early.'

'Anything you can do would be appreciated.'

'I will be blunt, then. We are all aware that Pakistan and China are in cahoots over this. Burma, too, but it is such a basket case that it is barely relevant. I can get a message right now to Hari Dixit to take his hand off that bloody nuclear trigger, if you come out in support of India.

Without reservation, of course. We don't have time to go through the "we are friends with both nations" business, like the Americans did with you in the Falklands.' Thapar checked his watch as if to emphasize what he was saying. 'If either Dixit or Khan give the order now, there could be a city destroyed in eleven minutes.'

'It is something we would need to discuss with the Americans and our European partners.'

'My friend Ratu Keni Vohra is at this minute with Joan Holden in Washington. Other meetings are going on throughout Europe. India is a democracy, Prime Minister. China and Pakistan are not.'

'Lord Thapar, are you threatening to escalate this conflict unless Britain publicly sides with India? I would hope that Hari Dixit is a more mature statesman than that.'

'Threats and reality are often confused. China is the threat. Pakistan is its foot-soldier. India has no superpower aspiration.'

'But it went nuclear.'

'Thank God we did. Or we would now be a colony of China's. Listen, if Hari Dixit knows the international community is on-side, he can afford to let India absorb its punishment and open a diplomatic channel. If you sit on the fence, he has no alternative but to fight.'

'You can talk to him?'

'I can get a message to him within five minutes.'

Anthony Pincher spoke to his Private Secretary on the intercom: 'Can you get me John Hastings again?'

'He's in the Situation Room, Prime Minister. He'll be at least half an hour.'

Hari Dixit, unshaven and frustrated, watched the broadcast from Hamid Khan in Pakistan on the BBC World Service. Khan himself did not appear, leaving a newscaster to deliver his historic message.

'Pakistan used its ultimate weapon of defence only because Indian military forces threatened to suck our nation away into oblivion. That has been its aim in the sixty years since partition. Last night, I made the terrible decision to defend our right to exist and we halted the Indian advance. But it was a terrible decision and I now pledge two things. Firstly, as soon as India declares a ceasefire, Pakistan will never use nuclear weapons again in this conflict. Secondly, as soon as peace is assured, I will step down as the leader of Pakistan. I call on the United States and the international community to support my pledge and persuade Prime Minister Dixit that this is the only way forward to avoid a nuclear conflict. Finally, I must remind all of you, that Pakistan carried out the nuclear strike on Pakistani soil. It did not breach the sovereignty of any other nation.'

The broadcast ended with the Pakistani national anthem, then cut to a studio discussion which Dixit muted with the remote control. 'What happens if we declare a ceasefire?' Dixit asked Unni Khrishnan, the Chief of Army Staff.

'They're well beyond the Line of Control in Kashmir. We have the huge loss of the armoured brigades from the nuclear strike. We have surrounded and cut off Sialkot. We could negotiate to hold our positions there. We would have to pull back from Lahore.'

Dixit glanced at the silent television screen running pictures of rioting and arson in Delhi. 'I can't think in this bloody dungeon,' he said. 'And I shouldn't be here while ordinary Indians are facing the threat of death.'

'Sir, the American President is insisting on speaking to you,' said an aide-de-camp.

'No,' snapped Dixit. 'I'll only speak to him after he has decided whose side he's on. Get me Hamid Khan instead. We'll give him one last chance. Link up Chandra Reddy, Prabhu Purie and the usual suspects with the call.'

Hamid Khan came on the phone keen to talk. 'The ceasefire will incorporate a referendum on Kashmir,' he said, immediately.

'There will be no ceasefire, yet, General,' said Dixit. 'You will release a statement announcing your withdrawal from Indian-controlled Kashmir. You will cease all hostilities. You have thirty minutes to do so. If we detect any aircraft movement or the hint of a missile launch, we will obliterate Pakistan with nuclear weapons.'

The Situation Room, The White House, Washington, DC

Local time: 2245 Sunday 8 May 2007
GMT: 0345 Monday 7 May 2007

'**Hamid Khan's stuffing** us around,' said Hastings. This was the second meeting of the Principals' Committee since the Pakistani strike. It had been timed to take in Khan's broadcast and then decide on as long-term and substantive strategy as possible. Hastings had added the Commerce Secretary, Stuart Hollingworth, to the committee for this reason.

'The Indians aren't accepting it,' said Joan Holden, when the broadcast ended. 'Kashmir is the main sticking point.'

'As always,' said Tom Bloodworth. 'At least the weather has cleared, so we have a good satellite view over most of the two countries. They're still fighting in the Kashmir Valley, hand-to-hand in some places.'

'Mr President,' said Ennio Barber impatiently, grasping printouts from the latest network opinion polls, 'if we dither any longer about backing India, we're going to take months to recover.' He unfolded a facsimile of the Monday's first edition of the *New York Times*. 'The *Times* pulled existing advertising to insert this on their op-ed page.'

The advertisement showed the picture of an atomic mushroom cloud superimposed on destroyed buildings and piles of bodies. The slogan read: 'India and America are nuclear democracies. Pakistan and China are nuclear dictatorships. Which do you support?'

'It was paid for by the Indian community in New York,' said Barber. 'The most successful economic ethnic community in the United States. They are paying for similar messages, television, radio and print across the country. Within twelve hours, about every American will be cheering for India just like it was a ball game.'

'Joan?' said Hastings.

'If we give our full support to India, we may have to take action against Pakistan to halt a nuclear escalation. I have no problem with that. I do have a problem with the knock-on effect. We will alienate the Islamic countries, possibly leading to the destabilization of Egypt and Saudi Arabia. We have been down that road before. It may be manageable. We will also alienate China, which has a defence agreement with Pakistan and all the baggage which goes with it. China's declaration of war on India and its invasion in the east has been eclipsed, but is very dangerous. What we need, therefore, is a comprehensive ceasefire. Then we pursue permanent settlements on all issues through the UN.'

'Stuart?' said the President.

'I am with Joan. Our trade with China is enormous, such that if it stopped buying our goods tomorrow between a million and two million people could lose their jobs. The comparison for India is barely a hundred thousand. In Seattle, for example, China keeps more than a hundred thousand people employed. Expand that out to families and you're talking of half a million people. That is the personal and domestic implication. Contracts guaranteed to American firms would go to our European and Japanese competitors, those who don't have to make the difficult decision.'

'We have already intercepted a communication between Paris and the commercial section of its Embassy in Beijing telling them to exploit the situation,' said Bloodworth, 'to stay neutral and snap up the contracts from any foreign firm whose government sides against China.'

'Exactly,' said Hollingworth. 'Then we have to look at

China's new membership of the World Trade Organization, freeing up a whole new area of trade, and the positive impact that has on the world economy. From the view of global business, it seems insane that one military dictator in a basket-case of a country can bring the world to the brink of nuclear war and economic chaos. There must be a better way.'

'Alvin,' said Hastings to the Defence Secretary. 'Give me your view.'

'I think we're all with Joan and Stuart,' said Jebb. 'Entering into hostilities with China would be a completely different ball game, as we found out during the Dragon Strike campaign. They have tested nuclear missiles which can reach the continental United States, and like it or not, the nuclear option is out there on the table. They have been good allies in securing peace elsewhere around the world, particularly on the Korean peninsula. When India declared China as the primary threat to its security in 1998, the Chinese were remarkably measured and mature in their response. When we bombed their Belgrade Embassy in 1999, they cut off all contact with us. Everything, apart from the ongoing negotiations on North Korea. We must assume that everything will stop again if we back India now. For defence purposes, it would mean policing three areas of potential hostility, the Indian Ocean, the South China Sea and the Gulf, which we would have to keep an eye on because of the Islamic support Joan mentioned which would swing in favour of Pakistan. Our satellite surveillance and our intelligence gathering and analysis capability would be stretched. We would have to step up substantially our anti-terrorist preventative measures on the assumption that America and Americans would be targeted. Should genuine hostilities break out, then we would be looking at calling up reservists, spending a lot more money and raising taxes – all of which would impact on your campaign for re-election.'

'Not good,' muttered Barber, who was scribbling notes and new estimates against his poll results.

'Let me give you a quick example,' continued Alvin Jebb. 'We're twenty aircraft short on the C-17 transport plane project, used to ferry troops and supplies to areas of operation. Budget cuts have left us with three less carrier groups than we had ten years ago, yet our commitments are increased. We have even had to reduce the gate-keepers on hostile ports.'

'Gate-keepers?' said Hastings.

'The attack submarines which keep watch on ships coming and going from any port, India, China, Russia. You name it. They record the signatures for naval intelligence. If it's a ship we can usually track it by satellite. If it's a submarine, we might deploy a second sub to track it and keep the first as the gate-keeper. We don't have enough money to watch every key port any more. There are numerous other examples, but our ability to get involved in two simultaneous regional conflicts is severely limited. To contemplate three would be madness.'

'Three?' said Barber, looking up from his notes, as he hadn't been fully concentrating.

'The Middle East, the sub-continent and the Asia–Pacific,' said Jebb.

'I'm with Alvin,' said Joan Holden. 'But I'm not convinced China would take it to the brink. As long as Saudi Arabia and Egypt stay on-side, we have no more risk of a flare-up in the Middle East than we did before. I think Stuart is veering too much towards the Sino-centric picture. The Council for Foreign Relations published a paper by the late Gerald Segal in 1999 entitled *Does China Matter?*. I don't agree with everything he said, but he's on the right track. In a nutshell, China accounts for not much more than 5 per cent of world trade. Only 2 per cent of our exports go there. Britain sells 0.5 per cent of its exports there, the same as it sells to Sri Lanka. Even for Japan the figure is only 6 per cent. True, multinationals such as Boeing, Bechtel and Motorola are heavily invested there, but 80 per cent of the foreign direct investment is from the East Asian ethnic Chinese. Last year, forty-five billion dollars went in and thirty-five billion went out in capital flight. If we contained China, like we did the Soviet Union, our economies would barely notice it. Theirs would collapse.'

'Alvin,' asked Hastings, 'do you go along with that? Does China matter? Because if it doesn't, we can wrap this goddamn war up by breakfast.'

'China is a second-rate military power, and as such is more like Iraq or Serbia was – a regional and not a global threat. We could defeat it in a conventional air, land or sea war in a matter of days. We could cripple its economy with sanctions. But I'm afraid life is not that simple. It has just brought on line the (East Wind) DF 41, the solid-fuel missile with a range of 8,000 miles. It already had the less accurate DF 5, which could hit the Continental United States. We think they have a DF 41 silo in Luoyang in Henan province under Unit 80304 of the Second Artillery, which handles the nuclear programme; one at Tonghua, about fifty miles north of the Korean border with Unit 80301; and one with Unit 80303 in the hills just outside of Kunming. Because the DF 41 is so new, the missiles would share silos with the lesser-ranged existing weapons. Unit 80303, for example, which also holds the DF 21s, range about 1,200 miles, would be used to attack India. China's doctrine is to be able to absorb a first strike and hit back. There is no way we could guarantee eradicating every silo and launch station in a first strike. Absolutely not. Nor could our own land-based theatre missile-defence system protect us against a Chinese strike. The whole emphasis of Chinese long-range power projection is its missile programme. To give an example of the detail they are concentrating on, their transporter erector launchers have been refined to make an erection and retraction within two minutes, meaning they can drive it out of a tunnel, fire the missile and get back into hiding again before we even know where it is. So yes, Mr President, we can defeat China, but we may lose a city or two in doing it and I am pretty certain no president would ever think the fight worth it.'

'And India, I take it, has nothing so lethal with which to threaten us,' said Hastings.

'More importantly, it has no reason to,' said Joan Holden. 'It is a democracy with an independent judiciary, a constitution which protects political debate, freedom of religion, the ownership of property. It might be flawed, but politically it's our way of life.'

'They also act like a bunch of assholes,' added Jebb.

'If I could add an extra warning to our dilemma,' said Tom Bloodworth. 'The technology which Alvin has referred to in the Chinese missile programme is only a fraction of what we believe they stole from us in the eighties and nineties. They haven't really started working with it yet. The classified information taken included material on seven different thermonuclear warheads: the W-88 Trident D-5, the W-56 Minuteman II, the W-62 Minuteman III, the W-70 Lance, the W-76 Trident C-4, the W-78 Minuteman III Mark 12A and the W-87 Peacekeeper. One of the twists is that it was probably American technology which helped create the neutron bomb used against the Indian forces. There is no way they could have gotten it so far advanced so quickly without it. I apologize if I sound angry about this, Mr President, but our stolen technology has led to

China building smaller, more versatile warheads, so, like Alvin said, they can fit more missiles into less silos. On top of that, they now have mobile and submarine launchers which can hit the United States.'

'We have, incidentally,' said Jebb, 'stepped security right up at the Los Alamos, Lawrence Livermore, Oak Ridge and Sandia laboratories where this type of research is taking place.'

'Fine,' said Hastings looking up at the clock. 'I'm well across the scandal of Chinese espionage, but I don't see the point of bringing it up right now.'

'For the past fifteen years, China has been pulled between inward-looking factions who want to concentrate on economic reform and more aggressive hawkish factions who are impatient for power status,' said Bloodworth. 'That debate is still going on and, if that damn prison rescue hadn't happened in Lhasa, I believe that President Tao would not have been prompted to push things to the brink. Ten years from now, however, the Chinese missile programme could be so advanced that we couldn't face it down. The moderate faction might have collapsed and war with China would be far bloodier than any hostilities which we embark on now.'

'I don't want a war with China,' said Hastings. 'Not ten years, not twenty years from now. Not ever.'

'We struck a deal after the Dragon Strike campaign,' said Bloodworth, 'and in a few years Beijing has bounced back again. Germany struck a deal after the First World War. Fifteen years later, Hitler was preparing for the Second World War. We nuked Japan, and it's been compliant ever since.'

'I don't like what I'm hearing,' said Hastings.

Zhongnanhai, Beijing, China

Local time: 1200 Monday 7 May 2007
GMT: 0400 Monday 7 May 2007

Jamie Song ushered the Russian Ambassador, Nikolai Baltin, into President Tao's official reception room in Longevity Hall. The windows, dripping with condensation, looked out over the Garden of Benevolence and beyond onto Nan Hai, or southern sea, the smaller of the two lakes in the compound.

The two men stood awkwardly in silence, waiting for Tao to arrive. They knew that anything they said would be recorded and this was not the time for small talk. Tao arrived grim-faced without an interpreter. Baltin was a fluent Mandarin speaker. Song was glad that the unsophisticated security chief, Tang Siju, was in the Western Hills, putting his hawkish views into practice in Tibet, rather than using them to wreck diplomacy in Zhongnanhai.

'You wanted to see me, and I am here,' said Tao, abruptly.

'Thank you, President Tao,' said Baltin. 'President Gorbunov is worried that the United States has everything to gain from the outbreak of war and that we – Russia and China – have everything to lose.'

'Has President Gorbunov sent you on the request of John Hastings?'

Baltin shook his head. 'He believes the United States will use this crisis to divide our strategic alliance, particularly your conflict with India.'

None of the men were sitting down, and Tao paced the room before answering. 'The long-term aim of India is to draw Tibet out of China and bring it under Indian influence, just like Nepal, Sikkim and Bhutan. If we show weakness, India will support a fully independent Tibet and win applause within the international community for doing so. I would not even be surprised if it offers to run an interim administration there, in other words, claiming its own suzerainty, which would be recognized by the Western powers.'

'We don't believe that is the case,' said Baltin.

'Well, we do,' said Tao. 'India and China have a difficult history. While we are naturally the Great Power in Asia, India has tried to assume that role through its colonial links with the West. We have still not forgotten the gracious way in which India treated us at the Afro-Asian Bandung Conference in 1955. Comrade Zhou Enlai gave the most memorable speech about the resentment of Western domination, which was applauded by all, particularly those Western puppets which resented our presence. "Most of the countries of Asia and Africa have suffered from colonialism," he said. "We are economically backward ... If we seek common ground to remove the misery imposed upon us it will be easy to for us to understand each other, respect each other, to help each other." Nehru embraced comrade Zhou afterwards.'

'Which is precisely what President Gorbunov would like you to do to Prime Minister Dixit.'

'I haven't finished,' snapped Tao. Baltin fell quiet, remembering the Chinese president's penchant for lecturing. 'Since the end of colonialism, India has purported to be the civilized face of Third World development. At Bandung, Nehru was gracious, like a father to an adopted child. Yet it was comrade Zhou who stole the show and no amount of embraces could hide the fact. While Nehru had been selling his books to Western publishers and dressing in Western suits, comrade Zhou had been commanding our fighters to rid China of corruption and oppression. The developing countries knew that Zhou was the genuine reformer. Nehru resented it deeply. Nehru's India had copied the Western democratic model and used English as its national language of communication. We pursued a more difficult path of finding our own way, the Asian way, which has proved more suitable to the culture of this region. We are now richer than India. Our people are better educated. Our hospitals and schools are better equipped. Our influence in global affairs is greater. The Chinese people are more confident.

'Yet India knows there is one weakness it can exploit and that is Tibet. In 1959, when the Dalai Lama escaped, Prime Minister Nehru travelled all the way to the Mussoorie Hill Station to greet him. This was a completely unfitting reception for a government to give the leader of a rebellion in a friendly neighbouring state. Your Russian troops have been in Chechnya to prevent separation, causing great bloodshed. We have done nothing like that in Tibet since putting down the rebellion in 1959. Even now, during the riots after the escape of prisoner Togden, our reaction has been constrained. Indian troops carried out that operation. The rebels are given sanctuary and supplies on Indian territory. The Dalai Lama, the inspirational leader of the rebellion, lives there. I sympathize with your President's concerns. I am worried, too. But I cannot allow the dismemberment of the Motherland in exchange for Russia's desire to lead a tripartite power bloc which might or might not work.

'So tell President Gorbunov to bring his influence to bear on India. An end to terrorism in Tibet. The expulsion of the Dalai Lama. The arrest of terrorists. The closing of their camps. Once that is announced, we will withdraw our troops from Arunachal Pradesh and then Russia can mediate in talks about our disputed border with India. Until then, the war continues.'

Without saying goodbye, Tao turned on his heels and left the room. Jamie Song escorted Baltin outside, so they could talk more freely.

'We are offering you six *Typhoon*-class nuclear-powered submarines,' said Baltin.

'President Tao sees it as a trick,' said Song. 'The issues on the table now will be solved within a few days. The submarines will take months of training and trials before we can put them to use.'

Baltin nodded. 'Do me one favour, then, Jamie. I understand the Americans are about to come down on the side of India, which will put them directly at odds with you. The Indian communities in Europe and the States are carrying out an impressive lobbying campaign, way smarter than anything the Chinese can do. Mushroom clouds, democracy, all that sort of thing. Get yourself on CNN and do something to neutralize it.'

Song laughed sarcastically: 'So while India and Pakistan are in the middle of a nuclear war, China goes on CNN.'

Cabinet Room, Downing Street, London

Local time: 0400 Monday 7 May 2007

'They want us to blow up Chinese ships in a Burmese naval base,' said Anthony Pincher.

'It is one of the most preposterous ideas in the history of modern conflict,' said Christopher Baker, looking at his Permanent Under-Secretary, Sir Malcolm Parton, for support.

'If the Chinese found out it was us,' said Sir Malcolm, 'our relationship would be set back generations. They would never forget it.'

'Does that matter?' said Pincher. 'My gut political instinct is to back India. This is the sort of action which would let us do it in a distinctive way, not as a lapdog to the Americans.'

Anchor: We're going from the crisis in India and Pakistan over to Beijing, China where we hope the Foreign Minister, Jamie Song, can shed some light on the terrible unfolding of events this evening. China is a long-term ally of Pakistan. It is at odds with India over Tibet. Seventeen hours ago, China invaded India, using the territory of another ally, Burma – or Myanmar – to move in. Jamie Song is calling from his car mobile so we apologize for the quality of the line. Foreign Minister, thank you for joining us. Firstly, on the nuclear strike. Hamid Khan has been unclear about whether he will launch another nuclear strike. Can you persuade him not to, for the sake of world peace?

Song: You speak about peace as if you can pluck it off trees. Yes, China wants peace. Our whole doctrine over the past fifty years has been to strengthen our political institutions and our economy. You can't do that while fighting wars. We are not expansionist and we did not start the present conflict.

Anchor: You invaded India. You supplied Pakistan with the neutron bomb.

Song: Indian troops invaded Tibet. We are merely defending our borders. I utterly refute the allegation that we supplied any nuclear material to Pakistan.

Anchor: All right, Foreign Minister, you say you're not expansionist, yet India claims that you have sent warships into the Indian Ocean.

Song: Technically, they are in the Andaman Sea. But you're right. China's oil supplies from the Middle East go through the Indian Ocean. We have a ship-visiting arrangement with the government of Myanmar. Given our reliance on that oil, it is only right that the Chinese navy is there to offer protection.

Anchor: Then you would have to take on the Indian navy.

Song: We hope it won't come to that. You will also note that the British, Australian, New Zealand and Singaporean navies are in the Andaman Sea as well and an American carrier group is in the Indian Ocean.

Anchor: Could we try to look ahead, Foreign Minister. I understand President Hastings is about to hold a brief news conference. He's expected to announce his support for the Indian government against Pakistan. What will be your reaction?

Song: He should examine the facts. India invaded both China and Pakistan. Pakistan exploded nuclear weapons over its own territory, not on Indian soil. India broke through the Line of Control in Kashmir to try to set up a new frontier ten miles inside Pakistani-controlled territory. India is hosting Tibetan terrorists. It is dangerously glib to talk about democracy and dictatorships. It might win him votes for the next election, but it will not create a better or safer world – that is if there is a world left for any of us to live in.

Anchor: I'm sorry, Foreign Minister. Should I take that as a warning for the President?

Song: If you wish to see it like that. India and China are not like Iraq and Kuwait or Belgrade and Kosovo. If we are threatened, we will defend ourselves, and as I pointed out just now, India has proved itself to be the most unpredictable and hazardous country on earth.

General Headquarters, Rawalpindi, Pakistan

Local time: 0930 Monday 7 May 2007
GMT: 0430 Monday 7 May 2007

'Get me President Hastings!' Hamid Khan had watched
Jamie Song's broadcast and taken it to be a message of
continuing support. He also remembered the words of the
Mullah al-Bishri: concentrate on Kashmir. If he won Kashmir, he would bring peace to South Asia, secure Pakistan
and win the respect of the Islamic and Western worlds.

'The White House is referring us to Ambassador Watkins
at the Embassy,' said Masood. Arthur Watkins, a career
State Department diplomat, was patched through to the
bunker at Chaklala.

'The United States is concerned that your statement was
not clear enough, General,' said Watkins.

'I want to discuss it personally with President Hastings,'
said Khan curtly.

'The President won't be taking your call, General. You
talk to me or no one at all.'

'I made my statement and now America must support
our call for peace.'

'The statement was premised on India's declaration of a
ceasefire. We need it to be a stand-alone announcement,
not conditional on any other action.'

'I have done that on nuclear strikes. I cannot make a
unilateral ceasefire on Kashmir.'

'In which case I am authorized to tell you that the
United States will throw its diplomatic support behind the
democratically elected government in India.'

'You have thought of the consequences?'

'That is what I am paid to do, General. And if it's any help, that is my personal view as well.'

'The Chinese will never allow it.'

'I don't think the Chinese have the authority to make American policy. The President will not be making his statement for another thirty minutes or so. You have time to think about it.'

As soon as Khan had finished the call, Masood said: 'They are waiting for your instructions, General.'

Two Chinese M-11 medium-range missiles, known locally as the Shaheen 1, were on mobile launchers, erected at 60 degrees, 800 metres apart, in cleared wooded area outside the town of Kagan. The border with Pakistani-controlled Kashmir was 13 kilometres to the east. Islamabad was 120 kilometres to the south. The target was the heart of the Kashmir Valley, the headquarters of XV Corps at the Badami Bagh Cantonment, which was set back on the other side of a hill from the busy area around Dal Lake and the market. Each missile was meant to have a conventional single 500 kilogram warhead.

'Missile launch from Pakistan!' shouted Unni Khrishnan.

'Target?' snapped back Hari Dixit.

'Uncertain, sir. We won't know until re-entry.'

'Warhead?'

'Not known.'

'Time to impact?'

'Estimated three minutes. Do we launch?'

'Launch site?'

'Kagan. Northern Pakistan. 34 degrees 47 North. 73 degrees 36 East.'

Dixit was silent, his eyes darting between his watch and the television screen. This was the moment of horrific farce about which so much had been talked and nothing had been done. Nine years since the nuclear tests and all they had were two defunct hotlines which no one ever answered. No system of checks had been set up. No negotiations to stop a false nuclear launch. Nothing to stop mistakes. When it had all started, he was a health minister in a far-away state and knew nothing at all about war.

'Get me Hamid Khan.'

'They're not picking up, sir,' said an aide-de-camp.

'Permission to counter-strike, sir,' said a voice which Dixit didn't even recognize.

'Confirm the number of enemy missiles?'

'Two, sir.'

'Time to impact two minutes twenty-eight seconds.'

'Waiting your instructions, sir.'

Except for the whirring of the air conditioning, there was complete quiet in the hot, claustrophobic bunker. The nuclear doctrine used in Asia, such as it existed, was one of revenge. There was no carefully balanced Mutually Assured Destruction, as in the Cold War, in which the United States and the Soviet Union would be deterred from attacking each other because nothing would be left of their countries once it was over. Nor were there checks on each other's nuclear arsenals. India and Pakistan were as the Cold War was in the 1950s, not in the 1980s. Within two minutes, an Indian city could be destroyed by a nuclear weapon, in which case Hari Dixit would unleash enough fire-power to eradicate Pakistan as a nation.

'Missiles on re-entry. Rajendra [phased-array radar] switched on. Akash [long-range surface-to-air missile] launched. One ... Two ... Three and Four.' India had deployed one of its six Russian-built integrated theatre-defence systems in Srinagar, throwing a 500-square kilo-metre protective umbrella around the city. The other five expanded the umbrella to cover the whole of northern Indian, threatened by Pakistan. The radar could detect an incoming ballistic missile 65 kilometres away, and the defending missile could hit descending targets 24 kilometres high, with an in-built active control mechanism which would guide it precisely onto the incoming Pakistani Shah-een. The system was meant to be able to track sixty-four targets simultaneously.

'Shaheen hit and destroyed.'

'One or two?'

'One, sir.'

'Chandra Reddy on the line.'

Many key Indian defence officials had remained outside the bunker, running operations on a war footing, but not protected from nuclear strike. Chandra Reddy, the Head of

External Intelligence, and the Foreign Minister Prabhu Purie were still working from South Block.

'I'm not responding,' said Dixit.

'Good. He wants you to retaliate,' said Reddy. 'We should do nothing.'

'Enemy missile ten seconds from impact, veering. It looks out of control.'

'Stay on the line,' said Dixit to Reddy.

'Impact, sir.'

'Where?'

'Military HQ. Unconfirmed. Yes. Military HQ. My God. No. Four impacts. Multiple warheads.'

'One has gone on the other side of the hill. Impact on Dal Lake market,' said Reddy. 'My God, thousands of people are there.'

Srinagar, Kashmir, India

Local time 1015 Monday 7 May 2007
GMT: 0445 Monday 7 May 2007

The fireball swept off the lawn of the Badami Bagh Cantonment with the wind, down towards the lake and into the market, sucking everything into its wake. The blasts of explosions from two separate warheads crushed together like the confluence of rivers. Barely anything survived in the first few seconds. Those on the outer fringes who did miraculously live spoke of the roaring winds of hell and the searing inferno which engulfed their loved ones in death. The flimsy buildings in central Srinagar caught light. Gas cylinders and fuel tanks blew up, as if smaller bombs had been planted in the most crowded streets. The victims tried to push their way out to open spaces. The weak were trampled to death. Stampedes took hold and panic swept through the city. Flames leapt into the sky, and after the enormous noise of explosions died down, screams for help could be heard, desperate, weak and sometimes horribly short and solitary until death took over. With their clothes in flames, many jumped into the cold waters of the Dal Lake only to be dragged down, or caught up in weeds and drowned there. The emergency services could do little. They could barely get into the streets, and had no equipment or medical services to deal with such a tragedy.

A single artillery shell or mortar landing in a crowded market place can do appalling damage. The destruction of a conventional missile warhead is unimaginable. The market was not a big one, nor was it buried within the warren of streets of old Srinagar, where the casualties would have been far higher. But it was by the Dal Lake, where traders set up stalls around the bus station, a place of transit, meeting, talking and buying, the first flavour of Kashmir which many visitors saw when they arrived.

More than two hundred soldiers died at the military headquarters, including the corps commander. By noon, it was clear that the missile strike had killed at least seven hundred Kashmiris in central Srinagar. Many more were expected to die, and by the end of the day the dreadful pictures of the aftermath of the attack were formulating the international policy which would last for generations.

Indian military HQ, Karwana, Haryana, India

Prabhu Purie, the Foreign Minister, and Chandra Reddy were on the line from Delhi with Hari Dixit and Chief of Army Staff, Unni Khrishnan. 'We have to kill his command and control centre,' said Hari Dixit.

'That is Chaklala, sir. Hamid Khan's bunker,' said Unni Khrishnan.

'Then we must strike it.'

'You could only be sure of success with a nuclear weapon.'

'Mani, what is your view?'

'Can't we bring in the Americans or the Russians and keep our own slate clean?'

'Chandraji?'

'He's made big blunder. My guess is he didn't intend to use multiple warheads. That was a cock-up. The missile we shot down was heading for the airfield. The one we failed to get was heading for the military headquarters. He would not have targeted the market. He has killed his own people. He could go one of two ways. Admit it and surrender. Or carry out another strike immediately to dampen the impact of this one. My guess is he's going to strike again.'

'Inside or outside Kashmir?'

'Impossible to say.'

Local time: 1155 Sunday 6 May 2007
GMT: 0455 Monday 7 May 2007

Question: President Hastings, the statements so far from the State Department and the Pentagon have not made clear where your support lies – with India or Pakistan. Could you clarify your position, please?

Hastings: I want a ceasefire then negotiations. But I want to say something about conflicts, and this one in particular. The grievances which caused this conflict go back to the partition of India in 1947. It is not a forward-looking issue, like the issues which tied us up during the Cold War. That was about the future, whether the political and economic system in the Western democracies or that of the Soviet Union was the more powerful one. The conflict between India and Pakistan is about the past. They have no issue with each other over their political systems and the basic concepts of democracy. This is not Pakistan fighting against the repression of Muslims in India as a whole. Or India defending Hindu rights in Pakistan. This war is about a piece of land called Kashmir. It's run by India, but claimed by Pakistan and it should have been sorted out as part of the overall independence deal, but it wasn't and that's why I'm standing here now.

It would be farcical if the American people were drawn into any kind of war over Kashmir, and we have to bear that in mind. A nuclear weapon might have been used, but the cause of the conflict remains the same.

Question: Sir, we're getting reports that Pakistan has launched a missile strike on the city of Srinagar in Kashmir.

It was conventional, but the Indians were seconds away from retaliating with a nuclear weapon.

Hastings: Yes. I saw those reports as I was coming here. Many innocent Indians have been killed and it might help me answer the first question, about which side I support. America and the American people support democracies. I spoke directly to General Hamid Khan about an hour ago. It is not my practice to talk with dictators, but these were exceptional circumstances. If you remember, President Clinton met directly with one of the former military rulers during his visit to South Asia in 2000. General Khan wanted my support in bringing about peace. I told the General that we needed an unequivocal declaration of a ceasefire. Hamid Khan's statement, which many of you might have heard, fell far short of that mark. Since then, he has launched a missile strike on Kashmir. It seems to me that we have a nightmare scenario of a desperate military dictator in a bunker with his finger on the nuclear button. In India, we have an elected Prime Minister, working with his democratically appointed ministers and institutions.

Question: Mr President, could you clarify—

Hastings: Sorry, Clarissa, for interrupting, but I want to add one detail, to give you an example of how this thing has played out over the last few hours. We are working with the Indians through normal channels, their ambassadors here and at the United Nations and their officials in Delhi. The Pakistani officials, on the other hand, say they have received no instructions from Islamabad. That situation speaks for itself, Clarissa.

Question: Yes. Thank you. Russia seems to be playing it neutral.

Hastings: Yes. I have spoken to President Gorbunov. We offered to help each other in whatever way would bring about peace quickest.

Question: But China seems to be taking a different line.

Hastings: Yes. And we expect it to. China is a long-standing ally of Pakistan's. It has a problem with India over Tibet. There is also healthy competition for these two great nations in their race for modernization. I know Joan Holden has been speaking to their Foreign Minister, Jamie Song, in Beijing and I don't see a problem with this. You are all probably more familiar with the way we worked with Russia in Europe and the Middle East. Our alliances might be different, but we are all working towards peace.

Question: Mr President, can you envisage any circumstances in which the United States will become militarily involved in this conflict?

Hastings: Only to save lives. And, I'm really sorry, I've just had a message that the Indian Prime Minister needs to speak to me urgently. I have to go.

RAF Upper Heyford, Gloucestershire, UK

Local time: 0530 Monday 7 May 2007

The suggestion of using the F-16 multi-role combat air-craft either from Incirlick in Turkey or one of the bases in the Gulf was dismissed in less than fifteen minutes. The host governments all had significant Islamic opinion to take into account. This strike was not worth upsetting it.

The second option, of using F-18 Hornets on board the 102,000 tonne USS *John C. Stennis* in the Gulf of Oman, was thrown out equally quickly. The aircraft's range was 1,600 kilometres and they could have completed their mission by refuelling 500 kilometres from the carrier and again on the way back, using tankers from Kuwait and Turkey. But with both options, American pilots' lives would be put at unnecessary risk. The aircraft would be over hostile territory, and liaising with Indian pilots who might have to provide cover would be impossible.

The aircraft chosen for the mission was a single Ameri-can B-52 bomber flying out of RAF Upper Heyford in England. It carried twenty BGM-109 Conventional Air-borne Cruise Missiles (CACMs) with special warheads. For four decades, the B-52 had been the mainstay of the American bomber force and when it was due to be finally scrapped in 2038 it would have been in service for eighty-two years. Technology had advanced tenfold since it flew its first mission. The B-52 was adapted accordingly and it remained the most versatile bomber in the American order of battle.

Shortly before it took off from the base in Gloucestershire, the crew saw the latest 116 Keyhole spy satellite photographs of the Rawalpindi cantonment area, under which Hamid Khan operated from the Pakistani war room. Throughout the night, other equally sensitive satellites had passed over the area, with optical equipment which cut through the darkness.

They also had access to special Doppler radar imagery gathered by a stealth AWACs aircraft flying high above Rawalpindi. It was the first time the United States had used the facility in a real conflict situation. Known as Ground Penetrating Radar (GPR) it could produce three-dimensional images of objects as far as 45 metres below ground or sea. Trials were as yet incomplete, but the implications were already enormous. Not only would it allow surveillance inside enemy bunkers, such as suspected nuclear facilities in North Korea or biological weapons bunkers in Iraq, it might also make the submarine, particularly those carrying nuclear missiles, a far more vulnerable weapon of war.

Ideally, the GPR is used on board a helicopter. The stiller it is the clearer the picture. But over enemy territory this is too risky. So the images fed back to Washington of the General Headquarters in Rawalpindi were not as clear as they could be, but the information was enough to characterize the target and therefore determine whether the special warheads to be used would be able to take it out of action. The underground tunnels linking the various Pakistani bunkers showed up clearly and confirmed for the first time the actual command and control centre being used by Hamid Khan.

The Americans' main concern was that Khan had taken to a mobile strategic communications system, of which the Pakistani DEFCOM was the most sophisticated, embracing both satellite and microwave links. It remained in the field and, as yet, undetected. Given that Khan was also head of government, he might have opted to use the Joint Operations Command (JOC), the centre for the Joint Services, which was better placed for direct liaison with the civilian government. But it was equally possible that Khan would feel more at home and physically secure on his own turf, which would be the General Headquarters in Rawalpindi – and this was confirmed by the GPR.

Analysts had picked out images of movement within that bunker and other specific targets believed to be the entrances, the control tower at the airfield, the officers' mess, the clinic and others. In one picture, three men were photographed going into the clinic, carrying boxes of supplies.

Indian Mirage-2000Hs, MiG-27MLs and SU30s continued to pound Pakistan air defences, and shortly before the B-52 was ready to launch aircraft descended to destroy key buildings in the complex, using fire and deep-penetration bombs.

The B-52 flying outside of Pakistan airspace over international waters south of Karachi carried twelve missiles externally and they launched those first. They were followed by four more from the bomb bay and four were held back in reserve. The type of warhead had never been used in modern conflict. John Hastings had told Dixit that the United States would not be involved in any offensive lethal action against Pakistan. But on advice from Alvin Jebb, the American Defence Secretary, he had agreed to use non-lethal weapons to neutralize Hamid Khan's command and control of nuclear weapons. Jebb was keen to test the weapons in a combat situation which he saw as a perfect, high-profile use of non-lethal weapons.

As the Tomahawks exactly hit their target, there was no fireball or wrenching explosion. That had been carried out by the Indians. Instead, almost farcically, a thin, fog-like foam was dispersed over specific areas. Immediately, it began hardening and within minutes had become as immovable as concrete, sealing the exits to the bunker like a glue. The Indian bombs had left hundreds of anti-personnel mines on the ground, demanding an exhaustive process before Hamid Khan and his staff could be got out.

It was impossible to know what contingency plans – if any – Khan had drawn up for this type of attack. But American SIGINT operators confirmed that Pakistan's command and control structure had gone dead, leaving individual commanders to fend for themselves. There was no communication from Hamid Khan's bunker, and, only when the conflict had ended did it become clear what had happened to him.

Eastern Air Command, Shillong, India

Local time: 1100 Monday 7 May 2007
GMT: 0530 Monday 7 May 2007

'Pakistan neutralized,' read the encrypted message.

Air Marshal Commodore Ravi Thapar received it in the code which had still not been deciphered by the United States and European experts. It was a simple message, leading to a battle plan he had already drawn up. The Chinese forces which had pushed into Arunachal Pradesh would now be cut off from behind and then destroyed.

Part of it was revenge for the dreadful defeat China inflicted on India in 1962. Part of it was sensible military strategy. The key targets were the bridges north and south of the Burmese town of Namya Ra, cutting off supplies for the Chinese troops coming in from Lashio and Mytkyina. Airfields at Mogaung and Bhamo were hit, destroying Chinese aircraft on the ground and rendering the runways unusable for several hours.

Then, after several hours' lull in the front-line fighting, Indian artillery opened up on the Chinese positions. Chinese aircraft from bases in Tibet were intercepted by India fighters and engaged in dogfights, leaving the ground troops vulnerable. Sensing defeat, the Chinese troops began a tactical withdrawal into Burma, but were cut off by three thousand Indian troops landed by helicopter and parachute behind the Chinese lines. Indian ground-attack aircraft took out Chinese anti-aircraft positions, then moved in with cannon fire, strafing the positions and the light armour the Chinese had brought in with them.

Once the element of surprise had ended, the Chinese

dug themselves in well. But they were running low on ammunition and supplies and it would be only a matter of time before they were defeated. Their attackers fought ferociously, taking huge risks in the mountainous terrain. In the first hours of fighting, they refused to take prisoners, even after the Chinese had shown the white flag.

Downing Street, London

Local time: 0600 Monday 7 May 2007

'**We're going over** to Downing Street now, where Anthony Pincher is on the line. This is the Prime Minister's first interview since news of the Pakistani nuclear attack broke just under six hours ago. Thank you for joining us, Prime Minister. I know you've been up all night. We have heard about the terrible Pakistani missile strike on Kashmir. Can you tell us the latest news about that?'

'Thank you, Michael,' said Pincher to the early morning presenter on BBC 5 Live radio. 'That was a tragedy, but thankfully things have moved on, to try to stop more bloodshed. As I speak an operation is underway to prevent any further use by Pakistan of nuclear weapons and, hopefully, force a ceasefire. I can't say too much about it, but I am convinced that this measure will go a long way to de-escalating the crisis.'

'Are any British troops involved?'

'No. Not in this operation.'

'You're implying, Prime Minister, that British troops are involved in another operation.'

'I'm not implying anything, except to say that the task force headed by HMS *Ocean* currently in the Bay of Bengal has been put on standby should it be needed.'

'But we are clearly supporting India, then?'

'As callers to your overnight programme have been pointing out, India is a democracy. We hope it doesn't come to supporting one side or another, but Great Britain supports democratic rule against any other.'

Prime Minister's Office, Singapore

Local time: 1430 Monday 7 May 2007
GMT: 0600 Monday 7 May 2007

'**John, I would** like you to regard this as a personal call,' said Anthony Pincher.

'Understood,' said Singapore's Prime Minister, John Chiu. 'I have just been listening to you on the radio. It appears you have taken sides already.'

'That's what I wanted to discuss, particularly Burma.'

'Yes. I couldn't imagine that a tiny city state like Singapore would be consulted on the greater geopolitical issues. What about Myanmar?' said Chiu, correcting Pincher on the official name of the country.

'There is a feeling among members of the Five Power Defence Agreement that China's use of Burma – or Myanmar – as a military staging post for invasion threatens the stability of South-East Asia.'

'Which members? Britain? Australia and New Zealand?'

'So far.'

'You want to know my view?'

'Yes.'

'It's bigger than Myanmar, Anthony, and you know it. That is what makes it so bloody complicated. I believe that ultimately China is trying to find a way of controlling the Straits of Malacca. The Dragon Strike campaign was merely a test of that. The Straits are one of the world's most strategic choke points. Through them travels all the Middle East oil supplies for Japan and China, which in ten or twenty years' time will become more and more reliant on oil imports. They have, therefore, a practical and geopolitical motivation for eyeing the Straits, and that combination has been the start of many wars. Should they ever succeed, they would also have access to the oil fields at the mouth of the Straits, and they would have to neutralize Singapore as we are by far the biggest port in the area.'

'How far away are they from achieving their goal?'

'The whole equation has changed in the past twenty-four hours, so it's impossible to say. The Malacca project has been underway now for fifteen years. In 1992, the Central Military Commission laid out the principle of creating a blue-water fleet, with an aircraft carrier and submarines. Internal documents committed China to building "the world's most powerful navy". A year later another document was issued outlining a doctrine known as "high-sea defence". It states that China could no longer accept the Indian Ocean as only an ocean of the Indians. I think the precise words were that the Indian Ocean was not India's ocean. In 1996, the plan was given a boost, or jolt of reality if you like, when the Americans sent a carrier group to the Straits of Taiwan and the Chinese realized they had nothing at all which could touch it. That alone eradicated any argument within the Communist Party about not pushing ahead with naval modernization.

'Now, you asked about Myanmar. China needs access at both sides of the Straits. To the east it can achieve it by setting up base on one of the Spratly Islands. To the west, it plans to use the two Cocos Islands and the sprawling Hanggyi Island naval base which are at either end of the Prepari Channel. Hanggyi Island is on the Irrawaddy delta coastline. Great and Little Cocos Islands are 240 kilometres to the south, and barely 15 kilometres from India's North Andaman Island. If you look at the map these are key strategic positions for monitoring shipping in and out of the Malacca Straits. Since 1994, Myanmar has officially leased the Cocos Islands to China. On Great Cocos it has built a maritime reconnaissance and electronic intelligence installation station. One of its main jobs is to monitor the Indian missile test site at Balasore on the Orissa coast. The Great Cocos Station has a 50-metre antenna tower, radar sites and other facilities for signals and electronic intelligence gathering with about a hundred Chinese staff working there. They've also dredged the harbour – it used to be a bleak fishing village – so that it can now take the 4,200 tonne *Ludu*-class destroyer and anything smaller.

'The Hanggyi Island base is far more sophisticated and has been built to take an aircraft carrier when China gets one, and strategic ICBM submarines. But it doesn't stop there. China has modernized ports in Sittwe in Western Arakan state and Zedetkyi Kyun or St Matthew's Island in the south-east, which directly threatens the northern entrance of the Malacca Straits. Basically, the Chinese military run the whole of that western coastline. It has equipped Myanmar with two *Jianghu*-class frigates with surface-to-surface missiles, *Hainan*-class fast-attack craft, other warships, crew to operate them and squadrons of fighter aircraft, the J-7 and A-5M ground-attack aircraft. It has rebuilt the Meiktila airbase, near Mandalay, and the smaller airfield at Lashio in the north-east. Both of those have been used in the operation against India. It has upgraded the road and rail system from its southern city of Kunming in Yunnan to a number of Myanmar ports – Akyab, Kyaukpyu and Mergui and others. The whole programme is run from the Chengdu Military Division, the same one which handles Tibet.

'Myanmar, or Burma as you call it, is nothing less than a military colony of China. So you ask me if Singapore is worried. What do you think, John? I'm as worried as hell.'

'I have an idea which might help,' said Pincher softly, sensing the frustration in John Chiu's voice.

'I'm not sure I want to hear it.'

'And it doesn't go further than the two of us?'

'Agreed.'

'Under the authority of the Five Power Defence Agreement, would your amphibious rapid deployment group want to take part in an operation to neutralize Chinese influence in the Indian Ocean?'

'You're serious?'

'Yes.'

'The agreement doesn't cover it.'

'It does if the stability of Singapore and Malaysia is threatened. From what you've just told me, it appears that stability is very much under threat.'

John Chiu was silent for at least a minute. 'If we have to choose a dominant regional power other than the United States, we would go for China over Japan, you know. We could never accept Japanese dominance after what they did during the Second World War.'

'I'm not sure the choices are so stark.'

'My answer, Anthony, is no. Singapore is a predominantly Chinese state. We will remain neutral in the international row. But you have my personal support and I suggest you try up the road in Malaysia. Their cultural Chinese links are far more tenuous than ours.'

'Understood.'

'But there is one other piece of intelligence we have picked up in the past three hours. It appears that President Lin Chung-ling of Taiwan is planning a formal declaration of independence.'

It took a few seconds for Anthony Pincher to change his focus to a completely different part of the world. He had thought he was fairly fluent in foreign affairs, but, as yet, he hadn't factored Taiwan into any of his thinking. 'Why on earth?' he asked.

'If he feels that China is sufficiently diverted by Tibet, India and Pakistan, he will sneak it into an interview scheduled with CNN within the next twenty-four hours.'

Prime Minister's Office, Canberra, Australia

'**The squad will** comprise two Australians, two New Zealanders, two Malays and the rest will be British. It will be under British command. All those involved have trained with the Special Boat Squadron. Our men have also spent time with the American navy SEALS.'

'The Malaysians are on board?' the Australian Prime Minister, Malcolm Smith, asked his Defence Minister, Keith Backhurst.

'They were very keen. The men have no identification and will be carrying a cyanide capsule in case of capture. I think some of it is one-upmanship over Singapore's refusal to take part.'

Smith laughed. 'All right. Let's do it.'

'There's one other piece of house-keeping we should wrap up at the same time,' said Backhurst. 'The Chinese also have a SIGINT site around Ban Sop Bau in Laos. It was used to monitor Vietnam, but since those hostilities have quietened down, they concentrate on picking up traffic between the South China Sea and the Indian Ocean. If we take it out, Australia will lead with the Thai and Filipino Special Forces. A unit left the peace-keeping force in Timor for Darwin yesterday and is about to arrive in Bangkok.'

'You are keen to do this?'

'The Timor campaign in 1999 was a turning point for many of us, Prime Minister. It was the first time we risked open hostility with an Asian neighbour in order to achieve a greater aim. People died, but strategically and politically it worked. There is a sense that we must take charge of our own security and the expansion of China is a key element of this.'

Great Cocos Island Naval Base, Myanmar/Burma

Local time: 1830 Monday 7 May 2007
GMT: 1300 Monday 7 May 2007

Crew from HMS *Ocean* slipped the Special Boat Squadron's Very Slender Vessel into the water from the amphibious loading hatch. Luckily the sea was choppy, stirred up by the foreplay of yet another cyclone heading into the Bay of Bengal. The waves would help conceal the VSV from radar operators and the moody dark clouds hid moonlight which could have lit them up in their final approaches to the base.

Sailing at 15 knots due south, the *Ocean* had taken just under a day to go from Cox's Bazaar to a point 80 kilometres off Cape Negrais, the most westerly point of the Irrawaddy Delta landfall. The *Ocean* slowed but didn't stop to let off the boat. Decoy radio communications were carried out in an easily breakable code, which British naval intelligence had confirmed that both the Chinese and the Indians had the ability to decipher. Messages concentrated on arrangements to sail west to join up with the American carrier group led by the USS *Ronald Reagan*.

The VSV was like a 16 metre-long, covered canoe, with a 3-metre cross-section so that it could punch its way through the waves swirling off the coast of Burma. This was an all-weather vessel. Whatever the conditions, it could put to sea and the storm approaching 320 kilometres to the south was not a deterrent. The two 750hp engines roared into life, and even in the heavy swell it was soon heading east towards the Burmese coast at almost 60 knots. The special design enabled the 30g impact usually experienced by speed-boat passengers to be reduced to only 3g, meaning that the men would arrive fresh for action and not exhausted by the buffeting of the waves or even suffering from sea-sickness. The eleven commandos were in a sealed section strapped into hydraulically braced seats. The crew was in a separate cockpit, slightly raised from the main cabin.

The *Ocean* had slowed where it did as a decoy to the Chinese who were monitoring its movements. The most strategic base was at Hanggyi Island where satellites had detected the Chinese *Luhu*-class destroyer *Haikou*, and a *Jianghu*-class frigate, *Tianjin*, together with at least one surfaced *Kilo*-class submarine. Interestingly, the far more sophisticated *Sovremenny*-class frigates had not been sent through the Malacca Straits into the front line of any naval war. They would have been lost to the Indian navy, meaning that the ships in Hanggyi were dispensable.

But Hanggyi was too well defended and too active. Indian and Western intelligence agencies knew pretty much what went on there and if anything went wrong with the mission the men would be on their own, facing certain death or capture and torture.

Their target was the base at Great Cocos Island, 320 kilometres to the south, far more secret, far quieter and only a few kilometres from Indian territory, to which they could make their escape, if necessary. The mission was to blow up a ship if they found one, photograph the base and leave. Once the raid was underway, the Indians would be notified. A single compressed burst code word would be sent to the *Ocean*, 270 kilometres away, passed onto Operations Headquarters in Northwood in London and then to Delhi. The whole process would take fifteen seconds.

Eight kilometres north of Great Cocos the VSV slowed to 20 knots, lessening the spray it was putting up, and making it easier to hide in the troughs of the waves. The long, thin design of the hull made it almost invisible to radar. The engine was enclosed and the heat contained, making it far more difficult to pick out with thermal-imaging equipment. 450 metres out, the VSV cut her engines, and the commandos went into the water with wet-suits and breathing apparatus. The port was in the Alexandra Channel on the southern side of the island. Working with maps compiled from satellite photographs, the raiding party made landfall halfway down the sharp and rocky eastern coastline. The island was no more than 8 kilometres long and barely 1,500 metres wide. The men had a clear run for the first 275 metres before having to take out the first Chinese watch post, killing the two guards on duty with silenced pistols. They took the tunic off one of the bodies for intelligence to establish the Chinese units deployed. The beginning of the naval port was marked by construction work, wooded land freshly cut back, a crane and earth-moving equipment. They could make out the darkened silhouettes of two ships in the harbour and figures on guard on the decks. More surprising was the hull, the conning tower well aft and an unusually wide, flat section of the top of the hull.

Two commandos photographed it using infrared lenses and, as a backup, one camera on long exposure with ordinary low-light film. Others took positions to ensure a safe escape. Four divers slipped into the water. They swam in pairs, attached to each other by a buddy-line, relying on the line to relay signals.

Then the mission was discovered. One of the Malay frogmen had trouble with his set. It's thought there was a leak of the carbon dioxide chemical in the oxygen rebreather. The Malay, who was swimming with a New Zealander, managed to give the signal of drowsiness, which could end up with a black-out. There was a risk that the blackness of the water, the noises under the surface of ships, propellers, generators, boats passing overhead could lead to an anxiety attack. The New Zealander had to let the Malay get to the surface to breathe fresh air as soon as possible.

He kept his nerve for the few seconds needed to finish the job. Luckily, the ship had a metallic hull, meaning that he could set his magnetic limpet mine on a short fuse. It was later identified through photographs as an old *Jianghi*-class frigate. Only the registration number 533 was visible on the photographs, listing it as the 1,700 tonne *Shaoguan*. Once the mine was attached, he pushed up to the surface, helping the Malay as he swam. They came up using the curves of the hull around the area of the propeller for cover. But it was exactly the time that a searchlight flitted across the water, picking up the ripples, then the movement and finally reflecting off the glass of his face mask. It was bad luck, which could have happened to anyone.

When the divers failed to respond to his challenge, a Chinese guard opened fire. The New Zealander fired four shots with his special Heckler and Koch underwater silenced pistol. The commandos on land divided into two groups as planned in the event of interception. The two photographers plus two cover men back-pedalled to the place of landfall. They sent a single burst message to the VSV, which came in on full engines to pick them up. Nothing that the Chinese had in the base could catch them and it would have been useless to put up an aircraft. The VSV waited just 90 metres off-shore for a second message. If it did not receive it within fifteen minutes, it was to head back to the HMS *Ocean*.

The remaining commandos kept the Chinese troops pinned down with sniper fire, while the divers tried to escape. What happened next was one of the most remarkable stories in Special Forces operations. Two companies of Chinese troops were sent out against the three snipers, while the port was lit up with searchlights. The Malay frogman, still disorientated, was shot dead within seconds. The New Zealander cut the buddy-line and went deep, with the other pair of divers. A single burst message sent to the VSV was relayed on to *Ocean*, then to Britain's joint-operations command at Northwood. The British Defence Secretary, David Guinness, personally telephoned Unni Khrishnan, who broke normal protocol by contacting the Commander of the Far Eastern Fleet at Port Blair in the Andaman Islands. A high-speed interceptor boat, capable of 40 knots, headed out from its base at Landfall Island to the territorial boundary just south of Little Cocos Island. Reddy then spoke to Unni Khrishnan who ordered the scrambling of ground-attack aircraft from Port Blair. They were over Little Cocos within minutes, using cannon to spread confusion among the Chinese. What the pilots hadn't banked on was the effectiveness of the Chinese air-defence system, which shot down two Indian aircraft before being taken out.

At the height of the airstrikes the *Shaoguan* exploded in a wall of fire. The three surviving divers had cleared the area, surfaced and commandeered an ageing *Carpentaria*-class river patrol craft, shooting the lone Burmese guard from the water before boarding. The New Zealand diver took over the 20mm heavy machine gun while the other two started the engine. They were spotted as they were gathering speed heading south out of the harbour. The New Zealander opened fire and was killed in the return fire. After that the boat reached its maximum speed of just over 25 knots and had a clear run to Indian territorial waters.

Attempts to intercept the commandos with a Chinese

fast patrol boat from Little Cocos Island was cut short by an Indian MiG-27 pilot who blew it out of the water.

Of the three snipers, holding back the Chinese ground troops, one Malay was killed, an Australian escaped and another New Zealander was shot and captured. It was his anonymous face which would later appear on television screens throughout the world as China used him to try and change the course of the war.

Western Hills, Military Headquarters, China

President Tao chaired the meeting in the conference room which looked out onto the main operations centre of the Chinese military's war headquarters. General Leung Liyin, Defence Minister and General Secretary of the Central Military Commission, was giving a gloomy summary of China's incursion into India. Also present were Tang Siju, the General Staff strategic planner, who was mainly tied up with Tibet, and the Foreign Minister, Jamie Song.

'We are cut off in Arunachal Pradesh,' said General Leung Liyin. 'The Indians have moved their airpower from the western front with Pakistan to the east against us. Our satellites show Indian aircraft at Kalaikunda, Barrakpore, Hashimara and Bagdogra in West Bengal and Tezpur and Chabua in Assam. Airports in Sikkim, in Gauhati and Jorhat in Assam and Itanagar in Arunachal Pradesh are supporting fighter and transport detachments. The main air-defence squadron is operating out of Hashimara, using MiG-23s and MiG-27s with maximum weapons loads because of the short range of the strikes. Indian airstrikes have cut the road north and destroyed the bridges, and are wearing down our positions. Artillery barrages are continuous. They have airdropped thousands of troops behind our lines. Some are Tibetans from the Special Frontier Force, which India said it had disbanded. None has been taken alive. They commit suicide with cyanide capsules rather than face capture.'

'Will we hold the territory?' said President Tao.

'At the present level we can hold for two or three days. We need to bring aircraft in from the north and the east to use against the paratroopers. Until we do that we cannot begin to repair the bridges.'

'It would mean weakening our defences along the Taiwan Straits?'

'Yes. If we were to bring an effective force to rout the Indians.'

'The Prime Minister of Singapore kindly telephoned me warning that President Lin might exploit our difficulties. He didn't say what, but Singaporean intelligence is second to none in East Asia. He also warned that our South-East Asian neighbours were uneasy about Myanmar's role in our dispute with India.'

'It's none of their business,' said Tang.

'Comrade Song, could you let me have your assessment.'

'It sounds as if Singapore is speaking with a forked tongue. Naturally, Taiwan will be planning the most effective measures to humiliate us. You don't need to be a spy to know that. I would also expect the Association of South-East Asian Nations to be worried about our relationship with Myanmar now that conflict has broken out. What I'm unsure of is whether Prime Minister John Chiu is acting as a messenger for the United States or on his own initiative. His warning, however, points up dangers in continuing our campaign.'

'We must also remember that as soon as we appear weak, internal forces of dissent might appear,' said Tang. 'I would forfeit Arunachal Pradesh and concentrate on Tibet and Taiwan.'

'Are we in danger of losing Myanmar's support?' asked Tao.

'It depends on Japan and ASEAN,' said Jamie Song. 'If ASEAN withdraws its tacit support for the regime and if

Japan withdraws its aid programme, the regime may look at its options.'

'I disagree,' said General Leung. 'Myanmar is run by a military government which relies on us for its international defence and its weapons. If Myanmar abandons us at this time, the government will fall within weeks.'

'How can you be sure of it?' said Song.

'I will make sure it happens, and they know it.' General Leung broke off abruptly as an aide walked into the room with a message on a computer printout. The meeting was silent as he read it, then passed it onto President Tao. 'This is a signals report from Little Cocos Island. The naval base at Great Cocos Island is under attack.'

'By India?' said Song

'That is unclear. It says that one of the enemy has been captured and he has a white face.'

President Tao slammed his hand on the table and shouted at Jamie Song: 'Call Ambassador Overhalt and tell him that while I have tolerated direct American participation in the action against Pakistan, I will not tolerate it attacking our military bases. I want a full explanation within thirty minutes, or we'll send a missile into Guam.'

Song retreated to a quieter spot to call Reece Overhalt. When he returned to the meeting, he said: 'The Americans know nothing about the raid. They were not involved.'

The Kremlin, Moscow, Russia

Local time: 1700 Monday 7 May 2007
GMT: 1400 Monday 7 May 2007

Instead of angrily picking up the telephone, President Gorbunov of Russia paced his office, hands behind his back, with music from Tchaikovsky's '1812 Overture' playing loudly around him. He had just received news of the American non-lethal airstrike on Pakistan and was watching BBC and CNN commentators announcing that Pakistan no longer existed as a functioning nation. The UN, backed by the European Union and the United States, had revealed that it was drawing up plans for running an interim government with a peace-keeping force of thirty thousand to ensure basic facilities such as power and water were functioning. Gorbunov had just absorbed that when another message came through about the Indian airstrikes against Chinese positions in Arunachal Pradesh, andthat was followed up by news of the raid on Great Cocos Island.

Gorbunov's bipolar world of the United States and Western Europe balanced by a strategic alliance of Russia, China and India was collapsing salami-style, slice by slice, with no defining event. This was why Gorbunov was deep in thought, because if no single event was great enough to force him to act, he would have to decide where the point of no return lay. If he waited beyond that, Russia would lose any power it had, switching within hours from the role of statesman in an unstable world to that of a pariah blocking peace.

He debated as to whether he should first call President

Tao in Beijing, Hari Dixit in India or John Hastings in the United States. Alternatively, he could muster support from the second-rank powers such as Iran, Syria, Indonesia or even muddy the waters by talking to Anthony Pincher in London, the French President, Jacques Duquan or the German Chancellor, Willhelm Braun.

If Gorbunov knew anything about politicians, it was their inability to handle embarrassment in a way which few military men would contemplate. A blindness enveloped a politician in a corner, and the two men fighting in the scramble for Asia were politicians through and through. The man with the most to lose was President Tao in Beijing, because Chinese culture had promoted shame high on the league table of faults. They called it 'face', and a Chinese losing face was like a Russian losing his soul. While Russia was still searching for her soul, China was close to becoming embarrassed internationally, and that would make her the most dangerous country in the world.

President Tao had only made one misjudgement in his planning, and even then the odds of events unfolding as they did were high. Tao had not anticipated India's ability to move its airpower from Pakistan to the eastern front at precisely the time China's forces inside India were so vulnerable. It was an easy mistake to make. Very few analysts would have predicted America's use of non-lethal weapons against Hamid Khan – particularly when he had pledged not to make another tactical nuclear strike. But then, Gorbunov himself was taken aback when Khan launched the missile into Srinagar. Such were the patterns of war, and it was a war which might be far from over.

The only man who could let the Chinese down without embarrassment was Hari Dixit. Gorbunov's call came through as Dixit was flying from the bunker in Haryana back to Delhi, the nuclear threat from Pakistan over. It was

a disjointed conversation, picking up the crackle of the
helicopter's intercom.

'Can you call it quits with China, Hari? Make peace.
Pakistan is defeated. There's no reason to fight.'

'If you can broker it, Vlad, I'll do it. We can't give
away Kashmir and we can't expel the Dalai Lama. We
can negotiate the border disputes, starting with reducing
troop levels. We can negotiate what they're doing in
Myanmar.'

'Can you give them an honourable withdrawal from
Arunachal Pradesh?'

'I can hardly hear you, Vlad. Tell President Tao that I'll
order a ceasefire now, right now, as long as his troops don't
try and fight their way out. If he agrees to back off and talk,
then we can wind everything down.'

The line to Beijing was much clearer and the Russian
President was patched through to the military headquarters
in the Western Hills.

'India has called a unilateral ceasefire in Arunachal
Pradesh,' Gorbunov told Tao. 'You can withdraw to the
former border, claim victory if you want, and then begin
talks on everything else.'

'You don't understand, Admiral Gorbunov. It's very
difficult,' said Tao slowly.

'Then explain it to me.'

'We are within a hair's breadth of losing Tibet unless we
send in the army like you had to in Chechnya. The
insurgency is far more entrenched than we had ever
thought. The SFF and other rebels are using India as their
base. It would be impossible for us to make peace with
India while this is going on.'

Gorbunov had not been directly involved in the
Chechnya campaign – but he was well aware of the deeply
entrenched national sentiment involved. Tao would prefer

to lose in Arunachal Pradesh rather than be seen to compromise in Tibet.

When Gorbunov called Hari Dixit again, the Indian Prime Minister had arrived in his office in Delhi's South Block. Much of the rioting had given way to celebrations, but buildings in Connaught Place were smouldering and communal killings were still continuing.

'Will you move in on the Tibetan bases? At least make a show of doing it.'

'While China is occupying our territory, it's politically very difficult. We have about twenty million Buddhists in India. They are only two per cent of the population, but it is a significant number of people. The Tibetan cause has a huge resonance here. There's also a growing anger about China's support for Pakistan. It might be defeated now. But it could rise up again and it did resort to using a nuclear weapon.'

'On Pakistani soil,' interjected Gorbunov.

'I'm not debating, Vlad, I'm explaining to you the issues with which we have to deal, so that you might be able to see a way to broker through a peace. If I announced a crackdown on Tibetan exiles, while invading Chinese troops were still on our soil, I'm not sure the Indian people would allow it. I'm not sure the party would, or the administration.'

'You mean you couldn't get it through?'

'I honestly don't think I could. On top of that, there would be an outcry from the Hollywood human rights activists on Tibet. That is not important domestically, but it has a huge impact internationally.'

'Tell me what you need, then.'

'As soon as Tao gets off our turf, I will reaffirm our policy of not allowing Tibetan exiles to partake in armed activity on Indian soil. I'll reinforce the border, put up air patrols and pass on information to Chinese intelligence. In return, he would have to allow an international human rights mission with a substantive Indian component to visit Lhasa and report on the consequences of the uprising.'

'And you'll keep the ceasefire?'

'At least until you get back to me.'

Before talking to Tao again, Gorbunov telephoned John Hastings in the White House. 'I think I have the makings of a peace agreement, but I need your guarantee that America will stay out until it's fixed.' Gorbunov outlined what he had brokered so far.

'Would Tao send the army into Tibet, Chechnya-style, or is he posturing?'

'We've been in a similar position,' said the Russian President. 'My bet is that he would move in, secure the territory again and pick up the pieces later. It would be twenty years before Tibetans get back the level of freedom they even have now. From the little I know of the American democratic process, it would put you in a very difficult position.'

'That could be the understatement of the year. You have my word we will give you the space to try to push through an agreement. Good luck.'

Prime Minister's Office, Wellington, New Zealand

Local time: 0500 Tuesday 8 May 2007
GMT: 1700 Monday 7 May 2007

Harriet Sheehan, the Prime Minister of New Zealand, looked at the photographs on her desk and felt the pressure of the people at the meeting for a decision. It showed the bruised face of Michael Hall, the SBS New Zealand commando sniper, who stayed behind on the Cocos Islands so his colleagues could escape. He had been shot in the leg and captured. The picture had been taken from a video, first released through the Burmese Embassy in Bangkok to the television news agencies and then broadcast around the world. The video showed Hall being jeered at by local citizens, and protected by Burmese troops. Then he was sitting at a table eating with the troops. The audio was clear and the Burmese conversation had already been translated. Sheehan felt that odd twinge of national pride when it became clear that Hall was living through his capture with true grit. The enemy had no idea of Hall's identity or his nationality. He could have been a Serb mercenary for all they knew, and despite clear signs of torture, Hall had not spoken once.

The New Zealand Defence Minister, Benjamin Leigh, broke the silence. 'The dead frogman was a Malay with no identification. I suggest, Prime Minister, that we say nothing whatsoever.'

'What about Hall's family?'

'They are in Palmerston North,' said Leigh. 'They are on side. Hall is dedicated to his work, so we don't expect problems from friends. If there are, we will cross that bridge when it happens.'

'And the British are taking the flak?' said Sheehan.

'Correct. Given our sensitive relationship with South-East Asia, if we can keep this quiet, so much the better.'

'We have one dead and one captured from the operation,' said Sheehan.

'I think it proves that this country can play with the biggest when the chips are down.'

Downing Street, London

There was a second set of photographs from the Cocos Islands raid which was classified for even the highest officials in the New Zealand government. Ever since New Zealand banned nuclear-armed warships from its waters in the eighties, it had been cut out of much of the intelligence loop. 'It appears this could be more serious than the capture of Michael Hall,' said Pincher, examining the picture taken with the infrared vision camera of the submarine surfaced next to the Great Cocos Island jetty.

'It dived as soon as firing broke out,' said John Stopping. 'According to naval intelligence, its permanent home is at Tsing Tao, the headquarters of the North Sea Fleet. In December last year it sailed down to Zhejiang, South Sea Fleet base, and was tracked by the USS *Hampton*, an American *Los Angeles*-class submarine. As far as we were aware, it was still at Zhejiang, but – to the embarrassment of the Americans more than anyone – it slipped out and no one knows when.'

'How?' said David Guinness, the Defence Secretary.

'Another *Los Angeles*-class submarine was redeployed from gate-keeping duties on Zhejiang because of budget cuts in February. The *Xia* must have gone out some time after that. The Malacca Straits are too shallow to send a submarine through submerged. It probably went through at night under cloud cover in the wake of a Chinese freighter to conceal its signature. Or it might have taken the longer route through the Sunda Straits, which divide

Java and Sumatra. Either way it has got into the Indian Ocean theatre undetected.'

'I'm sorry,' said Christopher Baker to John Stopping. 'I don't see how one Chinese submarine changes the situation as dramatically as you make out. We knew the Chinese maintain naval bases in Burma.'

Defence Secretary David Guinness had never rated the Foreign Secretary's intelligence highly. 'This is a photograph of a Chinese *Xia*-class type 92 strategic missile submarine from the 9th Submarine Fleet,' he told Baker bluntly. 'John Stopping has circulated the brief, of which you must have a copy. In peacetime, the *Xia* comes under the command of the People's Liberation Army – Navy. In wartime, it is commanded through the Central Military Commission, of which President Tao is the chairman. We presume the *Xia* is now under wartime command. It could be armed with the JL-2 submarine-launched ballistic missile. JL stands for Ju Lang, meaning Giant Wave, and its land-based equivalent is the DF-31 – DF meaning Dong Fang or East Wind. NATO knows it as the CSS-NX-4 with a range of 5,000 miles. It would either be kitted with three or four multiple re-entry warheads of up to 90 kilotons each, or a single warhead of 250 kilotons. This is a new SLBM system which was fitted in 1999, and if it works it would be comparable to our three-stage solid fuel submarine-launched Trident C-4.

'Up until now the *Xia*-class submarine has never been known to sail outside of the South China Sea. It is not clear whether this was because of operational difficulties or whether the Chinese, aware of Western and Russian anti-submarine warfare capabilities in the Pacific theatre, chose to keep their powder dry. In 1985, shortly after the first missile test from a submerged *Xia*, there was an intelligence report through Japan that the vessel had been lost, but this was found out to be misinformation planted by the Chinese. The type 094 photographed at the Great Cocos base was first deployed in 2003. The JL-2 was successfully tested in February 2004.

'It is possible that the *Xia* could be carrying the shorter range two-stage solid-propellant missile the JL-1, for which Nato's specification is CSS-NX-3. It had its first successful test in April 1982, from a *Golf*-class submarine, followed by a launch from the *Xia* in 1985, when we were told the vessel had been lost. The first successful *Xia* launch was September 1988. It is possible that the Chinese don't trust the bigger missile. The JL-1's range is just over 1,000 miles, which would give it a good range into southern and central India.'

'This is a nuclear missile?' the Prime Minister confirmed.

'Correct. Or at least the option is there. What this picture shows is that China has moved its nuclear threat from land-based to sea-based and added an extra theatre of war to its inventory.'

'And the situation right now is that we don't know where this submarine is.'

Local time: 1230 Monday 7 May 2007
GMT: 1730 Monday 7 May 2007

'If it's armed with the JL-1 and Beijing wants to threaten a substantive population centre, then it would be heading towards the eastern coastline,' said Alvin Jebb. 'It was photographed four hours ago, after which it dived. If it is travelling at 20 knots, it would be eighty miles north-west of Great Cocos Island.' Jebb put his finger on a map of the Indian Ocean spread out on the table and circled the spot. 'This is known as the area of probability where the *Xia* would be. The British have sent down their *Triumph* nuclear-powered attack submarine and the Australian *Collins*-class *Sheean*, which is diesel-electric. Luckily, they were with the HMS *Ocean* task force, about 200 miles north of Great Cocos Island. The *Triumph* has a dive speed of 32 knots. The *Sheean*'s is only 20 knots. They are the best chance we have at the moment of finding the *Xia*. The *Ronald Reagan* carrier group is still heading north, but is only off the coast of southern India. It could be another two days before it gets close to the area of probability.'

'What do the Indians have?' asked John Hastings.

'There is the *Bombay*, a *Delhi*-class destroyer inside the area of probability, which has begun searches, but its equipment is limited. The main eastern naval base is at Vishakhapatman. The *Godavari*-class frigate *Brahmaputra* left there two hours ago, together with the *Shankul* diesel-electric submarine. I might add that Indian submarine capability is not good.'

'And our chances of finding it?' said Hastings.

'If we are talking about the shorter range JL-1 scenario, there is a possibility, but it's remote. If the Xia is carrying the long-range JL-2 it could have gone anywhere from the Great Cocos and still be a threat to anywhere in India. The chances of finding it then are almost impossible. Or, if President Tao believes he has time on his hands, he could have sent the Xia, even with the JL-1, due south, with the view to getting it to double back on itself and confuse our search.'

'If the Chinese know that we know they have the Xia in the Bay of Bengal,' said Joan Holden, 'shouldn't we quit playing diplomatic cat and mouse, call President Tao and ask him what he's playing at?'

Hastings shook his head. 'A bad idea, I think. It would give him so much more leverage if I make the call. Let's try and find it first. I can't see any motive whatsoever for Tao to launch a nuclear strike against India. If he's posturing, let him posture for a while.'

Zhongnanhai, Beijing, China

The Indian ceasefire was open-ended and unilateral. President Tao had finished yet another conversation with the Russian President, whose peace brokering had become bogged down in detail.

'Hari Dixit will not hold on for ever,' warned Gorbunov. 'You will have to give him something.'

'Han Chinese are being slaughtered in Lhasa, Shigaze, Gyangze and Rutog. Those are just the places we know about. The Tibetans are getting their arms from India. They are going into Chinese areas, killing people and burning their houses. If you want, Vlad, send a Russian television crew in to show the world the atrocities that these so-called innocent Tibetans are committing. Do you remember Kosovo, how the Albanians drove out the Serbs after NATO had won their war for them? Well, the Chinese people feel the same about Tibet. We have done more to raise the quality of life for Tibetans than any other nation and we are being repaid with an orgy of killing. As the leader of China, I cannot agree peace with India until that stops. It would be impossible.'

Tao now looked out on the Central Sea from one of his offices, the smaller room which he used for thinking and which was decorated with some of his very personal momentos. It would take perhaps an hour at the most for Gorbunov to talk to Hari Dixit, who would have to call an end to the ceasefire. Just as Tao could not surrender in Arunachal Pradesh while the Tibetan uprising continued,

the Indian Prime Minister could not move against the Tibetan fighters while Chinese troops were in Arunachal Pradesh. Both men had painted themselves into a corner, and neither's bluff had yet been called.

Briefly, Tao wondered whether he could have acted in any other way, but concluded he could not. Ultimately, India was to blame. Had it disbanded the Special Frontier Force years ago, the Tibetans would never have had the resources to stage an uprising. The question now was not to look back, but to devise a way that China could win.

The People's Liberation Army had grown up on the doctrine of *yilie shengyou*, pitting the inferior against the superior. Despite the move towards missiles, submarines and high-technology warfare, that doctrine was very much in place. It assumed that China would opt to fight wars which other powers might not. It would take the risk of going into battle when it was not quite ready and win on courage and imagination. Without *yilie shengyou*, the Communist Party would never have defeated the Nationalists in 1949. After that, the Chinese Communist Party adopted another doctrine, of self-defence counter-attack, meaning that when it thought war was inevitable it should be fought on enemy and not Chinese territory. This was the pattern in the Korean War of 1950, against India in 1962 and against Vietnam in 1979. In China it was known 'to attack outside the door' or 'to strike beyond the gates'. The policy was loosely known as *xianfa zhiren*, which also meant that China would make the first strike and gain the initiative. But the psychology remained unchanged. China saw itself not as an expansionist power, but an inward-looking nation under threat, merely trying to protect itself.

With that doctrine in mind and Russian President Gorbunov's initiative stalled, Tao was considering at what level a strike should be made in order to achieve his goal. He

needed a quick end to the conflict, preferably one which would bring the international community back on side. It was known as *yizhan ershang*, winning a victory with one strike. The question facing Tao was where should he deliver that blow.

Kilo-class submarine 0821, type 877EKM, Bay of Bengal

Local time: 0147 Tuesday 8 May 2007
GMT: 2017 Monday 7 May 2007

The sonar operator on the Chinese *Kilo*-class submarine picked up the signature of a *Delhi*-class destroyer, but could not determine its exact identification as the *Bombay*. At 0207, the submarine came close enough to the surface to raise the satellite communication (SATCOM) mast, timed to catch signals from the Dong Feng Hong 6 Chinese military satellite passing overhead. The satellite was beaming down a constant brief message which was picked up by all Chinese military shipping and at the Menwith Hill Station in Britain and Pine Gap in Australia. Both were American-controlled facilities, run by the highly secretive National Security Agency (NSA), which eavesdropped on communications throughout the world. The order came as just one two-syllable word, *Houzi*, translating as 'monkey'.

Almost a thousand people worked at Pine Gap, near Alice Springs, intercepting telephone, radio and data links as well as satellite communications. The computer room alone was 5,600 square metres and there were more than twenty other service and support buildings. Yet when the Chinese satellite instruction made its debut in the massive Western listening station machine, there was nothing any-one could do to know what it meant. Only the senior Chinese army staff knew, together with the submarine commanders. Not even the communications officers who sent the message from the northern naval headquarters in Tsing Tao were aware of the significance of the signal.

It was luck more than anything that submarine 0821 had

to surface to pick up the twice-daily signal less than an hour after identifying the *Delhi*-class destroyer. It meant the Chinese could track the Indian warship for a minimum amount of time, lessening the risk of detection. The commander took the submarine just below the surface again, but within periscope depth. He verified the destroyer's position on the sonar and headed for the kill. Because it was dark and visibility was low, he decided to confirm the target with Electronic Surveillance Measures. He surfaced again using the ESM mast to absorb the electronic spectrum of the ship, taking in the destroyer's navigation radar, encrypted tactical communications and satellite communications. The data was cross-checked on the *Kilo*'s tactical weapons systems computer, giving the commander a near certain classification of the target. He verified that no unique signature had ever been taken of the Indian *Delhi*-class destroyers *Bangalore* and *Mysore*, deducing that his target must be one of those two ships.

She was sailing south-west on a course towards the Andaman Islands, her speed just under 20 knots, probably slowed because of the unsettled weather. There would be about four hundred men on board the ship, which was part of the cream of India's fleet. Unlike the Indian-designed and built Arjun battle tank or Light Combat indigenous fighter aircraft, the *Delhi* was considered a world-class warship and she sailed like a dream.

When he was 440 metres from the target, the submarine commander opted to go for an 'eyes only' attack using the periscope. Unlike the Americans, the Indians' skills at anti-submarine warfare were limited. The *Kilo* had been tracking the destroyer for more than an hour undetected. The two Westland Sea King helicopters remained strapped to the deck, indicating that the crew was not even suspecting an enemy presence.

When the submarine was 30 degrees on the bow of the target, the torpedo doors were opened. He would create a classic gyro-angle shot with a spread of three torpedoes to counteract the target speeding up or suddenly turning away. He waited until he was 900 metres from the destroyer, then he released the first torpedo at a bearing of 90 degrees to the target course. The second torpedo was fired at 5 degrees ahead of the bearing, and the third at 10 degrees behind.

As the 533mm torpedoes sped towards the target, the Indians had less than thirty seconds to react, which is why the commander had taken his vessel so dangerously close. The torpedoes did have a range of eight nautical miles and were wire-guided with active and passive homing at a speed of 40 knots. But the *Kilo* commander trusted little of that. He wanted to sight his target and fire.

The first torpedo, with an impact fuse, struck the destroyer aft, cutting the engines almost immediately. The second, with a proximity fuse, blew a hole amidships, sending uncontrollable litres of water streaming into the ship. If the destroyer had not been slowed immediately by the explosions, the third torpedo would have missed. As it was it clipped the propeller casing, blowing another hole in the stern. This decided the *Bangalore*'s fate. Within minutes the ship was sinking. She was lost with all hands. The only distress signal received was sent out after the second impact. Then the radio went dead.

In Zhongnanhai, President Tao was told of the success and hoped he had delivered China her victory with one strike, her *yizhan ershang*.

Prime Minister's Office, South Block, Delhi, India

Local time: 0300 Tuesday 8 May 2007
GMT: 2130 Monday 7 May 2007

'If we continue our ceasefire and show restraint, China will be condemned by the international community in such a way that it will never recover,' said the Foreign Minister Prabhu Purie.

'Whatever it does, China will recover,' said Hari Dixit, unable to contain his anger. 'China gunned down civilians in Tiananmen Square and within a year the Western leaders were kissing the asses of the men who ordered it. Now China is sinking our ships in our ocean, occupying our land, killing Buddhists in Tibet. If you are suggesting India surrenders now, you can bloody well resign.'

'No, Prime Minister,' Purie said firmly. 'I am merely saying that we should wait a few hours and get unequivocal international support. Then we can do whatever we damn well like.'

Zhongnanhai, Beijing, China

'He's British,' said Tang Siju. 'He confessed after we gave him truth drugs. It is impossible for even the best-trained man to resist giving away his nationality.'

'Is he a mercenary?'

'He is a member of the Special Boat Squadron. I suspect he was following orders which would have had the approval of the British government.'

'Comrade Song,' said Tao, turning to his Foreign Minister, 'what do you make of this?'

'The only motivation I can see for it is to create a power balance against us in South-East Asia. The British commando probably came from HMS *Ocean*, which is in the Bay of Bengal on exercises under the Five Power Defence Agreement. Technically, the Cocos Islands belong to Myanmar. Our lease on them has not been officially declared.'

'You're waffling, Foreign Minister,' said Tang. 'Britain is an American ally and the United States is intent on containing the power of China. We must strike back immediately and effectively. We have a *Song*-class submarine which has been following the *Ocean* task force for two days now.' Tang looked at his watch. 'The satellite is passing overhead in fifteen minutes. I suggest we give the commander his orders.'

Briefing

Taiwan

The island of Taiwan, 160 kilometres off the eastern Chinese coast, was governed by the Japanese from the 1890s and Taiwanese residents were given Japanese citizenship. For two years after the end of the Second World War it came under mainland Chinese control. Then, in 1949, when the government was overthrown by Mao Zedong's Communist Party, Taiwan became a stronghold for the fleeing nationalist forces. Taiwan made a remarkable development into a modern society under a mixture of military rule and American benevolence. Taiwan received a jolt of reality in the 1970s when the United States began its rapprochement with China, eventually cutting relations with Taiwan in favour of the mainland. The island continued to thrive. Martial law was lifted in 1987, the first ever direct presidential election was held in 1996 and its foreign reserves became among the highest in the world. Links with the United States remained strong. Taiwan remained protected by the 1979 Taiwan Relations Act. The act was designed to 'help maintain peace, security and stability in the Western Pacific'. It also maintained the 'capacity of the United States to resist any resort to force or other forms of coercion that would jeopardize the security, or the social or economic system, of the people on Taiwan'. It was deliberately woolly about America's obligation to go to war with China over Taiwan, but it left the option open.

Presidential Palace, Taipei, Taiwan

Local time: 0700 Tuesday 8 May 2007
GMT: 2300 Monday 7 May 2007

President Lin Chung-ling of Taiwan was born in the United States while his father was the Ambassador there in the 1960s. He was given the best American education and even held a United States passport, which he had to give up when he entered politics. He considered himself as much American as Chinese and certainly was more at home in the corridors of the State Department and the White House than he would be in Zhongnanhai and the Great Hall of the People.

The events of the past few days had thrown up an opportunity which Lin was convinced he could not let pass. For sixty years Taiwan had struggled in isolation, risen to the challenges and created one of the most modern Asian societies. Even the poorest Taiwanese were generations ahead of the Chinese peasants and right now a vulnerable China posed an enormous opportunity for Taiwan.

Lin had to strike while China was weak. It was pinned down in Tibet. The incursion into Arunachal Pradesh was as foolhardy as its invasion of Vietnam in 1979. International support had already been slipping from it. The decision to sink the Indian destroyer would bring condemnation from every quarter. Very rarely did such a succession of events come together in such a way.

President Lin Chung-ling had been elected with a landslide majority after he said he would attempt to see himself a citizen of Taiwan as a recognized independent country within his lifetime. Never had he dreamt the opportunity would come so quickly. He desk-topped his personal secretary to bring in the BBC film crew which was waiting outside to interview him. He had decided to make his announcement of Taiwan's independence on BBC rather than CNN to distance himself from his American benefactors. But it would be in the contemporary manner, announcing it to the world on live television.

The Oval Office, The White House, Washington, DC

Local time: 1830 Monday 7 May 2007
GMT: 2330 Monday 7 May 2007

'**They've hit the** British frigate *Grafton*,' said Tom Blood-worth. 'Two torpedoes. She's still afloat. More than twenty men dead.'

'What with?' said John Hastings.

'*Song*-class submarine, sir. She was damaged by depth charges and surfaced. The captain of HMS *Ocean* had to issue orders forbidding the men to open fire on the crew, they were so angry.'

'*Song*-class. Any significance?'

'It carries cruise missiles which it can fire from under-water – although the *Grafton* was hit with torpedoes. It's a diesel-electric vessel and we doubt the missiles have nuclear warheads. The *Song* is Chinese, broadly with eighties tech-nology. The main point, of course, is that the Chinese brought it way out of the usual theatre and used it effectively.'

'So how many more submarines do they have over there?'

'We don't know, John,' said Tom Bloodworth. 'We just have no idea.'

The President's personal secretary interrupted on the intercom. 'Joan Holden is on her way from State. She's suggested you get Alvin Jebb in from across the river, and tune in the BBC World Service. I'm changing the channels for you now, sir.'

Hastings moved away from his desk to the sofas in the middle of the room, just as the BBC interrupted its own breaking news report about HMS *Grafton* to go to its interview with President Lin of Taiwan. Because of the short notice given for the interview, the correspondent was only the local BBC stringer in Taipei. Unknown to the viewers he had already been told he had a maximum on-air time of two minutes thirty seconds. The editor of the day even questioned going to Taiwan for an unquantifiable announcement, believing the viewers wouldn't understand the link with the China–India conflict. At one stage, when it was thought the BBC would also have a live interview with the emotional mother of one of the naval officers killed on *Grafton*, the live segment from Taipei was to be cancelled. But a senior editor stepped in curtly. 'Our job is to inform and report breaking news. It is not to make people weep. Stick with Taipei.'

BBC: President Lin, thank you for joining us. As time is short, could you firstly give us your reaction to the Chinese naval offensive in the Bay of Bengal? British and Indian naval ships have been sunk, and there are even unconfirmed reports that a Chinese nuclear-armed submarine is steaming towards the Indian coast.

Lin: Yes. In the past few hours, China has forced me to make the most difficult decision of both my personal and political life. As the democratically elected President of Taiwan, I feel that we can no longer go on pulling the diplomatic wool over all our eyes. Unification with China, either under the mainland's system of dictatorship or our own system of democracy, will never happen in the foreseeable future. A compromise reunion, such as has been tried in Hong Kong, would not work and, more importantly, the Taiwanese people would not tolerate it. The brutal repression of Chinese citizens in Tibet, be they Tibetan or Han

Chinese, the invasion of India, a democratic neighbouring power, the exploitation of Myanmar or Burma for military means, upsetting the stability of South-East Asia, and the threatening naval offensive in the Bay of Bengal – these are not actions which the Taiwanese people can support. We abhor them.

BBC: But surely you are powerless against China? All but the poorest Third World governments have diplomatic relations not with Taiwan, but with China.

Lin: We have always been powerless, but we have become a leading light for both how the developing world should modernize and how it should handle the transition to democracy. So what I am saying is this. I have called an emergency session of both houses of Congress. They are ratifying a bill which will create the independent nation of Taiwan. At noon today, there will be nationwide celebrations to mark our transition. As from noon today, Taiwan will be an independent nation.

BBC: But you are already as good as independent. You raise your own taxes, issue your own visas, have your own defence force. Why risk stability?

Lin: The time has come for the international community to recognize that we are a nation in our own right. The policy of constructive engagement with a one-party state has merely strengthened China's ability to do what she is doing now. What we will celebrate at noon will be a beacon of political morality to the world.

Alvin Jebb and Joan Holden walked into the room together. 'Switch to CNN,' said Holden. 'Reece Overhalt just called saying Jamie Song is live, in vision from Beijing.'

Jebb was on his mobile to the Pentagon finding out the location of American naval forces in the Pacific. His expression indicated the news wasn't good. Bloodworth made a call from the President's Oval Office desk, took notes and moved extra satellite imagery over the eastern coast of China to watch troop and aircraft movements.

'Why didn't Lin tell us?' said Hastings.

'It would have been suicide for him and us,' said Holden, sitting down and pouring herself a coffee into the empty cup used by Bloodworth. 'Independence is about not consulting other powers. If he had, we would be accused of giving Lin permission.'

'Song's coming on,' said Bloodworth, finishing his call. Jebb shut down his mobile. The Oval Office fell quiet.

CNN: Within the past few minutes, Foreign Minister, Taiwan has announced its independence.

Song: Yes, I heard that, too, Mike. It's unfortunate.

CNN: President Lin described his announcement as a beacon of political morality to the world.

Song: Yes, I heard that, too, and his rather naive attempts to slur my government. The fact is, Mike, that India and China are in conflict right now over very complex issues regarding the sovereignty of both nations. It is not an immature conflict. It is the type of conflict which historically nations have fought, which you fought in your Civil War, your war in Vietnam, your conflict with Iraq and in Europe throughout much of the last century. Anyone who claims that the global economy, the Internet and all that are going to stop nations going to war against each other is naive in the extreme.

CNN: But was it necessary to sink the Indian destroyer *Bangalore* and cripple the British frigate *Grafton*, with at least 450 people dead?

Song: Let me try and answer that not in the emotional way in which you put the question but in the pragmatic way of geopolitics. We had intelligence information which we are making public on the Internet right now that the *Bombay* was under orders to sink a Chinese-flagged tanker heading for China with oil from the Middle East. We could not allow that to happen. It would be an infringement of all international shipping laws. We also have intelligence that this man – and I understand you have agreed to float the pictures over this interview – this man, Michael Hall, is a member of the British Royal Marines. He was captured while on a sabotage mission at our naval base on Great Cocos Island. That Britain attempted to interfere in this conflict is abhorrent; that it decided to interfere on the side of India is a wound which will take a long time to heal. It was only right therefore that we defend our territory.

CNN: Is it not Myanmar or Burmese territory?

Song: We have a lease to use it as a military base. If we attacked American facilities at Okinawa, Japan, it would be seen as an attack on United States forces.

CNN: All right, Foreign Minister. It seems that everyone is digging themselves deeper into the big holes. Pakistan is already finished. The UN calls it a non-functioning nation. You and India seem to be digging at the same speed, but both downwards. Taiwan has scooped its first shovelful of earth. How is China now going to dig itself out?

Song: We need help, and that's why I'm here, Mike. You've got a second video you've agreed to run. This was not shot by a Chinese television crew. We invited a neutral Russian crew to Lhasa. They picked their own interpreter and they were free to go anywhere.

Song fell silent and didn't speak throughout the first minute of the video. It showed a gang of Tibetan youths, brandishing modern weapons, moving in against a row of Chinese shops. They sprayed the shop-fronts with automatic weapons fire, shattering the windows, which fell out onto the pavement. Then they lit petrol bombs and threw them inside. The shop-owners mostly lived upstairs with their families and they came stumbling out, coughing, clutching their children and helping their elderly relations. As they emerged from the smoke, they were cut down in a hail of gunfire, women, children, the old, so fierce and unrelenting that those behind turned back and fled into their burning homes. One of the Tibetans moved forward, executing the wounded with a single gunshot to the head, until he ran out of bullets. Then he took out a machete, yanked up the body of a young woman by her hair. The camera unashamedly went close up on her face, her eyes danced around, between consciousness and shock. Her hands flailed out and the Tibetan began hacking at her neck with the machete to decapitate her. The crowd cheered and the CNN presenter came back into vision, looking utterly stunned.

CNN: We apologize. We should have brought you out of that footage earlier, but these were raw pictures, just fed in over the Reuters satellite from Beijing. I think we get your point, Foreign Minister.

Song: I would like to make an appeal to your audience. Do not force China into war over Tibet. What we have just seen shows that there are no good or bad guys in a struggle like this. It is a horrible thing and both sides are capable of terrible atrocities. Yes, both the Chinese and the Tibetans. We cannot simply give Tibet away now. Thousands of Chinese who have settled there could be slaughtered. I won't debate the rights and wrongs of that policy, because we all need to look forward. If you let us sort out the present crisis it will end soon. If you in the West interfere, there is bound to be a bloodbath even worse than the one you have just seen.

Hastings muted the television by remote. 'That is about the most disgusting thing I have ever seen in my life,' he said.

'Fortunately, we don't have treaty obligations in Tibet,' said Holden. 'But we do with Taiwan.'

Ennio Barber, the President's personal adviser, had until now stayed quiet. 'We have to get a statement out quickly,' he said. 'Or we'll be finding ourselves pushed towards war by Congress.'

'The Taiwan Relations Act is woolly about our obligation to use force to defend Taiwan,' said Holden.

'But the American people will expect it,' said Barber.

'Alvin, when can we get a carrier group into the area?' Hastings asked his Defence Secretary.

'The *Harry S. Truman* carrier group is just south of the Korean Straits heading out of the Sea of Japan. It'll take at least a day to get anywhere near Taiwan.'

'OK. Joan, I need to speak to Reece Overhalt in Beijing and get me Lin in Taiwan. Let's see if this is one Asian crisis we can defuse in a few phone calls.'

'**The passing of** the legislation we can ignore,' said Jamie Song. 'But if the celebrations go ahead, we will have to move in.'

'What do you mean, "move in"?' asked Reece Overhalt. The two men were standing on the balcony again, a sign from the Foreign Minister that the conversation was not being recorded.

'Reece, that is out of my hands. The military run our military strategy on Taiwan. When they take it over, I will be watching it on BBC and CNN just like you.'

'Give me your best- and worst-case scenarios, then.'

'Best case, we will have tests with DF-15 or some such short- or medium-range missile like we did during the presidential elections in 1996. Medium case is that we'll do that and blockade the Straits of Taiwan, throwing a cordon around the island, but not firing a shot unless attacked. Worst case is that we'll send a missile into the Parliament building as they're passing the independence legislation. Now tell me, what will John Hastings do?'

'They're sending the *Harry S. Truman* down from the Sea of Japan. We've got fighter crews on high alert in Okinawa. And that's about it. If you can hold off, we can hold off. We can handle the missile tests. The blockade would give us all room for negotiation and if no one wants war, it won't happen. If you send in a missile, I guess we'll have to knock out your missile bases. But like you, Jamie, that's not a threat. It's a guess from a non-executive ambassador.'

Jamie Song shook his head. 'I'll pass that on to my president, Reece. But I'm not sure even he will be in control of the Taiwan conflict. The military will not let Taiwan go.'

Military Headquarters, Western Hills, China

General Leung Liyin, the Chinese Defence Minister, was unable to control his anger when talking to President Tao. 'We have made it absolutely clear that if Taiwan declares independence we will attack. If we allow the declaration to go ahead, we will be weakened for generations. The Nationalists will have won the war in which our fathers fought. The Americans will increase its power in East Asia. Internal dissent will increase and the Communist Party will be lucky to stay in power. Total chaos will follow.'

'It could mean war against America,' said Tao softly.

Leung banged the table. 'They won't touch us. They know we could take out one of their cities with the DF-41. Their theatre missile-defence system cannot guarantee a missile will not get through. We are prepared to lose cities and the Americans are not. That is why we will win.'

Local time: 0930 Tuesday 8 May 2007
GMT: 0030 Tuesday 8 May 2007

Prime Minister Shigeto Wada put the telephone down from a conversation with John Hastings and thought hard, not about what the American President had said, but how he had said it. Wada's grandfather had been an administrative official in Taiwan and Wada himself had always looked on Taiwan's development with pride as if some of its success at least was down to the infrastructure and manner in which Japan had ruled the islands. Chinese military action against Taiwan now would not directly affect the treaty obligations the United States had with Japan. But given China's Dragon Strike campaign of a few years back and its expansion into the Indian Ocean, it was only inevitable that the two East Asian powers would come into conflict again, possibly sooner rather than later.

His intelligence chief General Shigehiko Ogawa had already predicted a horrific Chinese onslaught on Taiwan within a few hours, certainly before the celebrations were due to start at noon. John Hastings had spoken like a man who wished the problem would go away.

'We are talking to the Chinese and the Taiwanese about this,' Hastings had said. 'You can be assured we do everything to maintain peace in the Taiwan Straits.'

Wada was not convinced. He felt a tiredness in America, a sense that its days of fighting wars in Asia were over. It had given Japan and its neighbours a generous security umbrella for sixty years, and had allowed Japan two generations to grow out of the shame it felt after its defeat in the

Second World War. But time had to move on. Wada also faced a more practical difficulty. As soon as China attacked, he expected the United States to use its base at Okinawa as a launching point for military action against the mainland. That would put Japanese sovereign territory under a direct threat of Chinese attack.

The debate about Japan's defence role was not new, but Taiwan's declaration of independence had focused his thoughts. In the past five years, Japan had brought in Boeing 767 mid-air refuelling tankers for its F-14 fighters and launched the *Osumi* carrier, which could be used with either helicopters or jump-jets. It had put up four spy satellites, which gave it the best imagery in the region, and had brought in long-range air transport planes to deliver troops or rescue Japanese citizens from anywhere in the world.

Wada glanced at his desk-top screen to see the first official Chinese reaction to the Taiwanese announcement. It had come out quickly, but the words were familiar, showing a lack of imagination within the Chinese leadership.

'The Chinese government and people will not tolerate any action for Taiwan independence or any attempt to separate Taiwan from the motherland,' said the Xinhua statement. 'China's territory and sovereignty are indivisible. The Taiwan question is purely an internal matter for China. If there occurs any action for Taiwanese independence or any attempt by foreign forces to separate Taiwan from the motherland, the Chinese government and people will not sit back and do nothing.'

The fact that China had chosen to release the statement now was an almost certain indication that it would take military action. To do anything less would be an unacceptable loss of face to President Tao and the military.

Under the constitution, the Japanese navy could patrol 2,400 kilometres out to sea. One of its tasks was to keep shipping lanes open with Japanese minesweepers. It was also allowed to give logistical and medical support to American forces in combat in the region. Japanese forces were, of course, allowed to defend themselves if they came under attack. None of this conflicted with the constitutional declaration that Japan would 'for ever renounce war as a sovereign right'.

'John Chiu, the Prime Minister of Singapore, is on the telephone,' said Wada's long-serving personal assistant, whose desk was in the far corner of his large office.

'John, I can imagine the purpose of this call,' said Wada in English.

'Taiwan,' said Chiu. 'Our analysts believe China will attack within two hours.'

'I have the same reading.'

'I have just come out of an emergency Cabinet meeting and some members are listening in to this telephone call. Our conclusion was this. For many years our founding Prime Minister was of the view that Japan could never take the mantle of the main regional power in East Asia. However, China's policies in the recent years have made us uneasy about this view. The events of the past few days have led us to conclude that Singapore would support a strategic pact between India and Japan in Asia. Also we would remain politically neutral should you decide to defend the stability of East Asia in whatever manner you thought right during this current Taiwan crisis. Some time within the next half-century, we will see the American security umbrella close. We believe that now is the time to establish an Asian security umbrella, and we want to see it done not with one power, China, but with two – Japan and India. As you know, Singapore is predominantly Chinese and there will be domestic difficulties with our new thinking. This is why we will be muted in our public support, until we can sustain it. I'm sure you understand.'

Minutes after Wada had finished his call from John Chiu, Hari Dixit was on the line from Delhi. 'Prime Minister, this is a humbling call for me, but a frank one. It is also too late in the day, but in present circumstances that is beside the point. You have often approached us informally for closer ties and we have responded with insular arrogance. India has been an inward-looking nation, living on a false premise that it was a great country simply waiting for its time to come. We have had a jolt of reality in the past week and that is why I am calling you.'

'A call from the Prime Minister of India is always welcome,' said Wada.

'I believe the international community would support an alliance between our two democracies. I believe that right now it would support action against China. We will hit them on our eastern flank and win back Burma for the free world. We will support vigorously any action you take to contain China in its efforts to keep Taiwan.'

Military Headquarters, Western Hills, China

Local time: 0900 Tuesday 8 May 2007
GMT: 0100 Tuesday 8 May 2007

General Leung Liyin, the Chinese Defence Minister, was speaking in front of a wall map of the Taiwan Straits. President Tao was in the room, together with Tang Siju, and senior military officials. Jamie Song had not been asked to the briefing.

'80302 Unit of the Second Artillery will launch the DF-15 missile strike from the Huangshan 52 Base here in Jiangxi province. The launch control and command HQ will be with the 815th Brigade at Leping. We have an inventory of 150 missiles for the operation which are now being moved to pre-surveyed launch sites in Jiangxi and Fujian provinces. Unit 80301 in Shenyang in Liaioning province, just here, is on a high alert should we have to strike Okinawa. We hope this will not be necessary. We would use the DF-21 missile and the launch site would be here in Tonghua, just north of the Korean border.'

'Do you believe, comrade General, that we can defeat Taiwan, or merely use a missile strike as a means to get Lin to withdraw his declaration of independence?'

'If we decided to settle the issue once and for all, we would have to take action against the enemy's early warning radar sites, the SIGINT facilities, the command and control centres and power plants. If we did it swiftly in a single mortal blow [*zhiming daji*] we would need airstrikes and Special Forces operations. The first targets would be Taiwan's twenty-five early warning radar stations, which we would hit with anti-radiation missiles launched from aircraft. We would send Special Forces into some sites, such as the Chuan Kang Airbase. We have built a replica of the base in Gansu and have trained extensively to prepare for such an assault. We would also have to shoot down Taiwan's airborne early warning systems, which have taken off in the past hour. The enemy has eight key military airfields which we would have to take out; runways, barracks and control towers. Even if we succeed in shutting down the early warning apparatus, the command and control structure, the key missile sites and the airfields, we would only briefly have control of Taiwanese airspace. This first wave of operation would be fifteen minutes at best, but with both missile strikes and disruption of communication, we could complicate the enemy's response. We would follow it with a much bigger second wave, with precision-guided bombs which we hope would neutralize both the air-defence system and the command structure. This could be achieved within forty-five minutes. With control of the skies, we could impose a no-fly zone around Taiwan – including American aircraft – and then impose a sea blockade around the island. I would not suggest a land invasion, because it would be drawn out and costly.'

'Are you recommending it, comrade General?' said Tao.

General Leung was silent for what seemed to be an interminable amount of time. Then he said: 'No. It is the only way it can be done, but it is over-optimistic. We have two elements to consider. The first is that five years from now Taiwan will have a fully tested theatre missile-defence system. We are developing sophisticated jamming and chaff devices to confuse the enemy, but it would be far more difficult to conduct the plan I have just outlined. In normal circumstances, I would recommend implementing it now. But I am not convinced we have the resources to fight both

in Taiwan and on our western flank with India in Arunachal Pradesh.'

'Then what is your suggestion?'

Again Leung lapsed into silence. 'Population centres,' he
finally said. 'That would force America's hand and bring
Taiwan to its knees.'

'**The Taiwanese and** Japanese are giving us full access to their intelligence. Coupled with our own it provides a graphic picture. We have imagery of rail missile movements in Fujian province,' said Tom Bloodworth. 'Fighter aircraft are being flown into bases along the eastern coastline – Shantou, Xiamen, Quanzhou and Fuzhou. There is evidence of ground troops massing for a seaborne landing on the island chain of Pei-kan, Nan-kan and Pai-chuan, which are controlled by Taiwan.'

'The Japanese Defence Minister has telephoned saying they are deploying their forces towards the Taiwan Straits, including the helicopter carrier *Osumi*.'

'Surely they're not going to get involved?'

'He gave me the impression that they didn't mind if they did, providing we were on side,' said Jebb. 'Their intelligence analysts anticipate a Chinese missile strike within the hour.'

'What targets?' said Bloodworth.

'That's uncertain.'

'Lin is refusing to call off the celebrations,' said Holden. 'I talked to him directly.'

'John Chiu in Singapore corroborates with the Japanese,' said Hastings. 'He is convinced China will take military action.'

'Sir, we have to announce what we are going to do,' said Ennio Barber. 'The sending of a carrier group just isn't washing on Capitol Hill. They know it won't be there in time.'

'Sorry to interrupt, John,' said Bloodworth. 'We are getting reports in about an Indian missile strike on Burma.'

'The Chinese military there?'

'It seems to be wider spread, including airstrikes.' Bloodworth continued reading from the computer screen. 'Sorry. The report is that the Agni medium-range ballistic missile is being prepared for launch at a site just north of Calcutta. No indication of its target. The range is 1,600 miles, so it could hit Tibet or Burma. A lighter warhead could take it deep inside China itself, 2,000 to 2,500 miles range.'

'Get Hari Dixit on the line,' snapped Hastings.

'We've also got pictures of a Prithvi missile on a semi-erect mobile launch pad north of Dimapur on India's eastern tip. There's bad cloud cover there, so there could be a lot more of them, say around Tezpur or Imphal. Our ELINT and SIGINT people are picking up a big increase in military air traffic in eastern India. Just about every known airfield under the north-east military command is on a high alert. A massive influx of fighter and ground-attack aircraft are coming in from the west.'

'The Indian Prime Minister on the line, Mr President.'

John Hastings took the call on a mobile receiver, standing up, and put the conversation on open speaker. 'Hari, what are you up to in the east?'

'We're going to take back our territory and neutralize the threat posed by Myanmar's alliance with China.'

'I'm asking you to hold off. Wait until this Taiwan crisis has died down.'

'If we don't act during it, we will be defeated.'

'All right, Hari. I don't know if you've heard this from your own people, but we believe there's a Chinese nuclear-armed *Xia* submarine in the Indian Ocean. It can reach anywhere in India. We've got the *Ronald Reagan* carrier group looking for it. Four attack submarines are after it, but it is nowhere near the *Kilo* sub which sank the *Bombay*. No one wants China to launch from that sub. The country's vulnerable, confused and nervous right now. Do nothing, Hari. Be like Israel in the Gulf War. Take the punches, but don't hit back. Help me wind down the crisis and you have my word we'll work out a comprehensive Asian defence policy which will safeguard all our interests.'

Just before Dixit was able to reply, Bloodworth said: 'Chinese missile launch on Taiwan. Three, four – no, five launches from the Huangshan 52 base. They would be the DF-15s.'

Military Headquarters, Western Hills, China

Local time: 1000 Tuesday 8 May 2007
GMT: 0200 Tuesday 8 May 2007

'**Three minutes to** impact,' said Leung. 'The enemy's Patriot missiles have been activated. Four enemy air-defence missiles launched.' He turned to President Tao. 'We have fired sufficient missiles to ensure that we have at least two hits.'

Chiang Kai-Shek Memorial Square, Taipei, Taiwan

Local time: 1000 Tuesday 8 May 2007
GMT: 0200 Tuesday 8 May 2007

The air-raid sirens began as columns of school-children filed through into Chiang Kai-Shek Memorial Square. The palace at the head of the square, with its white walls and blue Chinese-style roof, housed a bronze statue of Chiang Kai-Shek. Although defeated by Mao Zedong, he had created this defiant island state which was now admired by Western democracies and Asian economic tigers alike. Soldiers stood solemnly on guard unaffected by the commotion going on around them. Even when the siren sounded, they did not look up. On either side of the square were the National Theatre and National Concert Hall and the square itself was used by thousands on special occasions. They gathered in 1992 for the first direct elections to the legislature, in 1996 for the first presidential elections and now, as Taiwan was about to declare independence, it was only fitting that the occasion be marked in Chiang Kai-Shek Memorial Square. School-children, unprepared and unrehearsed, some clutching lunch boxes, stood in pairs, holding hands nervously, while their teachers worried about how to arrange them. Officials handed out the red and blue Taiwanese flag for them to wave and a band started up with a ceremonial regiment from the army. To hold everyone's attention were huge screens strung up so they could see one from wherever they were, showing proceedings in the nearby Parliament buildings, where the Legislative Yuan was debating the vote on independence.

A decade earlier, the National Assembly voted by an

overwhelming majority of 261 to 8 to eliminate Taiwan's status as a province of China. By doing so, the Assembly was taking another tentative step towards complete independence. As a province, Taiwan accepted that it was part of mainland China. It appointed a governor and had its own provincial assembly, and the decision to end the facade meant severing yet another link of its bothersome relationship with the mainland.

The sirens did not create great consternation in the square. They were a regular element of city life in Taipei, as were the anti-aircraft batteries on the roofs of tall buildings. It was only when the children saw the streak of a missile flaming skywards and pointed excitedly that the teachers recognized something was wrong. Police from the cordon ran in and began the fruitless task of herding the children towards an air-raid shelter, and by the time the third Patriot missile had been fired, they were running in terror, but still with discipline, in pairs, holding hands, as they had been taught to since they were in kindergarten. Then Taiwanese fighter planes screamed overhead, so loud that people put their hands to their ears, and stopped dead in their tracks to watch, hoping that they alone would save them from the danger in the skies.

As soon as the planes had gone, a shrill electronic screeching came from the big screens around the square. The pictures juddered and you could see panic break out in the Parliament, that second-long expression on faces, the first instinctive movement of escape, before the screens went to black. Then the square shook. The troops broke formation and ran towards the rumbling noise of the explosion. Dust and then smoke rose up into view. Teachers and children screamed together, their lunch boxes falling to the ground, some losing their sandals, running, but not sure where, and then their sounds drowned out by more fighter planes flying low and loud over the centre of the city.

Two Chinese missiles scored a direct hit on the Parliament building, killing dozens of deputies and stopping the debate before the vote on independence had been taken. For President Tao, it was a constitutional master stroke. He had struck a civilian target at the heart of Taipei, as his military commanders had wanted. The dead were legitimate targets, and the law which would have embarrassed his presidency more than anything else remained off the statute books.

Military Headquarters, Western Hills, China

'**We have successfully** taken Pei-kan,' said Leung. 'Heavy shelling has been going for twenty minutes from Kinmen. We are exchanging fire. Taiwanese aircraft have attacked our base at Shantou, but our air defences are holding up well. The new Sector Operations Centres are taking individual control of their areas of defence through the integrated national defence system. Each sector is bringing in its own over the horizon and missile early-warning data and is directing our planes in the air. It is working far better than we expected.'

'Prime Minister Wada of Japan is on the line,' said an assistant to President Tao, who seemed hesitant before finally saying he would not take the call. It was the fifth time the Japanese Prime Minister had tried to talk directly to the Chinese president.

'Detection of Indian missiles being prepared for launch.'

All eyes looked up at the real-time screen, blurred but showing the distinctive shape from a satellite photograph of an Indian missile out of cover on a mobile launcher.

'The Agni,' said Leung. 'Where is it?'

'Eastern air command, Shillong.' The coordinates were given. 'From Tezu. Target range: Lanzhou, Xian, Chengdu, Chonqing, Wuhan, Guangzhou.'

'Take it out,' said Leung, without consulting President Tao, who nodded, knowing that power was slipping away and events were overtaking him. Leung dictated the order:

'Xining. Second Artillery. Unit 80306. Datong, Delingha and Da Qaidam launch bases. Range approximately 1,600 kilometres. Use the DF-21, low 200 kilometre trajectory to counter anti-missile defence system.'

By coincidence, Jamie Song was meeting Reece Overhalt when Japanese Ambassador Kazuo Nishimura insisted on an audience in a remarkably obstinate and un-Japanese manner. Overhalt and Nishimura had spoken barely an hour earlier, when Overhalt heard of Japan's plans to move in on the Taiwan Straits, and was now in the middle of relaying it to Jamie Song.

Song asked Nishimura in. The two television sets were both on with the volume low, but audible, showing BBC World and CNN, the pictures lagging behind events by only a few minutes. On the screen was the damaged facade of the Parliament building. Members staggering out, their clothes torn, some bleeding, and emergency vehicles arriving inside the complex.

'Foreign Minister, I insist you urge your President to speak to Prime Minister Wada. It is a great insult for him to ignore my Prime Minister's calls.'

Jamie Song shrugged. It was only mid-morning but he was sharing a malt whisky with Reece Overhalt. He offered a glass to Nishimura, who refused. 'Ambassador, the decisions are being made at our military headquarters in the Western Hills. In peacetime China, the tapestry of trade, diplomacy, commerce, politics and the military rumble along jostling for position with each other in the big picture. But in wartime, every voice is dampened except for that of the military. We are now in wartime. I imagine that the man in control of China is not President Tao, but General

Leung. This might last just the morning, or it might last for ever. I have no idea.'

Song hadn't bothered to offer Nishimura a seat. The ambassador sat down uninvited. 'Prime Minister Wada has made a decision to send Japanese forces to the Straits of Taiwan.'

'So Reece was saying. Personally, I think it is a mistake.'

'But your actions have been intolerable. They cannot be accepted in modern Asia.'

'I don't think so. Our territory was invaded by Indian troops, our oil supplies threatened by Indian warships, our naval base attacked by British forces, and Taiwan has chosen this very moment to make a declaration of independence. Tell me, Ambassador, what would you do in our situation? Just let it all happen? Give Tibet to India? Hand over our naval bases to the British? Let India control shipping in the Indian Ocean? Welcome Taiwan's separation from the Motherland?'

'There are channels. The United Nations.'

'What we call closing the door after the horse has bolted,' growled Overhalt.

'If you continue, you will become isolated by the international community,' said Nishimura. 'As I said, your actions are unacceptable.'

Jamie Song stood up. He was unshaven, his eyes were bloodshot and he clearly had not slept properly for several days. 'Get out!' he shouted. 'What right has Japan to tell us that our actions are unacceptable? What right have you to dictate levels of morality to me after slaughtering Chinese people and other Asians with impunity!' Song moved so quickly towards Nishimura that Reece Overhalt was also on his feet, ready to intervene. Song stopped half a metre away from the Japanese Ambassador and gripped his arm. 'Don't threaten China. Don't try to humiliate her. Don't boast about Indian–Japanese solidarity. Your country carried out the most horrendous atrocities and then rose up to try to claim the mantle of Asian power again. It will not happen. China will not let it happen. We will see this through to the end, believe me, and whatever decisions are being made now in the Western Hills, I, as a Chinese citizen, will support them without hesitation.'

When Nishimura had scuttled away, Song sank back down into his chair, looking at the television scenes of devastation from Taipei.

'Jamie, what do you think Leung will do?' asked Overhalt softly.

'Remember what Mao said? "The Chinese people will never be slaves again." We'll see it through, Reece. Even if it means the destruction of China.'

BBC Television Centre, London

Local time: 0330 Tuesday 8 May 2007

Robin Sutcliffe, the head of BBC Newsgathering, was woken at home. Fifteen minutes later a car was waiting to take him to work. He had packed an overnight bag. The call had come from the BBC's Chief Political Adviser, who herself was woken up by a call from the Home Office. The Home Office was reacting on advice passed through John Stopping's Joint Intelligence Committee, which had cleared the decision to alert the BBC with the Prime Minister.

Sutcliffe walked straight over to the horseshoe desk of banked television and computer screens on the first floor newsroom, the nerve centre of his department. He told the News Organizer and the Foreign Duty Editor to help arrange a core team to move immediately to Wood Norton, a manor house and country estate in the Cotswolds owned by BBC Resources and used mainly for hosting conferences.

Two correspondents who were working overnight in the Foreign Affairs Unit and for BBC News 24 were seconded, together with editors from Radio News bulletins and World Service Television. Sutcliffe insisted that the presenters, two each for radio and television, came from mainstream news, and not from the more controversial current affairs programmes such as *Newsnight* or the 5 Live chat shows. Luckily a long-serving presenter from the *Today* programme had just walked into the building. Radio Four's morning bulletin newsreader was also there. The television presenters were taken from News 24 and World Service.

Attempts were made to bring in a senior *Nine O'Clock News* presenter, but he did not arrive in time.

Sutcliffe was grateful for the BBC's shambolic but effective policy of retaining experienced staff. The faces and voices assigned to break news in times of crisis were more or less interchangeable. Sutcliffe telephoned the News Editor, who was his direct deputy, and asked him to come into Television Centre because he was opening up Wood Norton.

The Home Office had explained that a Chinese nuclear strike on a civilian population centre in India could not be ruled out in the next twenty-four hours. It was hoped the conflict could be contained. But the Home Secretary thought Wood Norton should be made ready just in case Television Centre in Wood Lane and Bush House in the Aldwych had to be closed down.

The Wood Norton bunker was hewn into a hillside close to the manor house. It was built at the beginning of the Cold War in the 1950s, and while other Cold War facilities in Britain were mothballed or sold off the BBC retained its ultimate crisis headquarters. As broadcasting equipment modernized and BBC studios were re-equipped, so was Wood Norton. It had been installed with the latest BBC computer network and digital video and audio links. It had the ability to take satellite picture feeds from and conduct live interviews with anywhere in the world.

Sutcliffe's core team was dropped off by coach at the manor house. Even though it was the middle of the night, there was still activity because the manor was hosting a special visit for fans of the radio serial *The Archers*, which was set in the area. The guests were breakfasting early to catch the Cotswold dawn. Sutcliffe led the team down a winding, woodland path. The massive metal door had already been opened by the caretaker, who had switched on the air conditioning and cleared away some of the mustiness. It reminded the older members of staff of the old Broadcasting House, drab but efficient, decorated with tough, institutional carpets and gloss grey paint on the walls.

The bunker was built on two floors, with a newsroom of about 180 square metres, off which ran two radio studios and one which had been converted to television. The camera backdrop was the BBC logo and the Union flag. Suggestions that there be a picture of the Houses of Parliament or another national symbol were rejected on the grounds that it might give a false impression. The BBC had to make it clear that it was not on the air from the banks of the River Thames. A second television studio had been set up in the newsroom itself, along the lines of the designs for News 24 and World at Television Centre.

On the lower level was a canteen, a dormitory which could sleep sixty staff, and at the far end a decontamination centre for those who might be affected by nuclear fallout. As they entered, each person was given an NBC suit, with syringes for the antidote to a chemical weapons attack, Fullers powder to decontaminate their own suit and a monitor to measure radio activity. For the first half-hour there was a cacophony of sound around the newsrooms as computer links were set up, the satellite desk was briefed, and the most senior correspondents in the field were told confidentially that they might suddenly be on air not to Television Centre, but to Wood Norton. The team had not been trained specifically for this situation, but once in, they settled down to their jobs as if they were back in London.

'At 0700, we will begin running dummy programming alongside the output from London,' Sutcliffe told the first bunker editorial meeting. 'Television and radio will have one channel each, BBC 1 and Radio 4. We will package material here and until we actually take over the presenters will substitute reporters here for the lives they would do with correspondents in the field. If we suddenly have to stop transmissions from Television Centre, it is imperative that the switch is unflustered, calm and without panic. Those few seconds will do everything to guide the national mood. At some stage, if war does break out, the government may take over editorial control. It is written in the charter. It is the law. Don't let's have any complaints about it. We hope to get a relief team down within twenty-four hours. Until then, we're on our own.'

'Yes, Mr President, Jamie Song told me personally that they would see it through to the end, even if it meant the destruction of China,' said Reece Overhalt on the secure line from the Embassy in Beijing. 'He quoted from Mao about never being slaves again.'

'Will President Tao take my call, for God's sake?'

'He's not in control, sir. The military is running China for the foreseeable future. As a personal friend, Song has promised me unrestricted access to his office unless we actually get as far as breaking off relations. If you look at it as the spectrum of Chinese politics, Song is at one end, our end, Leung is at the other, and President Tao is somewhere in the middle. Tao is at least in the bunker and I suspect he is keeping in touch with Song. So use me as the conduit and I'm pretty sure Song will get the message through.'

'Chinese missile launch,' Tom Bloodworth spoke in a precise, and relaxed manner, like an airline pilot addressing passengers about the flight path. 'Three missiles from separate launch sites in Xining area.'

'The Chinese have launched,' said Hastings to Overhalt. 'A base at Xining.'

'That's the site suspected of being used for India,' said Overhalt. 'The DF-21 site.'

'Second tranche launch,' said Bloodworth. 'Kunming area in Yunnan. Waiting for precise identification.'

No one spoke. They knew Bloodworth would have the details within seconds.

'Chuxiong, as I thought. Brigade headquarters from Unit 80303. DF-21s again. The Chinese have five ballistic missiles in the air. Xining launch is flying at low trajectory, 95 miles. Chuxiong, waiting for reading. Seem to be heading for 220 miles altitude.'

'Mr President,' said Overhalt, 'I'll stay on the line.'

'Less than four minutes to first impact,' said Bloodworth. 'Target area appears to be Tezu on the far eastern tip. This is a pre-emptive strike. Tezu was the base for the Indian missile launch which we stopped a few minutes ago.'

'So you mean their satellites had the same real-time imagery?' said Hastings.

'And they're going for Shillong. That's the Eastern Command HQ. Tezu comes under it.'

'They must have, sir. This is not a random action. Their missile sites are prepared and programmed to targets.'

'With our damn stolen technology. Reece, you still there?'

'Yes, Mr President.'

'Stay on the line until we ascertain what they're hitting and how hard. If it's a conventional strike against an Indian missile base, it'll be hard for us to complain. I don't like it but it seems to me to be a legitimate act of war. What we'll be needing from them, however, is a pledge that they will not go nuclear against India and that their missiles are not targeted against the United States.'

'I've just been speaking to Japanese Prime Minister Wada,' said Defence Secretary Alvin Jebb. 'He says Japanese warplanes have been patrolling an area to the north of Taiwan. He has both signals and electronic intelligence that a missile launch is imminent from Tonghua against the Okinawa facilities. That would be a strike against American forces, sir.'

'They wouldn't do it,' said Hastings, more to himself than in answer to Jebb.

'This thing is getting a momentum, sir. I wouldn't be so sure.'

The Kremlin, Moscow, Russia

Local time: 0900 Tuesday 8 May 2007
GMT: 0600 Tuesday 8 May 2007

The Cold War years of President Gorbunov's early career had centred on the few seconds that a nuclear exchange might become real. For decades the Soviet Union was on a constant exercise when conflict could suddenly break out from existing manoeuvres. The aim had been to exhaust and confuse, such that a decoy deployment staged for the enemy satellites could within seconds become a genuine step towards attack. For years in Moscow and finally as Pacific Fleet commander Gorbunov had lived and breathed it like a ritual. He could still recite weapons codes and coordinates. He knew without notes the sites which would be used for first strike and the surviving sites which would handle the second strikes. Even now, as President, he insisted on having the daily positions put on his desk of the *Typhoon*-class strategic missile submarines patrolling under the ice of the Arctic Circle. He had even insisted on changing the lax practice of not reconfirming the area known as the *polynya* every twelve hours. This was a patch of clear water, surrounded by ice, through which the missile could be launched. Gorbunov wanted the submarines no further than fifteen minutes from the nearest *polynya*.

Like China and America, Russia's intelligence-gathering machine picked up the Chinese missile launch. But unlike President Hastings, Gorbunov had arranged for a line to be kept open between his office and the Chinese operational command in the Western Hills. He was, after all, the main supplier of China's military hardware. On a separate telephone, he had a line to Hari Dixit, now back in the Prime Minister's office in Delhi's South Block. Neither party knew Gorbunov had direct access. More than any of the other two leaders, Gorbunov knew the split-second decision-making needed in nuclear warfare, and he had no intention of being called in at the fifty-ninth second, when a missile was midair and about to strike.

'Is it nuclear?' he said to his aide-de-camp, who checked on the line to the Western Hills.

'A conventional strike against missile sites at the Eastern Air Command in Shillong,' came back the reply. Gorbunov immediately repeated the message to Hari Dixit, then was on another line to John Hastings in the White House.

'What about Okinawa?' said the American President.

'I have nothing on that,' said Gorbunov.

'Well, if you're in touch with General Leung, tell him that if one piece of ordnance hurts one American, I will destroy his goddamn war machine for the next five thousand years.'

Gorbunov didn't pass on the message, but it confirmed very much what he feared. The orders which he personally would give over the next few minutes would also set back Russian–American relations for more than a decade. Ever since the end of the Cold War, however, the relationship had been one-sided, driven by the whims of Western money and Western democracies and caring little for the feelings of the Russian people. It was not an honourable position for the Motherland. Gorbunov was about to risk a change for the better.

The cornerstone of Russia's strategic force was the inter-continental ballistic missile, the SS-27 Topol-M. Because of funding problems, the Moscow Institute of Heat Engineering State Enterprise (MIT) – the sole Topol factory – could only produce ten to fifteen missiles a year. Russia had in service far fewer than the 450 missile level needed to maintain parity with the United States under the START II treaty. For the purposes of conflict, however, the figures were largely cosmetic. Gorbunov had about 150 missiles, enough to shift substantially the global balance of power.

The 45-tonne missile had had more than a dozen successful test flights since 1995. In December 1997, the first two Topol-M systems were put on alert for a trial period in the Taman Division at Tatischevo in the Saratov region, 725 kilometres south-east of Moscow near the border with Kazakhstan. Since then Russia had converted about a hundred silos of the defunct RS-20 missiles for use by the Topol-M. The plan was to have an equal number of silos and mobile launchers, which could be driven both on and off the road. Since coming to power, Gorbunov had insisted on a programme of constant exercises with the Topol-M mobile launch system. Tests in 1998 showed that the Topol-M could be converted to carry at least four manoeuvrable warheads and it could be launched with a short engine-burn time helping it to escape satellite detection.

By 2005, the Topol-M was deployed at Saratov, at Valday, 770 kilometres north of Moscow, in the silos in the southern Urals and Altay in Siberia. Gorbunov had also maintained a conflict launch capability at the Plesetsk test site, 800 kilometres north of Moscow, and at Kamchatka in the Far East.

He planned to use the Strategic Rocket Forces to the full, three hundred thousand troops divided into six separate armies, each comprising three to five divisions. The soldiers looked after security, transportation and above-ground maintenance. Officers manned launch stations and command posts underground. In total, Russia had three hundred launch control centres and twenty-eight missile bases, although some had been mothballed in the past ten years because of arms reduction. While the SS-27 Topol-M was the cream of the force, the SS-25s were better tested for road mobility and the SS-24 was the missile transported by rail. Two-thirds of the mobile missile force was deployed in the west of Russia to be used against Western Europe and one-third was still east of the Ural mountains for use against China. Either sector could strike the United States. All were in constant combat readiness with Gorbunov receiving daily reports of any maintenance problems which depleted his nuclear capability. Right now he had 4,486 nuclear devices at stationary, railway and mobile launch complexes and 672 launchers ready to be used. Before he gave his orders he set up quick response system between the Sixth Directorate of the Headquarters, Strategic Rocket Forces and the Twelfth Directorate of the Ministry of Defence, which represented the nuclear weapons line of command, with open lines from his office to both directorates.

Then he instructed overt activity at several nuclear storage and launch sites. Missiles were moved around by road and rail. They were brought out into clearings and elevated for launch. It was a crisp clear day over large areas of Russia and the American satellites were passing overhead.

Prime Minister's Office, South Block, Delhi, India

Local time: 1130 Tuesday 8 May 2007
GMT: 0600 Tuesday 8 May 2007

'**Eastern Air Command** outside of Shillong is a bloody mess,' said Chandra Reddy. 'We have lost our command and control ability for the operation in Arunachal Pradesh.'

'Casualties?' asked Hari Dixit.

'In the dozens, sir. The cantonment is outside the town. We're still checking, but there are no reports of large-scale civilian casualties. Air Marshal Ravi Thapar is among the dead. He refused to go into the bunker.'

'Damn fool,' muttered the Chief of Army Staff, Unni Khrishnan.

'John Hastings wants to speak to you from Washington,' said Prabhu Purie, the Foreign Minister. 'Joan Holden urges us not to respond.'

Dixit drummed his fingers on the table. 'Does she now. I will not be speaking to Hastings, and tell Holden this. We pulled back, on an American assurance which proved to be hollow. We have taken heavy casualties at Shillong. I have lost a personal friend, and our ability to conduct an operation against the invading Chinese troops has been severely weakened. If I was a suspicious man, I would imagine that the United States and China were working together against India. Certainly, that is what our free press will make of it. So tell Holden that the democratically elected government of India reserves the right to do whatever it chooses to neutralize the threat from China.' He turned to Chandra Reddy. 'Can you get me Gorbunov at the Kremlin?'

When the Russian President was on the line, he said, 'We may have to embark upon full-scale war with China.'

'That does not surprise me,' said Gorbunov.

'I would like an assurance that our arms supplies will continue.'

'You have it. I have anticipated the conflict and we have transport planes, engineers and technicians standing by to fly in spares and new equipment. But I must tell you this. We are doing exactly the same for China. We are abiding by our existing contracts, giving no more and no less. Should I withdraw supplies to you both, China would win because of its superior sea-launched submarine capability and land-based missile arsenal. It is also more able to absorb casualties. My policy is that whatever the stakes and whatever the outcome, this conflict must be confined within Asia without interference from Russia or the United States.'

Xinhua News Agency, Beijing, China

Local time: 1400 Tuesday 8 May 2007
GMT: 0600 Tuesday 8 May 2007

'**The loyal forces** of the Second Artillery Regiment of the People's Liberation Army have intervened to stop a splittist declaration of independence by illegal groups in the province of Taiwan. Taiwan is an inalienable part of China and is an internal matter for the Chinese government. Meanwhile, fishermen on the islands of Pei-kan, Nan-kan and Pai-chuan have asked Chinese troops for help in building cyclone shelters for their boats. The People's Liberation Army is now working on that task, despite being attacked by a small number of terrorists who are holed up on the islands. Chinese fishermen on the island of Kinmen [Quemoy] have also asked for help and Chinese troops are on their way.'

Prime Minister's Office, Tokyo, Japan

Local time: 1500 Tuesday 8 May 2007
GMT: 0600 Tuesday 8 May 2007

'John, you can't sit on the fence,' said Prime Minister Wada, on the phone to the American President. 'You have obligations both to Taiwan and to Japan. Matsu has fallen and within twelve hours they may have taken Kinmen. A carrier group arriving in twenty-four hours is just not enough.'

'Taiwan has nothing to do with our treaty obligations to Japan,' said Hastings.

'To be frank, it does. Taken in isolation, I might be able to agree with you. But given what China is doing in India, it is imperative that its aggression be contained.'

Local time: 0115 Tuesday 8 May 2007
GMT: 0615 Tuesday 8 May 2007

'**We're exchanging real-time** SIGINT and ELINT with Taiwan,' said Tom Bloodworth. 'We've identified targets along the eastern coastline for cruise missile attacks. We have an *Arleigh Burke*-class cruiser within range and a first strike of Tomahawk cruise missiles is ready to go. The Japanese have picked up ELINT that the Chinese may deploy a SATCOM jammer against the US NAVSTAR Global Positioning System.'

'They're that sophisticated?' said Hastings.

'We don't know. They may try. But anyway we'll be deploying the TLAM Block III system which incorporates jam-resistant GPS receivers. It will also mean we don't have to use the terrain features to guide the missile to target, which would take time to prepare. That's why we're ready to launch now.'

'I suppose it's no good me suggesting we don't,' said Joan Holden.

Ennio Barber answered before Hastings could. 'We have to go to the American people with at least one strike, Mr President. The polls want us to hit much harder. The talk shows are full of retrospective stuff about us being soft on China and coddling dictators. If we don't hit back at them we lose it all.'

'Ennio has a point,' said Alvin Jebb. 'Although I admit it reluctantly. A superpower which fails to use that power in time of crisis is no longer a superpower.'

'And we'll lose the election,' added Barber.

'I understand the domestic political angle,' said Holden. 'I disagree with Alvin about losing superpower status, and I am not sure what we will achieve with one missile strike.'

'We force through a ceasefire. It's a message of force,' said Jebb.

'Tom,' said Hastings, 'what is your view?'

'It won't force a ceasefire,' he said. 'The Chinese will not back down, because if they do they will be embarrassed. But I don't see that we have an alternative. If we strike over Taiwan, we might send a message to the Indians that we're out there and that they don't have to nuke China to survive. That's what we've got to keep our eye on. After all these years, Taiwan is turning out to be a sideshow to the real conflict.' Bloodworth suddenly became distracted by new information on his computer screen. 'Sorry, but we're getting reports of unusual deployments around the nuclear missile silos in Russia. Mr President, I think you had better talk to Gorbunov.'

Foreign Ministry, Beijing, China

Local time: 1430 Tuesday 8 May 2007
GMT: 0630 Tuesday 8 May 2007

'If American missiles hit the mainland, we'll be expelling you,' Jamie Song told his friend Reece Overhalt. 'The Embassy and your residence are surrounded by anti-American protesters. Don't even try to get back there. I will give you a car with Foreign Ministry number plates to take you to the airport. We've given permission for the Gulf-stream chartered by your Embassy to stay on the tarmac until you need it. I will send in Public Security Bureau police to the Embassy to help evacuate staff. I will do that now. They will be taken to the airport and put on any commercial flights out. CNN might be saying that the demonstrations are staged. Believe me, they are not. We're even worried that they might get out of hand and turn into a protest about our close relationship with the United States.'

'I'm urging them not to strike,' said Overhalt. 'If you can hold off the invasion of Kinmen, we can hold off the strikes.'

Song let out a tired, cynical laugh. 'Xinhua has announced it. China always does what it says it's going to do. We are the most predictable government in the world. Besides, you have no choice. If you don't strike, you lose it all, to Japan, to India, to Russia and to us.' Song got up. Despite his bloodshot eyes and drawn features, he looked immaculate in a tailor-made dark suit. 'I've promised to do CNN,' he said. 'It's only next door, so hang around and watch it. It'll probably be my last interview before Congress passes a new Trading with the Enemy Act with China.'

CNN: Foreign Minister, thank you for coming on to give us the Chinese perspective on the Taiwan dispute, and I would like to start on as optimistic a note as we can muster. Can you give us a timetable for the withdrawal of Chinese troops from Taiwan?

Song: I hope I can. But I would just like to make clear to the American people what we did and what we are trying to achieve. Our missile strike was very specific. We targeted the building and people inside who were about to issue a declaration of independence. We have always said we would take action and we did. For defensive purposes we will be putting military garrisons on islands previously occupied by Taiwanese troops. These are known in the US as Kinmen or Quemoy, and Matsu. They are about a hundred miles west of the island of Taiwan and dangerously close to our eastern coastline defences. Those operations are still ongoing and I believe the Taiwanese are putting up limited military resistance. I would expect us to be in full control by midday tomorrow.

CNN: Xinhua said that you were helping local fishermen build typhoon shelters.

Song: I don't edit Xinhua. You want to know what's happening and I'm telling you. This is too big to try to pit me against our official news agency.

CNN: All right, you occupy the islands. Then what?

Song: We will not strike Taiwan Island again as long as there are no further moves to declare independence. The National Assembly never passed the law. The celebrations did not go ahead, so I see no reason for conflict.

CNN: Except that the people of Taiwan want independence.

Song: They have it. They have more independence than the Kashmiris, the Chechens, the Texans, the Catholics of Northern Ireland and the Tibetans. All we are saying is this: Taiwan will not get a seat in the UN because China is a permanent member of the Security Council and we will veto its admittance. If John Hastings wants to recognize Taiwan's independence, China will break off relations with the United States. The same applies to any other government. What I suggest is that President Lin grows up. Instead of trying to score personal points for himself, he allows time for us to sort out the Taiwan question. It may not happen in my lifetime or his. But it could emerge peacefully, if he lets it.

CNN: The opinion polls in the US favour American intervention.

Song: Intervene in what? Unless you declare all-out war in China, I can't see what you can do. You strike one airfield on our east coast and we have a hundred more we can use. Just think what it took to get a deal with Serbia in 1999, and that's the size of just one county in one of our coastal provinces.

CNN: The feeling here is that Chinese aggression—

Song: Stop right there. Taiwan took advantage of a time when both President Hastings and President Tao were preoccupied with the much more serious problem with India. It was Taiwan, not us, which pushed the independence issue, knowing, and let me repeat that, knowing full well that both Japan and the United States could be militarily drawn into the dispute. If that is not the height of political cynicism and irresponsibility, I don't know what is. I just hope the American people understand that when they send their young men and women to risk their loves in conflict against us, it would only be to boost the ratings of a phony Taiwanese politician.

Local time: 0145 Tuesday 8 May 2007
GMT: 0645 Tuesday 8 May 2007

John Hastings turned away from the television screen. He said, looking at Bloodworth: 'Can we live with that? Has he given us the makings of a deal?'

'Overhalt says Jamie Song is not in direct contact with the President. He certainly doesn't have the authority of General Leung.'

'We're evacuating the Embassy staff on the basis of an ordered departure,' said Joan Holden. 'Apparently, the British Embassy has been burnt, with one diplomat dead. We've offered to take out their staff as long as it doesn't conflict with our "no double standard" rule. We have a line open to Reece at the Foreign Ministry. He seems to be camping in Jamie Song's office.'

'It's not a deal,' said Ennio Barber. 'It's an interview on CNN. Might I suggest that one missile strike could get President Tao to the phone? Once that conversation has taken place we can have a deal which won't cost us the election.'

'I don't like his reasoning,' said Bloodworth. 'But Ennio's idea might just work. I suggest two Tomahawks into two DF-15 launch sites in Fujian province. Our IMINT will throw up the coordinates.'

'All right,' said Hastings slowly. 'Do it.'

Military Headquarters, Western Hills, China

'**Two cruise missiles** have hit the control tower and runway at Xiamen civilian airfield,' said General Leung. 'We should respond by targeting Okinawa.'

'Not yet,' said President Tao. Holed up with the military, Tao had managed to cling on to the authority of his presidency. As soon as he emerged, leaving the general to his own devices, he would lose it. 'A missile launch on Okinawa would force us into a war which has no decisive end. It is against our doctrine of *yizhan ershang*, winning a victory with one strike. Let us try to follow the line which Comrade Song outlined on CNN. Let them strike us. We will use our air defences to intercept the missiles. We will not strike back. We will try to secure Matsu and Kinmen by the morning, and challenge the Western democracies to recognize Taiwan if they wish.'

General Leung: 'Then I suggest you tell President Hastings that. We occupy Matsu and Kinmen. Taiwan Island reverts to the status quo. They send no more missiles against our facilities.'

Local time: 0200 Tuesday 8 May 2007
GMT: 0700 Tuesday 8 May 2007

John Hastings had been on the telephone to President Tao for four minutes, using interpreters and patiently letting the Chinese leader run through his prepared script. Then Tao cut into his own lecture with what Hastings could only later describe as a high-pitched yelp. At the same time, Tom Bloodworth's voice broke through the hum of the war room: 'Indian missile. The Agni. Launch pad north of Allahabad. Waiting for coordinates.'

Tao left his line open but never returned to it. Analysts later described as gold dust the disjointed conversations recorded in Washington from the Chinese war head-quarters. They confirmed that China did have real-time satellite surveillance over India, which picked up the launch at exactly the same moment as it came through on Blood-worth's screen. The analysts also discovered – although only much later, when the conflict was over – that Tao himself remained in charge, and they were able to break down the command structure and the relationship between him, General Leung and their subordinates. But most signifi-cantly, ninety seconds after ending his conversation with Hastings, Tao's voice was identified as initiating the com-mand. Although Tao's mood and motive were hotly debated for months to come, it was widely believed that his decision had been made some time earlier and that India's missile launch was only the catalyst with which he chose to activate it.

Operational Directorate, South Block, Delhi, India

Local time: 1230 Tuesday 8 May 2007
GMT: 0700 Tuesday 8 May 2007

'**Target the Chinese** garrison in Namya Ra, Myanmar,' said Chandra Reddy. 'Target Chinese supply and airbase in Lashio. Target Chinese ELINT and SIGINT station on Little Cocos Island. Target Chinese naval ships at Hanggyi Island base on the Irrawaddy River delta. All targets are on Myanmar sovereign territory. None is in Tibet. One is in China itself – the DF-21 launch site in Chuxiong, used against Taiwan.'

'To show solidarity with the Americans and the Japanese,' said Hari Dixit.

'For symbolic reasons, they are all conventional missile strikes. We are using the Prithvi with single 500 kilogram warheads from bases in Arunachal Pradesh on targets in Myanmar, and from bases on the Andaman Islands to hit Hanggyi and Little Cocos Island. The Agni from Gorakhpur region is due to impact on Chuxiong. It has a single 1,000 kilogram warhead. Ground-attack aircraft are already in the air for an immediate follow up on Hanggyi and Little Cocos Island. The aim is to put all Indian Ocean and Bay of Bengal military activity to an end.'

Local time: 1205 Tuesday 8 May 2007
GMT: 0705 Tuesday 8 May 2007

President Tao's command came through as a two-syllable message picked up by the National Security Agency listening station at Menwith Hill in northern England, sent through to the NSA at CINCPAC headquarters in Hawaii and relayed immediately to the commander of the USS *Ronald Reagan.* It comprised yet another phrase, not encrypted, but compressed so that the transmission time was just a fraction of a second. *Long Huo,* it said, *Dragon Fire,* beamed down from the same orbiting Chinese satellite which had instructed the *Kilo*-class submarine to attack the *Bombay.* An encrypted and frequency-hopping signal almost certainly coming from the *Xia*-class nuclear armed submarine in the Bay of Bengal was sent back. The *Xia* could not pick up signals under water and must have been at least at periscope depth. It was daylight and unlucky that no ship was in the vicinity when the *Xia* came up. The NSA analysts put the vessel at about 150 kilometres south-west of the carrier group. A call was sent to all shipping, commercial and military, to look out for the submarine. Even then it was like finding a needle in a haystack.

The Indians were carrying out round-the-clock anti-submarine patrols in the area of probability where it was thought the *Xia* could be. The Americans were doing the same, and their experience and more sophisticated equipment, such as trailing kilometres of sonar buoys through the area of probability, meant that vast areas of sea were being eliminated. But none got a positive identification.

The water was deep and the *Xia* had dived. If it was carrying the JL-2, it could be fired from anywhere inside the Bay of Bengal and hit a target in India.

The *Xia* was under orders to receive messages every twelve hours, and as the Indian missile attack was detected it was on schedule to come up. Had Tao hesitated with his decision, it would have been another half-day before he could have given the command.

The Kremlin, Moscow, Russia

Local time: 1010 Tuesday 8 May 2007
GMT: 0710 Tuesday 8 May 2007

The news of the Indian launch reached President Gorbunov minutes after it got to the White House Situation Room. President Tao came through immediately and said in Russian: 'I have given the command. It is sea-launched.' He spoke in a manner which left Gorbunov certain as to what he meant. He also knew exactly the unstoppable process under which Tao had decided to operate. Once under the surface again, the commander of the *Xia* could receive no messages from the outside world. He would now be working side by side with his weapons engineer, preparing for the launch. Each man held separate keys and codes to verify each other's actions. When the missile was fired, there would be no doubt that it had been on the instructions of a legitimate government and that the men on the trigger were acting professionally and under orders.

Gorbunov telephoned John Hastings. 'I have intelligence that the Chinese have initiated a nuclear strike against India,' he said.

Hastings was silent for a long time. 'Are you in contact with President Tao?'

'I am.'

'Tell him to stop.'

'It is submarine-launched from the Bay of Bengal. Short of finding the vessel and destroying it, no one can revert the order.'

'Is Tao sane?'

'Perfectly. He sees it as a legitimate act of war. In discussions with him, he compared it to the American atomic bombing of Japan – necessary to bring about a decisive end to the conflict.'

'Then tell him that if his nuclear missile does strike India, the United States will obliterate his nuclear arsenal and his government with it. There won't be a China left to surrender.'

It was now Gorbunov's turn to use the silent pause. 'That is the main reason for my call,' he said eventually. 'Russia does not want American interference in this conflict. We understand your treaty obligations over Taiwan and Japan and have stayed silent at your conventional cruise missile strike on Xiamen. But if you threaten China with nuclear retaliation, Russia will have no alternative but to threaten the United States with a counter-strike.'

The conversation in English was being carried around the situation room on a speaker. The bustle of activity ended and the room became quiet.

'I'm not sure what you are saying, Vlad.'

'This is a conflict between India and China. Both you and I have tried to broker a peace and have failed. China has decided to use the nuclear option. India, so far, has not. You have yet to discuss this with your colleagues, but I suspect you will end up deciding not to risk losing an American city to save an Indian one. However, to posture and threaten will be dangerous for world peace. Therefore, see it as my doing you a favour, John. Should you make a statement threatening China, Russian missiles will be launched not against United States territory – I'll leave that to the Chinese – but against the Menwith Hill listening station in Britain and the Pine Gap listening station near Alice Springs in Australia. As well as damaging your intelligence-gathering capabilities, it will knock out the European Relay Ground Station for the space-based infrared theatre missile-defence system. That will eliminate your early warning mechanism for a missile strike from Russia. It will also split Western political resolve. The Australians and the British might think twice about your policies. Should you not then reconsider, we will be back on a Cold War footing of what we used to call Mutually Assured Destruction.'

'Why, Vlad? Why on earth are you doing this?'

'You've got to learn to balance power again, John. The Russian people feel you have walked all over them since the end of the Cold War. Vulnerable people who have lost their pride are dangerous. I am anticipating a way forward. If Tao is telling me the truth, India will decide her next actions, not Russia and not America.'

Local time: 0215 Tuesday 8 May 2007
GMT: 0715 Tuesday 8 May 2007

'**He could be** bluffing,' said Bloodworth.

'If he's not . . .' said Alvin Jebb.

Bloodworth pulled up a map of Russia's nuclear facilities and projected them onto a screen in the meeting room. 'Let's assume for a few minutes that we can do something. We could take out 12th Main Directorate offices here in Moscow with a conventional cruise missile strike. We could shut down the Tatishchevo launch base at 51° 40′ N, 45° 34′ E – again with a conventional strike. We could use tactical nuclear weapons against the Krasnoarmeyskoye storage facility south of Saratov, 51° 12′ N, 46° 02′ E. Only nuclear warheads would get into the ravined area which protects the bunkers. We would need tactical nuclear warheads against Malaya Sazanka, just south of Svobodnyl in the Far East, 51° 15′ N, 128° 1′ E. This is one of the older storage facilities, but it's still active. Again, we would need a nuclear strike against Mozhaysk, which is the closest storage bunker to Moscow at 55° 26′ N, 35° 46′ E. The satellite photograph, here, shows the soccer field within the perimeter fence, indicating the size of the facility we would be destroying. We could get away with a conventional strike at Nizhnyaya Tura on both the storage facility at 58° 37′ N, 59° 45′ E and the nuclear weapons production plant there. We might have to be careful because Nizhnyaya Tura works together with Sverdlovsk-45, the biological weapons research facility, which could release something like smallpox into the air when a missile smashes into it.' Bloodworth looked around the room. 'That is just a fraction of what my computer has thrown up.'

'We can't do anything, you mean?' said Hastings quietly.

'If we knocked out all of that and twice as much again, he could still do more damage to America and our allies than we could absorb.'

Local time: 1300 Tuesday 8 May 2007
GMT: 0730 Tuesday 8 May 2007

The swell of the sea around the submarine was identified by an alert analyst in Washington from a satellite transmission. Seconds after the swell, a generation of white water spread from the area as the submarine's missile doors opened. The sea began heaving violently, then it pitched and rolled as if a storm was whipping up. Outside the area of launch the sea was flat as it only could be shortly before a tropical monsoon. The water sprayed and frothed, and the satellite picked up fire, leaping from the sea, then when the missile cleared the surface, its thrusters took it skywards beyond the earth's atmosphere, before turning it to come down minutes later on its target.

On instructions from the Prime Minister, John Stopping by-passed the Home Office and called directly to Robin Sutcliffe in the broadcasting bunker at Wood Norton. He identified himself with a pre-arranged code. 'When can you begin broadcasts from Wood Norton?' said Stopping.

It was the morning peak time. Although the Taiwan conflict was high on the agenda, the bulletins were focusing on the sudden resignation of the Foreign Minister, Christopher Baker. He had been arrested for being drunk and disorderly in Pall Mall only a few hours earlier. He had been alone and carrying a briefcase of classified documents, which luckily had been kept safe and unopened by the police. India was ranking third in the running order. Shortly before going on air at 0600, the government in Delhi had shut down satellite broadcasts out of the country. Full censorship had been imposed. Journalists were banned from the front line in Arunachal Pradesh and the issues of conflict between China and India were considered obscure, given what else was around.

'We can switch any time at ninety seconds' notice,' said Sutcliffe. 'We are running simultaneous dummy programmes.'

'We would like you to wait until the 0730 news headlines are out the way and then switch. Say it is because of technical problems.'

'Why is it?'

'I am afraid I can't divulge. You can run your programmes as normal, but we might have to take over editorial control at any time under the terms of the charter.'

Many listeners, tuned into 5 Live, were unaware of the change because those channels kept operating. The *Today Programme* presenters had less of a problem in explaining the sudden change of broadcast venue than the two presenters fronting *Breakfast News*. They were replaced by a lone and less famous presenter with a bland corporate backdrop. The programmes schedules were maintained on the computer line, with the new presenters reading the same scripts as had been prepared in London. Sutcliffe decided that the packages at Television Centre should be used in preference to the lower-quality material which had been cobbled together at Wood Norton.

What remained a secret was that the BBC's programmes were going out from a nuclear bunker because British territory had been threatened with a strike from Russia.

Faced with a news blackout in Delhi, the BBC's Asia Correspondent, Martin Cartwright, had got straight on a plane to Bombay. On landing, he and his cameraman, Darren Scott, had taken a tortuous taxi journey to the financial district in the Fort area. If he could not report from the war zone or the seat of government, he planned to spin a story from India's economic centre, transmitting it illegally on a satellite telephone. Bombay was as restless, dirty and unmanageable as he had ever seen it, oblivious to the global conflict going on around. Cartwright and Scott had hardly slept in forty-eight hours, frustrated at the restrictions put on their reporting, made worse with their story being hi-jacked by the conflict over Taiwan. Cartwright was even more furious because Sutcliffe had overruled his plan to fly straight back to Taiwan. He was told it was already being covered by a more junior correspondent.

It was Scott who eventually came up with the idea of

just the two of them taking off to Bombay with a video-capable portable sat phone and the miniature SX edit pack. Scott said he could get Cartwright up for a two-way into the morning radio bulletins. They could then check into the Taj Hotel and have plenty of time to cut a piece of the *Nine O'Clock News*. If any pictures did come from Delhi or Arunachal Pradesh, they could drop them into the piece in London. As Cartwright and Scott inched through the streets in their taxi, beggars everywhere tapping on the windows, Scott checked out locations for pre-recorded two-ways in visions, which they could feed through the sat phone. He decided that the esplanade looking onto the Sea of Arabia outside the Taj Hotel would be as good as anywhere. The bustle of street-sleepers, traders and grubby children as a backdrop would show up India for what it really was. Cartwright liked it because he could contrast it with Shanghai. He would ask rhetorically why China's economic centre had built a beautiful waterside promenade where people went out to enjoy themselves, roller-blading, kite flying, taking pictures, buying ice-cream, living a life, yet the same in Bombay was a wretched place of poverty, where not even a drop of wealth had seeped through to the streets. He noted down the thought.

The waterfront was also a good spot for radio, giving a clear line to the Indian Ocean satellite, and close enough to the banking district and Stock Exchange for Cartwright to say he was reporting from the area. It was also near to Horniman Circle where the Town Hall had been the target of a Pakistani bomb just two days earlier. The area was still cordoned off, yet the stock exchange had only dipped by a few percentage points because of the war. Disappointedly, Cartwright decided his story would have to be about Indian resilience ploughing on in an atmosphere of business as usual. This was hardly a community living in panic.

Scott got through to Traffic, the BBC's communications centre, and was patched through to the radio studio in Wood Norton. The programme editor came on the line, asking if Cartwright could begin in fifteen seconds. They wanted an Indian reaction to the resignation of Christopher Baker. Cartwright was halfway through his objection that Baker was definitely not the story, when he heard the presenter's voice in the earpiece.

Presenter: We have finally got line to India, where our Asia Correspondent, Martin Cartwright, has managed to get to us from Bombay, or Mumbai as it is known locally. Before we talk about the situation there, Martin, can you tell us the impact Christopher Baker's suddenly leaving office will have on Britain's relations with India during this critical time?

Cartwright: Very little, I expect. India is in the middle of a serious border dispute with China. We've just learned since getting here that India has carried out a major missile attack on Chinese bases with the aim of pushing Chinese forces out of Burma – or Myanmar – and its naval forces out of the Bay of Bengal. I can't see Christopher Baker having much influence—

Presenter: I'm sorry to interrupt, but Mr Baker's supporters are saying that he was carrying out highly influential behind-the-scenes negotiations to try to bring about peace in South Asia, that he is a crucial player.

Cartwright: Well if he was, it didn't work because there's war. India is not a place where diplomatic secrets are easily kept, and no British or Indian journalist or diplomat has ever mentioned Christopher Baker as being a player. The only interest he ignited was about his mistresses.

Presenter: All right, very briefly, now, Martin, because we're running out of time, what is the atmosphere like in Bombay? We've had unconfirmed reports of mass panic in some areas.

Cartwright: The city centre itself is very much business as usual—

After that, the line went dead, but the tape was played over and over again; the explosion, the roaring air and then the silence were terribly and clearly audible – no more than five seconds of radio, painting a picture of sound for the first nuclear catastrophe of the twenty-first century.

Bombay/Mumbai, India

Local time: 1315 Tuesday 8 May 2007
GMT: 0745 Tuesday 8 May 2007

The temperature was 36°C, the day was clear with visibility of more than twenty-five kilometres and a light wind blew in from the south at 8.33 k.p.h. It was one of the hottest days of the year and many workers had stayed inside their air-conditioned offices for lunch away from the heat and humidity.

Those outside who instinctively looked towards the flash had their eyes burnt out. The ones who survived – and not many did – were blinded with third-degree burns to their eyes. The breeze whipped up into erratic gales which flung pedestrians at more than 160 k.p.h. to their deaths. Within about 0.1 milliseconds after the explosion, the radius of the fireball was about 14 metres. The ground at the centre exploded with heat. Tiles, granite, glass within a radius of 1,500 metres melted. Fires leapt out of wherever there were flammable materials, so that just about every building was alight, even four or five kilometres from where the warhead went off, forcing millions out onto the streets. Their clothes burst into flames as well, and afterwards bodies were found with clothing patterns etched onto their skins. The first thought of most was to head for water and thousands sought refuge on the sweeping beach along Marine Drive, or Sasoon Dock near the Gateway of India. The explosion had set off tremors in the ground like an earthquake and the sea swelled angrily around like water in an unsteady bowl. The sand exploded like popcorn, burning their feet and driving them towards the water. As they swam out, the fires proved to be faster and stronger. The victims were eventually incinerated by leaping fireballs which seemed to bounce out to sea in all directions killing everything in their paths. One moment the beaches were filled with the sound of shouting and crying. The next they were quiet apart from the roars of conflicting winds created by the nuclear explosion. Then, people would appear again chasing sanctuary until the next fireball engulfed them.

The citizens of Bombay were being killed by three direct impacts from the explosion: blast or shock, thermal radiation and prompt nuclear radiation. On top of this, there were the effects of the electromagnetic pulse in which they felt as if they were being smashed in the back by a hammer, then immediately hurled into boiling water or an inferno. Thousands more were cut up and killed by flying glass and debris or in secondary explosions of cars, motor-scooters and domestic gas cylinders.

Within twenty minutes of the explosion a circle of three kilometres radius from the blast was ravaged by the same type of firestorms as ripped through Hamburg, Dresden and Tokyo following the incendiary attacks during the Second World War, and of course, through Hiroshima and Nagasaki after the nuclear attack. The temperatures were 300°, 400°, no one ever knew. Those who did not flee their buildings were suffocated with carbon monoxide poisoning and died where they hid.

The fires created a massive vortex which sucked in air from the areas around it, building up yet more unpredictable winds, drawing in oxygen to feed the inferno at speeds of up to 80 k.p.h. At that stage, no one could survive.

It was then, almost half an hour after the missile struck, that satellite pictures picked up the first formation of the mushroom cloud. As the winds brought in fresh oxygen, the heat was pushed upwards, taking with it vaporized debris which became lethal, highly radioactive dust. Water droplets from the sea also condensed around radioactive particles and hours later fell to earth again, many kilometres away, as black rain.

Whether the missile had been targeted on the Fort area so the radiation cloud would be blown north over the highly populated areas of the city would remain a moot point for years to come. The Chinese claimed the coordinates were 19° 02′ N, 72° 56′ E, the Bhabha Atomic Research Centre (BARC) at Trombay twenty kilometres north-east of the main Fort financial district. Two of the research heavy water reactors there, the Cirus 40 MW and the Dhruva 100 MW, produced plutonium at the rate of 30 kilograms a year, enough for up to five nuclear bombs. Therefore, argued the Chinese, the site was a legitimate military target.

The fact was that the single 15 kiloton warhead exploded 185 metres directly above Fort, at a lower altitude but with the same velocity as the American strike on Hiroshima. The BARC complex was put out of action and the prevailing winds blew the fallout due north over the most heavily populated areas of Bombay. Just about every building was destroyed from the west coast to the east coast, the Sea of Arabia to Harbour Bay and from the southern coastal point in Colaba north through Fort, through the Chatrapathi Shivaji Terminus to the shacks of the Mohatta Market. Hardly anyone escaped alive – and that was only in the first hour.

The population density in the most crowded areas of Bombay was as high as 40,000 people per square kilometre. Given that it was lunchtime on a working day, the number of people in Fort was at least that. No one ever came up with even a roughly accurate figure, but for the record, the Indian government put the number killed in the first hour of the explosion at 200,000.

Operational Directorate, South Block, Delhi, India

Local time: 1415 Tuesday 8 May 2007
GMT: 0845 Tuesday 8 May 2007

'**We must retaliate,**' said Hari Dixit.

'No,' replied Unni Khrishnan, almost in a whisper. 'We must stop. If they strike again we are condemning the lives of another million people.'

Dixit shook his head: 'And if we don't we will lose India.'

'I don't care if your bloody government falls.'

'Neither do I. But if we capitulate now, we will lose our status as a nation. Are the Agnis ready for launch?'

'And if they target Delhi?'

'We die,' said Dixit.

'Four mobile sites are prepared,' said Khrishnan softly. 'Enemy targets are the military headquarters in Chengdu, the Western Hills in Beijing, Zhongnanhai and Shanghai.'

'We will not hit population centres.'

'They have.'

'We won't.'

'Then we lose.'

'We've lost already,' said the Indian Prime Minister.

'Then stop,' pleaded Khrishnan.

'We can't, Khrishnanji. Don't you understand, India can't surrender now.'

Operational Directorate, South Block, Delhi, India

Local time: 1510 Tuesday 8 May 2007
GMT: 0940 Tuesday 8 May 2007

'**They've launched from** Tibet,' said Unni Khrishnan. 'We should head for the bunker.'

'No,' said Hari Dixit. 'If the people of Delhi are to die in a nuclear attack, this captain is going to stay on the bridge.'

'President Gorbunov calling from Moscow,' said Khrishnan's aide de camp.

'Tao has called a ceasefire,' began Gorbunov.

'He's just launched,' said Dixit.

'Six minutes to impact,' said Unni Khrishnan.

'You have my word that China will carry out no more attacks.'

'Can they destroy the missile, mid-flight?'

'I don't know.'

'Listen, Vlad, within five minutes we could be vapourized. I don't regard it as a ceasefire. It's the act of high cynicism.'

'Agni ready for launch, Prime Minister,' said Unni Khrishnan.

Hari Dixit cut the line to Moscow: 'Go ahead,' he said.

Ground zero was between the North Block and the South Block. The fireball swept through the elegant buildings of pink Rajasthan sandstone, which collapsed into molten rubble incinerating everyone inside. The magnificent architectural buildings of Indian democracy were destroyed within seconds of the blast; India Gate, the Parliament

The Kremlin, Moscow, Russia

'**Are you threatening** me?' said President Gorbunov. He had taken the call from John Hastings, without interpreters or even his private secretary taking notes.

'I will repeat myself, Mr President,' said Hastings. 'You have five minutes to get an unequivocal ceasefire from both India and China. If you fail, we are going to obliterate China's military capabilities with nuclear and conventional weapons. If you threaten to strike the United States or Europe we will strike Russia. Your office will be ground zero. This is not a threat, Mr President, it is reality.'

'You are at risk of creating an even more dangerous situation.'

'I did not call you for a debate in international relations. I called to tell you what is going to happen.'

'And if I comply?'

'No one need know this conversation ever took place.'

Military Headquarters, Western Hills, China

Local time: 1730 Tuesday 8 May 2007
GMT: 0930 Tuesday 8 May 2007

'**Nuclear air-burst over** Chengdu?' said General Leung. 'Where, exactly?'

'Unclear. We have lost contact.'

President Tao remained silent. He sat in an office chair, his chin in his hands, staring at the huge map in the war room. Hari Dixit had more nerve than he had anticipated. If India and China slugged it out city for city, India would lose eventually, but China would not be an outright winner. The progress of the last quarter of a century would be wrecked, and the Motherland's standing in the international community would be in tatters. Yet if Tao stopped now, China would be a defeated nation. He pushed the chair back, stood up and walked over to the wall map, his shadow moving across it like a storm cloud.

The Situation Room, The White House, Washington, DC

'**The whole of** central Bombay is flattened,' said Tom Bloodworth. 'We're picking up the formation of a mushroom cloud. There are reports of black rain falling on the Tulsi Lake in the national park to the north of the city.'

John Hastings stood upright in the centre of the room, looking at the satellite imagery being translated into impact data on the map of Bombay.

'Reece Overhalt calling from Jamie Song's office,' said Joan Holden.

'President Tao gave the order for only one launch,' said Overhalt. 'He does not want to strike again.'

Bloodworth, on another phone, interrupted the President's conversation. 'Mr President, Hari Dixit is retaliating.'

'For Christ's sake tell him China's calling it a day,' yelled Hastings.

'That's not the point,' said Bloodworth.

'The Chinese are calling an emergency UN Security Council meeting,' Overhalt said to Hastings.

'Cynical bastards.'

'Two Agni launches from north-east India,' said Bloodworth.

'Get that shit Gorbunov on the phone,' snapped Hastings.

Building, the National Archives, the Supreme Court, then further out with temperatures still almost a million degrees, the path of destruction hitting Connaught Place, Janpath, and other landmarks of India's heritage. The glass walls on the newer buildings shattered immediately, with people and furniture instantaneously hurled outside. Then, like in Bombay, the firestorms reached the flimsier structures, the more densely crowded parts of the city, where people died in their tens of thousands.

Even ten miles away in places like Vasant, Vihar and Janakpuri, everyone outside was struck with severe burns and houses spontaneously caught light, causing unstoppable fires to rage through the slums killing those inside. Within the three kilometre radius of ground zero, nothing survived. The men in charge of the government of India were dead. The institutions which ran the country were out of action.

The Situation Room, The White House, Washington, DC

Local time: 0530 Tuesday 8 May 2007
GMT: 1030 Tuesday 8 May 2007

'**Dixit targeted the** Western Hills before he died,' said Tom Bloodworth. 'It must have been a 250 kiloton warhead to make the range.'

'Did it hit?'

'Yes, but the Chinese bunker is too well dug in. The only casualties are the villagers, fruit orchards and a few army barracks. There's a strong westerly wind. In nuclear terms the damage is minimal. We've just picked up new signals from the bunker, so their backup communications system must have kicked in.'

Hastings sat heavily in a chair, allowing the exhaustion to show for the first time in forty-eight hours. 'Hari Dixit refused to go for the civilian targets, didn't he?'

Bloodworth pointed to one of the computer screens. 'These are the latest satellite pictures from India. This is Delhi.' He changed the picture. 'This is Calcutta. Then Bangalore, Madras. It's going on everywhere.'

Even though ill-defined, the images showed streams of people fleeing the population centres of India. The main roads were too clogged with human life to take cars, carts or even motor-scooters. Vehicles were abandoned, as were possessions which hindered escape. The nuclear holocaust had instilled terror throughout the country.

'What about China?' said Hastings.

'There's cloud over Chengdu. So we don't know what's happening there. Tao has closed down all telecommunications. Even mobile phones. The television is showing a sitcom.' He brought up an overhead scene. 'This is Tiananmen Square, Beijing. The signs say it is closed for redecoration. This is the main road south. Traffic moving as normal. It's the same for Shanghai, Wuhan, Harbin. You name it, the Chinese are controlling it.'

'They've won, haven't they, Tom?'

'Won through their own brutality.'

'Damn right, they have,' said Hastings. 'They've won because they had nuclear weapons and they used them ruthlessly – just like we did in Hiroshima and Nagasaki.'

EPILOGUE

With medical and public services collapsed, the twenty million people affected by the nuclear attack in India were mostly left to fend for themselves. International agencies came in where they could, but the task was simply too enormous. The few not killed in the immediate explosion died of burns and infection over the following few days. Those who survived longer began to break out with illnesses. The symptoms were nausea, vomiting and loss of appetite; diarrhoea with blood; high fever; bleeding into the skin resulting in welts; ulceration of the mouth; bleeding from the gums, the rectum and the urinary tract; loss of hair and general weakness until death. The statistics were still being compiled when this report was written, but it was estimated that 60 per cent of the deaths were from burns and the blast itself, 20 per cent from radiation sickness and another 20 per cent from related injuries and illnesses. Many in this last category were the very young or very old. Scientists estimated that the radiation in the worst areas measured almost 500 rads an hour and that anything above 400 rads an hour (over a three-hour period) would kill at least half the people exposed to it. Given that most had no means of escape, many more than the specified 50 per cent would have died from it. A year later eight hundred thousand people were estimated to have died because of the attack.

*

Chengdu and the Western Hills outside Beijing were closed off completely. It is still not clear the extent of the casualties there, or how the Chinese emergency services handled the crisis. Experts assumed that because of its more disciplined society, the victims fared better than in India.

The United States led a global condemnation of China and introduced a package of potentially crippling sanctions. But these were ignored by Russia and most of the governments in South-East Asia. The Thai Prime Minister was the first high-level foreign leader to visit Beijing, followed by most of the South-East Asian heads of government, who publicly acknowledged China's new position as a world superpower. Dignitaries from the Middle East visited. The first Western leader was the German Chancellor, followed shortly by the French President. Britain maintained that a high-level visit was out of the question. It never confirmed that it had led the Special Forces raid on the Cocos Islands and it was never leaked out that for a few hours the BBC was broadcasting from the Wood Norton nuclear bunker.

The new Indian Prime Minister signed a substantive defence alliance with Japan allowing for joint exercises in the South China Sea and the Bay of Bengal, breaking Japan's commitment to confine its military activities to within 2,400 kilometres of its coastline. Russia attempted to initiate a three-power summit in Moscow with China and India, where it was announced that India would open border negotiations with China. At the eleventh hour India pulled out, refusing to send even a junior official. Chinese troops withdrew into Burma from Arunachal Pradesh. General Hamid Khan and his staff, including Captain

Masood, were dug out of the General Headquarters bunker by the first wave of UN troops to arrive in Pakistan. Khan was a broken man, conceding that his high-stakes plan to modernize Pakistan had failed. The country was run by an interim UN protectorate, but supported by the army. One of the options was to incorporate Pakistan back into the Indian federation, with a widespread international view that the partition had failed, but there was strong opposition to this from within Pakistan and the Islamic world. Chinese troops continued to occupy the outlying islands of Taiwan with no resistance from the local people. President Lin resigned and was replaced by a more moderate politician. Trade between the mainland and Taiwan boomed to such an extent that direct shipping and flights were allowed.

India held fresh elections and reconstruction work began in both Delhi and Bombay. The Bombay stock market was moved to Madras, but with the stated aim of rebuilding it on its original site once decontamination had been completed. The seat of government was temporarily set up in Calcutta.

Both John Hastings and the more hawkish Anthony Pincher were re-elected, with increased majorities, as were the leaders of New Zealand and Australia. Prime Minister Wada lost his election to more nationalistic forces in Japan. President Tao held a missile parade in Tiananmen Square with Jamie Song, Tang Siju and General Leung by his side on the balcony on the gate of the Forbidden City. Reece Overhalt, as doyen of the diplomatic corps, boycotted the ceremony. Shortly after that, both he and Jamie Song retired, with Song spending most of his time with his software companies in California.

The status of China in the twenty-first century was hotly debated in diplomatic and academic circles. But in reality, it had obtained power by force which would have taken it generations to obtain through peace.

SELECT BIBLIOGRAPHY
AND PAPERS

Afroze, Shaheen *Nuclear Rivalry and Non-nuclear Weapon States in South Asia: Policy Contingency Framework* 1995

Bajpai, Kanti P. etc. *Brass Tacks and Beyond: Perception of Management and Crisis in South Asia* 1995

Barber, Noel *From the Land of Lost Content* 1969

Bates, Bill *China: Can Engagement Work?* 1999

Bernstein, Richard and Munro, Ross H. *The Coming Conflict with China* 1997

Bhaumik, Subhir *The (North) East is Red* 1997

Byron, John and Pack, Robert *The Claws of the Dragon: Kang Sheng* 1992

Chalmers, Malcolm *Openness and Security Policy in South-east Asia* 1996

Chellaney, Brahma *After the Tests: India's Options* 1998

Cordingly, Major General Patrick *In the Eye of the Storm* 1996

Dean, Eddie *Rabuka: No Other Way* 1988

Dixit, J. N. *Across Borders: Fifty Years of India's Foreign Policy* 1998

Dixit, J. N. *Anatomy of a Flawed Inheritance* 1995

Evans, Richard *Deng Xiaoping and the Making of Modern China* 1993

Ghosh, Amitav *Countdown* 1999

Green, Michael J. and Self, Benjamin L. *Japan's Changing China Policy: From Commercial Liberalism to Reluctant Realism*

Han Suyin *Eldest Son Zhou Enlai and the Making of Modern China* 1993

Heisberg, François *Prospects for Nuclear Stability between India and Pakistan* 1998

Huntington, Samuel P. *The Clash of Civilizations and the Remaking of World Order* 1996

International Institute of Strategic Studies *Military Balance* 1999

Jeffrey, Robin *Asia: The Winning of Independence* 1981

Kalam, Abdul A. P. J. *India 2020: A Vision for the New Millennium* 1998

Khatak, Saba Gul *Security Discourses and the State of Pakistan* 1996

Lam, Willy Wo-Lap *China after Deng Xiaoping* 1995

Mahbubani Kishore 'The Pacific Impulse' 1995

Makhijani, Arjun *India's Nuclear Weapons Program: A Historical and Strategic Perspective* 1998

Malik, Zahid *Dr A. Q. Khan and the Islamic Bomb* 1992

Mason, Robert *Chickenhawk* 1983

Mattoo, Amitabh *India's Nuclear Status Quo* 1996

Mattoo, Amitabh *India's Nuclear Deterrent: Pokhran 11 and Beyond* 1999

Mehtab Ali Shah *The Kashmir Problem: a view from four provinces of Pakistan* 1995

Maxwell, Neville *India's China War* 1970

Menon, Rajan *Japan–Russia Relations and North-east Asian Security* 1996

Nehru, Jawaharlal *Glimpses of World History* 1934

Nehru, Jawaharlal *The Discovery of India* 1946

Nolan, Janne E. *Global Engagement: Cooperation and Security in the 21st Century* 1993

Nugent, Nicholas *Rajiv Gandhi: Son of a Dynasty* 1990

Pakistan Peace Commission *Pakistan–India Nuclear Peace Reader* 1999

Ramana, M. V. *Bombing Bombay: effects of nuclear weapons and a case study of a hypothetical explosion* 1999

Rohwer, Jim *Asia Rising* 1995

Roy, Denny *Assessing the Asia–Pacific 'Power Vacuum'* 1995

Rynhold, Jonathon *China's Cautious New Pragmatism in the Middle East* 1996

Segal, Gerald *Does China Matter?* 1999

Sheppard, Ben *The Ballistic Missile Programmes of India and Pakistan* 1998

Short, Philip *Mao. A Life* 1999

Singh, Jasjit *Nuclear India* 1998

Sparham, Ven. Dr Gareth *Why Beijing does not talk to the Dalai Lama* 1997

Stokes, Mark A. *China's Strategic Modernization* 1999

Sundarji, General K. *Blind Men of Hindoostan Indo-Pak Nuclear War* 1993

Talbott, Strobe *Dealing with the Bomb in South Asia* 1999

Vines, Steve *The Years of Living Dangerously* 1999

Wilkening, Dean A. *The Future of Russia's Strategic Nuclear Force* 1998

Wilson, Dick *Mao: The People's Emperor* 1979